Day's End

Lela Markham

Published by Breakwater Harbor Books

ISBN # 978-0-9981732-2-1 E-Book edition
ISBN # 978-0-9981732-3-8 Print edition

For permission requests, write to the author/publisher, addressed "Attention: Permissions Coordinator" at the address below:
Laurel Sliney
Aurorawatcher Publications
500 Ketchikan Avenue
Fairbanks, Alaska 99701
lelamarkham@gmail.com

A Word from Lela Markham

Thank you for reading my books. If you enjoyed this or any in the series, please take a moment to leave me a review at your favorite retailer. Only with your help can independent writers like me reach more readers. I appreciate it!

Transformation Project is at root a polemic against our rigged system of elites telling all of us "lessers" what to do while failing miserably on so many levels in their attempt to centrally manage the society. The political winds of change currently sweeping our nation have not altered my opinion that we're headed in a wrong direction and that the danger to all of us comes from those who would be our "leaders". Some of them mean well, but the belief that they are more qualified than ordinary people to "lead" us is the primary problem. Ultimately, I don't think politics will be what saves us, so you'll notice my characters don't really talk about partisan politics much. You know Rob is a "libertarian" elected to a non-partisan mayoral position. You can surmise Katharine Sullivan is a Democrat, but you'll notice some shifts in her politics in *Day's End* since reality has now set in. Shane says he's a fiscal conservative, but he didn't file an absentee ballot when he was overseas.

I don't believe politics – choosing who will be in charge this year or next – will save us. If there is any salvation coming our way, it will be from the actions of ordinary people living their everyday lives – milking cows and harvesting apples. I know the propaganda machines of today insist politics is the center of all power, but it's really just swapping one crazy train for another at periodic intervals. Until we start doing something differently, we cannot expect different results.

Apparently, *A Threatening Fragile* gored someone's sacred cow. I had some complaints about treating the military as the "bad guys", showing a rogue unit acting as jackbooted thugs. Contrary to the complaint, I do know a lot of military people. I live in a big military town – there are two Air Force bases and an Army base within an hour's drive of my home. I love many military people as friends and neighbors. Unfortunately, in an apocalyptic fiction someone – some group of someones -- has to be the bad guy and in considering the various potential villains, active-duty military and the agents of the federal bureaucracy drew the short straw. When the dice fell that way, I relied on history – what we know about actual rogue US Army units in other wars – to determine what might happen in the Transformation Project universe. I know many military people who would choose to act honorably in such situations, but I know enough who would not that I didn't feel my depiction was a stretch. If that makes you angry ... I don't like having my sacred cows gored either, but sometimes when they are I pause to ask myself if I was defending a mirage that I might need to let go of.

Lela Markham

Thanks!

This book is dedicated to my son Kyle because he is such a wonderful young man who is willing to lend his lush voice to an audio book for me. Keep an eye out for "Life As We Knew It" in audio form.

No book is the work of a single individual. The author gets all the glory but standing behind every published writer is a host of support personnel. Thank you to my editor, Dyane Forde, for the excellent job she did on the manuscript, and my husband and son for giving me cover design advice and final proof-reading.

Thank you to Sunrise, who spent many hours adoring me from the foot of the bed while I decided what came next. I will miss you, Golden Eyes, but since you've gone wild and free forever, I hope you aren't giving me a single thought.

This book contains short snippets of several hymns that have given me comfort during dark times. Although copyright laws allow my very incidental use, I want to thank Ludwig von Beethoven and Henry Van Dyke for writing the music and lyrics (respectively) of *Joyful, Joyful, We Adore Thee* (or Beethoven's 9th Symphony "Ode to Joy"), Horatio Spafford (*It is Well with My Soul*), Rich Mullins (*Calling Out Your Name*), Lewis E. Jones (*There's Power in the Blood*), the Gaither Vocal Band (*There's a Sweet Sweet Spirit*), and the anonymous slaves (or train porter) who wrote *Just a Closer Walk with Three.*

Table of Contents

"The white flashed back into a red ball in the southeast. They all knew what it was. It was Orlando, or McCoy Base, or both. It was the power supply for Timucuan County.

Thus the lights went out, and in that moment civilization in Fort Repose retreated a hundred years.

So ended The Day."

– **Pat Frank, Alas, Babylon**

Day's End

Book 4

Transformation Project

Prologue

When I think about those days of fire, it seems like years had passed between the bombs and the rebellion, but the transformation actually occurred over a few weeks. One day we were living the typical American lifestyle of mochas, cable television, and instant everything. The next we were worrying about radiation sickness and harvesting our crops. Some might say we were a little too attached to what we'd grown – that we didn't need to rise up against the USDA's attempt to confiscate our food, but Emmaus' residents saw it differently. If we gave up what was ours now, how did we know they would provide what we needed later?

We didn't, which explains the Cow Cop Rebellion. What happened after, though …

completely not our doing. That was just another crisis caused by others we had to deal with.

JT Delaney

Bleeding Kansas

Hutchinson, Kansas

Two weeks ago, Cai Delaney would not have thought this possible, but events in recent days had rolled back the calendar pages a century and a half—in Kansas of all places—as if the bleeding had never stopped.

While pushing a dolly of flour, no doubt confiscated from people who would be going hungry soon enough, Cai watched as the newest group of "volunteers" were stripped of their belongings within sight of the military's latest consequence for disobedience: what had once been a man, now sewed into a bag, hanging lifeless and putrid from a telephone pole.

"No one has seen April." Brian drew even with Cai, pushing a wheelbarrow filled with more bags of flour. The late afternoon sun turned his dark skin bronze. The air seemed marginally cooler than it had been yesterday, but Cai's clothes were still soaked with sweat and the sunburn on his neck prickled with salt. It did no good to complain. Showing human weakness risked more abuse.

"I heard some of the FEMA folks saying they sent a crew to Hays and it didn't return last night."

"I gotta find her, man."

"I wish you luck, but last night made it clear to me that I'm the next one up the telephone pole if I make Dershowitz mad. And how Wilkins interprets martial law is that they can do whatever they want to us. It's considered just punishment for our crimes."

Behind them, people cried out as they were stunned with the cattle prod. Guards broke out in cruel laughter. Brian glanced over his shoulder, dark blue eyes glittering with pent-up rage.

"Martial law, my ass. This is straight-up slavery."

They turned into a livestock barn and began unloading their dollies. Cai's shirt rubbed against his sunburn. A single booming sound rolled through the fairgrounds followed by a sound like firecrackers pattering. Cai paused in the midst of stacking a bag of flour on the pallet. Tat-tat-tat – pop-pop-pop.

"What is that?" Brian stared at the wall in that direction.

"Gunfire."

He could run or he could duck. Cai chose to duck down behind a stack of bags and Brian joined him.

"Are they executing people?"

"Lt. Wilkins is crazy enough that he might kill his slave labor force, but listen. Different weapons."

A random spattering of shots sounded here, there, far, and near. Cai thought they were becoming less frequent. He could hear men shouting. Was the madness dying down or …?

The soldier the prisoners called the Vulture came striding into view, drawing his weapon. He grabbed Brian by the shirt and dragged him from their screening. Vulture's gun came up as he bellowed that he would kill Brian if they didn't cooperate.

"We're just hiding here, man." Brian flinched back as the gun leveled at him.

"Dershowitz, we're just trying to stay out of the way of the gunfire." As if to underscore

Cai's words, a bullet dented the steel of the barn about ten feet up. Cai and Brian both flinched and tried to duck. The Vulture brought the gun around and his finger tightened on the trigger. Cai smacked his arm sideways and the bullet ricocheted off the concrete floor. There was no going back now. Brian and Cai jumped on Dershowitz to beat him. Cai had always been amazed that Shane could hold someone to the ground so easily. But it wasn't easy. The Vulture twisted away from him and scrambled for the gun. Brian cried out as Cai grabbed the Vulture's arm to stop him and then the gun came up and roared out fire and horror.

Near-Death Experience

Emmaus, Kansas

Shane Delaney refused to be an example for the cow cops. With his hands cuffed behind his back and a noose around his neck, his prospects looked grim. He'd broken the arm of one USDA agent with a lucky kick, but the other two agents took his feet off the ground and that took away his power to attack them, but not to free himself. Their commander argued with his father as the prisoners attacked the agents. The last thing Shane saw atop of the bridge was Rob draw his gun. Then he felt the open air at his back and he knew his prospects for survival were slim unless he got his hands free. Pain with a purpose was a light thing.

The rope burned a half-inch strip of fire across Shane's palm before it snapped hard at the bottom of its length, but he held on because pain was better than the alternative. Ignoring the pain, he pulled himself up the rope, so he could slide his left arm through the noose and hang with it under one arm and across his chest. Gritting his teeth, he reset his left thumb before wrapping his hand around the rope and paying attention to the screaming above him.

The girl hit the bottom of the rope, flopping like a marionette, jerking and dancing, her face purple and her eyes bulging. Shane swung over to catch her around the back and get the pressure off the noose. Her head lolled against his chest. He looked upward at the bridge where his father's ashen face floated. Rob disappeared, but Shane heard him yelling. Soon three faces appeared above him. The strain of pulling both Shane and the girl up to the railing showed on their faces.

"Take her," Shane croaked. "Dad, I'm good." He shook off Rob's hand, recognizing priorities.

'Good' was an overstatement. His legs wobbled as he rolled over the railing. His knees smacked the asphalt, but he didn't feel the impact. Sound dropped away as he felt something like a wall of thick glass drop between him and the bright colors and frenetic activity on the other side. All around him,

Emmaus and Mara folks were tying up USDA officers, one of whom lay bloodied and unmoving near one of the trucks. While Sharon Laughlin and Mace Kettridge checked the dead man's vitals. Rob and Frank Giffin, faces drawn and white above their beards, knelt over the girl Shane had rescued. Shane didn't think he knew her and he doubted he'd get the chance, but men like his father had to try to save people.

Sharon shook her head at something Mace said and lurched to her feet to check on Shane. She spoke some unknown dialect of Chinese to him, muted by the glass wall. She sat down in front of him, allowing him to pull her into his bubble.

"You look like you could use a cigarette."

"I never took it up." His own voice sounded alien to him. A trickle of blood ran from Sharon's hairline. Had the USDA been slapping women around too?

"Then you probably don't have one I could have?"

Shane wanted to laugh, but a shock shiver ran through him instead. Mark Ramirez came running from a truck near the top of the on-ramp, carrying a roll of duct tape and a plank that could be used as a back-board. Shane's teeth started chattering, but he moved to roll up on his knee. Sharon put a hand on his shoulder and another on his chest.

"They don't need you right now. How'd you get your hands loose?"

With the girl's head and shoulders secured to the board with duct tape, Frank and Mark carried the girl away on the improvised stretcher with Rob following them. Shane settled back onto his butt and tried to stop shaking. Sharon asked the question again.

"Trick I learned for getting out of handcuffs – dislocate your thumb."

"Doesn't that hurt?"

"Not as much as being hung would have." His voice had become his own again, almost.

Sharon snorted. Across the way, Rumdale, the USDA chief, had come out of the shock of being shot and was yelling at Mace that he needed a doctor. How dare he! Shane pulled himself to his feet and walked over to where Rumdale was handcuffed to the side of a truck. His legs less wobbly with each step and with hypervigilance returning, Shane became acutely aware of Jason Breen and one of his head guys walking onto the bridge.

"I need a doctor," Rumdale said.

Shane stared down at the chief's sweaty face. A wiser man than Rumdale would have been scared.

"Who shot you?"

"Your father, I think."

Shane considered the possibility. He'd been so busy trying not to die that he hadn't seen or heard the shot. He remembered Rob had drawn his gun, but Rumdale would be dead if Rob had fired.

"Nah. A Vietnam vet would have got you center of mass."

"Who cares? I need a doctor."

Shane wrapped his right hand around the USDA chief's bicep, making him howl. Blood welled up through the cloth.

"It's a crease. Bullet's not in there. I'm sure they'll get you some first aid eventually."

Rumdale ripped the air blue with swears as Shane wiped his blood-stained fingers on the cow cop's suit.

"You seen Frank?" Jason Breen had just arrived on the overpass, gazing around at the confusion.

"How are you related to me now?" Shane asked. "You're my brother's father-in-law. That makes me what to you?"

Jason frowned, which told Shane he wasn't making any sense. This was a first. He'd always been able to keep it together after nearly dying, before. Now, all the colors bled neon.

"Your friend, kid. I'm just a friend. I got a guy or two who would gladly put these guys down for you."

Shane scanned the bridge. A couple of the USDA female agents wept softly. Several of the men cringed at the sight of their dead coworker. Had there ever been a time when Shane cared about crap like this? Sunset shadows lengthened across the town as he looked out from the bridge. Right, this wasn't Miristan. Kansas ... the rules were different in Kansas.

"That's for my dad to decide. I think I've seen enough death for one day." Shane turned to Sharon, who had stripped a gun holster off a USDA agent and was now checking the mag. "You want to honcho this?"

She blinked at him, glanced around quickly, then grinned. "Yeah. Prisoners to jail, body to the morgue?"

"Right." The morgue seemed too good for any USDA agent, but Rob would want to follow the formalities.

"We'll get them there alive. Maybe a little bruised." Shane felt relief that Sharon was keeping her wits and humor about her. "Jason, can your guys get these trucks down to City Hall?"

"We can do that. Shane, you know about three of them headed east a few minutes before the hanging started?"

"No, I was too busy being hung to pay attention."

"Lucky says they're in sight. He'll get back with us when he can." Jason's key guy pocketed his cell.

"Don't chase them beyond the township line. My dad would care about jurisdiction, I think." Another shudder quaked through Shane, and he could feel the throb in his thumb now.

Lucky nodded and pulled out his cell again. Shane looked at the dead body.

"By the way, Frank— he beat that guy to a pulp with his own gun and then took an injured girl to the med center with my dad."

"That guy's dead."

"He probably shouldn't have been threatening to kill Frank. Guy takes that sort of crap seriously."

"You okay? You seem a little off-kilter."

"Near-death experiences do that. I need to get back to the airfield to retrieve my car."

"You don't need to be driving right now. Or handling a gun, which is the real reason you want to go there." Had Shane said that aloud? "Where else do you need to go?"

Shane tucked his hands into his armpits to stop them fluttering like leaves in a high wind. "City Hall."

The sky to the west turned purple, scarlet and gold as Jason dispatched more of his guys to help with securing prisoners and things Shane didn't currently have the attention span for. When Shane reminded him that Sharon was in charge, Jason relayed the information to his guys as Shane followed him off the overpass. Under other circumstances, Shane might have smiled at Sharon barking orders at Jason's men as if she'd always been their employer.

Why Don't I Feel Like a Hero?

Keri Lufgren wrapped her arms around her knees in a fruitless attempt to stop shivering. Tears flowed down her cheeks, mixing with the snot on her upper lip. She'd never shot anyone before. Her entire body convulsed, creating waves of cold and heat and the sensation of vomit pushing up against the back of her throat.

"What do you see?" Alice Ramirez asked Jos Osimowitz, who was using his detachable scope to view the overpass. Alice's dusky face tensed with concern as the 15-year-old boy carefully examined the activities atop the overpass a good half-mile away.

"Deputy Joe just got there and he's cuffing someone. Okay, he's standing the guy up and –

yeah, I think that's the guy Keri shot. He's walking. From the blood, I'd say you got his shoulder."

Keri surged to her feet and grabbed Jos' scope to look for herself. Seeing the USDA agent taken into custody, she sagged with relief, but then brought the scope up to view the overpass again.

"Did you see my dad or my brother?"

"After the shooting? Yes. From where I was up top, I could see Shane somehow avoid the hanging and also helping that girl. Your dad left with some other people carrying her. Then Shane left with…I think it was Jason Breen."

"Mark?" Alice asked.

"Yeah. I saw him helping with that girl. He was okay."

"What do we do?" Alice asked Keri, who handed the scope back to Jos before wiping at her cheeks.

"Give me a minute. I've never shot anyone before."

"My baby is alone, my husband just nearly died. I get that you're freaked, but I need to see to my family."

Of course, she did. Keri wiped her face again and bent to pick up her rifle. It clattered noisily against the spread-metal deck. Pointing the rifle in a safe direction, she checked the safety. She'd thumbed it on by rote, apparently.

"I hear you, though once you put Mocha on guard duty, Lisa's not moving more than a few feet and her face ought to be tongue-clean for good measure. I'll meet you at the car in a minute."

Alice headed down the ladder from the water tower's maintenance deck to the ground, Alex's hunting rifle over her back. Jos put a tentative hand on Keri's shoulder.

"You did what you had to do."

"I know that. He had a gun to my father's chest and he was about to hang my brother. It's just..." Keri took a shaky breath and let it out slowly. "Do you need a ride somewhere?"

"I came on my bike. I can get back that way. Just so you know, I was ready to do a head shot to stop him. I only hesitated because I was worried someone might be on the other side after it passed through him. I think I'm glad you took the shot first."

Keri laughed. If it sounded hysterical, it had been that sort of a day.

"I am too."

She climbed down the ladder. Her cell phone lay on the dashboard of her Durango, so she dialed her husband before getting in behind the wheel. Alex answered on the second ring.

"You okay?" He knew her voice and knew when she was upset.

"I'll tell you about it when we get home. Where are you?"

"Dennis and I are headed into town to drop him off. Mark is here. So's your dad. They're both okay. Apparently, the situation at the overpass is taken care of. Mark wasn't making a lot of sense."

"I'll let Alice know that he's okay. Have you heard from Poppy or Pete?"

"They're at the house."

"You're certain?"

"Yeah. She texted me to say she and Pete found Lisa asleep and Mocha wouldn't let Pete into the camper, but she let Poppy in. Where are you and Alice? What's going on?"

"I'll tell you later. I'll see you at the house then?"

"Whenever I can get away."

For the span of a heartbeat, Keri almost burst into tears. But she swallowed them back, mumbled "I love you", and then hung up before he could pursue it.

"Poppy and Pete are at the house." She squeezed the steering wheel with both hands as gooseflesh spread up her arms. The solidity of the steering wheel helped, but not enough.

"Maybe I should drive," Alice suggested.

Keri held up her shaking hands before her face and nodded.

"That might be a good idea."

Avoiding Rest & Relaxation

Emmaus, Kansas

Driving past people cleaning up the USDA mess replaced Shane's shock at almost dying. Now, he felt a resolute calm. People stood on their lawns looking stunned. Just across from Emmaus Road Baptist, a USDA agent lay dead on the grass. One of the Conophers wept on his front steps with a gun beside him, while his wife spread a sheet over the body. A block on, a homeowner trained an AR-15 on another cow cop tied to an oak tree. Further on, two ordinary people knelt beside a dead body, sobbing. The darkening of the blue sky as sunset came on surprised Shane. Hadn't it been noon five minutes ago?

Dennis Bishop came to meet him as he got out of Jason's truck. Dennis had been the copilot of a commuter plane that had set down at Emmaus Airfield during the initial crisis. Unable to go home because home was now a nuclear wasteland, Dennis was becoming a part of the community after only a couple of weeks.

"What's happening at Micah's place?"

"He's dead, but the rest of the family is this side of the veil."

"Tell me again why we're not shooting those pukes?" Jason looked ready to do the shooting himself right that moment. Though Shane understood his normal, human response, he decided against seeking revenge.

"Because we're not vigilantes and my father would be upset if I acted like one." *Rob is deep in my head and I didn't even know it.*

"Micah Lufgren never hurt anyone."

Shane agreed with Jason, but he couldn't take matters into his own hands knowing Rob would probably disagree. Dennis spoke up.

"We don't want to risk bringing the army down on our heads. Hanging onto food is more defensible than killing prisoners." Dennis sounded so reasonable. He hadn't watched a teenage girl strangle beside him a half-hour ago.

"What he said." Shane turned to Dennis because he knew how fruitless arguing with Jason was. "How do you even know what's going on?"

"I went to the med center with Alex to report Micah's death. Met your dad there. He said you'd probably show up here and I should make myself available to you."

"You your dad's deputy now, Shane?" Jason's teasing tone irritated, distracting Shane from asking if Kitty Vance would live. He didn't really want the answer anyway. He barely remembered Kitty Vance, but her father Dick was a close friend and Shane's heart, cold as it was these days, bled for the grief he would feel at her death.

"Yeah, actually. He even gave me a badge, but that and my gun are in my car, which is at the airfield. If you're going to be a jerk, why don't you go marshal your guys? We could use more guards on the off ramps. And you could find out if your guys retrieved those trucks. I'm pretty sure my dad would say don't kill anyone unless they are actively trying to kill you. Dennis, um …."

"Your father said you should see the nurse before you take on another task."

"Nurse?" The town's only remaining doctor and Shane's sister-in-law, Dr. Marnie Callahan

Delaney wouldn't have let a nurse go from the Medical Center with a critical case, but Dennis was leading him into City Hall.

"Come on."

Dennis led the way to the clerk's office where a first aid station had been hastily, manned by a dark-haired young woman Shane had never seen before. The way she and Dennis spoke to each other suggested she'd been on the commuter and had spent the radioactive rain at the salt mine together.

"Hi, I'm Christiana. You're ...?"

"Shane Delaney."

"He got hung," Frank Giffin spoke up from where he was providing first aid to a woman's eye. He seemed none the worse for having beaten a man to death under an hour ago.

"That's not actually true," Shane assured Christiana.

"They threw him off the bridge with a rope around his neck."

"Which I stopped from tightening."

Christiana focused on his right wrist which still sported the handcuff.

"How'd you get out of the cuffs?"

"Dislocated my left thumb."

"Excellent idea." It was hard to tell if she was impressed or being sarcastic. Shane admired people who could be both at the same time. "But let me see it."

In the end, after having examined him, she agreed that he'd reset the thumb correctly and that he already knew the exercises to speed healing.

"You probably shouldn't make a habit of dislocating your thumb." While dressing the rope burn on his right palm, she lectured him on hyper-mobile joints. Deputy Joe Kelly and Sharon came in with the prisoners, headed toward the holding cells. Shane itched to get back to work.

"If I were you, I'd go home and take the rest of the day to rest," Christiana said as she noted something on a clipboard. Shane watched the activity in the hall. "But I suspect that's not who you are, so good luck."

"Yeah, I don't do rest and relaxation" Joe returned from the cells, bringing Danny Hughes with him. Shane knew it was rude to just leave Christiana in mid-sentence, but he wanted the handcuff off more than he wanted to be polite.

"What are you doing with him?" Dennis's voice was curiously flat. They were holding

Danny for the murder of Dennis' coworker. Joe paused to unlock the cuff from Shane's wrist.

"We need the cells for the prisoners, but I don't like him in there with them," he explained.

"I'm not going to run away." Danny shot Joe a pleading look while subtly leaning away from Dennis. "I know what I did was wrong."

"How old are you?" Shane demanded.

The kid flinched. He didn't know Shane, and everyone in authority probably looked like a threat right now.

"Sixteen."

"That's why I don't want him in there." Joe looked at Shane as if he thought he was the new chief.

"You afraid you're going to corrupt him?" Dennis's voice dripped with contempt.

Joe looked flabbergasted. Shane held up a hand to silence Dennis.

"You have good instincts, Joe. You're going to make a good chief when Dad gets around to promoting you." That was more for Dennis than Joe, though he could see Joe's skepticism. "So, where are you taking him?"

"The d—old cells. There's a cot, and if he gets bored he can read old tax records."

"Reading 50-year-old tax records sounds like cruel and unusual punishment, but okay. What did you do with Rumdale?"

"I cuffed him to Bart's desk. Your mother is going to treat his arm before he goes to the cells. I left her the taser in case she needs it."

"Remember, that man is a mass murderer, so don't get careless with him."

Joe nodded and directed the cuffed Danny toward the back stairs that led down to what was known colloquially as "the dungeon." It was probably best that Joe had not called the old cells that in front of Danny. It seemed cruel to put a prisoner in "the dungeon." They really needed to decide what to do with the kid sooner rather than later. But he was the least of their concerns right now.

A group of people clattered down the stairs from the mayor's office, carrying rifles across their backs. As part of the Emmaus impromptu militia of distraction, they had scattered the organized efforts of the USDA to confiscate food and shoot townspeople for refusing. To Shane's knowledge, they'd managed not to kill anyone, so he guessed his first organized effort at creating a militia had gone well.

"I'm glad to see you're okay." Jazz Tully, a petite, athletic woman with reddish-brown hair and green eyes, carried an AR-15 across her back. Shane tried to reconcile that image to the one of her being a high school teacher, but he couldn't. They'd become friends in recent days. Though Shane knew it was a bad idea, he couldn't help being glad to see her. "We heard you were arrested on the radio." She paused, shaking her head. "Totally bad grammar, but you know what I mean."

"I'm fine. Has anyone heard—"

Shane faltered as Rob entered the lobby and walked their way. He had never seen that sort of look on his father's face before, not even when he'd done something manifestly inappropriate in his teenage years. Mayor Delaney looked like he wanted to shoot someone.

"Where is Rumdale?" His quiet voice vibrated with an undertone of rage that made several people turn and stare.

"Mom's fixing his arm in Bart's office." Before Shane even finished the sentence, Rob started up the stairs.

Dennis shifted from one foot to the other, watching him disappear up the stairs.

"I don't think I'd want to be whoever that is."

Who Do You Trust?

New York City, Holland Tunnel

"How long does it take to get there?" Julian Raines asked the driver, who said his name was Lou. Yancy was his last name, he explained.

Katharine Sullivan scarcely knew Julian and yet she felt like she'd known him all of her life and well enough to leave the city with him. She'd been about to embark from New York City and travel half a continent with him, but she admitted that she felt immense relief upon getting Joseph's text. Julian had been a good friend and she would advocate for Joseph to help him get back to Seattle, but she wanted to see her husband as soon as possible.

They had just cleared the checkpoint going into the Lincoln Tunnel, the high walls on either side embracing the truck as they dropped into the two-lane 1.5-mile long coffin.

"It'll take a while. There's a checkpoint at the other end. Maybe an hour."

Katharine texted that to Joseph, who said they were headed that way now. Perry, who normally shuttled the family about in helicopters, had somehow gotten her husband all the way to New Jersey. What a great story to hear on the way back to Kansas.

She had always hated tunnels. Even as a kid, going into one had always felt like being buried alive. It wasn't completely dark. The headlights of the other cars reflected off the tiled walls and roof. The only other light was small maintenance lights along the top of the wall, which caused shadows like prison bars to be cast against the righthand wall as the light showed through the railing of the pedestrian deck. The metaphor made her shiver. She especially hated that this was bumper to bumper, slow-crawl traffic, giving her time to wonder about the maintenance doors off the left-hand pedestrian deck. Probably for lighting. She wondered if any of them were for air.

Katharine glanced at her phone, seeing a message from her daughter Allison, dated two days ago. She hastily texted back, amazed that she had service in the tunnel.

> -Dad and I are fine. We're about to meet just outside the city. Hang in there. Tell Ren, we'll be there in a few days. Mom

Allison was no doubt safe and sound with her grandfather Ren spoiling her, but two days was a long time to not hear from someone in this crisis. Katharine expected a return text shortly. She looked up, smiling that the traffic now moved at a consistent pace. Then, her worst fear happened. Everything went dark, just like a tomb.

Hippocratic Oath & Other Myths

Emmaus, Kansas

"I've been shot," Mitchell Rumdale complained. "I need a doctor, not a nurse"

Clean cut and dressed in a suit jacket and tie, Rumdale must have cut a fine figure when he rolled into town and announced he was from the government and there to help them by relieving them of their stored food. Except for his sweaty light-brown hair and blood-encrusted jacket, he could have been anyone Jill passed on the street. Maybe mass murderers were all normal-looking before they went off the deep end.

"The doctor is busy with a critical patient right now."

Rumdale's complaining so irritated Jill Delaney that she grasped his upper arm just above the elbow to ply her scissors on the hastily applied bandana and then lopped off the suit and shirt sleeves above the wound. Rumdale whimpered.

"And, you're in luck. I'm an old Army nurse, so I could care less if you're in pain, so long as you're not bleeding out. It's a crease barely worth the first aid."

She really wanted to shoot him dead right where he sat. How many people were dead or dying because Rumdale had been blindly following orders? She'd known people like him in the Army. She had hated them then as she hated Rumdale and his squad now, but her feelings today were deeply, intensely personal. If she'd had a gun right then, he might not have survived five minutes.

"You take an oath to do no harm."

"That's doctors, not nurses, and if you wanted me to be kind to you, you shouldn't have tried to hang my son."

"He was hoarding food."

"That's rich coming from the guy who was going to take all the food and leave us starving."

"It's my job, and you would have gotten supplies later when you need—"

Jill tightened her fingers on his bicep and he groaned. She bandaged his arm but decided not to bother with an antibiotic shot or pain relief. Why waste resources? She had just cuffed Rumdale's injured arm to the table when Rob entered the examination room. Their gazes met. He shook his head almost imperceptibly.

Tears sprang into Jill's eyes. Kitty Vance had been such a sweet girl. How could everything in the world go so sideways in just a few short weeks?

Rob pulled his gun from its shoulder holster. Stunned, Jill got out of Rob's way as he advanced across the room. His hand didn't shake one bit as he put the barrel against Rumdale's forehead.

"Do you know what happens to a body when an inadequate noose snaps tight on the neck and the weight of that body stretches the spinal cord?

Rumdale babbled about the law and his orders as Rob thumbed off the safety and stood there, considering pulling the trigger. Blood swished in Jill's ears.

"That little girl died in terror and my son is going to have that image etched in his memory for a lifetime. It could as easily have been him dead. So, Agent Rumdale, you'd best make your peace because you're meeting whatever demon you worship." He pulled the trigger. The click of the cylinder thundered through the room and Jill flinched, remembering the sound from days past. But Rob stepped back from the gasping Rumdale as a puddle formed under his chair.

Shane appeared in the doorway, a smile warring with a curiously nervous expression. He had every right to enjoy what Rob had just done, but tormenting Rumdale wasn't over yet.

"What do you want me to do with him?" He unlocked the cuff from the desk and made no attempt at being gentle as he cuffed Rumdale's arms behind him. Rumdale didn't resist, breathing rapidly and shaking.

"I want him alone. I need to talk to the City Council before I decide what to do with him."

"Joe put that kid, Danny, in the old cells and the USDA agents in the new cells. I don't think it's a good idea to put the head back on the snake."

Rob caught a corner of his moustache between his teeth as he decided their next course of action.

"You know the electrical closet in the basement – the one with all the breakers?"

"Yeah." Shane's expression oozed disagreement.

"There's a small room at the back of that room. It's got the sewer cleanout and a cabinet that holds the old town switchboard. Here are the keys. Last I saw, it was empty, but if there's anything in there, pull it out. The light switch is outside on the wall to the right of the door. Leave it off. Chain him to the sewer pipe."

"Yes, sir."

Shane grabbed Rumdale by his injured arm, making him whimper and complain loudly as Shane dragged him toward the door, finally putting him to his knees with a thumb across the bandage.

"I have ways to hurt you that you haven't even thought of, man, so I suggest you shut up and walk like a good little prisoner because I'm inclined to kill you right now."

"I'm allowed a trial."

"This is martial law, Agent Rumdale, as you so enjoyed informing us," Rob corrected. "You violated the peace of the community and killed several people, so as mayor of Emmaus, I have full authority to hang you if I so choose." Rob's smile had just a hint of madness in it. "Give my son any more difficulty and you won't live to see another dawn."

"My pants --."

"Stink," Shane said, dragging the USDA agent to his feet to propel him out of the room.

Jill sat down hard on a chair. Rob pulled a magazine out of his back pocket and slapped it into his gun, re-holstered and squeezed her shoulder.

"I'm sorry, honey. I know you don't like to see that side of me."

"I don't." She wiped tears off her cheeks. "But if anything would bring that monster back to life …."

"Not completely. Apparently, not even someone trying to kill my son brings that to the fore anymore. I deliberately ejected the mag and cleared the pipe before I came into the room. I didn't want to, but .... Damn. If he just hadn't gone that far." Rob shook his head, voice raspy. "I hate to leave you to clean this up, but ...."

"No, I've got it." She stood up. Rob turned toward the door. "And, Rob ...." He turned back. "I want to be there." He looked confused. "When he hangs. I want to make sure that noose is loose enough that he strangles. Kitty Vance didn't deserve that. He does."

Rob's blue eyes widened in surprise, but then he nodded.

Jill stared at the urine on the floor. The smell triggered memories of shouts of medical staff and the associated smell of gunpowder on flesh. She shook herself and moved to clean up the mess, knowing that there was no time to indulge nightmares.

Dead Men Don't Sleep

Hutchinson, Kansas

Cai stared hard across the midway, willing himself not to think and failing utterly. Brian had sat with him for a while, but then Jared of FEMA had come to him with the duty roster for the "volunteers" and he'd gone to find out where his wife, April, was. He hadn't come back. Cai idly picked at the blood on his pants. He'd probably not have returned himself.

Vulture had deserved to be resisted. The worst of the worst in a rogue military unit, he was a bigot who hated black people and Brian was bi-racial married to a white woman. Who knew what he'd done to April. And Cai didn't doubt if the gun had been in Dershowitz's hand, Brian would be the one bleeding now ... or Cai ... or both. Still ....

How do you face your God when you've killed a man? Potentially ... probably ... hopefully not. He'd been circling around that drain for a while now, long enough for the sun to set and the carnage to be cleaned up out on the midway.

Mike Sanchez slid onto the bench next to him. Shane's friend from his mysterious last five years, a mercenary, a loyal guard dog. Cai hadn't thought it was him when he'd seen him earlier in the day, but the mercenary sergeant was a familiar face in total chaos. Shane apparently trusted him with his life and his brother didn't trust that many people.

"He died about five minutes ago. Myers isn't a doctor and he was gut shot."

"FEMA doesn't have a doctor onboard?" Cai croaked.

"Not one that wanted to step forward. Jared said there's at least one doctor among the prisoners, but his reply, when asked to help, would get TV stations removed from the airwaves."

Sanchez called Shane "Ric", but there were connections between the two men that said they were the same person – such as that Shane-ism. The thought the Vulture had bled out seemed a victory. Shane might have seen it that way and it could explain the haunted look in his eyes. Cai refused. A human being had died and he almost wanted to celebrate? Whatever he'd eaten for lunch pushed up against his glottis as the sound of the gun going off punched his head.

"You could use a shower." Sanchez didn't seem offended, as if he might be remarking on the price of tomatoes. "I'll find you some clean clothes. It'll be a few days before we can head toward Emmaus, but—"

Cai stumbled up and hung over a garbage can to puke. Two purges happened immediately, covering him in cold sweat and goose flesh. The third one suspended for a minute or two, then came dry heaves followed by tears.

"Your first kill is hard." Sanchez hadn't moved from the bench. He had a stronger head for the sound of puking than Shane did.

"I don't plan to make a habit of this," Cai rasped. Sanchez nodded soberly. Cai pulled his clothes around him, trying to get warm.

"Sometimes you don't have a choice. Man's trying to shoot you, what are you going to do?"

That way led through dark woods.

"That's not a justification."

"You sound like Ric."

Cai sniffled. The garbage can stank. He sat down on the bench again, cold sweat drying in the cooling night.

"We aren't all that similar."

"I don't know you well enough to say." Sanchez stared off into the gathering darkness. "Do you want to get drunk?"

"Not my thing." Cai wasn't good at it. He did stupid things when he drank. The son of a long- time sober alcoholic knew that was a hallmark sign that he shouldn't drink.

"It was supposed to be a comparison. Or a contrast ... er ... well, whatever."

Desperate for anything to distract him from the memories in his head, Cai examined what Sanchez had said.

"I know Shane has killed people."

"We're soldiers. It comes with the job. He's killed fewer than most. Why'd you do Dershowitz?"

"It was an accident. He was going to shoot Brian and I grabbed the gun to stop him. It went off."

It sounded like an excuse to Cai. A man was still dead.

"Into his liver. Lucky deflection. And, there you go. Ric could tell a similar story about his first time."

"It's my only time."

"That's what he said too."

Cai shuddered, remembering the haunted look in his brother's green eyes.

"He puke and cry too?"

"I don't know. I didn't know him until a couple of hours later."

"And?"

"CEO sent me out to find him. Found him in a bar about half-way down a bottle of whiskey. I asked him if he needed anything and he said, 'Help me polish off the bottle.' So, I did. I got drunk off my butt and he brought me back to the base. We've been friends ever since."

"That does sound like Shane. Everybody else gets blackout drunk and he ends up without a hangover."

"That's because he stops at a certain point."

"Is that his secret?"

"It's like a super power." Sanchez smiled at some memory they didn't share. "So, let's get you over to the shower trailer and I'll go find those clothes. By morning, we'll have gone through all the personal effects and, hopefully, find your ID and what-have-you."

Cai wiped the back of a hand across his forehead as they walked, feeling wrung out, empty, and not quite in contact with reality. He turned aside at a water fountain to rinse his mouth and face and drink a few mouthfuls of water. He'd not been to the shower trailer in his entire three days here. He felt like he was breaking the rules to even venture beyond the clearly defined lines prisoners had been allowed to operate within.

Sanchez buzzed in with his ID. Banks of lights came on at their entry. He opened a locker with the same ID and pulled out toiletries and a towel.

"Take as much time as you want. The FEMA folks are looking forward to using the trailer too, but they can wait."

"What happens to them?"

"Yeah, that's one of the reasons it will take a few days before I can head west. Waiting on my command to tell me what to do. So, those clothes... just toss them in the corner. You want them back or are they trash?"

"I don't have any others."

"Not a problem. Lots of fatigues around."

Cai sat down on a bench to pull off his shoes and peel off his socks. An overwhelming stench filled that corner of the shower room.

Sanchez raised an eyebrow. "Those pants are definitely trash and we don't have any little dark women here to do our washing."

Was he kidding? Cai didn't have the focus to decide. Just concentrate on the clothing and getting cleaned.

"Yeah, please get me some spare clothing. There's nothing sentimental here."

The shower's temperature was easily adjusted and it felt good to finally wash away the river he'd swam in days ago. The water sluicing down his sunburned neck and arms felt intermittently hot and cold. Mud collected by his feet as tears and snot mingled with the water on his chin. The memory of Dershowitz writhing in a pool of blood at his feet caused him to bend over and vomit into the drain. Gagging and cold, he scrubbed and rinsed, and wept.

When he stepped out of the shower, wrapping the towel around his waist, a stack of fresh clothing awaited him: military fatigue pants, a white undershirt, a black t-shirt, and a FEMA jacket. A razor, toothbrush, and toiletries sat atop the stack. He wiped fog from the mirror to look at his bruised face wit the scruff of rusty beard. His fingers shook so hard he nicked himself twice while shaving and it was difficult to button his shirt or tie his shoelaces. Just as he finished, the lights went out.

"Hello?" he called. Water dripped from his recently vacated shower. "Somebody here?"

Not a footstep, no sound of breathing. Probably the generator had turned off. Not an unusual occurrence here. He fumbled around to locate the jacket that had been part of the clothing stack and stuffed the toiletries in the pockets. He had never thought of being without these basic things before his time here and now he understood their value.

He felt along the wall until he found the door and let himself out into the virtual blackness of a new moon night.

Outside on the midway, the mercenaries held a meeting in the open-air pavilion that had served as a mess for the prisoners. Previous nights it had been lit by electric lights, but now they used two battery-powered lanterns hung from the framing.

"Have you heard from Wichita yet?" one of the lower-ranked mercenaries asked.

"Crispin hasn't gotten back to me." Sanchez aimed a flashlight at Cai as he neared the circle of light. "Oh, hey. This is Eric Faraday's brother, Cai."

There came a smattering of hellos. The demeanor of the mercenaries was much more casual than Cai had expected. This wasn't a military operation. No one was far from their weapons, but nobody reached for them as he approached. They reminded him of big cats relaxing in the sun—pent-up lethality temporarily calmed.

"Thank you for rescuing us," he told them.

"No big, man," someone said. "What was going on here was wrong. I used to be Army and it was wrong. Besides, a few of us owe our lives to Eric. Thailand, right?"

Cai blinked, uncertain of the meaning. Two or three of the group laughed softly.

"Just having one on you. Don't worry about it. If I'd had a clue this was coming, I'd be kicked back on the porch at my folks' place with a beer right now."

"Uh, I don't …." Was Shane AWOL? Did that even exist in mercenary circles?

"Don't worry about it," Sanchez reiterated, a sharp undertone to his voice. "Kriczek, go find Powell and see what's taking him so long getting the power back on. The FEMA folks promised dinner at sunset, so someone go find out what's happening with that."

"What should I do about Lawson?"

"Leave him where he is until morning. Maybe by then, I'll have heard from HQ." Sanchez turned to Cai. "You can bunk with us tonight in the CHU, decide what you want to do in the morning."

"I killed a man. I probably need to stay here until that's sorted."

Sanchez snorted.

"What happens in the field stays in the field. We ain't regular Army and this group wasn't either."

His dad Rob had said the military promoted soldiers to the level of their incompetence. Had that been what happened to Wilkins?

"One of my guys knew him back in the Box," Sanchez explained "Guy had a screw loose."

Putting it mildly. Did he say ...?

"You used the past tense."

"He and his aide put up a fight. Personally, I preferred to do this without killing and Wilkins and the aide ... and Dershowitz ... are the only ones who died. A couple of others are wounded, but they'll be fine."

"And the FEMA people?"

"Unless HQ tells me otherwise, I'm going to treat them as prisoners, just like you." Sanchez slowed near the military housing trailers and shined his flashlight about to see where the stairs led up into one of the trailers.

"But they weren't. They were cooperating."

"Were they? You know Wilkins had their chief agent killed the day after the military got here? And they were raping their women. So, I'm inclined to forgive any collaboration ... which, by the way, I learned from your brother."

"Like I said before, Shane and I aren't exactly alike."

"I've noticed."

Inside the CHU there were four beds in two tiered bunks. Mike showed Cai one of them.

"Sorry it's a lower bunk, but my guys were here first."

"That's fine. So what are you going to do with the soldiers?"

"If my HQ doesn't get back to me ... that'll be up to a vote of the prisoners ... former prisoners. You want some payback, that's how to do it, though they could probably use a good lawyer."

Sanchez fiddled around while he talked and finally a battery-powered lantern cast the room in muted tones. While he worked, Cai considered whether he could represent the soldiers who had enslaved and tortured him. Anxiety clawed at him. Before he could analyze it, Mike spoke.

"Home sweet home. I got a boatload of stuff to take care of and you look exhausted. Try to get some sleep, because we'll be up at 0600 ... um, 6 am."

"I know military time. My father was still in the Army when I was born ... Shane too."

"Yeah, he mentioned. Glad to know he wasn't deviating far from the truth."

Sanchez left him alone then to contemplate the horror of sleeping with a dead man in his bed.

Reconsideration

Emmaus, Kansas

Maggie Callahan had never been much of a lady and she'd worked hard to build her bar and grill into a successful business, so it didn't surprise Jacob to learn she'd shot a USDA agent who had tried to confiscate what grub she had left. Now she busily scrubbed blood off the floor of her dining room, only pausing when Jacob asked her if she could make a sandwich for him. She looked at her niece Missy, who sighed and said she would finish up the mopping.

"You okay, girlie?" Jacob asked. At 95 years old, he was old enough to be her father—or even grandfather—so that she didn't immediately bristle at the potential sexism in his question.

"He shouldn't of tried to take my stock. He won't be using his left arm for a few days, but he'll live. It's better than he deserved. Ham or roast beef?"

The USDA hadn't been interested in the dog food at the feedstore and they'd not caught onto the corn hidden in the building. Jacob had been clear with Shane and Rob both that he wasn't going to shoot anyone unless they were trying to kill someone, but he supposed any of the people who had resisted could have killed or injured someone. Maggie was handling it better than some. Her hands didn't shake while making the sandwich.

"Have you seen my daughter?" she asked.

He hadn't, yet. Maggie's daughter was married to Jacob's grandson and they lived in the same house. The clinic lay in the general direction he was headed so he said he'd tell Marnie to call her mother as soon as she had a moment. As the town's only doctor during a time of crisis, Marnie didn't have a lot of moments to spare.

Jacob parked his truck behind City Hall, which was usually not as busy as it was today. The mayor's impromptu deputies were trying to sort out what to do with the twenty-some prisoners in a drunk tank meant to hold eight at most, as well as what to do with them ultimately. Rob looked a curious combination of exhausted and excited, but Jacob was glad to see Lem hanging around, patiently waiting for them to have an opportunity to talk.

"Joe, can I have the keys to the dungeon?"

"Here you go." Joe Kelly, Emmaus' only remaining cop, handed over the keys. "The kid says he's not going to run away, so I let him have the whole area to himself rather than just one cell."

"You believed him?"

Joe chewed the inside of his lip for a moment before honesty won the war with his discretion.

"I don't think he meant to kill that pilot. He's young and he was scared. He'd had a horrible night and overreacted. Might as well let him be comfortable until Mayor Delaney convenes that coroner's inquest and they decide he deserves what happens."

Joe looked sad. Possibly too soft-hearted to be sheriff during the Apocalypse, Joe would have fit right into Emmaus 50 years ago. He'd been trained by Chief Bart Rawlston, who had not believed cops needed to be militarized or intimidating. Bart would have been better suited to the current circumstances, but he'd been among the first to die, a victim of the air-handling system going down in the City Hall bomb shelter where a hundred people had taken refuge against the radioactive rain. Two other deputies had died with him. Joe was sheriff by default, twenty years before he'd have earned the position.

Nobody had changed the lightbulb above the stairs since the old drunk tank had become file storage when they'd built the newer cells about forty years ago, the work of a mayor after Jacob had decided not to run again. He knew where they kept the flashlight behind the door and he used it to make his way down the narrow steps. Unlike the newer cells, the two cells here were separated from the stairs by open bars instead of a solid door. The boy Danny sat at a small table in the second cell, perusing a file. He stared at Jacob like he might a snake.

"I brought you some dinner."

Danny stood and came out to the common secured area, but didn't take the bag, eyes darting to the 357 under Jacob's left arm. He was still a teenager, with the soft cheeks of youth. His curly hair was trimmed short, but it wasn't truly the afro Jacob had thought it was the morning they'd met. His lips were full, but he was more "white" looking than most biracial men. What else had Jacob misremembered from that stressful morning?

"Where's Deputy Kelly or Mayor Delaney?"

"Busy." Jacob slid the bag between the bars and set it on the floor, then sat down on the bottom step.

Had he misjudged this kid in the heat of the moment?

"How are your bruises?"

"Bruises?

"From getting thrown around in the plane."

"Oh, that was more than a week ago. I guess I still have one on my hip. I deserved that."

Maybe he had misjudged him. A black kid waving a gun around and all. But the pilot was still dead.

"So, Joe thinks you didn't mean to kill the pilot."

The kid sighed.

"I didn't. He grabbed for the gun and it went off."

"That's not an excuse."

The kid's dark hazel eyes filled with tears briefly, but he blinked them back.

"I know. I'm kind of glad my grandma's probably dead, so I never have to tell her what I did."

He was still a kid and one raised by a good family.

"We're hanging a whole group of prisoners here in the next day or so. Do you think you ought to be one of them?"

"I killed a man, so …." Now he wiped tears off his cheeks. He left the bag where it was and sat down on the bunk, the weight of the world on his young shoulders. "Gran would say 'sorry doesn't cut it.'"

Gran sounded like Jacob's kind of parent. He nodded toward the table.

"You researching?"

"Deputy Kelly said I could earn my keep by neatening the files."

"There's an idea."

"I found a couple out of order. Those need to go in a different drawer, but I haven't found that drawer yet."

"You've only been down here an hour."

"I know he's just trying to give me something to do while I wait. Why are you still feeding me? I heard that dark-haired deputy telling Deputy Kelly not to feed the other prisoners."

"Dark-haired deputy? My grandson, Shane, I think. He's extremely pragmatic and doesn't believe in wasting resources on people who are going to die tomorrow. You're making yourself useful and you're just a kid. They're adults who came to steal our resources."

"You don't have to. If you're going to kill me, why feed me?"

Jacob remembered all the people in the Bible who had screwed up only to be used by God anyway.

"We haven't really had a chance to decide what to do with you yet. My wife's people, Wyandots, they used to make the killer pay back the family of the person killed, but in this case, he wasn't part of our community so we're not out anything from his death. But you have cost us a bit of food and some fuel and the folks from the commuter would probably like to see some justice done. If I said you had to work that off—that you owed me your life—what would you say?"

"I'm half-black."

"I noticed. So?"

"Are we talking about slavery?"

"Nope. My folks were anti-slavery. The town split on that topic. The Wyandots were pro-slavery. It was part of their culture and they saw nothing wrong with temporary slavery -- indentured servitude, of enemies and those who owed someone for something. But my folks were abolitionists. Slavery doesn't set well with me. But you killed a man. What are you willing to do to recompense that?"

To his credit, Danny didn't answer right away. He stared at the far wall long enough to make the silence uncomfortable before he finally answered.

"I'd be willing to work. I know what I did was wrong, and it beats staring at bars like this all day until someone gets around to executing me."

Jacob nodded.

"I'm not promising anything. Folks are in a killing mood right now. But I'll make a case for it."

"Seriously?"

"Uh-huh. You eat your food. I—"

The bulb in the middle of the ceiling grew uncomfortably bright and then the room plunged into blackness.

A Pleasant Walk before Dark

After Rob left to go tell the Vances about Kitty, Shane offered to walk Jazz to her car.

"I walked, but thanks." She had to smile at him because he was still looking out for others even after the day he'd had.

"I'll walk you then. If our calculations of their roster are correct, there are still three agents missing."

"Sure. I'll protect you if they come at us." She tweaked the strap of her AR-15. He tried to smile, but mirth had been squeezed out of him this afternoon. "Sorry." He nodded and they descended City Hall's front steps to head east along Emmus' main street.

The entire town glowed, porch lights blazing, front doors open, people milling and talking. One palm wrapped in bandages, the other hand black and blue, and ligature marks on both wrists, Shane didn't let his wounds slow him down. When people said "hi" he waved back, but he wasn't talking much. He kept his pace slow. Some tall people did that thinking she couldn't keep up, but he'd run with her, so she thought his slowness must just be exhaustion. Who wouldn't after the day he'd had?

"I can't imagine what you went through this afternoon." She shoved her hands into her pockets against the evening coolness. Shane shot her a sidelong glance, his full lips thinning as if in pain.

"It's not the worst nightmare I'll have." It might have been the most honest thing he'd said to her yet and so explained why he'd stiff-armed her several times. She breathed in the fragrance of blooming sage and monkshood, swallowing it into her depths.

"You almost make that sound like it's a good thing."

"It's not, but ... I think I prefer some of the other stuff to watching Kitty hang and unable to do anything about it." He stared at a fixed point of nothing, seeing something unpleasant. She'd seen him do that before. He had a gallery of nightmares to choose from. Daymares too, she guessed. He shrugged. "I don't know."

"What's going to happen to them?"

"The cow cops?"

She nodded, though that teasing nickname no longer seemed appropriate for a bunch of thieving, murdering tyrants. "That's up to my dad and the City Council. Rumdale I expect to be dead by this time tomorrow night. The others ... who cares?"

Jazz shivered at the frostbite in his tone. Her apartment was in the old aircraft factory not far from downtown. She tried to steer the conversation to less upsetting topics, telling him about the apple orchard behind his house, but he eventually held up a hand for her silence.

"Jazz, just ... walk with me. Don't try to ... It's not going to be better. Not tonight. Not for either one of us."

"I'm not the one who—"

"You've never fired your gun at someone before, have you?"

"Other than the guy at Walmart the other day?"

"I forgot about that. How did it feel today?"

"The other day it happened too quickly to really feel anything. But today ... scarily powerful ... like I had someone's life in my hands. I don't know. I just can't imagine telling my parents about that." Gooseflesh made her arms tingle. "Maybe they'll never be back anyway."

"I forgot to tell you this morning...Geo logged onto Facebook and marked himself as safe last night. There was no location listed."

"Oh, thank God! I need to call Michael to let him know. Thank you for checking. I can't imagine you hanging out on Face—"

She flinched at a high-pitched buzz from a nearby streetlight, which flared and blinked out. A smell like burning plastic and metal filled the air. Shane enveloped her in his arms, pushing her face into his chest and covering her head with his. And then the transformer on the corner pole exploded in a clap of thunder and a rain of sparks.

Burning Down

New York City, Holland Tunnel

Yancy slammed the hood and took the flashlight back from Julian. Down the line of cars in the tunnel were dozens of people doing the same thing—trying to figure out why their cars had just stopped working.

"It smells like ozone," Julian remarked. "Like a cooked hard drive."

"Blew a fuse, yeah, that happens, but everybody blowing a fuse at the same time—pretty big coincidence."

"Then what happened?" Katharine asked. It truly felt to her as if the billions of tons of rock and water above them were slowly lowering onto their heads.

"I read this book," one of the passengers from the cargo area said.

"I don't know," Yancy said, ignoring her. "Maybe some national security thing. The news reported a while back that hackers can hijack car computers. Maybe that's it."

"I read this book and it—"

"What now?" Julian asked Katharine.

"I don't know. My phone hasn't got any bars, but Joseph was going to meet us at the New Jersey side, so—"

"Hey, I read this book and it talked about—"

"Could you please stop?" Katharine told the younger woman. She hadn't stayed at the Casa Blanca. Katharine didn't know her and didn't want to know her. "We're trying to figure out what's going on, not talk about literature."

"Katharine, right? I'm Joline. I'm trying to tell you what I think happened."

Katharine wanted to snip at her, but the memory of another woman dying kept her from it. She should have been nicer to Lillian. Maybe she should be nicer to others.

"Alright, go on. You read a book and…?"

"The author is some sort of military expert, a university historian but he writes novels. In the book, someone set off a nuclear warhead very high up in the atmosphere and it caused an EMP that wiped out electricity all over the country. And it was like this. The cars just stopped working, except the really old ones."

"Well, thank you, Joline, for the Book of the Month update. Was there anything in the book about what to do in real life?" Julian sneered, voicing Katharine's initial thoughts but then the hair on the back of her next stood on end as she remembered her father-in-law, Ren, talking about the same sort of scenario and it being the reason for redoing the electrical system at the Shack.

"She might be on to something," she murmured. "I mean, this is obviously some sort of weird event and widespread. The cars stop, the headlights turn off, the tunnel lights are out."

"But your cell is still working," Julian pointed out. "The flashlight, my watch...."

"I think we should walk ahead and see just how far this traffic jam goes."

She couldn't read Julian's expression in the dark, but she didn't hear exasperation in his voice when he replied.

"Yeah. Let's just get our gear in case something keeps us from getting back here."

"I only got the one flashlight and I ain't loaning it to you," Yancy announced.

"That's fine. We can use our phones."

When they'd walked a few cars ahead, Julian whispered to her.

"What are you thinking?"

"Ever see the movie *Daylight*?"

"Sly Stallone? Sure. But that's totally bogus, you know."

"Hmm, but during Superstorm Sandy, the tunnels did flood, so ... I want out of here as soon as possible."

"Crank it over," a man called out from under the hood of a vintage Mercedes. The car sputtered to life, coughed a few times and then caught. "German technology. Now if we can just get these cars out of our way."

"What was wrong with it?" Julian asked.

"Fuse. It blows in this car kind of often, so I keep a spare in my tool box."

Julian suggested they climb up on the pedestrian walkway, which made the travel a little easier. A young mother rocked a baby to sleep while her toddler clung to his father's leg as the man tried to diagnose what was wrong with the car. Someone lit a cigarette. A man rhapsodized in Spanish when his old truck started, but he had to shut it down because there were dozens of cars in front of his.

To save battery on their phones, they relied on the lights of other trapped travelers. Katharine looked behind them and saw that Joline and several strangers were following them.

"What do you think?" she asked. The air in the tunnel felt thick and warm.

"I think it's a free country and if they want to follow the only sensible people in the tunnel, it's their prerogative."

"Where you going?" a man with a strong Queens accent demanded from out of the dimness.

"Ahead," Julian replied, then asked Katharine. "How far are we along the tunnel?"

"About halfway." Katharine pointed at the MTA station. "That's halfway. We get out of the tunnel faster by going that way," she pointed back toward Manhattan, "but that way is closer to our goal."

"Three-quarters of a mile?"

"About right."

Julian looked back toward Manhattan and then forward toward New Jersey.

"We should pick up the pace. Too bad Yancy wasn't offering a refund."

"That was unfortunate, but I don't care. I just want out of this deathtrap."

They passed a few cars, mostly older ones, that the owners managed to start briefly, but it merely filled the air with noxious fumes and so the owners shut them down within minutes.

Three-quarters of a mile took only about 20 minutes for two fit people to walk, but as they neared the New Jersey end a cop with a flashlight approached from the other direction.

"Turn around, folks. Go back to your cars."

"Why?" Julian asked.

"The storm doors closed and sealed. There's no way out this way."

"Why would they do that?" Katharine asked.

"According to one of the tunnel officers, it's standard procedure, an automatic thing to protect from flooding."

"Are you saying we're closed in here?" Katharine could feel the air being squeezed from her lungs.

"I don't know, ma'am. I'm headed to the other end to see about that now."

"Don't panic," Julian murmured. "We go back, we get out and we take a bridge over. It'll be fine."

Katharine took a deep breath and let it out slowly. The cop explained the reversal of direction to those who had been following them. They turned to follow him back. The desire to reach air and light caused them all to walk faster so that they neared Yancy's truck 15 minutes later. It was locked up and deserted. Katharine and Julian ran to catch up with the cop since he had a flashlight.

As they neared the Manhattan end, they could smell burning. The cop's flashlight didn't pick up any people, but a sliver of moonlight barely wide enough for a full-grown man to pass through provided access to the outside—after climbing over the crushed car that jammed the door. Someone had either kicked out the windows or they had shattered from the pressure. The occupants were gone.

A black-garbed mercenary met them at the top of the ramp. Katharine had never seen the city so dark, lit only by the fire of burning cars.

"It's hell out there, folks," the helmeted mercenary warned.

"What happened?" Officer Thomas, the cop, asked. He had finally gotten around to telling them his name.

Gunfire sounded a few blocks away. Everyone ducked and the mercenary scanned the street with anxious eyes, but the sounds moved away from them.

"Power outage, maybe, but we lost communications so…I don't know."

"Could it be an EMP?" Joline asked.

"A what?"

"Electro-magnetic pulse."

"Like on that old show with the pretty chick with the cat DNA? I guess."

Julian drew Katharine away from the others.

"New Jersey's that way. What do you think?"

Katharine checked her phone. Still no bars.

"The hotel might be safer," she suggested.

"Until we starve to death."

"Yes, we can't stay longer than tonight. Listen, we have no map. There's not light. Neither of us knows the territory and there are people shooting out here. Much as I want to meet Joseph tonight, I don't know if we can make it."

Julian rubbed the back of his neck. She could barely make him out against the darkness around them.

"You might have noticed I'm skilled at bartering, etc. You gotta trust me here. We gotta leave here now."

Julian's sophisticated accent dropped away for just a moment and working-class cadences cut through her fear of launching into the unknown. He wasn't just a software engineer from Seattle. He had shown skills that were useful in a crisis like this.

"All right," she relented. She followed him into the street and looked up at the stars that she had never been able to see from New York before. "That's the Big Dipper and Polaris, so that's north. That makes west over there."

"You sure?"

"Did a lot of star gazing in Kansas."

"We just go that way?"

"Not really, because there's no bridges right here." She tried to picture what she remembered of Manhattan in her mind's eye. "The George Washington Bridge is north."

"Okay. Let's go."

"It's a long way. Near the Bronx."

"How far is that?"

That took some calculation. New Yorkers measured distance in subway stops, not miles. Fortunately, she hadn't lived in New York for almost 20 years.

"Ten miles, maybe."

"You're kidding me! That's like walking all night through a war zone." Julian huffed. Somewhere gunfire sounded again. "We gotta go. This place is burning down. We gotta go."

"We can follow the river along the park. I don't know, though. Without lights ... might be kind of dangerous."

Less than a block away looters screamed in ecstasy while they smashed the windows of a Lexus. That no car alarm went off sent a cold shiver through Katharine's body.

"No more dangerous than it is right here. WE HAVE GOT TO GO NOW."

He drew her away down the block.

Fire

Wichita, Kansas

Ren Sullivan enjoyed the view of Crystal Lewis' legs. If he'd been twenty years younger...but he wasn't and though his bride had died three years ago, he still loved her enough not to cheat on her with a younger woman. Crystal and he had a strictly business relationship and Ren thought the outside package belied who Crystal really was.

The new governor of Kansas was a barracuda, a politically ambitious woman catapulted into the public eye by a radical form of feminism that had been replacing men with women in elections across the country. Donald "Harm" Harmon had invited her onto the ticket to strengthen his run and it had worked. Ren knew she was intelligent and conniving, but he was beginning to see how utterly ruthless she was.

Currently, she instructed Lyle Fuller to not distribute food to Murdock, McAdams, and Millair.

"We can't feed them all. We need to support the more useful residents. I know. It's unfortunate, but we simply have to make wise decisions now. There'll be UN shipments soon enough."

Ren focused on the paperwork before him. His tankers were bringing refined fuel to the Gulf Coast and he had trucks bringing what had already arrived north. The UN was still not releasing food to the states, but Bunnell & Wilson was providing aid to New York, Seattle and the refugee camps along the West Coast. Time would tell if the effort was enough. It comforted him knowing there was a three-year supply of food for 10 people at the Shack.

The lamp over the desk flared to twice its normal brightness and then popped off, the filament shattering. Ren flinched and turned toward Crystal, who straightened from her computer, pushing the power button.

"Oh, for heaven's sake!" she muttered as the room plunged into duskiness. "I'm the freaking governor. You'd think they could keep my lights on."

She rose and fumbled around to open the draperies. The sunset bathed the western sky in pinks and purple, casting everything in the room a shade of mauve.

"It's area wide."

Ren rose to join her at the large windows.

"It must be the power station," he reasoned, perplexed that there were no headlights shining in the streets.

"What is that smell?" Crystal wrinkled her delicate nose, sniffing.

"Ozone. Something must have cooked during the surge."

"Well, while there's still hot water, I'm going to go grab a shower. You should ask Troy to mix you a drink."

"I'm not ready for that yet. I prefer to wait until the work is done."

Ren turned to his desk and picked up the phone, but there was no signal, not even the persistent beeping of an out-of-order line. Crystal paused to take off her high heels and pushed through the door to the master bedroom. Ren jotted down an idea on his notepad, straightening as a pall of smoke tickled his nose. One of the Knights smoking indoors or—

Phil came charging into the room, face flushed.

"Sir, the building is on fire. We have to go right now!"

"Crystal, we need to go."

Crystal's Knights security team surged right behind Phil and his team of two SullCorp security officers.

"We need to go now, Governor."

Crystal grabbed her laptop and briefcase.

"We can't afford to lose the plans we've been working on. Grab that—"

Phil pulled Ren into the hallway as thick, black smoke poured down from the ceiling. Ren could hear Crystal's security team ordering her to move toward the hallway.

"We need to take the stairs, sir."

As the stairwell door closed behind them, Ren heard Crystal scream. He wanted to turn back, but the door said "No reentry" and occupants of other floors quickly surrounded them. Their progress slowed to a crawl as they moved shoulder to shoulder down to the parking garage, which also had smoke floating in the air.

"What the hell is going on?" Ren asked as Phil guided him toward an exit.

"We're not sure, sir. Some sort of power surge."

Ren and his security team forged out into the night air. He looked back at the building to see that two floors and the penthouse were fully involved in flames. The heat blew out the windows, shattering glass down on them. Knight Industries mercenaries met Ren's security forces to lead them across the courtyard to a nearby building. Ren blinked his scratchy eyes, wiping smoke-tears from his cheeks. One of the Knights spoke to Crispin, the Knights commander, via radio.

"He'll be here as soon as he finds a working vehicle. Something odd about that power surge."

"Where's Crystal—Governor Lewis?"

"We haven't heard from her team yet, sir."

"They should have been right behind us on the stairs."

"We haven't heard from them, sir."

Reality swirled around Ren and sat down on his lap. He stared at the burning building, realizing that he would never again admire Crystal's legs.

City Gone Mad

New York City

Across the street, two dark figures fought over a television set still in its box. Julian steered Katharine away. On 9th Avenue, people rushed by them as they walked huddled together like two lovers sharing an umbrella. That worked for about five blocks. They paused at 42th Street as a high-rise ahead and to the right blossomed into flame.

"Why would people set fire to an office building?" Julian stared at the building in awe as fire surged from floor to floor.

"If Joline is right about it being an EMP, I remember my father-in-law saying that would blow circuits and cook off wires. Wouldn't that catch a building on fire?"

"We're believing her now?"

"I don't know but it's a working theory. We should probably get away from here before there's a gas explosion."

Julian's eyes widened. They hurried passed a battered pickup with a camper shell. Julian paused to try the handle.

"What are you doing?"

"We need a weapon. It's locked, dammit." He glanced up to the sky and turned west again, pulling her along with him. Shattering glass drew their attention back toward the burning building.

"Run," Katharine advised. The ground beneath them rocked as the building's windows blew out. Fortunately, they'd put a block between them and the explosion that scorched the truck they'd been trying to break into. Something metal hurtled down the sidewalk, tumbling end over end. Julian ran back and retrieved a crowbar thrown clear of the explosion.

"This'll do," he decided aloud, hefting it.

Katharine scanned the street, nervous.

"I think we need to get off the main streets. That way is Riverside Park. We might have an easier time on the Esplanade." At least they'd be away from buildings that could fall on them or explode. Katharine led the way into a narrow residential street, deserted, though candlelight glowed behind some of the curtains.

"Where are we?"

"Clinton. Used to be called Hell's Kitchen."

"Really? I always thought…well, you know, Daredevil and all that. This is gentrification, right?"

"I suppose. Joseph used to live a few blocks from here when we were dating, back when gentrification meant nicer apartments. Now they're combining the apartments into full-homes, which is weird because that's how they started 100 years ago, as mansions."

Spouting the useless facts calmed her somehow. New York City blocks were long, but they only encountered people at a couple of intersections along the way, and they were pointing them toward safety. At least, Katharine hoped they knew where safety was. When they reached Riverside Park, they realized they weren't the only ones to have thought of it. A steady stream of humanity in all its many varieties headed north along the esplanade. Julian partially hid the crowbar in his coat while Katharine stared westward.

"What?"

"It's like New Jersey isn't there."

"It is and your husband is waiting for us there. We gotta keep moving."

"How do we get to him? Without cells, there's no way to communicate."

"We get out of this city first and then we figure it out. We gotta go now."

A large crowd had gathered at the ferry terminal, but Julian insisted they keep walking.

"There's no running lights on those ferries. I think they're dead in the water."

"They're saying some of them are just floating out in the river," some guy volunteered as they passed him.

"Then why are you waiting here?" Julian asked.

"I was picking up my wife and son. The Port Authority will figure it out, so I'm just going to wait."

Off to the east, they heard gun fire. Everybody ducked, but not many people ran. Katharine remembered Ren's advice for active shooter situations and pulled Julian with her down the walkway, walking as fast as she could without bursting into a sprint. Periodic gunfire punctuated a chain of explosions. Burning buildings lit their path.

"This is awful. Absolute hell," Katharine whispered.

"Hell of a honeymoon, that's for sure."

"Honeymoon?"

"Yeah, sort of."

"Distract me from the blisters and shin splints?"

He laughed, probably at the irony of them being surrounded by distractions.

"Not much to tell. Her name is Jenna and we were engaged to be married. Booked the Casa Blanca, had theater tickets, the whole nine."

"What happened?"

"She found out some things she didn't like."

"Like why you're suddenly sounding like a dock worker instead of a software engineer?"

"I am a software engineer. I didn't lie about that. My father's a dock worker though. Works the Washington State ferries."

"So Jenna's a snob?"

"Nah. Not really." Julian gave a homeless man who got too close a threatening look and the harmless old man scuttled away in fear. Julian took a deep breath and let it out in a burst of words. "I was a hacktivist. Got caught. Did two years in Leavenworth before they offered me a deal to design unhackable software. They even paid me for it. That worked into a job with Bunnell & Wilson working with Microsoft. But the massive salary they pay me wasn't enough to make her comfortable with my felony record."

"Hacktivist? Like Julian Assange?"

"My hero at the time, yes, but that got rubbed off in prison. Now I just want a normal life."

"I'm sorry."

"For what?"

"The girl, and the life. It looks like normal isn't where we're headed."

"You're not responsible for Jenna or this current mess. There's no apology needed."

"More like I empathize. My father's a sanitation worker and my mother's a meter maid." She smiled to herself. "It was years before I could admit that to Joseph and I've never told anyone else."

"Why?"

"Aren't you ashamed of your father?"

"No. He made a decent living to keep a roof over our heads and went into debt to help me with college. But then I screwed up, thinking I knew better than everyone else. If Bunnell & Wilson had not seen that a hacker had the potential for beating out other hackers, I'd have been paroled last year and probably be working a minimum wage job, disallowed from even touching a computer. Instead, I've been out eight years and I have a nice savings account even after I paid my dad back with interest."

"Maybe your father is better than mine."

Julian shrugged. Darkness enveloped this area of the dock.

"Did you come here to visit them?" he asked.

"No. I haven't seen them in a long time. My sister found me on Facebook, but things are complicated."

"Married to one of the richest men in the world. I guess it would be. What's that like anyway?" Did he sense how uncomfortable this topic was for her?

"Nice clothes, big house—it's my father-in-law's house, but it's nice. Ren Sullivan is one of the most down-to-earth rich men you'd ever want to meet. Changes his own lightbulbs and has been known to do a load of laundry and Joseph is a wonderful man, but … I don't know. I'm still amazed he got all the way here to get me without an entourage of servants."

They walked alone now, with groups far ahead and far behind. A solitary figure came from the darkest shadows. Suddenly, his arm went around Julian's throat, a knife pricking at his Adam's apple.

"I don't want no trouble, but you're going to give me your money."

Julian's eyes flared so wide there was white all the way around his iris. Katharine had spent her life pretending to be something she wasn't. She knew how to project calm when she was terrified.

"I've got it." Katharine held up her hands. She needed Julian to get out of this city. Things could turn badly for a woman alone in this chaos. "I'll have to take off my backpack."

The skinny white man with the windburned face nodded.

"You go easy or I'll gut your boyfriend."

"I hear you." Katharine slipped her arms out of the backpack straps and set it on the pavement. Of course, her money was in her bra, but she made a show of unzipping the pouch and wrapping her hand around the 22 like it was a money roll. The robber looked startled as she drew back the hammer.

"You slit his throat, I blow your head off. Or, you run away."

The guy dropped the knife and backed away, disappearing into the approaching crowd. Katharine tucked the gun into her side so as not to scare anyone.

"Jesus, woman! You are full of surprises." A hand to his throat, Julian stared around like he was trying to recover some measure of reality. The crowd passed. He followed her as she followed them. A little further on, she stopped to release the hammer, put the gun in her pocket. Now her hands were shaking as she donned the backpack again. "Where did you get the gun?"

"Lillian. Stanley gave it to me. He found it in her stuff."

"And you didn't think to tuck it into your pocket for easier access?"

"Hand guns are illegal in New York City. I thought if we were searched by security, it would be best hidden in my backpack rather than in my coat pocket. And, with so many security squads in the city, I honestly didn't worry about being mugged before we reached New Jersey. I wasn't expecting this. Let's get going."

"You want to give that to me?"

"No, I think the gun makes me a whole lot more frightening. Anyway, you've got a crowbar and can have the knife." She held it out to him. "Are felons allowed to have guns now?"

"Gun control laws are generally suspended during the Apocalypse, I think, but you make a good point. You seem to know how to use it." He closed the knife and slid it into his pocket.

"Everyone in Kansas is armed. I humored Joseph when he wanted to teach me, but now I'm glad I did. Let's go before that creep comes back."

They turned north again. The crowd bent around a dead body propped against a fence, drying gore coming from the side of his neck, his pockets turned out. Julian stopped to stare so Katharine stopped with him.

"Thank you for saving my life"

Katharine shuddered, then nodded, unable to think of what to say in reply. "You're welcome" seemed so inadequate. Julian touched her elbow and they turned away from this reminder of how close they'd come to dying. They continued walking northward.

Looking Eastward

New Jersey

Joseph Sullivan stared down the darkening ramp behind the soldier.

"There's no chance that barrier will open while the power's out?"

"None, sir." The young soldier seemed sincere and utterly unmovable. "I understand your concern, but if your wife was in the tunnel, she's probably headed back into the city by now."

"What other open routes are there out of the city, corporal?" Perry Carmichael asked. In ordinary circumstances, Perry served as Ren Sullivan's personal pilot, but in the evolving situation they were in Joseph had pressed him into service as a kind of chauffeur cum body guard for rescuing Katharine from New York City.

"Um, Holland would be closed too. The George Washington and the Verrazano Narrows."

Perry plucked at Joseph's jacket.

"We need to get back to the truck." His voice betrayed the slightest hint of stress.

"Why?" Joseph didn't argue as he followed Perry away from the entrance to the Lincoln Tunnel, fully aware that his Columbia University education had not prepared him for this situation that Perry seemed imminently qualified for. He just wanted to understand why Perry made the decisions he made.

"It's a working vehicle and you've probably noticed there are not a lot of those."

"You're afraid it will be stolen? What causes all the vehicles to stop working all of a sudden?"

"Theoretically? An EMP."

"A what?"

"Nuclear bomb detonated high in the atmosphere. We used to make fun of the idea when I was in the Air Force, but I had a jet's nav system shut down on me once during a solar storm over Alaska, so...."

"Does that mean we're being irradiated? Shouldn't we take shelter?"

"The corporal was wearing a rad badge which was in the green range, so I think we're fine. What do you want to do?"

"Go to the George, see if we can get across."

"That's right. You went to school here. You know the city."

"I also know Katharine. If she was in the Lincoln Tunnel, she'd go back to the hotel for safety."

"That could be some real hostile territory, sir."

To their left, they heard gunfire.

"Like it isn't already hostile here?"

They'd left the old truck they'd borrowed from a Missouri farmer in a small park just north of the Holland Tunnel. As they approached, two men worked to jimmy the lock with a slim-jim.

"Hey! What do you think you're doing to my truck?"

They turned and one of them reached for his back pocket, but Perry already had his gun out and pointed at the man's head. They hesitated a split second and ran, leaving the metal bar still sticking up between the window and the door casing. Perry scanned the area for more threats, but most of the people in the vicinity seemed concerned with their own problems. He tossed the metal bar in the bed under the canopy.

“This could go sideways really easily. We should go to the Washington Bridge to assess the situation, but we'll likely end up coming back to a stripped truck if we leave it. And without a vehicle, I don't think we're making it back to Kansas.”

Joseph stared at him. Perry had been incredibly optimistic for most of this trip. His complete honesty drove home the severity of the situation.

They turned the truck north. Joseph tried to see the city on the far side of the river, but it was utterly dark.

“What do you think is going on over there?” Joseph shivered.

“Nothing good. New York without power...not a good situation. Twenty New York blocks is a long way. A woman alone and unarmed. I don't know.”

They were nearing the end of the George Washington Bridge, but the onramp was clogged with broken-down cars and people trying to start them.

"We're not driving across that bridge. It's total gridlock."

"One of us needs to stay with the truck." Perry reflexively checked his gun, so Joseph did the same. "Sir, I can't." Perry's voice cracked. "If you go, I have to go with you. If I go, you have to go with me. Watching each other's back is the only way this works. But if we leave the truck, we lose our best means for getting back to Kansas. Your daughter needs you as much as she needs your wife. I think we should stay here and wait to see if Mrs. Sullivan makes it to us."

"She could go in any direction once she's off the bridge."

"She could, so I say we build a bonfire. It'll attract people in the dark. It'll attract Mrs. Sullivan."

"And if she doesn't come? Maybe she's gone back to the hotel."

"Maybe communications will be back tomorrow. You don't dive into a firefight without any idea of what is going on. In the morning, we may know what we actually need to know."

Joseph stared at the sweep of the bridge, a dark structure against the stars that were usually so hard to see near the city. He nodded, sighing.

"I'm going to go gather stuff to burn," Perry explained. "I need your word that you're not going to go anywhere." He waited for Joseph's answer.

"I just gave it to you, Perry. I won't go anywhere. I'll get started with the base fire. And, I thought we agreed ... I'm Joseph, right?"

Perry looked toward the unreachable city. "Joseph, I'm sorry we can't rush across that bridge to find her."

"No ... you're right. We can't do this on foot."

He stared at the city again, seeing flickers of light here and there.

"What is that?" Perry asked.

"Probably working vehicles, but – Maybe people carrying flashlights. They're moving too slowly to be cars, but they are definitely moving. That's Riverside Park, people using the esplanade as a route north and south. If Kat didn't go back to the hotel, she would be one of them."

Perry pointed to a bright pinpoint of light in Lower Manhattan.

"And that?"

Joseph swallowed tightly and rolled down his window.

"I think that's a high rise on fire."

Perry rubbed his face. He'd aged since leaving Kansas. Joseph couldn't believe it had only been a few days. How could the world have gone so completely mad in such a short time? Had they really been that fragile all along?

"Katharine's in that."

"And there's absolutely nothing we can do to help her right now. It would take us hours to cross that bridge and, in a city that large, we have no idea how to find her. We could miss her by a block and not even know it. She knew where we were. It just makes sense for us to stay put and for her to come to us. And if she doesn't come, then we reassess in the morning."

Much as Joseph's instincts said to go find his wife, his logic insisted Perry was right. He knew portions of Manhattan fairly well, but he could get lost between subway stops. Katharine had grown up there. She knew her way around.

And, yet, an unarmed woman in a city gone mad… This was going to be the hardest night of his life.

Who We Don't Want to Be

New York City

Katharine's stomach growled and Julian's echoed. They glanced at each other, laughing ruefully. They agreed they needed food and detoured into a neighborhood to the east to find it. Across the street from the park lay old brownstones that had been converted into apartments. Julian tried doors, but nobody answered. New Yorkers didn't open their doors to strangers on a good night, let alone during Armageddon.

Katharine found a basement door unlocked. Her flashlight beam bounced off washing machines, dryers and a set of vending machines. The warmth of Julian's body touched her back. He pushed by her, opening his wallet. She smiled as he attempted to feed the dollar bill into the receiver.

"Right. No power." He pulled out the crowbar and smack the front window of the vending machine. It shattered into a pile of tiny little pieces. "What would you like, m'lady?"

Katharine unzipped her backpack.

"I say we take it all. And see if you can force that soda machine."

While she emptied the vending machine, he rammed the crowbar into the side of the machine and popped open the front. They were fitting bottles of cola into his backpack when the inner door at the top of the stairs opened.

"Who's down there? I've got a gun."

"So, do we," Julian hollered back. "We don't want trouble. We just need supplies. Stay upstairs and there's no problem."

Silence echoed off the walls for a long moment and then the door closed and a bolt slid back into place. Katharine heard Julian swallow in the darkness and then mutter a swear word.

"This is not who I want to be."

"Our way out of here is on the other side of that river and we need strength enough to make it."

"I know." Julian shined his phone's flashlight at the vending machine, mouth moving silently. He pulled two bills from his wallet and dropped them in the bottom of the vending machine. "Let's go."

"Right behind you." He went out the door ahead of her and Katherine grabbed the two bills and tucked them into her bra. That $40 might come in handy on the way to Kansas.

The bridge was only about a half-hour's walk further on. Katherine had driven over the bridge once or twice as a passenger in a car, but of course, she'd not been paying attention as she'd been engrossed by the artistry of the iconic bridge. They wandered up a grassy strip to the concrete lower deck, nibbling chocolate and washing it down with soda. With sugar and fluids replenished, they faced west, walking down the right double-lane, weaving between all the stalled cars. Some owners still tried to get their cars going, but most had given up and joined Julian and Katharine on their eerie walk through the darkness.

"How much further?" Beyond the railing, it had begun to rain. Despite the food in their system, the hours of walking were wearing on them and Katharine's back was starting to ache. She had to check his watch since their phones were no longer registering time.

"Maybe three hours. I don't think I can walk any further, though. My feet are numb."

"Oh, thank God. I thought you'd never admit that. I'm exhausted. It's got to be past midnight. Let's rest."

"Where? It's not safe out here."

"You don't think I can protect you?"

"I think I had to protect you not so long ago and that should have taught you something."

"That New Yorkers are badasses, yeah. But look around. Most of these people are just like us, trying to get away from Badass City. I guess we could see if someone left their car unlocked."

That quickly became a faint hope. People had assumed they could come back for their cars and so had locked them. While the crowd kept walking west, Julian indicated a spot between one of the broken-down cars and the concrete railing.

"Keep your backpack on. We'll catch a few hours and then push on to Jersey."

It wasn't much of a shelter, but the upper deck provided a roof and the car would screen them from sight. Katharine put her hand in her pocket where the gun rested. Slowly, the blood returned to her feet and ache replaced numbness. Images of fires mixed with Lillian's death and an occasional flicker of Joseph's face flitted through her mind as her head settled back against the concrete. And, then, almost without knowing it, between one breath and the next, she fell asleep.

A Last Hint of Normality

Emmaus, Kansas

Alex Lufgren smiled as the lightbulb over the desk glowed when he flipped the switch on.

"See, it was just a brownout," he told Keri. "The surge blew the bulbs. No biggie."

"But we're still on the windmill, aren't we?" She seemed better today after her adventure yesterday. He couldn't quite reconcile his wife the school teacher with a sniper in a water tower, but he certainly understood why she'd done it.

"You mean our windmill, not the power plant's turbine?" She nodded. "Yeah." He turned on the radio that sat in the windowsill. The dial lit up, but he couldn't pull in KERB, so he turned it off. "Town power must still be out."

He picked up his cell from the hutch where they charged them. “No bars.”

Keri picked up hers.

“Actually, mine’s dead.” She turned the black screen to him.

“Really? The surge protector’s supposed to be top quality. Too bad I bought it at a Radio Shack in Denver; no refund.”

Keri tried the surge protector’s power switch and then tried to reset its onboard breaker, but nothing happened.

“Nope. I think it’s fried.”

Alex’s teenaged sister Poppy clattered down the stairs, waving her phone around, signing that it was broken. Poppy, like most Lufgrens, had been born deaf and texting kept her in touch with people. Alex took it from her and tried to power it up, even plugging it in, but it was dead too.

“My friends, how me call?”

“Don’t know. Maybe go see?”

She stomped her foot at Alex’ suggestion. Keri signed for her to go upstairs and get ready for school. Poppy made a show of making as much noise as possible going up the stairs.

“She does that deliberately, doesn’t she?”

“She knows I can hear it even if she can’t and she’s had fourteen years to learn what irritates me." Alex turned at the sound of the kitchen door. Farm hand Mark Ramirez yawned.

"How you feeling?" Alex asked him.

"Surprisingly good for a man who stared death in the face yesterday. Keri, can Alice catch a ride to town with you? We're getting low on gas."

"Yeah, of course. Coffee in a few minutes."

Mark thanked her. He had a towel under his arm.

"Can I use your shower, boss?" he asked Alex.

"You know where it is. And you know you can use our gas pump, right?"

"I think we might want to ration it, use it for what we need rather than random trips into town."

Alex had a family recipe for making ethanol, but since he didn't have a still, it wouldn't do them a lot of good. They had more immediate concerns anyway. The Ramirez family needed to move into the house as the nights were getting cold.

"Put this bulb in the bathroom socket," Alex said as Mark headed up the stairs. "That brownout seems to have gotten them all."

Pete Ramirez came in the back door, tapping on his phone screen.

"That's weird. The network is down again."

"It happens," Alex assured him. "Rural Kansas, nuclear Armageddon."

"Eggs?" Keri asked.

Alice Ramirez set her preschooler Lisa on the floor inside the door, assuring Keri that she could cook for her family. "You don't have to make breakfast for us."

"You're family now. If you weren't before, you are now after helping me defend the town."

"You want to gather eggs while I get the milking theater going?" Alex asked Pete.

The teenager followed him outside. It was still dark and Alex paused to stare out across the prairie. Mocha, the chocolate Lab, leapt over the paddock fence to herd the goats toward the milking shed.

"Odd." Alex stared at the sky.

"What?" Pete asked.

"I can usually see the town lights reflected off the clouds."

"You enjoy that? I thought people lived in the country to avoid light pollution and all that crap."

Kid had a point, but Alex still felt out of sorts. "I'm used to it," he explained.

Keri surprised Alex while he was monitoring the milking theater. Her battery was dead. Mark, a certified mechanic who seemed to speak car, offered to check it out. He came back wiping grease off his fingers when Alex was filling the chiller bottles and reported that he'd sent the three women to town in an old beater Subaru because something was wrong with every other vehicle he tried. He also reported that the phone lines were completely down, so he thought he'd try to figure out what was wrong with Alex's newer trucker instead of going to the mine.

"It's some sort of timing issue, I think."

"I can't deal with it right now," Alex explained. "I need to get this milk over to the dairy. Still, it's weird that a bunch of our vehicles are suddenly not working all at the same time."

"That's what I'm thinking."

"Could be an EMP." Pete held a wire basket filled with the eggs he'd been gathering.

"A what?" Mark paused on his way to the door.

"Electromagnetic pulse."

"That's science fiction." Alex scoffed, but when Mark looked thoughtful, he stopped.

"The transformer at the bottom of your lane blew last night. That explains the blown electronics and light bulbs. But that wouldn't have affected the cars. An EMP could affect all of them."

"So why does everything work in here?"

Mark looked at Pete.

"Because you're old school and have mostly analog stuff that doesn't blow easily," the teenager said. "That's for when you lose power and have to go on the windmill, right?"

"The windmill also saves me a boatload in electricity."

Mark explained that modern cars had a lot of electronics and were sensitive to static, while older cars had heavier wiring and no computers. Because Alex's "new" truck was not that new, it was running while Keri's Tahoe was not. Mark believed he could bypass the computer and the truck might run just fine.

With his livelihood in the back of his big farm truck, Alex just couldn't be bothered with the details. He thanked Mark for his contribution, lined Pete out for the next few hours of work and fired up the truck, which seemed to be working just fine. The sun just blushed the eastern horizon with seashell pink and blue as he turned west on the Old 24 toward Mara Wells.

Bad Petrol & Other Myths

Missouri

Dawn painted the eastern sky when Javi moved and woke her. Amisi Ceylon sat up, keeping her sleeping bag wrapped around her against the cold while trying to stretch out the aches of sleeping on the hard ground. The tarp she'd pulled over them crackled.

"What is it?" Javi asked.

"Nothing. It's dawn."

"You going to take this blindfold off?"

Last night had started out pleasantly enough for this adventure they'd been living together for the last week. It was going to be her first camp out and she thought maybe the reserve Javi shielded himself with was finally starting to dissolve. At least he was starting to trust her with details of his real life, like having been in the Army.

And then he'd gone blind. She couldn't explain it. One moment he could see and the next he couldn't. Being a doctor, she had a med kit with her and she diagnosed flash blindness, except there'd been no light strong enough to do that ... unless it had happened while her eyes were closed, so briefly that it affected him, but not her. Whatever had happened, it had turned the hero of their team into someone utterly dependent upon her.

"No, not yet. Look, I don't know what caused it. I'm not an ophthalmologist, but I saw a few cases in the ER and they always treated it with a period of time letting the eyes rest."

"And you said it usually fixes itself."

"Yeah, usually." That he'd lost his vision so suddenly worried her. He'd complained of his corneas burning—a symptom of flash-burn—and the sudden blindness suggested retinal damage. "If your cones are trying to heal themselves, too much light right now might set them back, so I think we just need to wait, unless we go to a hospital where someone more qualified than I am can help you."

"No." There was a sharpness to his tone that said this was one of those topics on which he would not entertain arguments. "You're right. I'll take it easy today. You can drive."

"Where are we going?"

"Further west."

She'd accepted that the price she paid for his help was that he kept secrets. But now, he needed to let go of his reticence because he couldn't see to get where he needed to go. It was not easy for him.

"Much further and we'll be in Denver, which seems unhealthy."

Denver was among the several cities that had been irradiated by suitcase nukes two weeks ago.

"We're not going that far."

"Colorado Springs to see your kids?"

He smiled. He seriously needed a shave and a shower, but that would have to wait until they could take off the blindfold.

"You guessed correctly that there's no kids. I've never been married. That safe house I told you about is near a town called Emmaus, Kansas."

"I'll consult the map as soon as it gets light enough to see. In the meantime, maybe you could talk me through restarting the fire."

"Is it dead?"

He probably knew how to stock a fire so it burned all night, but she'd done her best last night. Her childhood in Cairo had been upper-class. She'd never needed to build a fire. This was all new to her.

A tendril of smoke attested to a little bit of life. Tying her ringlets in a bandana for safety, she piled dried grass on the coals and blew until she was dizzy. It finally caught and she added larger and larger sticks until it burned steadily. He talked her through making coffee and how to use the CO2 heater to warm MREs.

"This feels so weird," Javi admitted as she handed him a pouch of sausage and they fumbled to get it set right in his hand. "I've never felt this helpless in my entire life."

His voice quavered. She suspected he had felt that helpless before … as a small child caught up in the foster care system. That was the fire that had refined who he was. Ami sat down on her sleeping bag with MRE portions spread around her.

"It'll be okay." She silently praised herself for sounding more certain than she felt. An awkward silence ensued while Javi struggled to dissect the sausage he couldn't see and she refrained from trying to help. After eating a muffin portion, she gathered up the oddments to keep for later meals.

"I should start packing the car."

"Yeah. Um...okay. Here's the thing: I can't protect us like this."

She paused in the act of shaking out her sleeping bag. "The next town should have a motel. We'll both sleep better in warmth and with a roof."

Javi cocked his head as if trying to read her expression with his ears.

"We have no idea what could be coming our way."

"You're right, but I've been wearing this gun for days now and.... You're going to have to trust me for the next day or two. Besides, you could use some antibiotics and I haven't got those."

She helped him put on his shoes and shirt and sit in the passenger seat while she packed the camp. He asked for the keys to turn on the radio.

"That's weird," she said as she watched him fumble.

"What?"

"That's the AM dial and you're not picking up ghost channels even."

"That is a little weird."

Ami slid into the driver's seat and adjusted it for her shorter legs. Starting the car, she turned down the road they'd come in on.

"What's with the car? It's running really rough."

"No clue. I don't know much about cars." She stopped at the gate.

"What's up?"

"You closed the gate. I have to open it."

"Um, that's going to be complicated." Then he confessed to locking the gate.

In the end, she put the picks in the lock and he fished around until he felt the tumblers. She hated that he felt so uncertain being led by her but, of course, he wasn't used to being blind. She hoped this wouldn't last so long that he would become used to depending on her. He grunted when he smacked his head on the door frame as he tried to climb back into the car.

"Sorry. I'm not used to helping someone sit in a car."

He rubbed his upper temporal bone where a slight lump was forming.

"It's fine. I've got a thick skull."

He fumbled around with his left hand trying to find the seatbelt receiver. She wanted to jump in and help, but she didn't want to insult him. He finally requested.

"Helpless is not a good feeling."

"We're going to find a motel and you're going to sleep all day. I'll find you some antibiotics and you'll be fine."

"Great. Glad we have the next twenty-four hours figured out."

Driving to the nearest town proved to be something of an obstacle course because of all the cars abandoned on the highway. Javi frowned when she told him about the third one.

"Maybe some sort of wide-area dampening field? Our car sounds like it's been affected."

"Bad petrol, maybe. Used to happen all the time in Egypt."

St. Cloud, Missouri, had set up a checkpoint on Route 61. The local police officer looked over their IDs and registration and asked to look in the cargo area. When Ami escorted him back there, he asked about Javi's bandages.

"He got careless with white gas." Ami had no idea what white gas was, but she remembered a patient in the ER with flash-blindness from some sort of explosion involving the mysterious vapor. Or was it a liquid?

"One of our officers was temporarily blinded last night by what he says was a flash of light in the sky."

"Hmm, that's interesting."

"You sure you don't want to change your story?"

"No, I don't, Officer. Is this sky-flash anything to do with the broken-down cars?"

"We don't know, yet." He closed the cargo hatch. "I think the Budget still has a few rooms. Grocery store's been cleaned out. I'd take those MREs into the room with you tonight. Folks around here are scared, you know? It's good you're armed."

Ami nodded.

"Thanks for the heads-up."

Javi waited in the car while she went into the Budget Inn to secure a room.

"The power's been out all day." The balding front desk clerk with the high voice leaned back in his chair with his chubby hands folded over his paunch. "No magic fingers. No hot water. Even the vending machines ain't working."

"That's fine. Two beds are all we need. And is there a pharmacy in town?"

"There is, but the USDA was here and cleaned most of it out."

"The USDA? I thought they inspected crops and certified milk."

"Yeah, well, apparently they confiscate crops and medicines during times of national crisis. But it's just two blocks up on the right. It's a Walgreens."

Javi had the heels of his hands to his temples when she got back to the car.

"Headache?"

"Yes, and my eyes are burning."

"Suddenly or...?"

"It's been growing and I wasn't complaining."

"You have to tell me your symptoms. I need to find a pharmacy and you need to rest in a darkened room."

He didn't argue while she drove around to the room and helped him inside. Remembering that he had always taken the bed closest to the door, she guided him to the one closer to the bathroom and folded back the covers.

"You should try to sleep. I'll be back in an hour."

"You can't leave me here like this."

"I must. You need rest and I need to get you medication."

"I'm completely helpless without you."

"The door will be locked."

"Where's my gun?"

"Not where you can access it. You can't see and I'll not have you shooting me because you're in a panic."

"I can't do this alone."

"Sleep? Of course, you can. Now, I have to go."

His death grip on her wrist might have restrained her had she not been trained in techniques to release herself from patient grabs. When she got her wrist free, she backed up so he couldn't grab her again. He smelled of fear and sweat.

"I will be back. I promise."

"I don't believe you."

"No, from what you've said you've not had much reason to trust in your life, but I keep my word. And, I owe you my life. I won't abandon you, but I also won't let you be permanently blinded by your own fear."

She reached the door as he cocked his head, trying to define the room and locate her. He'd be good at that if she gave him time to make use of his other four senses. She slipped out the door and locked it firmly behind her.

Not A Ray of Sunshine

People finally left Rob's office just after dawn, so after a few minutes of staring at the desktop and praying silently, he walked out into the lobby of what served as a police station for the town. Shane and Jace Welton stood at the counter staring at something.

"What's the situation?" Rob asked, seeing it was a map.

"I drove east about twenty miles, then swept south, came back through Beulah. Every transformer is fried." Shane didn't look tired, but he had to be going into his second day without sleep.

"Same to the west and north." Jace acted as city engineer and he looked exhausted.

Rob sighed. They'd lost the elementary school and several houses in fires, but at least no more people had died since the USDA had been arrested. "So, that means—"

"It gets worse. The generator farm in Beulah was on fire." Shane shrugged to show he couldn't explain it.

"It had to be an EMP," Jace said. "Some things are working, like the old work trucks, for example, and my watch. But the grid is shattered."

"The turbines?"

"Not moving when there's wind," Shane reported. "It's outside of my area of expertise, but I'm thinking they're not working because something's fried inside. I did see a couple of old windmills turning, so ...." He shrugged. "I thought about going to Alex's to see if he's got power from his windmill, but I'm starting to see double."

"Yeah." Rob feared falling asleep on his feet if he closed his eyes. "What about the telephones?"

Shane looked at Jace.

"I only know what I've read, but the old ding-a-ling system probably would work if the switches aren't fried, which they probably are."

"You're talking about the old rotary phones?"

"Well, any land-based phone system—assuming it wasn't replaced by fiber-optics and assuming the switch between the two phones was not destroyed by the pulse."

"Is there a way to bypass the switches?" Shane never paused to grieve. Rob appreciated his forward thinking.

"Maybe. I'll let you know."

"You got a working car or are we walking?" Rob asked Shane.

"My Jeep is outside."

Jace announced he was taking the work truck and headed toward the front stairs. Rob followed Shane toward the back stairs. Joe slept on the couch in Bart's office.

He had to stop calling it Bart's office and find the time to tell Joe he'd been promoted by circumstance.

Rob wondered why Shane's Jeep was working, but he was beginning to understand that his son wouldn't give him direct answers to direct questions, so he didn't bother. Shane rubbed both hands across his face before sliding the car in gear.

"Do you need me to drive?"

"Have you slept more recently than I have?"

"Maybe by an hour or two. When did you sleep?"

Shane took a moment to answer as he finessed his way over the sidewalk to avoid two crashed and abandoned cars.

"I think I caught about five hours night before last."

"You know your body will eventually demand you take care of it?"

"That's what they tell me."

Rob glanced down at the console where Shane's cell phone lit up with a message.

"How the hell is that thing working?"

Shane's gaze flickered over to it.

"I suspect the case acts as a faraday cage." He pulled over to the curb to look at the screen. He smiled briefly and texted back to the sender.

"Do they know what's going on?"

"It's just a check-in." Shane put the phone back on the console and pulled away from the curb. He acted like the subject had passed.

"Aren't the towers fried?" Shane frowned. After a moment, Rob growled. "You won't answer."

"When you were in the Army, could you tell friends and family everything?"

"Did you know this was coming?"

Shane's eyes flashed and he sped up a little. "Why am I not surprised you asked me that question?"

"You were prepared."

The car slowed slightly as Shane's jaw muscles rippled and then he relaxed a little. "I was just playing with the car. Improving the suspension, stuff like that. They hardened the vehicles at BW and I thought it was a good idea. My communications gear is government-issued. I got lucky. That doesn't mean I knew this was coming. Jace was saying that the government has mostly not prepped for this, so we may not need to worry about anyone following up on the USDA, at least not for a while."

Rob rubbed a hand over his face and scratched his beard.

"Something on your mind?"

"What I do with them. We lost a bag silo and three trucks full of food, mostly from people who didn't hide theirs well enough. That's people starving later this winter."

"I heard there are 20 people dead already."

"Eighteen between the two towns. What did Beulah look like when you drove through?"

"There were a whole lot of dead bodies wearing USDA jackets piled up in the back of a truck outside the court house and enough National Guard on the roof to make me not want to stop for a visit. I'm going to guess some Beulah folks died. So, it seems your only decision is the method of execution."

Rob stared as his middle child calmly discussing the execution of government agents.

"You willing to pull that trigger, son?"

A long pause ensued.

"Yeah, if you need me to." Shane's voice was soft and utterly controlled.

"Don't you have enough nightmares?"

"Don't you?" Shane's counter caught Rob by surprise.

"My point exactly," he said. "There's got to be a better way than that."

Shane sighed. "So, your alternative?"

"Not there yet."

Shane pulled behind Jill's Tahoe in the driveway of the house that had sheltered five generations of Delaneys. The live oaks to either side of the walkway were just starting to turn toward their fall colors.

"You don't think your mom's going anywhere?" Rob pointed to the Tahoe.

"Not with that car."

Shane got his duffle bag out of the back, but before he lifted it onto his shoulder he pulled out the tablet. Rob wondered what else was in that go-bag.

"Is it working?"

"It's got no signal, but yeah. I need sleep before I can deal with it."

Jill met them at the back door. Shane's nose wrinkled.

"What's burning?"

"I've checked for actual fire. I think it's all the fried electronics. Must have been an incredible surge."

Rob exchanged an astonished glance with Shane. While they'd figured it out in the heat of the moment, Jill had been at home. With no television or Internet, she'd been in the dark literally and figuratively.

"It was an EMP, Mom."

Her mouth twitched like she might laugh, but then she sobered.

"Power's not coming back on, at least not for a good long while, and we're probably going to need to address it ourselves."

Jill looked at Rob for verification or the announcement of a joke. When she saw his face, she sat down in a kitchen chair, gasping.

"Aren't I just a ray of sunshine? Going to bed now." Shane left the kitchen.

"He's running on empty." How else to explain their son's flat affect?

"He's a realist." Jill's gaze swept the kitchen, eyes settling on the electric stove with all the bells and whistles he'd installed three years ago. "We kept the food, but now I'm not sure how to cook it."

"We'll figure it out, honey. I've got to get some sleep, too."

"Marnie never came home and my car isn't working. Can I take your truck to go check on her?"

"My truck broke down with the EMP last night. It's a brick with wheels now."

"I don't suppose Shane would let me borrow his car."

"You better catch him before he goes to sleep, but don't enter the room, because if he's already asleep—"

"He's you after you came back from Vietnam. I know that, maybe better than you." She moved to leave the kitchen, then paused. "I'm scared. For the first time, I'm really scared."

"I hear you. Listen." He told her briefly about what was going on with the USDA agents. "Not all of them participated in the killing and abuse, but most people are going to want to see the others die."

"Rumdale at least."

"What you said about hanging him?"

"I still feel that way, but ... I'm supposed to forgive him."

"That doesn't mean he's walking away from this."

"No. He's dangerous to us and other communities."

"Do I give the others a pass?"

"I don't know."

"Do you have an inquest report?" Jacob stood in the door between the living room and kitchen.

"I started a partial one at City Hall," Rob explained. "It's hand-written for now."

"I'll give you a ride over there, Jill. We can check on Marnie and type up that report."

"There's no electricity."

"I saw an old typewriter down in the storage when I was feeding that kid, Danny. Probably the one I used when I was mayor. While you get some sleep, Rob, I'll convene an inquest jury and see what they say. This shouldn't be one man's decision, and we need to make one before our prisoners start consuming resources."

Rob's 95-year-old father was still spry and in possession of all his faculties. He'd been an invaluable part of Rob's crisis management during this chaotic time.

"I figured you'd want to let them walk away down the interstate."

"I do, except for Rumdale. I don't want to see the man dead, but I recognize he can't live through this. People are going to want justice. I'll work on volunteers for that too."

Jacob's energy seemed too bright and active compared to Rob's exhaustion.

"You sleep last night, Pa?"

"I did, but I also spent time praying. You'll have my recommendations when you wake up. Jill, you need to do anything before we go?"

"You should eat."

Jacob looked around the kitchen, then barked a short laugh.

"It's too warm to fire up that cooker there. I'll take a bread and butter sandwich and one for that kid Danny at the jail. Make it two, so we cover lunch too."

Jill moved to take care of that while Rob stared at the old wood-and-coal cookstove in the corner near the steps to the mudroom.

"Ma used to use that sometimes, didn't she?"

"Yup. We still have a couple of barrels of coal out in the garage. We'll need more to get through the winter. I think you've got enough wood for the living room stove and we can supplement with corn cobs. Have to figure all that out tomorrow. Deal with the objects in view now."

A knock on the backdoor announced Jazz Tully, who shared Shane's forward-looking view. With school canceled on account of the fire, she wanted to get started harvesting the crab apples from the old orchard out back

Rob watched his father and the young teacher interact and thought his father had quite a crush on Ms. Tully. After they left to get the chainsaw out of the garage, Jill turned and wrapped her arms around Rob.

"It's going to be okay." Her hair tickled his nose as he mumbled into it.

"No, it won't be, but we'll get through it as a family. I just wonder how Cai's going to get home."

"He's smart. He'll figure it out."

"I want to believe that."

"Then do. I've got to get some sleep, darlin'. Wake me about noon."

She nodded. When he looked back at her assembling the sandwiches, he saw her wipe away a tear, but he knew she'd never admit to that if he asked.

Set Back

The MacArthur Dairy sat just northwest of Mara Wells. Only two days ago, a collection of farm buildings had stood on a gentle rise as the prairie continued its tilt toward the Rockies. Now smoke rose from the collapsed barn and destroyed production building, the stench of roasted cow entrails making Alex gag as he got out of the truck. Several black-faced workers turned toward him, but then turned back to their work of breaking apart the smoldering debris. A man broke away from the work to greet him.

"You brought milk to sell?"

"I did. What happened?"

"Some sort of massive electrical surge. Something caught fire and we were only able to save 10 cows and none of the production facility. Sorry, there was no way to let people know that we're having a fire sale."

"Alex Lufgren, by the way." They shook hands, Alex's hand coming away with soot "I'm sorry for your loss. Was anyone hurt?"

"I'm Abe MacArthur. We had a few smoke inhalation problems, nobody really hurt. Losing the cows is the biggest hit. There's no way to rebuild right now, but I'll be working those 10 cows to their utmost. How many do you have?"

"About the same. Over in Emmaus."

"Emmaus? That used to be the buckle of the dairy belt for this part of Kansas. My father used to talk about the Lufgrens over there. Said they were marvelous dairymen."

"We've always had cows." Lufgrens weren't a prideful bunch, so Alex had not heard of this legendary status.

"You pasteurize and chill it yourself?" Alex nodded. "You still have electricity?"

"We have an old windmill. It's still working."

Abe looked at the turbine that stood behind his burned-out facility.

"Of course, we didn't think of that when we built the new facility. Tore down our old one. That new-fangled one there hasn't moved all morning, despite the wind. Frustrating. Can I send a man or two to check out yours, see if they can recreate it?"

"Sure. Lufgren's Crossing. Northeast corner. Yellow farm house, red barn."

"Do you have the means to bottle your milk?"

"I don't."

"Pity." Abe scratched his sooty beard. "But you can dispense it to people in pitchers if you have to. Without the USDA looking over your shoulder, you could sell to your town. I suspect we won't see the government until spring, if then. Good luck."

"You too."

Alex gazed around the former dairy. This area had been marginal farm land begging to become pasturage. The house and remaining barn were new, as were the buildings that had burned. It would be cold and windy here this winter. Alex suspected MacArthur Dairy would be out of business by spring. But he prayed it wouldn't be.

"I'd better get this back before it spoils."

Alex drove away with emptiness in his chest. Until now, the end of the world had been theoretical to him, but now it had affected his business and he was scrambling to save his resources and find a way to make the new situation work for his family's survival.

Greyeyes

Wyandot Lake shimmered silver in the morning sunlight as Mick Parker drove past the sign announcing the Wendat Reservation. Trees dressed in their fall colors waved in the breeze to either side of the asphalt strip. Beyond the trees lay cleared corn fields now tilled with winter wheat. The tribal police department had been gutted by fire and several cars had their hoods up with people bent over the engines.

Scruffy houses edged the shore of the lake. Parker turned into Porcupine Street and pulled up at the edge of a weedy lawn where two men and a woman were working on a truck. The woman cast a suspicious gaze their way.

"Wait here," Frank Giffin told him. Jason Breen had sent out his truckers in twos so that one of them would be in charge and Frank was the designated leader here. "These people can get a little touchy."

Frank got out of the car. "I'm looking for Ed Greyeyes."

The three exchanged glances and then the taller of the men wiped his hands on a rag, moving to meet Frank. Ed was middle-aged, with curly almost-black hair and the grey eyes that were characteristic of the family.

"What do you want?"

"I'm Frank Giffin from Emmaus. Jacob Delaney asked me to check on you."

"That's nice of Uncle Israel. We're good here. A few buildings burned down, half the cars aren't working, whole Rez has no power, but we're working on it. How are things in Emmaus?"

"About the same. If you've got anything to trade, or can get anything to trade, talk to Jacob or Jason Breen at Liberty Trucking. We're trying to establish a network."

Ed tugged on his Foo-Manchu beard. Frank had been married to a Wyandot gal before he'd gone to prison and knew that the slowness was not a sign of mental lethargy. It was a cultural thing. You didn't speak until you were fairly certain of what you wanted to say. He wondered what had happened to Ana after she'd divorced him. She didn't live on the Rez anymore, he knew.

"That sounds like a good idea. We don't have anything to trade. though. The USDA took it all with the help of some BIA agents." Ed muttered a descriptive swear word under his breath. "They took it to that facility at the east end of the lake."

"Have you folks tried to reclaim it?"

"It's not an easy facility to get into and we've been dealing with broken cars and stuff. Some people believed the BIA were just storing the grain for us, but then the lights went out and nobody is answering the door. Now we're worried about making it through the winter. How'd things go in Emmaus?"

"We fought back and have a couple dozen USDA agents in the jail."

Ed smiled, which transformed his somber Indian face into something soft and friendly.

"Good for you. We'll have to reclaim our corn and create that network. People here are pissed and we're ready to fight."

"Plan it well, man. Keep yourselves safe."

"Safe? That's for ordinary days."

Frank got back into the truck and Parker drove toward the other end of the lake. When he told Parker about what had happened on the reservation, the younger man shook his head, smacking the heel of his hand across the steering wheel.

"I'm for killing every last one of them."

Frank nodded. He didn't feel at all guilty about clubbing the USDA agent to death. Those people got what they deserved. It was worth the restless night to get one of them.

The USDA facility at Wyandot Lake lay just past the Forestry complex. Both buildings were silent and dark, like most buildings since the blackout. Emmaus had "borrowed" a forestry plane to stop a corn field fire that had put a serious dent in their winter food stores. He didn't see where they'd returned it yet, not that Frank cared. The USDA building was a stack of offices at one end of a large warehouse wing. Several trucks were behind the high fence topped with concertina wire.

Frank pushed the buzzer beside the door, but nobody came. He tried pounding on the door but still got no response. Parker joined him at the truck.

"It's all locked up and I couldn't see anyone in the lobby windows. So, I don't know. What do you think?"

"I think we're heading back. We can't break into this with just the two of us. But Wyandot's ready to fight and Emmaus might throw in with them for the right reason."

They drove south. Frank twisted in the seat and watched the building as they drove. Just before they dropped over a rise that blocked his sight, he saw a flicker of movement in one of the upper windows.

ready to fight and Blemous might throw in with them for that reason.

They drove south. Frank twisted in the seat and watched the building as they drove across. Before they dropped over a rise that blocked it from sight, he saw a flicker of movement in one of the upper windows.

Stirring Trouble

Shane paused at Lufgren's Crossing and stared south toward the Delaney Airfield. His handler Grant Rigby was dealing with his own issues from the pulse, but he'd taken a few minutes to apprise Shane of what he knew. Cai was alive and somewhere that Rigby wouldn't identify because he knew Shane would go to get him. He'd reiterated that the thumb drives in Shane's safe were important enough to be dangerous. Whenever Rigby's equipment was back up and running, he'd let Shane know what was going on out there and try to unlock the Jericho Springs Hotel. Apparently, the pulse had fried the electronic brain, so it now considered Shane to be an intruder...a problem since it held resources Shane needed.

Alex's big farm truck passed by with a little toot of the horn. Shane hadn't come out here to visit with his brother-in-law and best friend, but he had information Alex needed to know, so he followed him up the driveway to the farm house.

Keri bolted off the porch, followed by Poppy. Keri talked a blue streak for a good minute before she sobbed and buried her face in Alex' shirt. Poppy explained what Keri had said: the elementary school had burned down and the school board members considered the school year for all age groups to done.

"Bummer for teachers, I guess." Shane laughed at the dirty look his sister gave him. "I know. I'm a jerk. But we need people working, not teaching. That's a sad fact, but it is a fact."

"So, we just don't teach kids to read or do math?" she snapped.

"Of course not, but winter is coming and a lot of those children you care so much about are going to starve or freeze to death before spring. School isn't that much of a priority under those circumstances."

"They're children. Are we going back to the Industrial Revolution and kids working in factories?"

"You're being hysterical." Shane hated overly-emotional people. Just keep the important objects in view and do what you had to do to survive.

Keri looked at Alex, who looked like a deer caught in headlights.

"You agree with him?"

Alex was a brave man.

"I agree there's a lot to do that we normally do by machine. We maybe need to consider our priorities."

Shane waited for Keri to explode, but Alex apparently could talk sense to her. She sighed instead and asked sincerely what an unemployed teacher was supposed to do during the Apocalypse.

Shane's radio squealed.

"Maverick, what's your twenty? Over."

"Maverick here, Pathfinder. Lufgren Crossing, over."

"Bastiat's Ghost has a couple of jobs for you. You used to climb over the Arikaree Breaks, right? Over."

"Yeah. Over."

"Ever run across some coal fields? Over."

"It rings a vague bell, but that might have been in another country. Does Jacob think there's some there? Over."

"We're going to look at some USDA maps here at City Hall. If we find it, are you willing to drive a truck over there? Over."

"Yes, sir. We could probably make it a community event if we let Jason Breen in on it. Over."

"There's safety in numbers. Anyone who can is fine by me. For now, I need you to go to the feed store and sell some flour to Anders McAuliff. Over."

"What is he trading and what's the exchange rate?"

"Salt, of course, and bag for bag."

"When."

"Forty-five minutes from now."

"I'll stop at Jason's on my way there. Over."

"Sounds good. Over."

"Over and out."

Shane looked up to see Keri staring at him.

"What?"

"I think I just found a way to make myself useful."

Shane opened his mouth intending to say "no", but he saw shades of Jill in her daughter and he thought better of it.

"If Alex is willing to provide a truck and you can talk someone firearms-proficient into being your shotgun, then yeah. The more the merrier."

Alex had been in heated conversation with Poppy and so hadn't heard any of their exchange. Far more traditional than Shane, he probably wouldn't appreciate Shane getting ahead of him, but he was already there, so .... Wow, Poppy really had become a teenager, demanding and irrational.

"I gotta go," he announced in spoken word and sign. Alex told Poppy to close her mouth and turned to Shane.

"You and I should actually plan a conversation, I guess," he said.

"It's not my fault." Shane laughed. "Seriously, I don't remember this town being so exciting when I was younger."

Alex, the son of Deaf parents, was a master at reading expressions and body language in the Hearing. He cocked his head, looking from Shane to Keri and back again.

"What have you two done?"

"Not my fight." Shane moved toward his Jeep.

"It's not what we've done, but what we're going to do tomorrow." Keri put a restraining hand on Alex' arm to force him to have the conversation with her rather than Shane, who slid behind the wheel of the Jeep and drove off. He watched in the rearview mirror to see Alex' reaction. He didn't like it, but that didn't mean he would try to stop her either.

Ami's Secret

Javi was asleep when she got back to the room. Ami lugged in the valuables, though she wasn't sure if the electronics actually still worked. When she laid her briefcase on the table, she glanced at Javi, but his face remained slack, his chest rising and falling regularly. She opened the blinds and unzipped the briefcase so it could be opened flat. Her laptop appeared to be dead, but that wasn't what she was after. She hadn't been able to do this since finding the briefcase in the bushes near where she'd left her car before it was stolen. Javi thought he was a master at keeping secrets, but he'd not caught onto her secret yet. She pulled the six vials out of their pouch and their protective packing. She'd been worried they might have been cracked or in some way compromised, but they seemed fine.

Ami had been drinking a glass of wine with a colleague at a conference meet and greet when she'd seen Samira through the crowd. Samira smiled and hugged her like any two friends might. They'd been close acquaintances in medical school, amongst the handful of Middle Eastern students there. Samira's politics had been a little radical for Ami's tastes. There'd been a lot of anger at the administration for supposed profiling and immigration restraints that Ami had not experienced personally. Still, Samira had become a good and capable doctor. Ami hadn't expected to see her at the conference in Harrisburg, but they were all research scientists, so it wasn't really that odd that she'd be there. They retired to Ami's room and gossiped about their colleagues. Ami went to the bathroom and come back to a note and the beaded and padded purse sitting in the middle of her bed. The note read:

Something's going to happen soon and these are the six most important vials in the world. You can save the world, if you can make them work.

Ami tried to call Samira, only to find she was not on the conference list and didn't have a room in the hotel. She'd seriously considered calling the police, but she imagined the embarrassment if it turned out to be a joke. She had decided to take the vials back to Chicago to see what they were really about. To see if she really could save the world.

"Whatever the hell that means." Ami's muttered comment caused Javi to grunt from the bed. She put the vials back in their protective purse. One vial wouldn't go fully inside, so she pulled out all of the vials and tipped the purse upside down. A thumb drive slid out onto the table. She'd been so freaked by the circumstances, she'd not thoroughly investigated the purse.

This was more than a science experiment. The thumb drive might contain vital information. Too bad her laptop wouldn't turn on. If she'd found the thumb drive the first night, she'd have had a better idea of what was going on now.

Javi muttered softly in his sleep. Ami put the vials back in the purse, wedging the thumb drive behind them and then put the purse in the pouch of her briefcase where the vials seemed most safe. She had no idea what Samira had been talking about, but since they were both virologists it seemed certain that Samira knew something Ami did not. She needed a laboratory where she could figure out what she had and a working computer. She wondered if Emmaus, Kansas, had a medical center or at least a high school biology lab.

Javi reached a hand up to touch the bandages.

"Stop that."

"I forgot. Dreamed I could see."

She closed the blinds, turned on the flashlight and directed the beam so it bounced off the wall, providing enough light to take the bandage off. Javi blinked, eyes tearing.

"They burn."

"But can you see anything?"

"Blurry shapes. Could just be because I'm crying."

"Could be, but the irritation suggests we need to treat it." She tested his sight with a pen light. His pupils were reacting to light now. The constriction caused him to flinch in pain. The conjunctiva was blood shot and the retinal sensitivity was concerning. "So, lay back and let me get this done."

The pink eye solution eased the sting. She rebandaged his eyes and made him take the amoxicillin.

"I feel like a little kid," Javi told her after swallowing two teaspoons of the pink stuff.

"It's all they had. Infection would damage your eyes permanently, so you'll have to survive the infantilization."

"Ooo, big words! So, want to listen to a movie?"

"There's no electricity, remember?" Ami opened the blinds and turned off the flashlight.

"Still? That's weird."

"It is weird. Cars in the street, no hydro. It's like a Third World country out there.

"We're still in Missouri, right? I guess that's kind of like a Third World country."

"Except Egypt doesn't have trailer houses. Does everyone in this state live in a trailer?"

Javi shrugged. Ami consulted the map by the light from the window.

"I didn't realize this was Route 66. Is that the legendary one?"

"I don't know. I guess. I've mostly been on the coasts. Do we have any food?"

"Just MREs. Nothing's open." She explained about the USDA. He listened to her description, then asked questions.

"We saw it developing on our way," Javi pointed out. "Now it's all over. There's an executive order that allows whoever is in charge to do this."

"Who is in charge?" Ami asked.

"Not sure. Ellerby was the designated survivor."

"Does chicken burrito bowl sound good?" He nodded, pushing up to sit against the headboard. "So, who is this Ellerby?" she asked.

"Head of Homeland Security, so technically my boss."

"Why do I sense that is not a good thing?"

Javi frowned, then sighed. Maybe he was beginning to trust her a bit.

"He wrote a doctoral dissertation on just this scenario. Multiple city suitcase nukes disrupting transportation, supply and communications networks. It's not a good feeling knowing your boss ended the country and is now probably in charge of its dismantling."

The CO2 was bubbling. Ami started to prepare her chicken noodles and vegetables.

"I'm not disbelieving you, but a dissertation … How many years ago was that?"

"Twenty-ish."

"Couldn't he just be far-seeing?"

Javi cocked his head. "Maybe. But a guy writes about it and then it happens when he's in power."

"Hasn't he only been the head of Homeland for a couple of years?"

"He was Director of National Security under the last president."

"Who was only in office for a few years. What's he been doing for the last twenty years?"

Javi scratched the five-o'clock shadow on his chin, seemingly at a loss for words.

"It wasn't part of my assignment to find out."

"What was your assignment?"

He sighed, shrugged, then laughed and changed the subject "What does blurry shapes mean?"

"It's better than it was last night. That's a good sign."

He tried to hide it, but blindness scared him and Ami couldn't do anything to put that fear to rest. He rubbed his forehead.

"Have you checked the routes west?"

"I'm making dinner now, but yes. Kansas City is off limits because of radiation. We have to swing south to Springfield and then the Kansas Guard is sending everyone to Wichita."

"Why?"

"I have no idea, but it makes me nervous. It's currently the provisional capital since Topeka is so close to Kansas City. I think we can get off on the side roads and avoid Wichita."

"Won't that bring us kind of close to Kansas City?"

"I didn't say it was a good plan."

"You're joking, right?"

"If you really want to get to this Emmaus, that's our only choice."

"You aren't telling people that's where we're going, are you?"

"Yes, of course, I am. Why wouldn't I give random strangers my entire life story and tell them exactly where I'm going? And while I was at it, I told them I have an assassin in tow."

"You think you're funny. It's not."

"You're going to have to trust me. I distrust people probably more than you do. I've been telling them your original cover story, that we're headed to Colorado Springs to visit you kids. Apparently, Cheyenne Mountain requires that you go through Limon, Colorado, which isn't that far from Emmaus. And, we're going there because there is a … what did you call it?"

"A safe house. And I think my handler might be there."

"And what do I do when we get there?"

"Don't worry. You're with me. And being a doctor doesn't hurt. You have skills. They'll have power and communications. They might be able to find your sister."

She wanted to believe Chris was alive, but she knew the danger of false hope, so she handed him the MRE entrée.

"I think I probably need something, like a bib or a towel."

She got a towel out of the bathroom. This motel wasn't as clean as some of the ones they'd stayed at, but since there was no hot water, she supposed they wouldn't be using the shower.

"What time is it?"

"Afternoon."

"I want to get on the road early in the morning."

"No," she said.

"What?"

"Your eyes need to be treated every four hours and that requires low light. We need to stay here tomorrow."

Javi opened his mouth to protest but then spooned up some food.

"You're not going to argue?"

"If I did, it would be fruitless. I can see blurry shapes in a darkened room. I can't go anywhere on my own. When you left, I tried to put the chain on, but I tripped over the other bed and got all turned around. Never did find the door. When I finally got back to the bed, I was exhausted." He spooned more food into his mouth, then spoke around it. "Much as I hate it, you're in charge until I can see again." He caught his lower lip in his teeth. "I'm not used to needing help and … I'm scared."

She had no words of comfort beyond what she'd already given him. He wasn't as blind as he'd been last night. She patted him on the knee and then turned to her meal. All they could do was wait.

Voluntary Trade

Alice wondered if illegals felt this odd receiving wages in cash. Mae had no other way to pay her, of course, with the banks closed and the Internet down. Mae Osimowitz carefully noted the amount like the honest woman she was. She'd even calculated the taxes, which she sealed into an envelope with Alice's name on it.

"I feel like I'm breaking the law." Mae grinned. "It's the best I can do."

"I know."

They left the office to go into the market itself. The shelves were mostly empty. The coolers along one side were dark. The front windows and door had been filled in with plywood to replace the glass that had been broken. "I don't know if I'll even be able to stay open now that there's no power. The generator's blown. If Jos hadn't smelled that cooler catching fire, the whole building might have gone up. These are not good times."

"No. They're truly bad times."

"Even if I had electricity, I'm running out of stock. I'm so sorry."

"It's fine. Alex and Keri say we can stay through the winter. I'll make myself useful in other ways."

"I know you will. For the time you worked here, you're the best employee I ever had."

Alice laughed and it felt perfectly natural to hug the middle-aged woman who had been her employer for only a couple of very long weeks.

The bell at the door tinkled and Mae turned to see who was there. Jos straightened up from cleaning a shelf as Jason Breen nodded at the grocer.

"What can I do for you, Jason?"

"It's probably what we can do for each other. I've got men headed out looking for trade. You want in on it?"

"What do you mean by that?"

"Well, I don't really want to bother with selling things piecemeal. That's your bailiwick. I'd take, a cut of course. I'm not a charity."

"I'm not either. But if we can agree to terms, I know you'll keep them."

"Granmae, he could help us retrieve the food stores from hiding." Jason shot a sideways glance at Jos.

"For five percent, agreed?"

Jos waited for Mae to decide with a quick nod of her head.

"You go with them to assure he's honest." Jos nodded, tossing his cloth onto the shelf.

"Now, Mae, I don't do the cartage myself. I have employees to do that."

"That's fine. When will they be available?"

"We can go now. I just don't want you thinking I jump at your command."

"Didn't think that, but we're paying you five percent so .... Could you give Alice a ride back to Lufgren's Crossing? It's on your way."

Jason's craggy face split in a big grin.

"You hid it in the Wolf's Head Mine, didn't you? That was either a brilliant move or utterly insane."

"It's in better shape than you might think," Jos said.

"I'd have to go inside to vet that and I'm not doing that, just in case you're wrong."

"I'm not. Are we ready to go?"

"Sure." Alice and Mae embraced one last time and then the three went out the door to Jason's truck. While Jos and Alice belted in, Jason keyed his radio mic.

"Liberty Base, this is Liberty 1. I need two guys with the 3-ton panel to meet me at Lufgren's Crossing. Over."

"This is Liberty Base. When? Over."

"Twenty minutes. Over."

"They'll be there. Over."

"Over and out."

Jason hung up the mic and put the truck in gear.

"So, whose idea was it to use the mine?"

"Mine," Jos answered.

"How'd you know it wasn't collapsed?"

"Granmae and I went there last year to scatter my grandfather's ashes. It's in pretty good shape. She explained her father always believed there was more silver there, so Grandpa and Stan reinforced it back in the 1970s."

"They find any silver?"

"No, so they stopped, but the main shaft and an abandoned tunnel are in decent shape."

"Genius idea to hide the groceries in there," Alice said. "But why is Mae acting as if you're out of business."

"Because we had no idea how we were getting it back to the store. We used her nephew to move it there and he's not exactly reliable."

Jason laughed.

"Paul ... how a decent hard-working man like Stan could produce that ... at least Randi turned out okay."

Jos grinned and shrugged. Alice noticed that the trees they passed were starting to turn yellow. They passed the trailer court where at least three trailers had burned following the EMP. A woman leading a goat off a trailer waved at them. It was a good community. Alice worried about her parents in Texas, but she knew Mark wouldn't risk their kids out on the highways now, not when they had a place to stay for the winter.

The panel truck was just pulling up when they reached Alex's farm. Jason pulled up the long driveway to drop Alice at the house.

"Thank you for the ride."

"Just being neighborly." Jason waited for Jos to slide over into Alice's seat and then drove away. Keri met Alice on the back porch.

"You're home early."

"Mae can't afford me, at least for now. What are you doing here?"

"The school burned down."

"Oh, that's awful!" Alice home-schooled Pete, so she really felt less sad than she hoped she sounded, but Keri wasn't ready to hear her true thoughts. She hugged her friend instead.

"I'm good." Keri's aqua eyes misted briefly, belying her words. "There's a lot of work to do, anyway."

"Yeah. But I know it's hard for you."

Keri nodded and controlled herself. After explaining where everybody else was, she asked, "Want to help me grind corn?"

Alice loved these people's attitude. The world ends and they just take care of what needs to be done. Maybe when they woke up tomorrow, the apocalypse would be canceled and they'd have their winter food supply laid in.

"I will do whatever I must to get through this coming winter."

Keri smiled. She seemed fully recovered from yesterday's shooting. "I'm glad you're here. Alex and Poppy are lovely but having a vocal conversation with someone certainly helps the work go lighter."

"Well, then let's get started then. So, how do you grind corn?"

Not All His Fault

Cai's fever broke in the afternoon and he woke to the distant sounds of the fairgrounds. The sweat had dried on his body and his teeth no longer chattered, so he supposed whatever it was had passed. He wondered if the nightmares of Dershowitz dying ever would. He'd awakened the whole CHU twice last night before his temperature had spiked and they'd moved him to this room by himself. Sanchez had left a tray of food and a dozen bottles of water earlier today. Cai wasn't hungry. He drank some water and sat with his back against the wall, feeling like a wrung-out washcloth and wishing he could remember what Marnie looked like.

A knock on the door startled him. Sanchez followed the knock without permission.

"How you feeling?"

"Better."

"Good. You might want to eat something."

"Not hungry yet."

"It takes some men that way."

"Murder?"

"Self-defense. So, Myers thinks you were just dehydrated and sunburned. You ran a pretty good fever, though, so it makes sense that you slept all day. I brought you a sandwich and I'll take this plate away. You should eat. Whatever that voice in your head is saying right now, you need to do the opposite."

"I want to go home."

"Yeah? I bet you really don't."

"Why? Because Shane chose to run in the other direction? I am not my brother!"

"No, you're not Ric—who never compares himself to you, by the way. But that's not the reason. It's because almost nobody wants their family to see them afterwards. It'll take you a few days to get past that."

"Get past having a conscience?"

Sanchez shrugged and picked up the plate. At the door he paused.

"You're a lot more like Ric than you think you are."

He'd closed the door behind him before Cai thought to ask what that meant. Cai was pulling on the Army pants when another knock came from the door. Brian entered.

"How are you feeling?"

"Exhausted. How are you?"

Brian sighed and sat down on the opposite bunk.

"I still hear the gun going off."

Cai nodded before reaching for the black undershirt.

"I keep seeing that pool of blood. It looked darker than expected."

"He deserved it."

"I don't … it's a comforting thought, but I can't."

"But you helped to end slavery, man. There's nothing to be ashamed of in that."

"It was martial law …."

"No, it was slavery. And now they're talking about what to do with the soldiers and the FEMA people."

"What do you think they should do with them?"

"Well, they wanted to be slavers. Maybe not all the FEMA people, but ...." Brian sighed. "Those Army guys, though, deserve to know what we went through."

Cai stared at Brian, shock silencing any reply. Brian rubbed a hand over his curls. Did he recognize the irony of his statement?

"So, I'm headed out to find April soon as they'll let me."

"What's stopping you?" Could slaving others come naturally and the mercenaries were already bending that way?

"Needing a vehicle and food. There might have been hope of finding either before the USDA and FEMA pillaged the area, but now people aren't so trusting of strangers."

"Yeah. It's going to take a really long time to get over that feeling that I'm about to be zapped in the ribs for anything, like looking at someone the wrong way or for failing to answer quickly enough or answering too quickly."

"We wouldn't have survived our thirty days. I'm trying not to think about what April might be going through."

"It'll be okay. Just believe that. And whatever she's gone through, it'll be okay once you're with her. Where are you going after you find her?"

"Wichita. Her mom's there. I think. Actually, I don't know."

"Good luck." The bunks were just far enough apart that they could hug. It was hard to believe they'd only known each other for a few days. They felt like brothers now.

"She's going to be fine. And, if Wichita doesn't work out or you can't figure out how to get there, come to Emmaus."

"To do what? Neither of us are farmers."

Cai snorted.

"I'm a lawyer. Hard-working people can always find a place. What did you do anyway before?"

"I'm a physical therapist and April is a speech therapist."

"My wife would probably love the help. She's the only doctor, now."

"I'll think about it. The sergeant seems to be a friend."

"I'll ask him if he can help you in some way. April wasn't the only woman taken, so he ought to care."

Brian avoided Cai's gaze. "I grew up thinking I could trust the Army and that mercenaries were greedy. Now...."

Cai thought of his father's dress uniform hanging up in the attic. Had his father not told the whole truth about the military? Was the dark underbelly a wholesale reality or an isolated anomaly?

"Yeah." The one-word grunt was all he could manage and it said everything he needed to say.

Finding Kate

New Jersey

The bridge vaulted out into the fog, grey water lapping at its supports. Joseph rubbed his face, trying to keep his eyes open but finding it increasingly difficult. He'd been staring across the river at the burning city all night and now nearly all day. From time to time, people disgorged from the bridge, coming down one of the access roads. It no longer mattered if people walked there as so few cars were functioning. The rain had slacked off and fog had crept in, limiting sight distance and diminishing what little sunlight made it through the clouds.

A pall of smoke hung in the fog. How many buildings had burned during the night? He could only hope Katharine had not been in any of them.

Perry tapped on the glass and Joseph unlocked the far door to let him in. He brought two cups and a thermos of coffee.

"Thanks."

"Is it possible we missed her?" Perry asked after a sip of coffee.

"Why?"

"Well, she would go to this end of the Lincoln Tunnel, right?"

"Probably. But we would have seen her."

"Both of us dozed off a few times last night. I just don't want to risk missing her entirely by not going to check."

"Maybe you're right." Joseph sighed. "I don't know. She had to come this way."

"There's a lot of area to cover. We can give it a half hour and then go check."

The warmth of the coffee soothed the ache of anxiety in Joseph's chest. Outside, the silvery world changed, clouds shredding like rose-colored cotton candy against a lilac sky. Under ordinary circumstances he'd have had his camera out.

"Can you imagine being in one of those high towers with no elevators?" Perry wondered aloud.

"It would be hell, even if it wasn't on fire."

They sipped coffee in silence. They could see the river and the harbor better now. One of the ferries was beached just below them. Another was floating far off course toward the ocean. There were people trying to maneuver the currents in life rafts. A third ferry was headed sideways toward the bridge. If it hit one of those supports .... Joseph felt a cold hand rush down his back.

"So much destruction," he murmured. "What if we can't find her? How long do we wait before looking?"

"As long as it takes. She's a smart woman and she knows her way around New York. She'll make it over the bridge and we will find her."

Joseph finished his cup of coffee, ignoring the enormous emptiness inside him.

"Let's go check the Lincoln Tunnel."

Perry downed his cup and started the truck. Several people looked in their direction. A working vehicle was precious now. Perry drove south, making his way around discarded vehicles. Up ahead, a woman in jeans and a ski jacket walked beside a man in a dark car coat. Both wore hiking boots and carried backpacks. Joseph had hiked enough with Katharine to know what his wife looked like from behind. He began frantically rolling down his window.

"Katharine! Katharine Sullivan?"

She turned and for a moment his heart sank. Katharine never looked so disheveled. This couldn't be her. But then he jumped out of the truck and ran to embrace his wife, who caught him in a furious hug before bursting into hysterical tears mixed with laughter.

Letting in the Light

Emmaus

Dan McAuliff stepped out of the spiral staircase into the main room of the converted missile silo he called home. Several of the men in his community had had family arrive just before yesterday's EMP and they were making the best use of the first free times they'd had in five years. Children laughed and adults held hands, spread in small family groups around the common area. Dan poured himself a cup of coffee in the large kitchen that occupied one wall of the soaring commons.

Rod Patterson held up a coffee cup in salute.

"I'm a genius with great timing."

"I don't doubt it, but perhaps you'd like to enlighten me."

"When I designed the solar array, I set it up so that there are shutters which close at sunset. I did that thinking to keep snow and dust off the panels. I also hardened the turbine to assure it wouldn't fry during an EMP event. And, so our electrical plant shut down during the event, but it just needed a few linkages repaired and, viola, lights. Water heater's back on. The boiler is tomorrow. Concrete partially protected this level. We lost some LED displays, but we still have working DVDs."

"What about communications?"

"We have listening, not that there's a lot out there to listen to right now, other than Emmaus has short range radios. They're working on getting coal. You gotta love the practicality." He turned his laptop around. "And there's this curious signal here."

A single blip off to the southwest blinked.

"Someone who hardened their network?"

"It's the Jericho B&B."

Dan stopped breathing for a moment before offering an assessment.

"I'm pretty sure that was the FBI listening post."

"I know and, ordinarily, there'd be so many competing signals that you'd never even notice, but now it sticks out like a sore thumb. What's more, these folks are utterly silent, like they're listening."

Dan rubbed the back of his neck.

"Can they listen to us?"

"We broadcasted to our families when we first got here, so probably they heard that. I've got Fineseth writing a scrambling program. Before, we didn't think we were doing anything illegal, so it never occurred to me."

Dan sighed. It wasn't Patterson's fault that the FBI might have overheard their earlier broadcast and it certainly hadn't been his fault five years ago when they'd thought they were just creating a commune based on the dangerous idea of liberty.

"We weren't doing anything unlawful." Dan felt no need to justify his belief. The Founders would have been proud of his efforts. Unfortunately, none of them were innocent any longer. "Don't tell anyone and don't do anything more than monitor."

"I thought you'd say that. You know Shane Delaney's here?"

Dan blinked at the news.

"You sure?"

"His father used his call sign and I recognized his voice. What do you want me to do about it?"

Of course, the Delaneys had no reason to hide the return of their younger son. Dan sipped coffee to give himself time to think. Shane had been a pawn in the effort to put him in prison, but he had done what he'd done. What did Dan want Patterson or anyone else to do about it?

"Nothing for now. It might be a good idea to get the town on our side. They are certainly in better shape to defend the town than we are and that was an impressive bit they did with the USDA. I'm wondering who came up with that. Send Kletti to talk with Andrew Bennett. Let them know we're willing to work in trade for food."

"What if Delaney moves to re-arrest us? He's had time to get higher in the FBI. Could be connected with that listening post."

"If he reaches out, I'll see him. Otherwise, just keep an eye out and we'll see where things end up."

"Yes, sir." Patterson sighed. "It's going to be a long, dark winter."

Dan nodded, then drained his coffee cup. He bent over to pull a drill with a screw bit out of Patterson's tool bag.

"Where are you going?"

Dan smiled and walked away, stepping around the kids play with toy trucks and the couples leaning on one another. The only above-ground part of the refurbished silo facility was the large main floor with lounges, the kitchen and dining areas, and a group meeting area. The vaulted ceiling allowed for a mezzanine library with access to a deck that faced south, so wouldn't be visible from surrounding farms. He let himself out the door there. In a few minutes, the plywood that had been blocking one of the windows had been removed. He returned to the now transformed space. What a difference it made to open an 8x4 area of window. The light hit the blocked windows on the other side and reflected down into the gathering space.

"We still don't want to attract any attention, so we'll need to cover this with drapes for the night, but we can have a little light." Everyone turned to look at him standing on the balcony and then someone clapped and everyone joined in. He scanned the group. They were mostly good people who had believed him when he said they could create a better world from the ashes of one about to destroy itself. Only one adult wasn't clapping. Josh Callahan was staring around as if the applause was the dumbest thing he'd ever seen. Was he right or did Dan need to be worried about that one?

An Offer He'd Better Refuse

Wichita

His clothes smelled of smoke still, but since they were the only ones he had, Ren Sullivan didn't complain. It had all happened so fast. One minute he'd been plotting the recovery of the area with Gov. Lewis and the next smoke had billowed into the room. By the time they got out, the entire building had been involved. Thank God Phil was a take-charge kind of guy who didn't head for the elevators. Lewis and her security detail had not been seen again. The stairs had proven to Ren that he was indeed getting old—at least his knees were.

The Knights had brought them to SullCorp Headquarters, which had electricity, unlike the rest of the city. That was a testament to Phil's thinking ahead. It was at least equal to the far-sightedness of the engineers of Bunnell & Wilson.

The Knights commander, Crispin, had explained that Acting Governor Lewis had said he was her second and, since she was presumed dead, he was their priority now. Ren felt very safe with all those Bunnell & Wilson's mercenaries protecting him, but it didn't really solve the crucial problem. The power had gone out, every transformer in the city had fried, and they were now cut off from communication. SullCorp had power, thanks to generators that had been hardened against EMP, but Ren couldn't even call the Columbus hub, which is where he had hoped to find Joseph and Perry. Nor could he call Emmaus, which truly worried him. He was even now concerned for that gold-digger daughter-in-law of his. New York City without power would be hell on earth. Ren cared far less for the people of Wichita or his world-wide business empire than he did his family, though he was surprised to discover he was actually fond of Katharine.

Despite being cut off from his worldwide company network, it took less than 24 hours for the US Army to track him down. Spring, an intern who had no way to get home to distant family, was acting as his receptionist. Young and inexperienced, she walked Captain Armstrong right to Ren's office unannounced. With no choice but to take the meeting, Ren sat back in his brown, leather executive chair and let his gaze wander to the wood paneling in his corner office before the captain started talking. No, he wasn't going to fire Spring, but they were going to have a talk when all was said and done.

"Acting Governor Lewis named you as her provisional lieutenant governor in the event anything happened to her," Captain Armstrong said. "It's my mission to take you into protective custody to assure continuity here in Kansas."

"You know I'm a libertarian, right? I can't think of anyone further from the Democratic Party that Harmon and Lewis were elected under."

"We don't really care about your politics, sir. We need someone to be in charge."

"There's a reason I never ran for public office."

"We don't care if you're electable, sir. We need someone to be in charge."

"And I need someone to run my company, which is me."

“We don’t care if you’re in business, sir. You can keep doing that. We just need someone to be in charge.”

“And if I decline?”

“I’m authorized to take Lyle Fuller into custody.” Lyle Fuller had been Crystal’s public relations officer cum major domo. Lewis had been on the phone with him moments before her death, telling him not to distribute food to a working-class neighborhood.

“So you don’t care who is in charge so long as someone is?”

Armstrong smiled and nodded.

“I need to think a few minutes. Spring,” he called, “can you provide these gentlemen with some coffee and breakfast?”

She nodded. He could tell she knew she’d screwed up and was trying to look at once professional and contrite. That was an impossible combination for a twenty-year-old. Armstrong recognized he was being maneuvered.

“Sir, I—”

“--will give me the courtesy of a half-hour to consider my options!”

Armstrong’s eyes narrowed.

“I’ll put a guard on your door.”

“I’m under arrest, then?”

"That's not how I would put it, but I do have my orders."

Ren looked at Phil and Crispin.

"These men are my advisors. They will stay with me while I make my decision."

Armstrong had been well-trained in controlling his expressions, but Ren wasn't fooled as he withdrew from the office.

"Tell me what you think," he said, pointing at Phil first.

"There are about twenty-five men stationed outside."

"And, you?" Ren asked Crispin.

"We have nearly two hundred on-site and another several hundred in the city."

"If it came to blows?"

"Our trucks are working. They marched up, which indicates to me that they haven't got vehicles. I'm confirming that with the larger force now." Crispin indicated his tablet.

"If I go with them ...."

"You'll be a puppet," Phil said. "It's clear that's what they want you for."

"Where is Armstrong getting his orders from?"

"No idea," Crispin said. "According to my communications network, the Army is pretty much silent. They've picked up some short-distance radios and we're trying to get ears on Cheyenne Mountain but, so far, it's radio silence."

"What do you recommend?"

"Stall them for the full half-hour. Let me get my men in place. How do you feel about body count?"

Ren hadn't thought about that question and Crispin didn't push him for an immediate answer, just started detailing his men through the secure network. While he turned aside to do that, Ren gestured for Phil to sit down and talk.

"Do you still trust him?"

"He's not lied to us yet. And what happened at the Governor's wasn't something we can pin on him. He lost five guys when Lewis ordered them into that elevator."

Ren leaned back in his chair for a moment, taking a deep interest in the wood grain of his desk top. When he looked at Crispin again, the man stopped working on his tablet.

"Who is in charge of you?"

"You're the client, Mr. Sullivan, so you are in charge of me."

"If Carson Wilson calls you and says otherwise?"

"He won't. In the ten years I've worked for Knight Industries, he has never overruled a client. But if he did, I'd remind him of the oath he asked me to sign, which says the client's wishes come first. I can let you read that, sir, if you like."

Ren nodded and Crispin returned to tapping on his tablet. A few moments later, the tablet he'd loaned Phil dinged and SullCorp's head of security turned it around for Ren to read a signed and notarized oath.

"Fuller is a sycophant. He'll do whatever they want." Ren rubbed his chin. He really needed a shave. "What's the name of that sergeant you sent after Cai Delaney?"

"Sanchez."

"And his orders following that?"

"To go to Emmaus and deliver that package to your granddaughter."

"Have you been able to speak with him since?"

"The connections that far out aren't very stable, but they survived the taking of the FEMA base in Hutchinson and your man is safe."

"And you're certain he'll go to Emmaus?"

"I'm certain he'll try."

There was that. This was not a normal situation. The best anyone could do is try.

"And if I order you to take out Armstrong's men, what prevents you from deciding to hold me hostage to control power in Kansas?"

"Why would I do that, sir? Prisoners don't generally pay their captors for the service. But, I can see where you might be concerned. I'm authorized to make contracts with people."

"Are you?" Now they were talking Ren Sullivan's language. A moment later, a beep from the tablet in front of Ren found a simple contract for protection. Crispin's men would work for room and board, but eventually, fees would cost Ren up to a million dollars through spring. It specified that Ren and Phil were in charge except in a few narrow exceptions. Phil nodded. Ren signed it and sent it back. "The body count should be as low as possible. Disarmament should be the goal."

Crispin nodded and Ren sat back to see what would transpire over the next hour.

A Haunting in Emmaus

Joe had just finished his verbal report to Rob when Carl Sullivan came up to the counter outside Rob's office. Rob thanked Joe for his information and rose to meet his oldest friend. Although they were the same age, Carl's schizophrenia had taken a toll on his body, leaving him fat and out of breath. Despite his mental illness, Carl had made himself useful in this crisis by monitoring his short-wave radio.

"What do you have for me, Carl?"

"I heard you talking on the radio about coal."

"Ah! It was a good idea, but we can't find an open mine anywhere in Kansas or Nebraska."

"Not an open one, but there used to be a lot of mines around here."

"Mostly in the southeast, right?"

"Yeah, but there were mines this part of the state too. I used to drive a truck for one before I went into the Army."

"How far away?"

"Maybe an hour and a half. Over in Arikaree Breaks."

Shane came in from the back stairs.

"Do you remember Carl?" Rob asked.

"Sure." Shane held out his hand to shake, but Carl stared at a point behind him, leaving Shane's hand hovering in open air. "Nice to see you again." Shane hooked his thumb in his belt, trying not to look awkward.

"Carl tells me there's a coal field within driving distance."

"I told you I'd seen one."

"But you don't remember where it is," Carl said. "I remember it."

"Didn't you used to climb over in the Arikaree Breaks, Shane?"

"Yes. And, you're right, Carl. That is where I saw it."

"Pit mine, right?"

"Yeah. We were looking for a wall we hadn't climbed yet and we discovered it. Coal is a crappy climbing surface, so I put it out of my mind, and, frankly, I don't remember how to get there."

"Too many years?" Carl was teasing and Shane knew it.

"Probably too much pot."

Carl chuckled. Rob tried not to look distressed by how casually Shane mentioned getting high.

"You got a map?"

"Just one of the state. That's not going to have enough detail, right?" Rob pulled it out from under the counter.

"Let's see it."

Rob spread the map on the counter and Carl leaned in to gaze at it.

"I'm willing to run a quarry team if we can do it with basic equipment." Shane leaned in towards the map also. "We can't be going underground or dynamiting. We're not coal miners and I'm not taking a huge risk with peoples' lives."

"That's rational." Rob appreciated that Shane, always so bold, had clearly learned to think ahead. "How many people do you think you could gather for this operation?"

"Don't know. I ran into Jason outside the feed store. He can send a truck, but he's limited by what's working. Have you found the mine yet?"

Carl shook his head.

"This map's not giving the detail. The library didn't burn down, right?"

"True. It's getting late and it's going to be hard to see without electricity. You want to meet me there in the morning and we'll see what we can find?"

"I gotta go, Dad. Promised Mom I'd move the refrigerator onto the porch and Jacob wants me to figure out how to extend the hand pump back up into the living space. Let me know what you found. I'll see about gathering a crew."

Rob waited for Shane to descend the stairs and turned to Carl.

"You got something bugging you?"

Carl sighed.

"Your boy ... you know he's haunted, right?"

Rob opened his mouth to justify Shane's sometimes odd behavior, but an icy hand clenched his gut instead. His mother Vi had said that Carl had known his brother EJ was suicidal long before they found him hanging in the garage. He faced Carl full-on. "Tell me what you see."

Shelter

New Jersey

Perry came out of the Hackensack Travelodge and slid into the driver's seat. Julian gave him a curious look.

"They're closed. If we had food, they'd have rented us a room in exchange."

Julian glanced into the bed of the truck where Joseph and Katharine had fallen asleep after the ecstasy of finding one another again.

"So, what do we do?"

The youngest in the group by ten years, there was something about Julian that said he'd lived, and Perry appreciated that. Being responsible for two people was more than enough.

"I don't know. Find shelter, someplace we can park the truck. You know the area at all?"

"I'm from Seattle. I've pretty much never been between the Hudson and the Cascades. Well, there was a trip to Yosemite when I was a kid, but my parents were in charge then. Naw, I don't know this area at all."

Perry started the truck and turned west again, weaving past abandoned cars. At his suggestion, Julian looked at one of the maps in the glovebox and suggested Glenn Rock Borough Park, but, driving past, they could see hundreds of people gathered around campfires, so Perry continued on.

"If we lose this truck we're walking, so the last place we want to be is somewhere we can be overpowered."

"My thought too. So, pulling over to the side of the road wouldn't be a winning choice either?"

"No. Better someplace we can pull in and not be too visible."

They drove for several minutes, Perry trying to get back to the main road they'd left to check out the campground.

"Whoa, check it."

"What?" Perry scanned the buildings to both sides, confused. Julian pointed to an oil service station on their left.

"I'd swear the garage door wasn't completely closed."

Perry drove around the building and Julian jumped out to try the service bay door, which seemed to have a half-inch gap at the bottom. It halted its upward movement about two feet up, so he dropped onto his back and wriggled under it. The door closed briefly and then he pushed it all the way up. Perry backed in over the service well and shut the truck down while Julian closed and locked the overhead door with a screw driver through the track. He pointed to a control unit on the wall and the overhead door track.

"Must have failed in the pulse."

"Our modern world ... oh, so fragile. This'll do. Check around. See what's here."

The garage resided in a well-cared-for older building that had seen a good cleaning lately. Perry was in the well looking at the underside of the truck when Julian returned with a half-empty bottle of scotch and four paper cups. Perry joined him at the tailgate.

"Cash register's empty, but I found this. What did you find?"

"No food, but I'm giving the old girl a tune-up tonight since the resources are here." He pointed to the array of hoses and reservoirs on the back wall of the service bay. "It might help us to get all the way back to Kansas."

"Sounds good. That's halfway to where I need to go." Julian sighed. He filled two cups with scotch and offered Perry one of them. It was a cheap brand, but all alcohol has the same effect.

"Ren Sullivan owes you. He'll get you to wherever you want to go." Julian blushed. "Something?"

Julian sipped his scotch before answering.

"It's horrible, but I did think of that when I offered to help her get out of the city."

"In a world gone mad, the safest place to be standing is next to someone loved by the rich and powerful. And, you got her out of the city."

"It was mutual. My idea of the truck through the tunnel exploded in my face and if I'd been alone, I would have gone back to the hotel. But she knew the city, so all I had to do was convince her we could make it, if we did it together."

"What were you planning to do after you got across the bridge? If you'd missed us ...?"

"Walk west and hope you found us, I guess. Find someone with a working vehicle to take us west. Steal a car if necessary."

"Well, that's practical. Tomorrow, we'll pick up a fourth sleeping bag and you can share my tent. Why don't you climb into the front and get some sleep while I tune her up? Then you can drive in the morning so I can get some shuteye."

"Sounds good."

Julian took the sleeping bag and left Perry to study the underside of the truck by the uncertain glow of a battery-powered lantern. Outside Perry heard loud voices trying to whisper. He turned the lantern way down and watched from under the bumper, but he couldn't see any movement from the door. After a while, the voices faded and he turned up the lantern to get back to work.

The farmer who had lent them the truck had kept good care of his equipment. The oil needed to be changed, but not desperately and there were no leaking hoses or cracked gaskets. It was simply an old truck needing care if it was going to get them all the way home. Perry fully planned to get the Sullivans back to Emmaus and then take the truck back to its owner. He knew Ren would appreciate that he didn't welsh on a deal. He wondered if the helicopter they'd left with the farmer could be started since the pulse. Or maybe the pulse had just affected the east. That seemed a faint hope.

He finished the tune-up and ascended the stairs out of the well. It was darker than hell outside and not much lighter in the garage so that he was surprised to see Katharine pouring herself a cup of scotch at the work bench. She poured another cup and offered it to him. She took a sip, blinking.

"I think they use this to clean grease off engines." She grinned at Perry's joke. "Thank you for coming to find us. I was not looking forward to going into the city."

"It was more hellish than usual. New Yorkers do not do well with the unexpected."

"Julian was telling me. I can't imagine what it took from both of you to get out of there."

"What is it soldiers say? We had each other's back. So, what are the odds of us getting all the way to Kansas in this old bucket of rust?"

"It's in pretty good shape for a vehicle with 300,000 miles on it. I'm more worried that someone is going to try to take it from us."

"I have a gun." She pulled it out of her pocket to put it on the workbench. He deflected her hand gently.

"Let's not point that at me, okay?"

"Sorry. That's one of the rules, yeah?"

They said it together: "Always keep your gun pointed in a safe direction."

He picked it up, flipped the wheel out, dumped the rounds, and inspected the chambers. It was a cheap 22, but it would do the job if it came to that. Its main drawback was that it only had five rounds.

"You got any other ammo?"

"I was surprised it came with ammunition. The woman who bought it knew a thing or two about guns, I think."

He reloaded the gun and gave it back to her. She put it in her coat pocket.

"We run into trouble, let me and Joseph handle it unless you don't have a choice. Get in the cab of the truck. Whatever you do, don't let them take the truck away from you. The kid armed?"

"No. And I'm not sure he wants to be."

"He probably should be, but I'm not going to force anyone to be sensible. I'm frankly surprised you have a gun. I thought you were opposed."

She sipped more scotch.

"The world ended and suddenly, being disarmed feels like a really good opportunity to end up dead or raped."

"Yeah." Perry downed the last swallow of the scotch in his cup. Breathing out felt like he imagined dragon breath to be. "So, I sent the kid looking around this place, but this is all he came up with. I'm going to poke around myself."

"I'm going to have another cup."

"By all means, just make it your last one. We're on the road at dawn."

She nodded. The front of the shop had a customer lobby with a popcorn popper, vinyl sofas, a television and a counter with a cash register. The drawer stood open and empty. Perry snagged some bottles of oil and power steering fluid and a jug of antifreeze. The flashlight beam bounced off displays of belts and he gathered two sets for just in case. If nothing else, they could perhaps trade belts for food or gas. With that thought, he decided to fill a carboard box with as many as he could fit and another box with fluids.

He doubted he'd find anything in the office, but one of the file drawers contained a couple of cans of olives, five tins of sardines, a can of tuna and a box of crackers. It was better than going hungry. In the well-scrubbed bathroom, he decided to wash up a bit. He really needed a shave, but it felt good to be sort of clean. He was relieving himself when the front lobby lit up with headlights. Someone began banging on the door. He hesitated for a moment, thinking it could be the owner, but what owner would bang on the door? He stepped out of the lobby with his gun drawn and shined his flashlight beam right at the young man with the metal pipe in his hand. The kid flinched and back-peddled, diving into his car and disappearing into the night. Joseph had joined Katharine by the scotch. He at least had his gun out. Julian had sat up and produced his wrecking bar.

"Looter."

"You gotta wonder where the police are." Joseph holstered his gun. Julian lay back down.

"You mean the people with the brand-new cars that are lumps of steel and composite now?"

Joseph nodded in the lantern light.

"I hadn't thought of that. How long until dawn?"

"Another hour. Let the kid get a bit more sleep. You can flip him for driving, I guess."

"I'm perfectly willing to let him drive. Perry, how are we for gasoline?"

"We're not, but we'll work it out."

Perry put the cap back on the scotch bottle and stowed it with the auto parts. Katharine made a plate of olives and tuna and they left some for Julian. They filled water bottles and cleaned up before the sun came up. Joseph left an IOU in the office. And then Julian woke, ate his breakfast, cleaned up in the bathroom and then got behind the wheel of the truck with Joseph riding shotgun. Perry slept in the back.

Technical Difficulties

Emmaus

Assuming they could find coal, the long-mothballed furnace looked like it could burn it. Shane had figured out how to adjust the air, and providing the initial spark wasn't a problem. The old coal bin had long ago been replaced by the storm cellar and he couldn't foresee the folks giving that up. It didn't matter, anyway, since the auger had been removed and Jacob couldn't remember what had happened to it. The auger had been stored behind the furnace, but somehow, it had been moved and no one knew where it had gone. Still, Shane thought there would be plenty of volunteers to shovel coal as the winter encroached. Nobody in Miristan's high mountain village of Padaresh ever complained that it wasn't their turn to feed the fire when the wind was racing out of the mountains.

The landing at the top of the stairs groaned and Shane glanced behind him to see who it was.

"I thought you were working on the hand pump." Rob stopped about six steps from the bottom, knowing how Shane felt about others sharing his oxygen in tight places.

"I was. I need some pipe to extend it into the mudroom. I even found the hole in the floor where it used to be. I have to get the pipe threaded and move the pie cabinet over about four inches. Then I decided to look at the furnace."

"And?"

"Assuming we can find coal, it should work with some modifications and reconnecting the exhaust pipe to the chimney. Unfortunately, there's no way to get the heat to the rest of the house."

"It'll keep the ground floor warm. What do you need to finish it?"

"Replace the old auger port with a functional door. I think I can weld one up or … I don't know. It's hard to think down here."

"Oh, c'mon. There's as much room down here as there is upstairs. The ceiling's a foot lower and the windows are ... er ...."

"Non-existent?"

"Dirty. But you could open the bulkhead doors if needed."

Shane let his gaze sweep the basement. Opening the bulkhead doors for air flow would just increase his paranoia at someone sneaking up on him. Like the attic, the basement held a collection of generational cast-offs. He wondered if his parents knew about him and Marnie in the bed with the white iron headboard. As she was his sister-in-law now, he hoped not. The memory warmed his cheeks, but he trusted his tan to hide the evidence.

"I'm not trying to get out of the work. I just hate being down here. Feels like I'm being smothered."

"You always were like that. Most babies like to be swaddled. Cai did and so did Keri. You would fight the covers and bellow your little heart out. Vi was the one who figured out you wanted to be free. She'd even strip you down to your diaper to make you happy."

"Yeah, that sounds like me ... closet nudist, functional anarchist. I can't do anything more here tonight."

Rob turned and went back up the stairs so Shane could follow him. A single battery-powered lantern lit the kitchen and mudroom where the stairs came up.

"Where is everybody?"

"Pa and Jill went to bed. Marnie is taking a shift with David Vance, I guess. I wanted to catch you to talk."

"What about?"

"You know you can talk to me, right?"

"We've already had the birds and the bees talk, Dad."

"Yeah, thank you for that. I had questions." Shane snorted. Rob smiled, but then he sighed. "We haven't had the war talk."

Shane felt like the air had been sucked from the room.

"I wasn't a soldier, Dad."

"People were shooting at you, right?"

Shane wished it had been that simple.

"I don't want to talk about it, not now anyway. You can't just spring this on me. And, you can't make me tell you."

"No. And, we don't have to talk tonight. I just want you to know that you can talk to me. It's not like sex outside of marriage or smoking pot or drinking. I absolutely know what you're going through and I think I can help you."

Shane sighed, infinitely sad, absolutely aware of the weight he'd been carrying for so long.

"I get to think about it, right?"

"Of course. I told you a while ago that if you wanted, all you had to do was listen. That's the gift Pa gave me when I really needed it and it's the offer I give you. I think once you know you're not alone, it'll get easier."

"Should it?" Rob's eyebrow raised. "I think you've figured out that I played both ends against the middle and ...." Shane let his breath out really slowly. "I just really can't talk about it."

"Don't give me crap about agreements you signed. The government doesn't appear to be functioning. You *can* talk about it."

"That's not .... It's not happening tonight. Don't push."

Shane waited for Rob to do exactly what Shane had forbidden, but his father had experienced Shane with his back against a wall and apparently knew when the conversation was over. He threw his hands up like he'd been arrested.

"Good night. Just ... when you're ready ... or when the load gets too heavy. Okay?"

Shane nodded. Rob sighed and left the kitchen. Shane stared at the cookstove, willing the dark shadows to retreat into the darker ones. Kitty Vance danced in his mind, briefly. Something dark stirred in a corner. He dropped to the floor to do 100 pushups until the burn in his arms vanquished all demons and he spied hope of sleep.

Fateful Decisions

Anders McAuliff had hoped to visit his brother's compound today, but when he'd been called to City Hall for a dawn-hour emergency session of the Town Council, he'd tabled that plan. He had to give it to Jacob Delaney. The old man knew how to produce a report and he wasn't missing any beats. He'd interviewed people in Mara Wells and Emmaus to determine what specific USDA agents had done in their invasion of the two towns. Anderson, Isenberg and Dolachek had all beaten and/or killed people. An as-yet-unidentified agent had beaten David Vance into a coma for the "crime" of resisting confiscation. Rumdale was responsible for what his agents had done. That left a dozen of USDA agents who had done the job they were ordered to do in a way consistent with humanity. The coroner's inquest recommended a course of action. His job complete, Jacob sat down and let the City Council decide its next action.

"I think it's clear what we should do," Cass Bradford said. "These agents attacked our communities and we can't let that stand. I say we execute them all."

"Including Danny Hughes?" Rob asked the question because the discussion had touched on what to do with the young man who had killed the pilot of a commuter plane the morning after the bombs.

"We can't afford to feed him," Anders remarked. "And Jacob saw him commit murder."

Jacob surprised Anders by shifting his weight from one buttock to the other.

"Something to say, Pa?" Rob asked.

"There was a wall between me and that kid. More I think about it, it might have been an accident."

"He's not a wild dog you think you've tamed." Shane had been there as a witness and technically should have left the chamber, but like Stan Osimowitz and some others, he'd pulled up a chair to listen and now apparently thought he could offer an opinion.

"You think I just got attached?" Jacob asked, his gaze sharp on his favorite grandson.

"Shane, if you've got something to say, you should say it," Ted Murdock said.

Shane had apparently expected to be shushed by his elders, so he hesitated for a moment before speaking.

"My experience is that if you leave portions of the enemy alive, they come back to haunt you."

"These are Americans, same as us," Hiram Schoenfeld said.

"Is this still America?" Stan Osimowitz asked. "It sure looked a lot like another country the other day."

Jacob started to say something, hesitated.

"Say what you need to say, Grandpa," Shane encouraged.

"To a man whose only tool is a hammer, everything looks like a nail. You're so recent from a warzone that you don't recognize that this isn't one."

"Isn't it? Agents from some government were attacking civilians. That's how war works."

"If we stick to that path, that's where we'll end up." Jacob directed his remarks to Rob now. "I've no argument with hanging Rumdale.

The man is a menace. The others should be made to watch and then released to go off down the road. I get that we need to show that attacking our community has consequences. But maybe we don't want to give the feds too much evidence that we've gone rogue."

"Are you becoming a statist?" Lisa Maguire teased.

"No, but I don't want anyone making an example of Emmaus or Mara Wells, either."

"Call the question," Anders said.

"I'm not sure discussion is over." Rob could never have gotten away with that in ordinary times, but Anders doubted letting everyone speak was a martial law court standard either. "What do you folks think?"

"I wish we knew what the law says." Like Anders, Ted Murdock hadn't attempted to memorize the town charter, because it was readily available online until the pulse had wiped the server.

"It's martial law," Jacob responded. Jacob had lived before computers. He'd been the mayor for two terms. He probably had memorized the charter, back when memorizing was something people did. "Rob can make these decisions, according to the City charter."

Rob leaned back in his chair, fingering his beard.

"Vote," he said.

The six council members voted 6-0 to hang Rumdale, 5-1 to hang Isenberg, Dolachek and Anderson, 3-3 to hang the others and 3-3 to hang Danny Hughes. Ted Murdock dutifully noted the tally. Everyone waited on Rob, who looked like he wished he'd lost last year's election to Anders.

"We release the others far enough out that they can't return here easily. Pa, you and Dennis Bishop get to decide what is appropriate for Danny since you are his only real victims here. Do any of you would-be killers want to volunteer to hang the others?"

Eyes widened and Anders' pulse began to race in his ears.

"You're the military leader during martial law, Rob," Ted Murdock reminded.

"I stopped killing people after I came back from Vietnam and I won't set aside that vow now." Anders didn't believe that Rob was a coward, but he wondered why a leader would decide not to be involved in as important an action as this one. Anders thought about volunteering, but the words wouldn't spring into his throat.

"I'll do it." Frank Giffin, one of the witnesses, seemed comfortable. "I already killed one of them. Ain't going to get anymore muck on my soul than that."

Stan Osimowitz looked like he'd swallowed a lime the whole time Frank was talking, but as soon as the ex-convict subsided, he nodded.

"I'll help with that. Gary Carter didn't deserve the way he died and my people are going to expect his killer to pay."

Shane Delaney's gaze was aimed at his boots as his hand drifted toward his shoulder when Sharon Laughlin sprang to her feet.

"I'll make the third," she said. The crowd gasped. "They were going to hang me because I refused to let them into my house. If that's a reason to die, then trying to hang someone for that is surely an even better reason to die. And, if nobody has any objections, I'll gladly read the sentence to the prisoners."

Shane looked like he'd been hit by a 2x4, staring up at Sharon as if he'd never seen anything like her before. Rob wiped tears from his eyes and proclaimed that the execution would take place at a time and place of the executioners' choosing and that the entire USDA entourage would be expected to watch. The meeting dismissed, Anders swallowed the big empty feeling that moral cowardice had left in the middle of his chest. He wanted those people dead, but what did it mean that he didn't want to do it himself? Apparently, he'd thought that aloud because Rob paused as he was passing him.

"Killing someone is not as easy as some folks think. It's easy to pronounce judgment, but hard to live with the outcome."

The three volunteer executioners stayed seated as the crowd bent around them. They didn't even speak to one another. And, though Anders noticed this and sympathized with them, he didn't speak to them either.

Wichita Burning

Ren stood at the windows of his office and watched Wichita go up in flames. Not all of it, of course. It only seemed that way. Haze obscured the early morning sky. Phil and Crispin had explained that a lot of the haze came from smoke grenades used to flush out military troops as the Knights advanced. They'd connected SullCorp headquarters with Eisenhower Airport and now were advancing toward McConnell Air Force Base in an attempt to divide and conquer the military. The reports said it was working. Unable to fly, the Air Force was unable to help the Army, which didn't have a secure base of operations in the city.

Crispin came into Ren's peripheral vision.

"I'm not going to bark 'sit-rep'. What's going on out there?"

"Thank you, sir. I always thought that was military machismo, even when I was in the military. We've quartered the northern part of the city and we're working on the southern part. We've got absorbed National Guard troops joining us. Some of the Army have surrendered, but a large contingent has occupied St. Francis Hospital. Getting them out won't be easy."

"You mean it'll cost lives on both sides? What's the butcher's bill so far?"

"We've minimized casualties. These days our body armor goes a long way toward protecting us. Not just our side, but theirs. We've mostly had wounded and we've taken a fair number of prisoners. We're stripping them and holding them at Eck Stadium, except for the commanders. They've been isolated in whatever containment we can manage for now. What do you want us to do about St. Francis?"

"Can we contain them there and starve them out?"

"No telling about their on-hand food supply, but we can shut off the water. Without electricity, the air handling system already doesn't work. If we get a hot day or two …."

"Surrender is they lay down their arms and remove their armor and they walk away."

"That's a lot of hostile folks way too close to my troops. If they coordinate with one another …."

Ren nodded, considering the possibility.

"How many are we talking about?"

"Fifty to 100."

"And the other captured troops?"

"Over a thousand."

"I don't think killing them is the right move."

"No, sir, but after we pacify the city, we'll start sending out groups to establish communication with our outlying troops. We could drop these prisoners at remote locations, scatter them, make it harder for them to form a counterstrike."

"Sounds good. What's your take on these National Guard turncoats?"

"Most of them were forcibly inducted into the Army during the first few days after the Incident. I think they honestly want to be on the right side."

"After the main fighting is over, I want to talk to their commanders. I'll also want to talk to the Army commanders."

"By evening, we ought to be in operational control of the city. I'll let you know when later in the day."

So far, Crispin had done exactly what he said he would do. Ren put that tight feeling in his gut down to his own prejudice. Crispin was a mercenary, a former soldier who had decided to work for money while pretending to be a soldier still. Or, you could look at it as he was still a soldier but one who had retained his freedom and the right to negotiate while getting paid a much better salary for it to boot. Knowing that didn't mean Ren felt good about what he was doing. He'd served in the Navy as a fighter pilot and he still wanted to believe that the US military was honorable and had not been trying to enslave him or anyone else.

Ren hoped he could reach an agreement with the Army commanders and end hostilities. His concern was really not the men and women who were in Wichita. Crispin reported that Cheyenne Mountain was utterly silent and that filled Ren with dread. What could possibly be happening there that could explain why they weren't prepping reinforcements here? Crispin said these sorts of hostilities were happening in at least a dozen remaining cities since the blackout. Sometimes it was the National Guard against the Army. Other times it was the Knights against the Army and the National Guard. In Columbus, it appeared to be a local militia that had had enough and Crispin wasn't sure they wouldn't turn on the handful of Knights there once they were done with kicking the military's butts. In some places, it appeared the military was winning, but not in most. The military struggled when their hierarchy was disrupted, and first the bombs and then the EMP had majorly disrupted their hierarchical communications network. The Knights still had theirs and that made all the difference.

But Cheyenne Mountain's silence didn't mean they weren't still there and wouldn't come bursting out to impose martial law once more when they were ready, and, probably at the worst possible time.

Settling In

Jericho Ghost Town

Grant Rigby rolled over and yawned, surprised to see sunlight glittering through the window and bouncing off the honey-toned walls and white casework. He sat up, listening to the sounds of laughter from the back yard. His mother-in-law, Madelaine, was playing some silly game with his two daughters and they sounded like they were having a wonderful time now that they were finally allowed outside.

Grant, his father-in-law, Jim, and his adult son, Dylan, had worked most of the night on the radio tower that was the listening station's link to the world. Grant hadn't intended to sleep so late, but Emily must have slipped out of bed while he was still half-comatose. He'd been sleeping really well since they'd moved to Jericho Springs, where their closest neighbor was across a substantial wood lot. Still, it surprised him that sleep came so easily now, since it hadn't been like that for years.

He donned jeans and a sweat shirt, brushed his teeth in the on-suite bathroom and headed down the back stairs to the hidden telemetry room under the garage. Dylan was already there, bare feet up on the table, keyboard in his lap, watching the static-filled monitors.

"What's with the crappy resolution?" Grant asked.

"The pulse fried a lot of stuff. Some of my favorite traffic cams died. Can I break into one of those bottles of bourbon for the wake?" Dylan wouldn't even be twenty until next month.

"Those are for trade. What the heck is going on out there?"

Since they were now working with the children in the house, the father and son counter-intelligence team was trying to cut swear words out of their language.

"We're mostly on satellite, hence the crappy resolution. That's Wichita and those are B&W Knights going up against the US Army and, from what I can tell, they're kicking ass. Of course, it helps when your HQ is bringing in arms and backup."

"Cheyenne Mountain isn't helping the Army?"

"They're shuttered. In my training, I remember them talking about how Shalimar and Toro Boro would go silent sometimes and they'd think they'd been abandoned, until they launched a counter-offensive. But even the Utah Data Center is perplexed about what's going on with NORAD."

"Is it possible they took a fatal hit?"

"It was partially hardened against EMP, but your guess is as good as mine. I don't know who is in charge in Wichita, but whoever is giving the orders is being careful with the body count and they've managed about a 60% conversion of the National Guard to their side."

"I guess as wars go, that's better than some. What about the rest of the world?"

"Seattle took a big hit with the Pulse. Ditto Silicon Valley. B&W is still functioning. How well, I'm not exactly certain. Oddly, I'm picking up communications from Ft. Lewis in Tacoma."

"What about New York?"

"Shambles. Fried grid, toasted communications. I think the UN building caught fire. The Freedom tower is now melted modern art. They've got ferries floating dead in the harbor. A military jetliner crashed at JFK."

"And Marshal Ellerby?"

"No idea. I looked for him for over an hour, and I put facial rec on to help locate him, but so far, nothing."

"So, did you do what I asked you to do?"

"I did. The Army contained all of the hot spots before the Pulse rendered them helpless. Of course, a lot of the surrounding area was contaminated, but the risk of radioactive rain has been substantially reduced. All of those cities will remain no-go zones for at least a decade, but there's hope for the future, I guess."

"Any news on the Pulse itself?"

"Not from America. We are mostly radio silent. Seattle still has some chatter, everything else is scarily quiet. Europe is speculating a North Korean tanker or maybe an Iranian one, using a SCUD missile lobbing a missile into the upper atmosphere."

"That would mean they intended to fry the grid."

"Yeah. And China is claiming they detected not one, but two missiles – one from the Gulf of Mexico and the other from off the California coast. Background radiation shouldn't jump substantially, but we're about the only people for 3000 miles that have any form of communications. Well, Emmaus has short-range radios. Your boy is spending tomorrow playing coal miner. Is there anything that guy can't do or won't try?"

"Not much. He's claustrophobic, but I've never met anyone who could control it as well as he does. There's a place he goes to in his head where what's going on around him just doesn't affect him."

"Until later?"

"Yeah. The psyche can only sustain so much before it begins to react. Shane had hit that wall, which is why he came home."

"He seems to be doing better here."

"He's busier here. That's not necessarily a good thing long-term, but for now ...."

Grant tapped some keys on his board and growled.

"What?" Dylan asked.

"That EMP hit southern Canada, too."

"Yeah, but Alaska and Hawaii are both still broadcasting loud and clear. Their governors are arguing with the military about sovereignty, but Alaska seems to have worked that out."

"How so?"

"Francene Maracle was there when the bombs went off. She's taken command in the line of succession and the military is complying."

Grant scuttled backwards in his chair to see what was on one of Dylan's three screens. It was the front page of the Anchorage Daily News.

"Good for them. Good for her. Anything about what she plans to do here?"

"Not so far, but I've got a bot on it."

"Good. I'm going to see if I can pull up archive data from just before the pulse, see if geosynch captured anything. You said Utah Data Center is still working. Can you get me inside?"

"Maybe. Where is that in my priority list?"

"Secondary."

"Okeydokey. Do you want cloaking or do we not care at this point?"

"Cloaking for now. We still need to pretend like we're a B&B. Speaking of which, what about our friends in the missile silo?"

"I think they might be on to us. They went radio-silent abruptly earlier today."

Grant sat back in his chair and stared at the ceiling for a long while. He knew Shane's opinion that the militia had never really been a threat to national or even domestic security, and he recognized that he and Dylan couldn't do anything about them now except monitor their activities, but he worried about what they might be up to.

"You think they're down or masking?"

"Fineseth and Patterson have got big reputations."

"See what you can do to get back in." Grant opened a bot program he'd set up several days ago, checking to see what safe houses were active. They didn't need to be fighting over satellite bandwidth and focus. Once he knew it was safe, he needed to reach out to other localities and, hopefully, find Chavez.

Awaiting Sentencing

Galena Carboy tried to shift her weight from one buttock to another, which woke Isenberg, whose head had settled on her shoulder some time ago. He snorted and flailed.

"What's wrong?" Tanaka asked. He sat directly across from Isenberg and had probably been kicked.

"Nothing. It's just really tight in here." It wasn't only tight but pitch black. Not even the emergency light was on. The bucket under the bench-bunk really needed to be emptied, but nobody had come to bring them food, though there was a water tap in the corner.

"What do you think is happening?"

"Your guess is as good as mine." Nobody had said word one to them since the door had been closed, and Galena was relatively certain that had been a couple of days ago. They were all dirty, achy from sleeping on concrete, hungry and scared. As the ranking officer in the cell, they expected her to have the answers, but she only knew what they knew.

"Do you think Rumdale is still alive?"

"What difference does it make?" Reinhold sounded sarcastic. "He should be dead. He couldn't have had orders to kill Americans for trying to hang onto food."

"The cities needed food," Anderson said. Galena bit her tongue. Anderson had killed that man in the last town ... what had it been called? Something "Wells". There'd been no reason for that. The man hadn't been armed and plenty of the townsfolk had said he'd been a faithful Quaker.

"We were following orders," Dolachak said. He'd shot someone here in Emmaus. Cranston was dead, another creep who deserved to be gone.

Kelan and Jeremy were waiting for her at home. Would they ever know what happened to her? What would Kelan tell Jeremy about her and why she'd never come home? You just couldn't say you were following orders and do crap like they'd done there. Before she realized it, she'd said it aloud.

"If we have any chance of getting out of this, we can't say we were following orders. We have to admit what we did as a group and hope they'll only want to kill those who are truly guilty."

"We're all guilty," Isenberg snapped.

"Yes, that's true. We're all guilty, and whatever these people decide to do is completely our fault, but if we admit our mistake, some of us might survive this mess."

Light flooded into the room as the door clanged open. Blinking, Galena saw three figures enter the secure area outside the cells. A uniformed deputy closed the door, holding a lantern, while a dark-haired man in jeans waited with an AR-15 at the ready. The older woman approached with keys in her hand. She'd once been a little heavy set, but now seemed raw-boned.

"Dolachek, Isenberg, and Anderson, please stand. The rest of you stay seated, cross your legs at the ankles and put your hands on your head."

Some of them must have hesitated because the man with the rifle spoke up as the woman hesitated to insert the keys.

"If you argue, if you make a move toward Sharon, if you so much as look left when one of us says look right, I will shoot you. It won't ruin my day. It'll just shorten your life."

The three who had been called out were standing now and everyone else was in the required position.

"Those standing, hands on your head and ankles crossed," Sharon ordered. She opened the door of the right-hand cell and signaled for Dolachek to come to her. After relocking the door, she then zip-stripped his hands behind him. She muscled him around and ordered him to sit down, then moved to the door of the left-hand cell. She called Isenberg out, relocked the door and secured him before calling out the weeping Anderson who begged her to understand that she hadn't meant to kill anyone.

"I'm sure Gary's wife won't believe that." Sharon forced her to sit down and moved on.

When all three were sitting on the floor, the uniformed deputy ran a chain through their arms and led them out of the cell enclosure, Sharon covering them with the AR-15. The dark-haired guy stayed behind. He'd given up the rifle, but he wasn't unarmed. Galena guessed the sweat shirt he wore over a t-shirt hid a semi-auto pistol. The short time she'd spent training for dealing with hostile citizens also informed her that his loose-armed-but-ready-to-pounce stance meant he didn't need a weapon to end her life.

"Which one of you is Galena Carboy?" the man asked. There'd really been no hope that they didn't have her name, but she *had* hoped. No use hiding now.

"I am." She indicated she meant to stand and he nodded. As she stood, she signaled the others to stay where they were. "Where are you taking my people?"

"Those three are having their charges read to them and then they're spending the night separated from you. Tell me what happened in Mara Wells, Galena."

"That was the town we were in before we came here, right?" He nodded. His face was cast in shadows because the lantern was behind him. He wanted to see her. He didn't want her to see him. "We were collecting food there. Rumdale said we needed to send a message that you lot couldn't get away with nonsense and some of our people got a little over-zealous."

"Which people?"

Her people held their breath. A few should have been worried, but they hadn't killed anyone. Being abusive jerks didn't mean they should be dead, right?

"You already took them."

"Those are the only bad apples, huh?" She could hear the derision in his voice.

"A couple of the others aren't here. I assume you killed them already."

"I didn't kill anyone. I was too busy being hung."

He's the mayor's son. Damn!

"Rumdale let the power go to his head. I should have done something about it, but I didn't realize how bad it had become until we got here."

"You're not a soldier. It's not what you signed up for. You're an innocent caught up in other people's power wake?"

True enough, but she knew a test when she heard one.

"Hell, no. I'm responsible for what I did and, as Rumdale's second, I am responsible for what I failed to stop. I can only say I'm sorry and offer myself in exchange for my people."

He didn't speak for a moment, but she could feel his gaze upon her. He pulled out a sheet of paper and used a flashlight to light it fully.

"Who is this?" It was a drawing of Cranston standing over a man on his knees, a gun to the man's forehead.

"That's Tom Cranston. I'm told he was shot by someone here in Emmaus."

"House on Mission Road," Tanaka added.

The mayor's son stared at Tanaka for a moment, then stuffed the picture back in his hip pocket and set the flashlight on the floor. She heard him sigh before he spoke.

"The three we took are already forfeit. But keep talking. You might save a few of the lives here. Tell me about Wyandot Lake." She felt her entire crew in both cells hold their breath. Some of them so deserved to go with the other three, but she wouldn't help the town to do it.

"It's a USDA facility north of here."

"How much of our stuff went there?"

What did she care about anyone else besides herself, the people in these cells and her husband and son?

"Not much because it was already full."

"With whose stuff?"

"Mara Wells, the reservation over there, and a town called Goodland. But mostly I don't know because we weren't the only unit in the area."

"Yeah. I saw a truckload of dead cow cops the other day. Any idea who set fire to our fields?"

"Not my unit. In fact, I'd be surprised if it was the USDA. We don't burn food."

"What do you know about Cole Packard?"

Her heart thudded up into her throat. The rest of her squad didn't know that name, but Rumdale had talked about him. Her hesitation told him what he needed to know. There was no use to pretending that she didn't know him.

"He's Forest Service and is connected with Wyandot Lake in some way. It was his idea to approach some of the larger towns with an offer to hold their grain for them."

"Was that really going to happen?"

"What do you think?"

"I think I used to lie to people in the Middle East, too."

When Kelan had come back from Miristan, he'd talked about the mercenaries who had been the primary fighting force there. He told it like a horror story, made more terrifying because he'd been telling the absolute truth. She'd never thought to meet one herself. She was the USDA, for God's sake. They inspected cows. They never should have been here doing things that would piss off a mercenary. She could only hope he was alone and that he was truly as reasonable as he sounded.

"What's going to happen to us?"

He walked over to pick up the lantern and flashlight from the floor.

"It could be worse." His face was now visible. Handsome and young, but oh, so cynical. "You aren't dead yet."

He locked the security door behind him and the light faded from the little window in the door. The cell block sunk into blackness once more.

"Are they going to kill us?" Lammers asked, her voice childlike in the dark.

"Your guess is as good as mine, but Rumdale and those three...yeah."

"What about me?" Raskin asked. "I cracked that kid in the skull."

"I don't know."

Galena settled back against the wall. There wasn't anything else to do. Morning would come and something would happen or maybe they'd just leave them here to starve. That guy who had just interrogated her seemed like the sort of guy who wouldn't scruple against just that.

Aid Center

Santa Fe

Alicia stirred, fighting free of the heavy quilts she'd layered on her bed last night. Despite the sunshine seeping through the curtains, the room was still cold. She winced at the hacking cough she heard as she neared Magdala's door.

"Mami, how are you?"

"You shouldn't come in here. I'm probably contagious." Magdala's usually lively brown eyes were crusty and her nose red. She seemed thinner and smaller than just the day before. "Is there anymore cough medicine?"

"No. I'll bring you some water. Maybe Popi's truck is working. I could go to the store if it is."

"You be careful out there. We don't know what's going on."

"I know." Alicia withdrew to the kitchen where she made tea and sliced the last lemon into a pitcher of water.

Her mother had come home from work night before last complaining of a sore throat and headache. When the lights had gone out, Alicia had figured the power would come back on in a while, but it had now been more than thirty-six hours. The Casanedas' house had burned down that first night. Unable to get her van started, Mrs. Vega had left it in the middle of the road. Strange booms and gunfire were heard in the distance.

Alicia's phone still worked, except there was no signal. She didn't know how to contact her husband Mike in Wichita, but if she could, she'd tell him they needed him right now. Magdala had planned well. They had a generator and extra propane, a nice store of wood for the kiva, but she needed medicine and that meant they weren't self-sufficient.

Magdala told her to leave the tray on the dresser. Her cough sounded worse than it had even a half hour before. Alicia dressed, donning a loose shirt to cover her bump and went to the garage to see if her father's old truck would start. She had already tried Magdala and Mike's cars and been unable to get a spark from the engines. As a final thought before setting out, she donned the 45-cal Mike had insisted she keep. The concealed carry belt no longer fit, but Magdala had a shoulder harness and a jacket to go over.

Popi's truck hadn't been started in a couple of years, but after it sprayed blue exhaust out the tailpipe, Alicia was able to back it out and drive to the nearest market. However, Johnnie's was closed. The Walmart was also locked up tight. A nose to the glass revealed the shelves had been stripped. She tried a pharmacy on Galisteo, but it was closed, too, and the front window, smashed. She looked around for observers and decided to risk it, stepping across the glass. She found a couple of packages of Sudafed and slipped them into her jacket.

Trying to get around a snarl of broken down cars on Paseo de Peralto, she turned down the Old Santa Fe Trail on her way back home and had to stop because a FEMA truck was blocking what was left of the road next to a command trailer. A red-headed man turned and frowned at her, then his face relaxed as he came up to her window. She recognized him from a few days before.

"Alicia, yes?"

"Yes." Her pulse hammered in her neck. He'd given them an extra ration card for the baby and hinted he might expect payment...though what good a ration card to stripped grocery stores would do, she wasn't certain. "What's going on?"

"Best guess is an EMP. Do you know what that is?"

"I've seen a movie. My mother's sick. I'm looking for antibiotics."

"Hmm, I could maybe get you some." Ron Bannon reached up and caressed a tendril of hair that had worked loose of her messy bun. "Can you reimburse me?"

Her heart began to beat faster. She wanted to smile coyly and try to convince him to give her what she needed without a price, but her skin crawled. Fortunately, another aid worker came over.

"Leave the lady alone, Ron."

"Of course, Dr. Perrin."

The doctor was a little younger than her parents, clean cut, wearing green scrubs.

"Did I hear you say your mother is sick? What are her symptoms?"

"We thought it was a cold – coughing, sneezing, sore throat – but it's not getting better."

Dr. Perrin's face sobered, became analytical.

"You appear asymptomatic."

"I've been fine so far. No symptoms."

"You seem flushed."

"I'm pregnant."

Perrin gazed at her for a long minute.

"Antibiotics won't do anything. It's a virus. Some sort of flu. We've had about 50 cases over the last two days. What is your mother's lifestyle?"

"Lifestyle? She works, she paints and she hangs out at home working in her garden."

"What does she do for a living?"

"She's a public bus driver."

"That's a common denominator. Commuters, transportation workers." His mouth twisted. "There's been no deaths so far, which is why we're not quarantining people, but it's a tough one. Really takes it out of the patients. You can try cool baths to keep the fever down, aspirin. You've already been exposed, but you should wear a mask and gloves in her presence and be hyper about cleaning any and all surfaces – boiling water or bleach. Try to keep yourself clean. If you wait here, I'll bring you some scrubs, masks and disinfectant."

While she waited for him to return, Alicia's cell buzzed. She'd had no bars since the blackout but it was still keeping time and she didn't have a watch. Now she had reception. The trailer had a comm dish on the roof, which would explain the service. She texted Mike, begging him to come to Santa Fe RIGHT NOW.

Dr. Perrin walked up to her window with a box.

"Push as much water into her as you can. She'll spike a fever and that's burn the virus out."

Thanking him for his kindness, Alicia backed out to the intersection and drove home. When she got there, she sat in the garage for a very long time, staring at her cell phone. Where was her husband and why wasn't he here with her?

Doing My Job

Mitchel Rumdale's arms were numb and he had to go to the bathroom again. At some point, he'd finally been unable to hold it any longer and he'd gone in his pants. Were these people trying to humiliate him for doing his job? Didn't they realize the risk they were taking in doing that? When his superiors learned of this, they'd send the Army in to quell this uprising.

The numbness in his arms didn't extend to the bullet wound in his shoulder which throbbed and itched, and he thought sometimes that it might be bleeding, again. How long did they think they could hold him in these conditions?

He might have dozed off for a while because the sound of the door unlocking startled him. His eyes teared as lantern light filled the small room where he was chained to a sewer pipe.

Mayor Delaney entered and closed the door behind himself. He tucked the keys deep in his jeans pocket before sitting down on the floor with his back against the far wall.

"How you doing?" he asked.

"I want to speak with a lawyer."

"Small town, only one lawyer still living. He's out of town."

"Let me go, then. You can't hold me."

"You're wrong. It's martial law and I have been tasked with deciding your fate."

"My fate? I'm from the government. You can't decide my fate."

"Sure, I can. I can put a bullet in your brain right now. Fate decided. Tell me why, besides who you work for, that I shouldn't do that."

"I was doing my job."

"That sounds familiar. I was a soldier once in a foreign land and I did things like what you did in my town."

"Then you should understand that I had an uprising to deal with and that doesn't make it easy."

"That's what I used to say and, you know, I don't think my justifications convinced any of my victims, or the families I took them from."

"I have a family. Two girls and a boy."

"So did Gary Carter, Dick Vance, Micah Lufgren, Kitty Vance, David Vance, Kellen Josephson, Shane Delaney, and the others your people beat and abused. My son has a family that loves him."

"Your son was hoarding food."

"From our perspective, you were the ones hoarding food and we were just trying not to starve this winter."

"That wasn't your call to make."

"Living isn't our call to make?"

"More food would have come later."

"And if it didn't?"

Mitchel tried to shift his weight, which jostled his arm and, for a moment, pain seared through him.

"You stupid hillbilly! That isn't your call to make. You're lucky the Army didn't come to collect your food because you'd all be dead. This is ridiculous. We were doing our jobs."

Delaney scratched his beard.

"I was hoping you'd give me a reason to save your life, but you clearly don't understand what you did or why we fought back. Tell me about Micah Lufgren."

"Who?"

"Deaf farmer. You threatened his family, confiscated his corn, and shot him in the head for not talking to you."

"That's not what happened. He threatened violence toward my officers."

Delaney laughed.

"You do know there are other people who can sign who have talked to the Lufgrens? And they've given statements."

"They're lying."

"Micah Lufgren has been a member of this community his entire life. I grew up with his uncle. I believe his wife, son, and daughters more than I believe you, a stranger who tried to steal our food."

"And that's the problem. You believe liars over those of us who have been entrusted with running the country."

Delaney had a deep, throaty laugh. The hick seemed genuinely amused.

"Before you worked for the government, what were you doing?"

"Why does that matter?"

"I'm still trying to find a reason to save your life. What were you doing?"

"I was hired right out of college as an agriculture engineer."

"I don't denigrate ag engineers. This is a farming community. So, you were a college student before you worked for the government. What qualifies you to tell me how to live my life, or whether or not my family should let go of its food in the hopes that more would replace it before they went hungry?"

"I work for the Department of Agriculture."

"Who owns the USDA?"

"Who owns ...? It's a government agency. What the hell are you trying to get at?"

"The people of the United States own the USDA. In other words, I own your agency and *you* work for *me*. So, when I told you not to take the food, you should have listened. You had no authority to kill people whose only crime was refusing to give up their property."

"You're a mad man. You just can't have people doing what they want, not when terrorists bomb twenty cities. The government is trying to keep things going and you people need to get out of our way."

Delaney stood up. Mitchel flinched back from his looming presence.

"For the murder of Micah Lufgren, Gary Carter, Kitty Vance, Richard Vance, Kellen Josephson, and Christopher Merrick, you are found guilty and will hang for your crimes tomorrow at dawn. For the attempted murder of David Vance, Robert Shoenfeld, Frank Giffin, Sharon Laughlin, Mark Ramirez, and Shane Delaney, you are found guilty and will hang for your crimes tomorrow at dawn. For the assault of twenty-four other people, you are found guilty and will hang for your crimes tomorrow at dawn."

"I didn't do all those things."

"No, but you were the leader of the ones who did. The ones who killed the others will hang beside you."

"You can't do this! You can't take the law into your own hands."

"This is not my decision alone. A council of townspeople met, discussed the facts, and voted on your fate. If you'd given me the right answers just now, I'd have reconvened the tribunal and asked them to reconsider, but I think the world is best rid of men like you. I'm sorry for your wife and children, but I can't let you go on to oppress other towns."

Mitchel called him every dirty name he could think of as Delaney unlocked the door and let himself out, taking the lantern with him, which plunged Mitchel into darkness once more. Kicking, tugging on the zip ties that held his hands, screaming curse words, he watched while the light faded from under the door and left him in utter silence. Delaney's words echoed in Mitchel's mind. He would never see Renee and the kids again. His son's six-year-old face flickered through his mind.

"I was doing my job," he said to the uncaring darkness.

"For your crimes, you will be hanged at dawn tomorrow."

The memory of Shane Delaney's fingers tightening on his bicep seared through his mind. These people didn't care. They were going to murder him and his officers for doing their jobs.

Tears spilled down his cheeks, and there was no one to witness them or care about them.

Pyrrhic Victory

Beulah

Stan Osimowitz stopped at the top of the off ramp where a connex blocked the lane. Stan couldn't see any movement in the area, but that didn't mean no one was there. He shut off the Mustang.

"What do you think?" Rob asked.

"I don't know. You said Shane came here yesterday and saw bodies?"

"A whole truckload of USDA agents, he said."

Given what Stan had agreed to do tomorrow, he had no real problem with dead USDA agents, but the apparent abandonment of the checkpoint was concerning.

"Did he see anyone else?"

"He claimed there were snipers on the roof and that the transformer farm was on fire."

"Well, we smelled that. I guess they put the fire out and then took a nap. We walk."

"We could take the onramp off."

"It was blocked when I was last here."

They locked up the car and approached the connex. Nothing moved. Rob put his hand on his gun as he pushed past the barricade. Nothing happened. Stan followed him, slightly comforted that Rob was still walking hoping his old friend's instincts remained true Beyond the connex a second connex sat at ninety degrees to the first one, followed by a collection of trucks and cars, some of them with keys still in the ignition.

"You see any snipers on that roof?" Rob indicated the courthouse that stood tall among surrounding buildings.

"I don't, and that's concerning because it was bristling when I was last here."

"Shane is not easily intimidated and he said he was nervous to stop."

Stan rubbed the back of his neck where the hairs were standing on end.

"I think we should split up." Rob had stopped walking. "You walk up straight because they know you, and I'll go through the woods and parking lot. If there's trouble, hopefully, they won't open fire on you."

Spreading out made sense. Just one sniper up on that roof could take them both out in two shots right now. He nodded and kept walking down the offramp. Rob stepped over the guardrail and disappeared into the trees.

At the bottom of the off-ramp, the road split in two directions. Stan took the one that led past the court house. He'd lost track of where Rob might be, which made sense. Rob had been a Ranger, skilled in disappearing into the foliage so that the Viet Cong couldn't see him. Stan, as an interrogator, had never needed to disappear to that degree, though he'd done his fair share of killing.

Flies buzzed in the bed of a truck that smelled of salt and iron. A shadow moving between trees distracted Stan a moment and turned out to be a dog disappearing into the understory. Rob slipped along the front of the courthouse as Stan neared the front entrance.

"Nothing's moving."

"I saw movement in an upper window when I was back in the trees. You want to try that door?"

"And risk getting shot?"

"There is that."

They both stared at the door for a moment and then Stan muttered a swear word under his breath before trying the door. It was locked.

"You smell that?" Rob asked.

"The blood or the cigarette smoke?"

"Soldiers smoke. These days they do it outside."

Rob stepped over the railing of the front steps and ghosted around the corner. Stan followed, trying to remember to lift his feet as they wove between the lilac bushes. Rob indicated a can of gravel near the rear entrance, one of the butts there still smoking slightly. The door was ajar. The back hallway had once been the post office's loading dock. Now it was the employee lounge, a plant-filled space with art on the walls. Rob held the door to ease it shut. He and Stan took the left-hand stairs to the main floor, watching each other's backs, hands on their guns, but not drawing them.

The two young soldiers reached for their service weapons as soon as they saw them, but Stan and Rob had served in a nasty war and they were prepared to see them rather than be surprised.

"Easy," Rob whispered as he disarmed the taller of the soldiers. Stan disarmed the other. "We're not looking to hurt anyone. I'm Rob Delaney, mayor of Emmaus, and this is Stan Osimowitz, mayor of Mara Wells. We're here to see Gus Hornsby."

The two soldiers exchanged furtive glances. The taller of the two spoke.

"Sergeant Major Hornsby is upstairs in the infirmary. You're going to want to talk to Sergeant Murphy."

"That radio work?" Rob asked.

"It does."

"We're just not interested in walking into a trap."

"Yes, sir. I can call him."

Since Stan had been here before, he waited with the soldiers while Murphy came down the stairs from the higher floors, but Rob slipped around the corner in case things were not what they seemed.

Stan remembered meeting Murphy briefly during an earlier visit, so he signaled Rob that it was safe to join them.

"What happened here?"

"The USDA came with the Army and they had inside information. They poisoned the town well before we even knew they were coming. We didn't suspect anything until people started to get sick. Then they attacked. We were outgunned, but the townspeople rallied and we won. Well, I guess you could call it a victory. The few of them ran away and left us here to die surrounded by towns that aren't going to come to our rescue."

"Lots of us have friends and family in Beulah," Rob said. "My sister is married to a man whose brother lives here. I guess he still lives here. We'll do what we can to help. How many National Guardsmen are left?"

"Nine."

"Damn, son! No wonder you don't even have a sniper on the roof." Stan figured it was best to keep things light. Murphy had had a tough go of it and he needed to know it wasn't the end of the world.

"Yeah. Three of us are wounded, two critically. We don't have a medic and we're out of first aid supplies."

"My daughter-in-law can look at your injured. Do we know what shape the town is in?"

"The poison was pretty wide-spread," the taller of the two soldiers reported. "I checked some houses around here yesterday. I found two people alive but I don't think they're alive now. They didn't want to come in with me, so...."

Rob looked older than his years, as old as Stan felt. He pulled out his radio and tried to pull up anyone. On the third channel, he got Anders McAuliff, who was manning the eastern off-ramp at Emmaus. They spoke back and forth for a couple of exchanges and then he turned to Murphy.

"Marnie can't come. We'd be risking our doctor in hostile territory, but we've got some first aid workers coming with vehicles and we can transfer people to the med center. I'd like your remaining six to hang here. One of our townsfolks is putting together a squad to sweep the houses. Emmaus has plenty of water."

"Thank you. We'll help in any way we can."

"Now, can we see our friend?"

"Of course, sir. Jones, take them upstairs. Hopefully, the colonel is still alive. He's got sepsis. It's been touch-and-go all day."

Rob and Stan sighed, exchanged tired gazes and followed the shorter of the soldiers to the stairs.

Hard Work

Emmaus

Shane admired Jazz Tully's hard work. She had spent yesterday single-handedly filling the Big-I's cargo bed with crabapples four feet deep. Jacob smiled as he surveyed the load.

"These'll make good cider. I drove out to talk to Trish Vance this morning and she is expecting you. James said he'd have the still all cleaned and ready to go and he's got way and enough cobs to keep the fire going for the time it takes."

"You're sure this will work, then?" Shane asked.

"Yeah. Trish's Pa and I used to make cider ourselves. Don't you remember?"

"I remember Dad reaming you three ways to Sunday for letting me drink it, yeah."

"There wasn't enough alcohol in that to make a church mouse drunk. And that's just what we want. Just enough to preserve it, but not enough to where it is leaching the Vitamin C out of it."

"How many gallons will we get out of this?" Jazz asked.

"Not nearly enough, but hopefully it will be enough to prevent scurvy." Jacob picked up an apple that had missed the truck and bit into it. "These wouldn't be bad eatin' apples if we'd taken care of the trees. That's something to be doing now before it gets cold."

"I cut some of the dead limbs. Thanks for the book on that, by the way."

"I like engaged students." Jacob grinned. The old man had a crush on her and Shane could see why. She was nothing like Vi except in her matter-of-fact way of doing what needed to be done. "The bad news is I can't figure out how to heat that building. Nick pulled the old furnace out and that new-fangled thing needs equipment and electronics we don't have to work."

"It's okay." Her voice caught. "Some of the other tenants have already moved out. Tara's talking about going to her aunt's house and Missy Callahan is going home to her mom."

"You moving back to Mara Wells?" Hope and dread warred in Shane's chest.

Jazz sighed and, in that space, Jacob did the unexpected.

"No need for that. We've got a bedroom free."

Shane stared at the old man. Had he lost his mind?

"You ask Dad and Mom about that?"

"I don't need to." Jacob wasn't correcting him, just stating fact. "It's my house as much as it is theirs. If I don't want a friend to freeze to death this winter, then that's my choice."

He'd quit-claimed the house to Rob and Jill years ago, but his name was beside theirs on the title and they were always quick to point out that the house was as much his as it was theirs. Of course, Jacob could invite Jazz to live with them for the winter. But why?

"We'd better get these over to the Vance's," Shane said to Jazz.

"Thank you, Jacob." She utterly ignored Shane. "Thank you for understanding. Michael's offered me food from the pantry, so I'll be able to contribute that way."

"And having another hunter who can hit the broad side of a barn can't hurt either," Jacob assured her.

Shane decided to count to ten rather than say anything he shouldn't.

"Where are those apple branches?" the old man asked just before Shane slammed the driver's door on the two of them.

The radio on his belt crackled.

"Maverick, what's your twenty? Over."

"Pathfinder, I'm in the Big I in the backyard. We're just loaded up with the harvest. What do you need? Over."

"I'm back from Beulah and Carl and I met here at the library. I think we found the coal bed. It's been abandoned for decades, but if this USGS map is correct, there are still accessible deposits. Over."

"Then getting these apples out of the Big I is important." Jazz opened the passenger door and scrambled up into the cab. "When are you wanting me to go? Over."

"It depends on how quickly we can assemble a group to go with you. Over."

"Jason's working on sending a couple of trucks and I'm swinging by Bennett's after Vances. Over."

"Coal mining?" Jazz pulled off her gloves and rubbed her nose with a roughened hand. "Do you feel like we just stepped back about fifty years?"

"Kind of. This is assuming that behemoth in the basement will even work. I have my doubts."

"Jacob says it was appropriately mothballed when he replaced it with the boiler."

"Yeah, well, he may remember it like it was only yesterday, but that was actually fifty years ago." Shane started the International Harvester truck and eased it into gear. "Thanks for doing this." He jerked a thumb at the bedful of apples. "I don't think any of us had time for it."

"Is it enough to earn a winter with your family?" Shane opened his mouth to answer, but he couldn't think of the words. "I sensed your discomfort."

"It's not...well, it is and it isn't. You become off-limits if you're living in my parents' house, and a part of me objects."

"And the other part of you?"

"Is relieved...or not." He paused while he threaded the big truck down his parents' driveway and then onto Little Turtle Street. "I might be feeling slightly conflicted."

"So, I'm not delusional?"

"No, though I probably am."

Shane wheeled to the right and up onto a sidewalk to avoid a tangle of vehicles that hadn't been removed yet. He'd determined the best route earlier today, aware that the width of the Big I had to be taken into account. His right mirror missed the Stattlers' oak by less than a hand-width and one of the cars by half.

"You don't strike me as out of contact with reality."

"More like an extreme realist. If Stan, Sharon, and Frank hadn't stepped forward, I'd be hanging four people tomorrow morning. That sort of drama and dating don't really go together." She froze, staring at the steering wheel rather than his face. "It's nothing personal. I just don't think we met at the right time of my life."

"You think I can't handle it?"

"I don't think anyone can handle it."

They rode in silence until he finally turned onto Willow Creek Run.

"Just so you know. I've lived a bit. I'm not a sheltered little farm girl who needs to be protected from the worldly man." The way she said "worldly man" made it sound like a horror film character. "I told you I had dated Paul Osimowitz. What do you think that means?"

"It means you were a really poor judge of character, which, hopefully, you've outgrown. And, if I ever raise a hand to you, you'll probably blow my face off. And, I don't want to introduce you to my demons. If you care about yourself, you don't want to get to know them either."

Jazz stared out across the cleared fields. Alex or Poppy was mowing the last of the hay from the Greyeyes' allotment, dragging an ancient mower behind one of Alex' older trucks.

"Maybe someday you'll trust me enough to tell me about them."

"We'll get to know each other pretty well this winter, so maybe. But, I haven't even told Jacob about them, yet."

"Are you afraid he can't handle knowing?"

"Maybe I'm afraid I can't handle him knowing."

He couldn't believe he'd said that aloud. She watched a big dust devil as it raced across a stubbled field, shredding when it hit a fringe of trees.

"Jacob loves you, Shane. You can hear it in his voice when he says your name. I don't think there's anything he can't handle knowing about you."

"But I don't know that, you see?"

Shane turned into the Vance farm then, so the conversation ended. Trish Vance looked like she hadn't stopped crying since Dick's death. Shane wasn't sure what to do for her, but Jazz asked her how she was doing and reported on David's condition: still comatose, but Marnie was hopeful.

James had scrubbed and scalded the still and brought a large supply of corn cobs into the smoking shed for fuel. Shane remembered the visits here when he'd been a kid. Jacob had hardly let him have more than a sip of cider. That had been a big year. He'd tossed Rance Conopher out of Nick's that year, lost his virginity to Marnie, and beat Paul Osimowitz at wrestling. He'd also started smoking pot and hanging out with Marnie's little brother, Josh. There'd been a winding road to this point ever since.

"Nevada's going to bring me into town tomorrow to sit with David. I just needed…." Trish misted up. "It's just really …."

Shane found the flickers of his grandmother, Vi, in Trish's face disconcerting. Rumor was that Vi's brother, Lai, had been her father, but rumors weren't truth until you started to see evidence with your own eyes.

"They're hanging Rumdale and Dolachek tomorrow." James straightened from the fire. "I don't know if that will provide any sort of closure for you, but it'll be at dawn on the roof of City Hall."

"Why there?" James asked softly.

"There's already gallows there from the old days. I think it was last used in the 1940s, but Jace says it still works."

Trish burst into tears and fled. James took a deep breath and let it out very slowly.

"My dad wouldn't like us seeking revenge." His voice was husky with tears. "I don't think we'll go, but I know it helps me to know they'll not be able to hurt anyone else."

Shane agreed. Smart people avoiding killing people if they had a choice. He wished he'd been smarter or luckier.

After they'd unloaded the apples into the huge copper vat, Shane and Jazz swung over to the Delaney ranch to check on the horses and to retrieve something from the apartment above the stables. Nevada Randolph and her daughter, Kim, were feeding the horses when they got there. Kim's arm was in a cast, so Nevada was doing all the work, but it was clear Kim was the one who knew the feeding regime.

Rocket tossed her mane and shoved her nose hard against Shane's shoulder.

“She seems to know you.” A tall, slender girl with light brown hair caught up in a simple pony tail, Kim clearly enjoyed the horses.

“She does at that.” Shane rubbed the roan mare between the eyes. “She was my horse before I ran off.” His eyes grew unfocused. “I’d sometimes drive up on weekends just to ride her when I was in college.”

“Then maybe you could exercise her?” Nevada said. “She’s ripping the heck out of my hands and I’m terrified to even saddle her.”

“She’s definitely a fun ride.” Shane held Rocket’s halter with one hand while undoing the gate of the stall with the other. She tossed her head, recognizing how close freedom was, but aware of his restraining hand. He led her into the paddock and stood softly speaking into her ear for a moment before vaulting onto her bare back. She danced sideways, but then realized he wasn’t going to fall off, so she trotted crisply around the paddock, tossing her mane and snorting. Five times around and she settled to a walk. He dismounted.

“Wow! I’ve never seen her so calm with another rider. And without a bit or saddle. Cai has to fight her.” Kim cast Shane an admiring glance.

“She recognizes a maverick same as her.” Shane led the mare back into the stall. “I wish I had time to take her for a full ride, but I've got stuff to do."

They pulled hay bales away from the door to Jacob's apartment. Without any power, the only light was from the large windows, the western ones showing the sun racing toward the horizon. Shane shone his flashlight around the room at all the tubs and bags of food.

"How did he know?" Jazz asked.

"They were children during the Depression. A generation of hoarders."

It took time to haul everything to the hay mow where Shane rigged up a pallet to the winch and lowered the load to the bed of the Big I, all except the part Jacob had designated for Nevada and Kim.

"Do you have any idea how we are going to heat this place this winter?" Nevada asked when Kim was not within earshot.

"Jacob has a whole load of corn cobs from the allotment. I'm headed out to get coal tomorrow, but as soon as I get back, I'll bring them by."

"Thank you. We are so blessed to be here and not in Seattle right now. I can't imagine what's happening in the big cities."

An icy hand slide down Shane's back like a premonition. All he could do was nod and call out to Jazz that it was time to go. Andrew Bennett waited for them on the other side of the creek.

"Something up?" Shane asked.

Andrew nodded at Jazz before answering Shane.

"I saw your truck there and figured I'd catch whichever of you was here. Only coz you probably should know for your own safety. Dan McAuliff's back."

Shane hadn't expected that, but he realized he wasn't surprised.

"Anders didn't mention this morning."

"He might not know. There's a whole bunch of them at the silo. Josh Callahan's one of them."

Dan could be reasoned with, but Josh probably couldn't. It was mixed news, like so much in his life. "Yeah, okay."

"You aren't worried about repercussions?"

"I can take care of myself. I wonder how they got out of prison. I can't imagine Dan killing anyone, but five years in Supermax might change a man. Thanks for letting me know. I sort of thought that would be against your principles."

"Turning him into the cops would be against my principles. Not warning you of potential danger would also be against them."

Shane grinned involuntarily.

"It's interesting to hear other people as completely consistent as my grandfather."

"He's a good man."

"He is. So, you talk to anyone at the silo yet?"

"Yes."

"And?"

"They still have electricity and they're willing to work for food."

"Did you ask Dan about his feelings?"

"I didn't talk to him. Kletti mentioned your dad, but I didn't mention you were home."

Shane glanced west where the sunset started painting the sky purple.

"What would you say if he asked?"

"That you'd do things differently if you had to do them all over again."

Shane nodded.

"That's about right. If he wants to talk, is your house neutral territory?"

"Unarmed, yeah."

"Good enough. We gotta go."

"I hear you. We got enough corn cobs to heat the place, but if you need a working truck to haul coal, let me know."

"I was going to swing over to your place on the way back to town, but we spent too much time here. You have to crew it with a driver and someone to ride shotgun, just in case."

"We even have gasoline."

"And this coal is for …."

"One of my brothers has a coal burner, but I'm giving my share to Trisha Vance."

"You're a good man, Andrew," Jazz said.

"Ain't nothing good in me besides Jesus, but you know that already."

"We gotta go." Shane preferred to avoid the topic. Shane waited until he was steering down Willow Creek Run before he glanced at Jazz. "You a church-goer?"

"I wasn't for a while, but yeah."

"How'd Andrew know that? I thought you just met the other day."

She shot him a sidelong glance accompanied by a smirk.

"There's a secret handshake. Didn't you see us give it?"

"Seriously."

"You can tell by how we fix our hair."

"You're mocking me."

"A little. You grew up in a family of Christians and you don't know how we might know one another."

"I'm not a Christian."

"I know. For a very secretive person, you have been remarkably honest about that."

"That might be another reason for you and me not to go where our instincts are driving us, because I am never going to become one."

"You sound so certain."

She smiled at him. Not knowing how to respond without sounding hostile, Shane drove the rest of the way back to the house in silence.

Past Doesn't Always Smell Sweet

Rob parked one of the town work trucks in Sharon Laughlin's driveway and walked slowly toward the porch. Sharon sat in a rocker, watching the sunset's outrageous shades of purple and orange.

"Mind if I sit with you for a while?"

"There's a free rocker."

He paused long enough to admire the beautiful quilt tossed over it. He struggled to imagine Sharon's rough hands doing such fine work, but she'd won blue ribbons for her quilts.

"You want to know why I volunteered, don't you?"

"You just never seemed like the blood thirsty type to me."

"Not much I feel so passionate about that it makes my blood boil. Except maybe your boy."

"Shane?"

"Yeah. He looks so much like EJ."

"That's right. You dated in high school, didn't you?"

"And we got back together for a while when he came back. He asked me to marry him."

Rob stopped rocking, stunned.

"My parents never mentioned it."

"I don't think they ever knew. He was ... I think today they call it manic. At first, it seemed like the old EJ except brighter, more exciting. And I was thrilled to be engaged. But we knew my pa would say no way unless he had a job, so we didn't tell anyone. We'd meet up at the old barn, sleep in the hay loft. He did manage to get a job over at the brake factory in Mara. But, I don't know what happened. A month later, he'd lost the job and he was talking like a crazy man. I know now what was going on, but back then ... I just didn't. The night I found out I was pregnant, he hung himself."

Her eyes glittered for a second.

"Did he know?"

"No. I was just counting on my fingers and I knew. I was going to tell him, but he never came to the barn because he was hanging in your parents' garage."

Rob didn't want that image in his head. "What happened to the baby?"

"My parents wouldn't let me keep her. In those days, it was closed adoption, so I've never been able to find out. I put a memo in the file about twenty years ago, but I've never heard from anyone, so I'm thinking her adoptive parents never told her. That, or she was so comfortable with them that she didn't need to know."

"I'm sorry."

"It's okay. I'm hoping my choice meant she had a father. I certainly wouldn't have given her one."

Rob nodded.

"My brother ruined you for other men?"

"Ruined me for love. There were men when I first got back from Wichita, but I couldn't find any reason to go on a second date. Love means loss in my experience, and I didn't want to go through that again. So, I took to dressing mannish and giving men the cold shoulder. Then my parents died and I had to work the farm. There were other men then, but I knew they didn't want me. They wanted my land. The ones that wanted me … well …. You remember Celia Franich?”

“Vaguely.”

“She started hanging around me back before you and Jill came back to town. At first, I thought she was just a friend, but then it turned weird and I told her I wasn’t interested. I don’t think I like women that way.”

“Some of your neighbors have doubts.”

“Some of my neighbors should mind their own business. I loved him, Rob. I don’t grieve him anymore, but the other day when I saw Shane for the first time in years … my god, but they look alike. Except for the eye color.”

“And that has something to do with why you volunteered to hang some people?”

“Your boy was going to, but I can’t let him. He’s already got haunts in his eyes, same as the ones I saw in EJ. He seems less damaged, but he doesn’t need to kill any more people than are absolutely necessary in a world gone mad.”

“You’re right there, but it’s Jill and my responsibility, not yours.”

“I don’t think you need more haunts, either, Rob.”

“There are some nightmares you never get rid of.”

"I expect not. At least my haunts won't be for long."

Rob took in breath to tell her they could live thirty-odd more years when he remembered her personal bio.

"Is it back?"

"It's been back. Found a lump on my rib last Christmas. They removed it, but it was too late. I was taking pills, but Marnie can't get anymore. I might make summer."

"I'm sorry to hear that."

"I'm not really. It's been a good life. My niece turned out well and I'd be sad to miss her children, if I thought she was going to have any. But, she was off traveling overseas when this happened, and if she's got any sense, Annabel will stay there until we sort out our mess. But, really, I don't mind moving on."

"Sharon ..."

"No, Rob. You need to listen, not talk. I've planted the winter wheat. Most of the land is in hay. It was getting too much for me, all that corn and wheat. But the ground's real fertile. It would make someone younger a good living. They could grow grain or a truck garden."

She was right, of course. How many times had Jill told him to listen to the kids instead of a lecture? Fewer times than Pa and Vi had.

"You have a will?"

"Annabel gets the savings, if they're still there. I had about a half-million in stocks and bonds. If she doesn't claim it in five years, it goes to the college as an endowment. The land goes to Shane."

Rob blinked at her.

"He's no farmer."

"Lots of people who aren't farmers are going to wish they were by the end of this. Alex Lufgren can teach him what he needs to know, or he can lease out the land. I know he won't want the house since he's got the hotel, but he could rent it out or whatever."

"He's going to want to know why a woman he barely knows gave him a really nice piece of property."

"And, you're not going to say it's because he reminds me of his uncle who committed suicide."

"No. I don't think he needs that comparison."

"Absolutely. So, my reason is that I admire what he's doing here in this crisis. That's what I'm telling you, so you don't have to lie. I've got an appointment with Brandon at the bank tomorrow to register my new will. I'm naming you my executor."

Since the bombs, he and Jill had both been approached to be executors of about two dozen wills each, so this didn't surprise him at all. He nodded, accepting the responsibility.

"What about your personal stuff?"

"I'll work on that and attach it to the will when I know. Probably label what goes to who. It's not like I have a lot of jewelry or art. Mostly it's my quilts and pottery, and I plan on gifting those personally before I pass. My will won't be hard. I'll be clear, I promise."

"You always have been. I'm surprised you kept EJ a secret all these years."

"I didn't intend to. Nobody asked so it seemed ridiculous to proclaim him the love of my life. So, now that my will is taken care of, there's one other bit."

Rob turned toward her and saw a pleased look on her face. He knew that expression from when she'd sat in the audience as Annabel had graduated from the local community college. Besides his son, what young life did she plan to transform this winter?

Brothers

With the ending of the work day, Anders McAuliff stood by his truck thinking about going home to his empty house and taking a shower. Usually, he'd be planning a hot date with the television, but that might never happen again.

He paused at the end of the mine road, considering whether to turn right to drive home or left for the uncomfortable meeting he kept putting off.

Wolf Creek Run was quiet. He saw some figures out in the darkening fields wielding scythes in the hay. Hard work, farming without equipment.

County Road N was clogged with Bennett vehicles. It was too dark to see what they were doing, but it would be like the brothers to come up with an innovative way to do something in a new way. Their ingenuity was one of the things he loved about Emmaus. He so wished he'd told Rogan to come west before the Pulse. Anders pulled into the compound road. The compound looked deserted behind a closed and locked gate. He knew that wasn't true. He pressed the horn, let silence reign after. When he didn't see any movement, he laid on the horn longer. A man who wasn't his brother came out of the gloom.

"You're Anders, right?"

"That's right."

"Stop drawing attention to us or you'll regret it. Dan'll be up in a minute. Just sit out here and enjoy the solitude."

The man melted back into the cooling darkness. Anders leaned against his truck, feeling the warmth of the engine. The waning moon cast everything in a rime of cold silver. Dan's hair reflected it, raising gooseflesh on Ander's neck when his brother suddenly emerged from the night like a movie Count Dracula. The first man reappeared to unlock the gate.

"I'll be back. You can trust me with the key, Kowalsky."

Kowalsky whistled as if to alert a watcher in the dark and headed back toward the building.

"Let's sit in the truck." Dan moved toward the passenger door. Anders unlocked it, still surprised that it worked. Who knew it was a good idea to keep a truck twenty years?

They sat staring out the windshield for several minutes before starting to talk about things that didn't really matter, like whether they each had enough food to get through the winter. Finally, Anders asked how Dan and his men had gotten out of prison.

"Bureaucracy. I was at Leavenworth when the bombs hit and most of my guys were there. We got out between radioactive rain and before the Pulse hit. How long have you known I was here?"

"The day after the cornfield fire, but we were hiding crap from the USDA so I couldn't get here." They talked a little about their situations. Anders thought his ex-wife and adult children were safe in Columbus and he hesitated to risk the highways now. Dan asked if Anders had heard from his ex-wife. Margie had taken a settlement from Anders and withdrawn from contact after that. She and Dan had not had children, so there was nothing to tie them together after he'd been sentenced to 25 years in federal prison. Anders expressed sorrow that she hadn't tried to keep in touch with Dan, but his brother seemed to have moved on.

"I appreciated your efforts, you know, getting me the best lawyer money could buy. And, thanks for getting them to return my books and journals."

Anders nodded. An uncomfortable silence descended. What needed to be said pushed its way to the fore.

"Were you planning to overthrow the government?"

Dan laughed softly, ruefully.

"No, but I did see this coming. Broad strokes anyway. I was hoping to wake people up so they'd be ready. They weren't, were they?"

Anders shook his head, infinitely sad.

"I hope Margie is somewhere safe, on a beach, in another country." Dan smiled. "So, don't be a stranger. If you need somewhere to come when the fecal matter hits the oscillating rotor, you're welcome here."

"I hear you. For now, the town needs good leadership. I'm on the City Council."

"Maybe I should have been more pro-government."

Anders knew Dan wasn't serious. Dan reached for the door handle, then paused.

"It's going to get bad this winter. You know that?"

"Yeah. Oh, I brought this." Anders held out the key. "Somehow the FBI missed a huge weapons cache off-property."

"You didn't tell them?" Dan took the key.

"Weird, huh? When I found it, I'd had time to reconsider the wisdom of cooperating with them."

They laughed and it almost warmed Anders' heart.

"Come by for coffee sometime." Dan slid out of the car and closed the door. Anders turned on the headlights to make it easier for him to unlock and relock the gate and then walk back toward the building. A dark shadow moved on the roof, evidence that these men were no longer the harmless community they once had been. Anders turned around to head home.

Dawn Truth-Seeking

Jacob flipped the page to finish 2 Chronicles 32 and the life of Hezekiah and paused, hearing a bedroom door opening and a dog's claws tapping on the wood floor. He glanced at the dark window. Shane tossed and turned half the night, which had probably caused Jacob to awaken. Sighing, he decided to give up reading, turned off his headlamp, set the Bible aside, and listened. Shane took Glister out into the backyard. When the generator wasn't running, the house had no water pressure, so the boy spent a few minutes standing on the edge of the yard staring into the trees, while Glister stretched to the end of his leash. Jacob donned his dungarees and a flannel shirt and went to brush his teeth. Glister nuzzled his hand as he passed him in the kitchen.

Shane straightened from the fire he was building in the barbecue pit as Jacob approached.

"Sneaking up on me in the dark might not be the wisest choice, old man."

Shane wasn't wearing a gun, but he didn't need a weapon.

"You knew it was me, though, didn't you?"

Shane returned to blowing on the fire. Jacob prepared the coffee.

When the pot had brewed, Shane joined Jacob on the steps, a storm lantern between them. Had it only been a couple of weeks since that first night after Shane came home when they'd sat here on the porch steps and talked? So much had happened that it felt longer than that—like a year—but it really had only been a few weeks. And in that time, Jacob had learned that his grandson was haunted by a demon older than Jacob.

"Have you given up sleep?" Jacob asked.

"I think sleep has given up on me."

"How long has it been?"

"The night before the hanging."

"She haunting you?"

Shane stared at him, fear flickering in his eyes. "What is it you think you know, old man?"

"I know war comes home with you." Shane's respect for Jacob kept him silent while Jacob sipped his coffee. "I went to war for a vaunted cause, and I came home to parades. We liberated all these people from concentration camps, got rid of one of history's bloodiest bastards. And, I still wake up in the middle of the night seeing some German soldier dying from my bullet in his guts, crying for his mother just as I would have been. I know that specters from war follow you home, and you can only avoid them so long before they eat your face like one of them monsters in the horror flicks."

Shane licked his lips, eyes narrowing.

"That hit close to where you live?"

Shane wrapped his long fingers around his cup, gazing into the lightening darkness.

"I didn't go to war for a vaunted cause or end a bastard who needed to be put down. In the long run, I'm not even sure I was protecting the country. A bunch of goat-herders are really no danger to us."

"You don't think they did this?"

"No. I don't think they did the bombs. Someone far more sophisticated did this. Which means that there's no grace that can cover what I did."

"You cannot sin enough to run out of grace, boy. You need to know that. And, forgiving yourself can only come when you accept it." Shane grimaced, head twitching sideways in rejection. "You're not there yet, so I'll tell you something else I know. You see things." For the first time, Shane made eye contact, like a man seeing a snake within striking distance. "A woman dressed in a burqa, I think." Shane's next breath didn't come. "The Greyeyes men all struggled with depression. The ones who went to war more so than the ones who drank themselves to death."

"I'm not my dad, Jacob."

"You got self-control, I'll give you that. What you don't have is Jesus, and the only Greyeyes man I know who made it to a ripe old age was my father-in-law who did."

Shane opened his mouth to protest and then snapped it shut.

"Don't worry," he muttered. "You won't find me dangling from the garage rafters by my neck." Jacob winced.

"I'm not an enemy, boy. Man throws you a lifeline, you don't set it on fire."

Shane winced now, too, and a look of shame crossed his face. But before they could pursue it further, Rob came out the back door.

"Any coffee left?"

Shane, master of avoidance, swept the lantern up and headed into the house.

"We have to get ready."

Rob stretched an arm across the door, other hand on Shane's chest.

"You're going to Arikaree Breaks and dropping off the USDA agents we're not killing along the way. So, you do need to get ready, but you won't be going to the hanging."

Jacob could feel the heat of Shane's anger.

"I didn't miss the first hanging. Why should I miss this one?"

"Do you think you need any more nightmares? Seeing people swinging won't cure them."

Shane muttered a swear word and looked like he might slug Rob, but then he paused. The explosion Jacob expected never happened.

"When do you want us at the courthouse?"

"Just after dawn."

Shane looked at the sky, which was lightening but not blushing with colors yet

"Not long then. I'll do as you say, but I need to go wake Jazz. She's Keri's shotgun."

Rob didn't move.

"It might seem wrong to you, son, but I'm trying to shield you."

"I'm not twelve, Dad." His gaze shifted to Jacob. "But, I'm trying to listen to wiser voices."

Jacob nodded ever so slightly. Rob dropped his arm and Shane headed indoors. Rob turned to Jacob.

"Are you planning to attend?"

"I've seen enough people hang in my life, son."

Rob's eyes widened. "Of course. I ... that was insensitive."

Jacob briefly remembered the creak of hemp rope rubbing against old timbers and saw the man-shaped shadow flickering across the floor. One ... two ... three ... four ... five ... forty-year-old grieving over now.

"Unfortunately for you, you have to be there. But, I'm going to go talk to that boy, Danny."

"Dennis and you decide what to do with him?"

"Dennis doesn't care. Or, er, he admits he shouldn't care. He hadn't known the pilot even twenty-four hours. We'll never know what actually happened that day. I'm not sure Danny even knows. It's all mixed up with his fear and guilt and what he wishes it could have been. If Sharon wants him, I can't think of too many people more qualified than she is to put him to work. But I need your word and hers that the boy is free to go come harvest next year with at least two weeks of rations and a firearm to protect himself with."

"You have my word, Pa."

Good enough.

"We need to be thinking about conserving gas. When you're ready, I'll be checking the oil on the truck."

"Yes, sir. Jill wanted to go, too."

"Why? It's not cheap entertainment."

"He tried to hang her son, Pa. Would Vi have wanted to see him dead?"

"Before you went to war, yes. She sort of lost the image of you as an innocent after that."

Rob sighed and nodded, then went to go find his wife. Jacob stared at the side door of the garage. It had been years since parking in there made him cry, but today, he congratulated himself for parking in the driveway.

A Hanging in Emmaus

When Joe and Sharon led the chained prisoners onto the roof, Rob wished he'd chosen to go to the old basement with Jacob instead of upstairs with Jill. Too late now. In the uncertain light of dawn, the uncondemned USDA folks looked pale and sick. The council had voted not to feed them and Rob hadn't rebelled. Stan, Anders McAuliff and Frank Giffin brought the condemned out last.

Rumdale still smelled of piss, but he solemnly mounted the platform. The days chained to the sewer pipe in darkness had apparently proved to him that they weren't going to change their minds if he begged. The others struggled, begging to be allowed to live. Jason Breen stood before the platform, an AR-

15 at the ready. Apparently, the three executioners had already decided how this would play out. Sharon placed the noose on each of them. Stan put a sack over each head. Frank made sure the knot on each noose was properly positioned. All three put their hands on the big lever that controlled the trapdoor.

Joe turned away and Rob stared at the roof as the trap door dropped open with a finality and four bodies snapped hard against the end of the nooses. Jill covered her mouth, face contorting. There was no dancing. Well-placed knots ensured that death came quickly; the smell of urine permeated the pre-dawn air. The surviving prisoners cried out and wept. Jason Breen and two of his men stepped forward to remove the bodies. Joe sniffled.

"Shane'll be waiting out front with the Big I. Remember to give him the key to the restraints," Rob said around the huge lump in his throat.

Frank helped Joe lead the prisoners away. Jill wiped tears off her cheeks. Backlit by a pastel sunrise, she watched as Jason and his men cleared away the bodies.

"You're right," she said. "There's no closure. I'm going to check on Marnie."

They hugged, both fighting back tears. It was a fearsome thing to stand as witnesses at an execution.

When she'd left, Rob put his hands on the roof parapet. He didn't think he'd ever view the sunrise or sunset from this roof again. The joy had been sucked clean out of what had been a mayoral perk. Jason Breen came into his peripheral vision.

"Something you should know."

"Besides we've become Death? What?"

"Dan McAuliff's back."

"Shane told me last night."

"You got any plans about that?"

"With what army?" Rob shook his head. "Shane doesn't care, and I am holding out hope that McAuliff doesn't want revenge."

"He doesn't. Josh might, but Shane can still take him."

Rob considered the oddity that Josh's father took Shane's side, but he didn't care enough to ask why. They admired the sunrise a moment.

"This was the right thing to do. It sends a message that nobody should mess with us."

"You're part of us?"

"As long as it's voluntary, yeah. For now."

"I haven't got the means nor the inclination to enforce anything involuntary."

"Then we understand one another. I sent some guys out looking for trade. Mae's in. So's Marnie. What about the town?"

"People can make their own decisions. Ask Jacob if he needs to restock for the feed store."

Nodding, Jason looked across the roof. "I gotta go help bury them. I know you hate this, but they had it coming."

Rob couldn't nod. He waited for everyone to leave the roof. He missed the cooing of the pigeons.

God, I know vengeance is Yours and not mine. But what else could I do?

Maybe there was an invisible dome between him and God. Today, he felt more alone in the universe than at any other time in the last thirty-five years.

Reprieve

Danny Hughes heard the door at the top of the stairs unlock. He managed to reach for his pants before the old man reached the bottom step. It was hard to tell with someone that old; was he here to deliver bad news or just not smiling? Danny finished zipping his pants while the old man ruminated.

"They're hanging people upstairs."

Danny sat down on the bunk. Mr. Delaney sat on the stairs.

"Have they said...?"

"They listened to me and decided not to kill you. We're going to wait until dawn and then I'll take you somewhere. You'll pay your debt by serving. After the harvest is in next fall, you'll be given a choice to stay as a productive member of the community or head on down the road with provisions and protection."

A two-ton weigh lifted off his chest and settled onto his shoulders.

"I killed a man. One year doesn't seem like much."

"You'll live with that. I can't tell you it'll go away because it won't. But working off a little of that will help you, as well as one of our community members. You aren't a slave. You're more like an indentured servant. You have rights within the terms of your service. I wrote them out." He held up an envelope, which he handed through the bars. Danny hesitated. Did it send the wrong message that he wanted to know?

The list, written in lovely long-hand, wasn't easy for him to read because nobody learned that anymore, but it was simple enough. His terms of service were to be home every night at this lady's house and to do the work assigned by her and others. He could be worked up to twelve hours a day and six days a week, but he couldn't be abused or starved. He had a right to speak his mind, go to church, and receive due process if accused of a crime. If he walked away, nobody would stop him. But he couldn't take food or anything else with him or he'd be hunted for thievery and made to suffer the assigned consequences.

"Who signed these?"

"Myself, the mayor, and Sharon Laughlin, the lady who's taking custody of you. We'll be your parole board."

Danny sighed and reached for his shirt. He'd been wearing it for weeks now and it reeked.

"There's something you ought to know. We got hit by some sort of power outage." Danny nodded. Deputy Kelly had put him to work cranking a charger for the lanterns and radios. "You knew that. But the power's not come back. And I don't know if it ever will."

"What does that mean?"

"Imagine all the work it will take to do all the things we used machines for. Young, strong men like you will be the ones doing most of that work."

Danny finished tying his shoelaces and stood.

"So, can we go now? I don't want to seem impatient, but it's like being buried alive in here, and I haven't seen the sun since that day."

Mr. Delaney looked at his watch, shining a flashlight on it.

"It's time, I think." He unlocked the block doors and Danny did something he'd come to believe would never happen: he stepped into freedom. Well, a kind of freedom, one with responsibility and consequences.

Outside the front doors, the old man's green pickup waited in front of a string of four large trucks. Some people were being lifted into the back of a white farm truck and being chained to the slats.

Was there a difference between him and them? He didn't feel like there was. He was being given a chance to prove there was a difference. Or, he could just walk away with nothing but the clothes on his back. Getting into the green truck seemed like a much wiser idea.

What She Can't Save

Dr. Marnie Callahan wrote TOD 6:17 am on the chart, took a deep breath and set the pen down. National Guard Commander Gus Hornsby lay dead in the bed. She might have been able to save him if she'd been able to do surgery soon after he was shot and if she'd had his blood type on hand. A call for donors hadn't produced any B negatives willing to part with their bodily fluids. Or, maybe it was just that they didn't live within earshot of the clinic.

It truly felt like the 1880's. Everyone was isolated from everyone else by a mere couple of miles, without radio, or television, or enough internal combustion engines.

Marnie scrubbed her hands with alcohol and soap then rinsed them and her face in cold water before going into the darkened room where David Vance remained in a lightening coma. They'd moved him into his examining room yesterday when she'd agreed to care for the folks from Beulah. The advantage was you could view him through the window at one end. He smelled of urine. While she struggled to change the pad between his legs, she reasoned that it was a good sign. He'd been holding his bladder yesterday. He'd peed twice during the night. As disgusting as it was, it was a sign that his brainstem was still functioning.

He was subtly turning toward the left and that was a worrying sign. She had no idea what was going on beneath the bandage wrapping his head. When she peeled back his eyelids, she could see his brain was under pressure, but how much and what was causing it was impossible to tell without modern equipment. If it got worse, she could try to relieve it by drilling into his skull, but she'd not been properly trained for that, and it might not work anyway. A simple skull fracture, yes, but removing bone fragments from his brain without amplification—

It was an impossible situation.

In the other room, the three Beulah folks awaited care from Lila who was changing a bandage. Marnie washed her hands again and moved to take care of the patient in the furthest bed. She cut the bandage away and gagged as she smelled the infection. The wound had improved from yesterday, but their stock of antibiotics was running down quickly. Damn Stan Osimowicz for bringing more people into the community. Yeah, help your neighbor, but who really was your neighbor in a situation like this? Not National Guardsmen who had tried to kill her husband Cai only two weeks before. Doctors trained for impossible situations where there were no good answers, but Marnie was still human. Had she been given a choice, she would have let the National Guardsmen take care of themselves.

Finishing the bandage, she withdrew to the hallway to sit on the floor and cry. Eventually, Lila came out to sit beside her.

"Babies make us emotional."

"Yeah, so do dead patients."

Lila simply sighed and changed the subject.

"David opened his eyes last night."

"He did?"

"I pinched his titty and they opened. He didn't react to me, but that's improvement and I'll take it." Good news balanced bad.

"Hornsby died a few minutes ago."

"We knew that was going to happen. He leaked into his gut. We don't have enough antibiotics to counter that. Probably shouldn't have wasted them on him." Lila pushed herself up the wall. "I'll have Mace take him to the morgue. Vin spent all day yesterday over at Beulah helping them bury the dead, now he's headed to the Breaks to mine coal. I suppose I should go home and make sure Melanie is taking care of those kids."

"How's her ankle?"

"She ain't gonna die from it. Abigail should be here soon. You ought to head home and get some sleep."

At the other end of the building, someone banged on the front door. Lila went to answer it, while Marnie peeled herself off the floor. This was no time for self-pity. Jill came around the corner and gave her a hug.

"You've been here long enough. Go home. I'll take a shift."

"Seriously?"

"I'm rusty, but I was doing this before you were born. You go on."

Marnie started to turn toward the office, but then turned back. "Thank you." Jill nodded and smiled like it was the most ordinary thing in the world. These weren't ordinary times, and

Jill had to know that she was performing a miracle just by being here. "No, seriously. There's only so far one person can go before they are out of steam, and I need a break. Thank you."

"You don't have to suffer. Just tell us when you need help. I'm not the only old nurse around who could take a shift here."

"How did …?" Marnie struggled to find the words. They'd just hung people on the roof of City Hall. How could that even be their reality now?

Jill's smile grew plastic.

"Knowing they deserved it doesn't change the fact that I consented to kill four people today." She pulled herself up to her full height. "How's David?"

Marnie outlined the status of each patient. By the time she was finished, the nurse Abigail was there and Lila had left to check on her family. Marnie gave Jill one final hug and then headed home. She walked because she and Cai no longer owned a working automobile.

Feeling in the Dark

Missouri

Javi felt around the end of the bed and reached a searching hand for the wall, brushing and catching hold of a door frame. Ami wasn't breathing, but she wasn't offering to help either. It wasn't a complicated journey. There was a sink and counter and then the toilet. He'd decided yesterday that it was better to feel silly than to make a mess in the bathroom, so he sat down. It smelled stale in here because the water pressure was almost non-existent, so flushing was mostly useless. He'd insisted Ami take him to the nearby woods this morning and he suspected she'd taken care of her own needs there too. Without such precautions, the room would quickly become unlivable.

When he returned to the main room, he could hear her putting things away…getting ready to leave. Provided his eyes continue making progress, they would set out tomorrow morning. Ami needed to fill the gas tank before then. He knew that, but he hated being left. He didn't know how much help she would be in any incident, but she wasn't blind and that meant she was more use than he would be.

"I really could use a shave."

"Do you trust me to shave you?" she asked.

"Trust another human being near my jugular with a razor? Maybe I'll grow one of those old-man beards…like that giant guy with the blue cow."

"I think it was an ox."

"What the hell is an ox?"

He shouldn't have been bantering. He'd missed the edge of the bed and stumbled into the wardrobe…or was it the TV cabinet.

"I'm lost," he admitted. She was already there, guiding his hand to the foot of the bed. He fumbled his way to the pillows and sat down. "This is frustrating."

"You could see better this morning and your right conjunctivity is no longer bloodshot.

No promises, but if you continue healing at this rate, we should be able to take the blindfold off tomorrow."

"And get on the road?"

"That depends on how sensitive your eyes are to light, but perhaps. What are you going to do while I'm away?"

"Nap. Is this dozing off thing my body trying to heal itself?"

"I believe so. I'm sorry I have to leave you here alone, but the bandages raise too much attention."

"I understand. See you in an hour or so." A brave front did nothing to alleviate the echoing hollow in his chest as the door closed and locked. Only the plan he'd had in mind since she'd announced this outing kept him from curling into a ball with the pillow over his head.

He listened for the car backing away from the curb and crossing the parking lot. She'd gone. Now he could find out what she had been keeping as a secret.

Javi eased the blindfold up onto his forehead and slowly removed the gauze pads from his eyes. There were a lot of tears as his eyes adjusted. She'd left the blinds closed, but the slats let in enough light that he could make out the general shape of things. Her blue briefcase sat on the table next to maps and MRE sides. He found that if he kept his eyes narrowed, the tears stopped flooding so he could see a bit.

He put the briefcase on her bed and unzipped it. With his back to the window, he could see the contents – a handful of files, a medical kit, and a beaded purse that seemed very much out of character for Dr. Ceylon. He eased it out of the briefcase.

"I'm a virologist," she'd explained that first morning at breakfast.

Did viruses come in vials with twist-off lids? And what was on the thumb drive? His tablet rested on the table as well and it came on when he opened the case. He couldn't see well enough to read text, so the first few files he opened were useless to him. He was so engrossed in trying to figure it out that he didn't hear her drive up and only heard the key in the lock.

"What are you doing?" she demanded as he tried to shield his eyes from the overwhelming light from the door. "Are you trying to cause permanent damage?"

She closed the door with a finality, but his eyes were already in full retreat, plunging him into helpless blindness.

"Who the hell are you?" he demanded as she steered him toward his bed.

"Who are you to question me?" she snapped. "I've never lied to you. Sit down. Let's treat your eyes and bandage them again and then we can have a good row about who is up to what."

He had little choice. She wouldn't treat his eyes if she meant to kill him ... right?

While he was laying on his back as she washed out his eyes and treated them, she explained about her friend Samira and the mysterious package she had left her.

"I don't know what's in those vials until I can get to a lab ... or access that thumb drive."

"While the notebook still has a charge, you should check it out."

Amisi sighed as she rebandaged his eyes.

"I should be getting gasoline, but I worried that you were helpless by yourself. Then I thought I hadn't locked the door."

He was flattered by her concern for him.

"Take a few minutes to check the flash drive and then you can go get gasoline. And I promise I'll take a nap and stay out of your things." It was his turn to sigh. "Paranoia is part of the job. And, yesterday, I heard you getting into something and not telling me about it."

"Why didn't you just ask me?"

"A direct question would give you an opportunity to lie and out me knowing. Playing dumb is a better way of gleaning information."

"Do you consider me to be a subject of interest, Mr. Pulgarin?"

Her use of his false name lay between them. He reached in the general direction of her voice, fingers tangling in her curls. She chuckled as he hooked his fingers behind her neck and pulled her toward him.

"I was beginning to wonder," she murmured as he missed her mouth entirely and got her ear.

"A little out of practice. And, blind, which complicates things. And getting a headache." A throb behind his right eye threatened to grow.

"And it's perhaps a complication we want to avoid." She disentangled her hair from his fingers, sat back. He fumbled for and caught her hand.

"It's not necessarily what I want. It's just...if I tell you who I am, you can't tell anyone."

"Do you trust me that much?"

"I'm taking you with me to the safe house. Does that sound like I don't trust you? It's just been so long since I could be honest that I don't know how. It's also made me deeply suspicious of everyone."

"I wasn't really trying to keep anything from you. I just...we didn't know each other a week ago. And you are secretive...."

"Not really. I maintained a cover for years and then I changed my identity just a few days before we knew each other. But that wasn't me. It was a role I took on to hide. But then I rescued you and...I didn't want to be a made-up person with you. I wanted to be me. Which it would be wonderful if I knew who me was, but I'm still rediscovering him."

She laughed.

"That's the nicest compliment anyone has ever given me – that they wanted to be themselves with me."

He did, though the throb was growing in size.

"Javier Chavez."

"Not Pulgarin?"

"No. It's not even my mother's maiden name. I've had lots of names over the years."

"And you work for the government?" He nodded. That made the throb worse. "The *American* government?"

"What was the American government, yes. I shouldn't have spied on you. And, now, I really need that nap."

"You need some aspirin?"

"Yeah." She got it for him.

"Just so you know, you deserve this pain. Taking off the bandages was foolhardy."

"The consequences of being impulsive and paranoid are occurring. Go get gas. I'll be here when you get back."

"Thank you for sharing it with me."

He couldn't do anything more than that for now, though he so wanted to. He rolled over and buried his face in the pillow and waited for her to let herself out the door. He remembered her fountain of black curls and her eyes like aged amber and he prayed to the universe he'd be able to see them again soon.

Behind him, he listened while she used his tablet to check out the thumbdrive. When she muttered *xara*, he turned toward her.

"What?"

"It's encrypted," she explained. "Assuming this thumb drive was for me, I've got to figure out what the password might be. And now the tablet is out of power, so this will have to wait until we get to our destination." She heaved a deep sigh and he could hear her putting things away. Then she walked over to him and planted a kiss on his mouth. "I'll be back," she assured and then was gone before he and his aching head could think of what else they might do.

I Don't Care Where You Go

Northwest Kansas

The sky blushed with sunrise pastels when the USDA prisoners had been restrained in the bed of the Big-I. An hour later, Shane pulled the Big I over on Highway 36 just outside of St. Lucy. The rest of the convoy of five trucks pulled over behind him. He climbed up into the bed of the Big I and unlocked the long chain that had run through handcuffs to restrain the prisoners. Jos Osimowitz unlocked their handcuffs.

"Are you going to shoot us?" Galena Carboy stared uncertainly at Keri's AR15.

"You didn't kill anyone." Shane pointed northeast. "Bird City's about two miles that way. Limon is that way." He pointed south. "Of course, you probably want to avoid Denver, so make sure you turn toward the Springs."

The other cow cops dropped off the back of the truck and moved away from Keri and her rifle.

"That's it?" The strain of the last few days showed in Carboy's face and her blond hair needed a shampoo.

"You know Rumdale deserved what happened to him. And, you know what will happen to you if we see your faces again."

Carboy looked like she might suffocate.

"I'm sorry for Rumdale. Our original orders didn't involve killing people."

"That's why you're alive. My father and grandfather understand what it means to follow orders, but you were still part of the invasion. Anyway, if you make Colorado Springs, maybe they won't shoot you for insubordination. Or, you could be smart and go home to Omaha, to that man and kid in your wallet." She looked stunned. "It's about a three-week walk to Limon and about four weeks to Omaha, so I'd get started."

Carboy's forehead creased. "We haven't eaten since you arrested us. Can we at least have water?"

Shane acted like he'd done this a thousand times. Jos tossed him a soda bottle that had been refilled with water. Shane handed it to Carboy. Maybe his time in the Middle East had involved just such releases of prisoners.

"That's more than David Vance will get to drink today, assuming today isn't the date on his death certificate. So, Limon, St. Lucy, Sherman, Bird City, whatever." He pointed in the directions of those settlements. "I wouldn't keep talking to me, though because I voted to kill all of you, and I am tempted to take matters into my own hands."

Carboy's eyes widened and she hastily joined her compatriots as they conferred at the side of the road.

"Load up," Shane hollered and climbed back into the Big-I. The last Keri saw of the USDA group was in the rearview mirror.

Jazz offered Keri some water from her canteen after Keri had pulled Alex' hay truck in behind Shane. The hay truck's heater was stuck on, so they were already sweating. Shane had inexplicably brought Jos as his shotgun rider and was letting the boy drive now. Each truck had two men in it, sort of.

"You notice we're the only women on this trip?"

Jazz handed her a half-sandwich.

"You take some meaning from that?"

"Shane tried to talk me out of it. He stopped short of forbidding me from joining the convoy because he knew I'd just go it alone, but he really wanted to argue with me."

"You think he's a sexist?"

"Shane? Not by any stretch of the imagination. He just thinks this is dangerous."

"He doesn't want me along."

Keri nodded.

"That too." Jazz pursed her lips, considering her cheese and tomato as if it were a doubtful dish. "He's still giving you mixed messages, isn't he?"

"He says he's attracted to me, but then he says I should stay away. And, I should probably be more careful after that stupidity with Paul. But I don't get that vibe from Shane."

"Shane and Paul couldn't be more different without being different species, but something did happen to him. Just be careful. Maybe even take his advice. He's trying to warn you."

"Or, trying to keep me at bay."

"You saw what he's capable of. I don't think he'd ever turn that on someone he cared about. Still, you might not want to care too deeply for a man who can turn off his emotions to that degree."

"You don't think Alex, in a similar situation, could?"

Keri rolled up her window as they turned off onto a gravel road. Sweet Alex able to gun down people whose only crime was radiation sickness? She couldn't reconcile the image. She might have said that of Shane before he'd gone to war.

"You should ask Marnie about it."

"Marnie? Why?"

"They dated all throughout high school and college, but they were friends even in elementary school. I don't think anyone has ever known him better than she did. Alex was his best friend, but …."

"Guys don't really share with each other unless they're forced to. At least my brothers never did. You have to wonder how they can spend so much time together and not talk. Wow, it's hot in here."

Gradually, the canyons of Kanopolis enveloped them. Keri had heard about Smoky Hill and the Arikaree Breaks her whole life. The sandstone cliffs were irresistible to rock climbers constrained by the lack of vertical surfaces in Kansas outside a few converted silos. Shane had been here before. Jos paused at a Y in the gravel road before turning left. The road passed through deep woods and then through a narrow canyon. A few more turns and they were on a road that hadn't seen maintenance in decades. Jos pulled to a stop at a rusted metal fence beside some ramshackle buildings and a dump truck half-full of coal. Beyond, Keri could see the rim of an unnatural canyon.

Shane came to her window.

"It looks like someone might be manning the line shack. I'm going to go talk to them. Let the others know. Let's not do anything threatening. They've got someone up on the bluff over there."

He made a show of pointing where he wanted her to look before walking toward the open door of the office.

Drought

Santa Fe

A curtain twitched on the bedroom window of the Acevedos house. Alicia hadn't seen anyone all morning while she picked pecans from the big trees in the front yard. People were scared and reverting to behaviors that fit their mental state, reminding her of the first San Diego neighborhood she lived in before she met Mike. Most of her neighbors had been illegal aliens and so they hid behind curtains when times were uncertain.

The Acevedos had been in Santa Fe since before Santa Fe had been in America, which made her wonder why they were hiding behind their curtains. These pecans were calories and their pecan trees were ripe too. Yet all along the street, no one was out harvesting them, even as she was leading the way.

She paused on the ladder to stretch her back and she heard a sound behind her. The Pachecos were setting up a ladder in front of their pecan tree. Mrs. Pacheco waved companionable. Alicia returned the gesture.

She had circled the tree and reached as far as the 10-foot step ladder would allow. She'd do the other tree tomorrow. She lugged the ladder into the garage where her father's truck was parked. She climbed under it to put the plug back in the drain and pull the catchment tray out. Doing what Mike had taught her, she filled the engine with the new oil and then used a funnel to pour the old oil into the bottle. She couldn't do anything about the filthy air filter until she found a store that was open, but Magdala had had an oil filter and she'd been a good student when Mike had taught her this basic auto repair.

In the house, Alicia crept into her mother's bedroom, wearing gloves and a mask, dumping the trash can that was filled with used tissues. Magdala snored while she slept. She was coughing less, but her fever had been intermittently high. She's sat in a cool bathtub for about a half-hour last night and then slept all night. It worried Alicia that she didn't want to eat or even smoke a cigarette.

House cleaning taken care of, Alicia stripped off her clothes and turned on the shower. The pipes vibrated violently and a trickle of rust ran out of the faucet. No way! She'd assumed city water would continue. She waited, but nothing changed. Muttering swear words in Spanish, she used a handful of baby wipes to give herself a sponge bath. Without water, things could go very badly. She couldn't believe Magdala didn't have a contingency for this, but her mother was exhausted from her illness and it wasn't really a disaster yet. They had some drinking water and there were some good-sized rivers that ran through Santa Fe. It was just a matter of filling buckets and transporting the water back to the house. Easy, right?

New Plans

Hutchinson

The techs among the Knights and FEMA folk suggested EMP. Cai thought that sounded like science fiction, but he'd have said that about nuking a dozen cities just a couple of weeks ago. Sanchez called a gathering of all the "free folks" at Hutchinson Fairgrounds. That apt descriptor sounded like something out of a fantasy novel Cai had read. The "unfree folks" were the surviving soldiers, now locked in the connexes where they had held Cai and other prisoners only a few days before. The food and water Sanchez provided them with was probably more than they had earned, but Cai thought that might be PTSD talking. He'd spent days under the thumbs of these soldiers and he no longer saw military personnel with the same warm fuzzy feelings he'd once had.

They gathered under the pavilion where meals had been served under martial law. Cai couldn't shake the feeling he violated some law by walking across the midway without a box in his arms. Amazing that a few days as a slave could take at least that long to wear off. Several of the other former prisoners had already left. Brian had headed to Hays in hopes of finding April, refusing Cai's offer to wait until Cai could give him a ride.

"You can pick me up on the way, if you see me." He'd set out on a bicycle not twenty minutes ago, with a backpack of food and a sidearm taken from one of the soldiers.

Cai approached the crowded pavilion. The mercenaries' rifles were slung over their backs and a few of the FEMA folks were now armed. Jared saw Cai approaching and met him. Yesterday, Cai had wanted to imprison Jared with the soldiers, but now he understood the FEMA agents had been prisoners too.

"I'm sorry," Jared said. "If I'd known they were watching us through the cameras I wouldn't have agreed to send a message for you and you might not have been arrested."

"I'd already been arrested. They just hadn't locked me in a connex yet. What did they do to you?"

Jared swallowed tightly, but he answered. "My dad never took a belt to me. Now I know why kids whose dads did were so compliant. Dershowitz really enjoyed his work."

Cai swallowed. He wasn't ready to admit Dershowitz deserved what had happened to him, but he was edging closer to it.

"Then they locked me in one of those connexes too. By morning, I'd have agreed to anything to avoid their sanction."

"You were locked there too?" Cai's skepticism must have resonated.

"You were singing hymns. That ate at my heart. I knew I should have backed you up, but ...." Jared looked stricken.

"I get it, man. I understand."

Following Jared, he took a seat near the front of the crowd. Jared explained that without trucks they couldn't deliver the food to the cities. The conversation went back and forth for a while before Helen DeWald spoke up. Cai hardly recognized her. Her face was bruised and there was a flinchy quality to her eyes that he thought he might see in his own, if he looked in a mirror. Still, she suggested they become a hub center for the nearby communities.

"Nobody expected the power to go off and stay off when we confiscated the food. We were sure there'd be resupply in a few weeks. Given the transportation issue, maybe that's the best we can do. But to do it, we'll need security."

Not all of Sanchez' mercenaries were able to stay. Some cited family, some cited needing to get back to Wichita. A handful said they could stay and Sanchez said he'd talk to HQ about sending more.

"What about the mechanic?" Jared hoped to get more trucks going.

"Lawson is going back to his family in Wichita," Sanchez said.

"Are we sure we want to let him just walk away?" one of his men asked.

"He didn't do anything."

"Because I had my gun to his head."

"And, we're not at war with the Army. We had to stop what was happening here because it was rogue, but we're not at war with them. Besides, Lawson was National Guard before the bombs. He just got off-track."

"He killed a man."

"Shut it." Jacobson's voice crackled with authority. Sanchez seemed new to authority, but he straightened at that point.

"Lawson is free to go. I had him held because I wasn't sure which side he'd be on, but now that it's done, he's free."

That decided, Jared wanted to know what would happen to the Army prisoners.

"The part of the crew that is returning to Wichita is taking them back for a military trial."

Cai listened to them and understood they were people nostalgic for the old order but already facing their new reality. The distribution center would become a trading hub, and discussions were already underway with the people in town about working together. Some of the FEMA agents were leaving with Sanchez' crew, hoping to return to families. At least one said he'd be bringing his family back with him.

Sanchez signaled for Cai to follow him toward the command center.

"We're leaving in the morning. Our truck is already running, but I have to make sure my guys understand what's going on here."

"What do you need me to do?"

"How are you at mechanics?"

"Not as good as Shane, but I know my way around a twenty-year-old engine."

"Go ask Lawson to put you to work. Most of the FEMA and military vehicles are dead, but a few are only damaged. Lawson has figured out how to get around the damages. Basically, anywhere you can help gets you and me on the road that much sooner."

Cai nodded. He sensed suppressed anxiety from Sanchez, but he didn't know him well enough to ask him about it.

Lawson was up to his elbows in a truck's engine when Cai walked up, introduced himself and explained Sanchez had sent him. Lawson dropped down to the pavement and stared at him, a crease between his eyes.

"I know you, don't I?"

"I don't think so. Cai Delaney." Cai held out his hand to shake, but Lawson didn't look friendly.

"Delaney … you got a brother named, Shane?"

"I do. You two serve together … or, er …."

"No, we met out Kanorado way. He put two in my vest while you watched."

"Uh …." The power of speech deserted Cai as he remembered Shane's actions that first night.

Lawson chuckled ruefully, rubbing his chest reflexively.

"I get that you'd be dead right now if he hadn't. But you gotta know, if they'd let me be armed right now, I'd show you what it feels like."

Cai's heart hammered against his ribs. His voice still shook a little when he spoke.

"I didn't know he was going to do it. And, not that it probably helps any, but he said he deliberately aimed for your vest."

"It doesn't. Anyway, I'm trying to bypass the blown relays on this electrical harness. You know anything about carburetors?"

"I've rebuilt a couple of them."

"Good. Over there on the table. If you've got any questions, ask."

Cai turned to the folding table under the market awning and saw how Lawson had laid everything out to reconfigure the two carburetors sitting there. If it got Sanchez and him on the road to Marnie that much quicker, Cai was more than willing to do it.

Open for Business

Arikaree Breaks, Kansas

The mine shack had been abandoned for decades, but someone had hastily cleaned it up so recently dust still floated in the air. Despite being open carry, the three who greeted him didn't seem the dangerous sort. One of the men held out a hand to shake. He was in his early forties, his belly starting to lap over his belt.

"Bob Lee Donavan. My wife Bethany and that there's Darryl, my brother. You come for coal?"

"Yes. Last time I was in the area, this site had been abandoned."

"Right. We had that thought right after the rain stopped. The county sheriff asked us to secure the resource." They didn't seem to be lying and were probably just locals the sheriff trusted, sort of like how Rob trusted Shane or Anders McAuliff to take on a mission and follow their own path to making it happen.

"We want to fill five trucks. What'll that cost us?"

"Corn. Salt. Precious metals."

"We have salt and corn. One bag each per truck?"

"Two bags each," Bethany said. A fading redhead about the same age as her husband, she definitely needed to work out.

"We can do that."

"And ten percent of the coal you mine." Darryl was older than his brother but in better shape. If it came to a fight, Shane would have chosen to put him down first. Darryl's addition explained the truck outside. Shane looked at Bob Lee, who appeared to be the front man for this operation.

"Five percent."

Bob Lee laughed, but his tone was admiring. "You know your way around the apocalypse. Five percent. Food and salt now. Coal when you leave." Bob Lee probably owned a car dealership.

"In writing."

"We've got a ledger." Bethany indicated the two-part invoice book and a ballpoint pen. Shane signed it and so did Bob Lee. Shane walked out of the shed into the blinding light of day. Jason's crew had the salt and one of the Bennetts was carrying the corn, evidence that they'd been listening at the door. It only took a moment to make the trade. Then Bethany opened the gate and they drove down the long incline into the pit, which was pleasantly shaded with cottonwood trees that had grown up in the decades since the pit's abandonment. The clay sides exposed layers of coal. People were already at work, trundling wheelbarrows through the woods. Shane examined the left-hand cliff.

"That'll do nicely with my climbing gear and we won't have to waste time with wheelbarrows."

"Why is everyone else going back into the woods?" Jazz asked.

"They opted for shade. In a couple of hours, we'll be in the full sun and it'll get hot, but the work will go faster and we aren't in view of their overwatch."

"Overwatch?"

"That's what we called snipers in the service," Vin explained. "You sure this is such a good idea, man?"

“I’m hoping they’re just prepped for trouble. I didn’t get a hinky jibe from them. And ultimately, we need the coal and we didn’t come all this way to go back empty-handed.” Andrew nodded as Shane saw a man coming their way. “Get your hard hats on and let’s get to work.”

“Evan Kendrick.” The man held out his hand. Shane and Andrew Bennett exchanged glances before shaking hands.

“We already paid up top.” Shane wanted to get that out of the way right at the outset.

“I wasn’t trying to shake you down, man. I’m just saying howdy. A bunch of us are working together in the woods. We got a fire going and some places to sit. You can join us if you need to heat food or whatever. If you’re staying the night, it’s not a bad place to set up tents.”

“Thank you.” Andrew exchanged a few more pleasantries with Evan. They parted on friendly terms and Andrew turned back to Shane. “Do you trust anyone?”

“Myself, sometimes.”

“That’s no way to live, man.”

“I didn’t say it was.” Shane turned toward the other Emmaus folks, signing for Noah. “We’ll try to get out of here by sunset. Going back in the night might not be that safe and the sniper worries me, even if it's a wise precaution. So, let's get busy. Jos and I are going up top. Andrew, you're in charge down here. Remember, folks. We'll be prying into a whole lot of soft rock, but when that rock hits the ground, it won't be a nerf ball, so stay back until you're sure we've stopped descaling. Jos, you don't touch the wall unless everyone is back at the trucks, right?"

Jos had climbed enough that Shane didn't need to help him rig his belt, so Shane free-climbed the wall to tie off the top anchors. He had to go a bit back into the tree line to find sufficiently robust trees to tie to. Now he could see that the quarry had been larger at one time. They'd stripped off the first layer and then started on the next layer, but they'd only done part of the tier before they stopped. As there was still coal visible in the clay walls, the mine hadn't been played out. He supposed the environmental movement had closed it down.

The wind shifted from the north and brought the smell of cigarette smoke to Shane's nose. Despite his unease over someone up here with a rifle, the flash might have been binoculars or a spotting scope. It was also entirely possible he was paranoid.

While he rigged the anchors, Shane contemplated checking out the overwatch, but the smell of smoke had shredded on the wind and the second-growth wood was silent except for the buzz of insects. He could be borrowing trouble for their group by being too bold.

Deciding that, he slipped over the edge. As he rappelled down to meet Jos at the top of the coal belt, Kitty Vance's purple face filled his mind. He belayed to wait for Jos to join him by a sizeable protrusion of coal, with a nearby crack perfect for a cam. He pulled up his dust mask and donned a pair of heavy gloves. Kitty wavered off into shadows cast by the sun shining through the trees. The days were getting shorter. He didn't have time to waste grieving.

Gridlock

New Jersey

Perry stopped in the traffic lane, growling. Joseph looked out through the windshield at a mile-long traffic jam before Warrington. The huge interchange was clogged with permanent gridlock. They all got out to investigate, but there were too many vehicles to push out of the way.

"There's no chance to cross the Delaware here. There's a bridge at Portland, but we're down to half a tank of gasoline. I, uh, confiscated a barrel pump that wasn't being used, but it's going to take a while to get any gasoline out of an underground tank with it."

Raines opened his mouth as if to say something, but then nodded. Joseph appreciated his willingness to hold any criticisms he might have. They found an unmanned Sunoco where the service ports had been left open by the last people to have used it. Perry rubbed his chin, looking like a man trying not to look distressed.

"We can't trust the fuel isn't mixed with water."

"No, but if we pump it into a bucket first, we can check for it." A computer programmer by trade, Raines seemed remarkably comfortable with working-class tasks. There was no reason to distrust him, and Joseph knew he should be grateful to him for getting Katharine out of New York, but something tugged at his stomach every time he thought of the long trip back to Kansas.

Pumping gasoline out of an underground tank was slow, smelly work. None of them could crank for more than about fifteen minutes and the tank filled slowly. Every time they switched, the pump would lose prime and there'd to several minutes of cranking fruitlessly until the gasoline resume flowing. People on foot stopped and demanded to know what they were doing. Most continued on. Finally, a man stopped.

"What a nice pickup you got here. How come you got that pickup?" He smiled in a forced friendly way.

"We own it." Perry slipped his left hand into his jacket while unzipping it with his right so the stranger could see the butt of his gun under his arm. Katharine had her hand in her coat pocket. Joseph decided to put his hand on his gun, though he really didn't want to shoot anyone. Raines gestured with the crowbar.

"Seriously, mister. You need to value your life more than transportation."

Outnumbered and unarmed, the man looked desperate.

"I'm a good man, but my family's waiting for me. It'll take me all day to walk home and something bad could happen to them by then. I gotta get there."

Perry and Joseph exchanged glances. When Joseph nodded, Perry sighed.

"If you help fill the tank, we'll give you a ride to the closest place we get to your house."

"Bless you," the man said and relieved Joseph from cranking.

A woman leading a little boy by the hand stopped next and begged a ride. By the time they headed west again, they had four extra people in their truck. The woman and boy insisted on getting off at a neighborhood that had been devastated by fire. The last they saw of them, they were walking down the middle of the road calling a man's name.

The second man to join them got out a few miles on and was happily greeted on the front lawn by his wife and two children. The first man finally got off at the top of a country lane. He thanked them again and then hurried toward his house. Joseph wondered if there would be a happy ending. He would never know.

Perry slowed to a crawl and Joseph raised his head from where he and Katharine were resting in the camper shell.

"What's going on?" Kat asked.

"People walking in the road. I guess pedestrians rule now," Joseph answered.

"Maybe we should start charging for rides."

Joseph kissed her. "You always make me laugh."

"I'm not actually joking. We are going to need to find food soon and it seems like we could use the resource we have to get the resources we need."

So practical, so working class. She reminded him of his grandmother on his mother's side. He tapped on the window that separated the shell from the cab. Raines slid it open. Perry listened while he explained.

"You have a point. Next time we pass just a few people walking, we can make the offer. I don't want to stop in a big crowd. It's too easy for a bunch of unarmed people to overpower four of us."

Raines nodded. He and Perry seemed to be hitting it off, which bugged Joseph for some reason. They continued down the highway until they encountered several women walking together and made their offer. One of the women said she had food at her house and they all piled in. They'd knocked the heels off their shoes and were all headed to Portland. They were neighbors who had found each other on the way from Ft. Lee and were now in the second day of walking. One woman thanked them profusely about three times, terrified for her kids who were home alone.

When they got to Portland, they waited in the truck while the woman who had offered food went into her house. It seemed to take a while, but she finally came out with a grocery sack of potatoes and a bag of partially thawed frozen chicken. Her husband came out onto the porch to watch the exchange, a small child clinging to his legs and a shotgun cradled in his arms. What must have happened over the last day to make him feel it was necessary?

Joseph took the bag, thanking her and waved at her husband before going to the truck. He counted it a victory that the man didn't shoot him.

Julian walked the woman who had been worried about her children to the house across the street. As they passed the bushes, the woman flinched and shrieked, then ran up to the porch, pounding on the door. Julian covered his mouth and nose, staring at something behind the bushes. The woman kept banging on the door. Perry got out of the truck to join Julian, looking distressed.

"Stay here." Joseph handed Katharine the shopping bag and went to join the other two men. Now the woman was hugging two middle-graders and all three of them were crying. A man lay in a congealed pool of blood behind the bushes.

Julian nodded toward the porch.

"There's a blood trail down the stairs and along the path. The older kid must have shot him."

"Why?" Joseph asked.

"It looks pretty peaceful right now, but at night, with two kids home alone in a house possibly full of food, and no cops and no way to call them...You get the picture." Julian went to the porch and spoke with the woman. She nodded and pointed to a shed. Julian came out with two shovels and a garden spade.

"This isn't any of our business." Katharine had come to check on them. She looked disgusted by the dead body, and she wasn't the delicate type.

"We can't leave this family to deal with this alone." Perry took one of the shovels from Julian. "And, I wouldn't want to confront this every time I came out my front door."

Katharine growled.

In the end, they chose not to deprive Nancy and her children of their shovels, and they buried the man in an overgrown yard down the block. Nancy had stopped crying by the time they brought the shovels back.

"Thank you. Thank you for getting me here and for taking care of ... of that. This is horrible! I wish I had something to give you."

"It's fine." Katharine smiled warmly and patted her on the shoulder. "We were glad to do it. Will your boy be okay?"

"Yes, I'm not worried about him. It was my daughter who shot him."

"Oh, my!"

"She didn't have a choice. He got a hold of Jeffrey and there was no other way. But that doesn't make it any easier."

"No, of course not."

When they climbed back into the truck, Katharine sighed.

"What is this world devolving into? This looks like a nice town."

"Nice is for safe times." Perry sounded sad. "We should get back on the road."

The bridge at Portland was also clogged with broken cars. As they turned south onto Highway 40 hoping for a bridge in Belvedere, Joseph and Katharine stared into blank spaces, sitting next to each other without touching as the enormity of what had befallen just one community sank in.

True Friend

Arikaree Breaks, Kansas

Shane inserted his wrecking bar into a crack in the clay near a bulge of coal. Jos, clipped off to an anchor on the wall, bracing Shane so he wouldn't swing out from the wall as he levered the coal off the formation. The coal tumbled down the clay face and rolled toward the trucks. Andrew Bennet and Noah Lufgren moved in to break the rubble into small enough chunks to load into wheelbarrows to transport the short distance to the trucks where the others used buckets on ropes to pull the coal up and dump into the beds.

Shane waited while Jos reset the anchor and then he swung toward the right to reach the next clinker. Of course, they had to wait for

Andrew and Zachary to be done. They drank water and Shane suggested Jos reapply sunscreen.

"Don't you burn?"

"Not in the United States."

Jos gave him a quizzical look. Shane laughed.

"Closer to the equator, if I stay in the sun too long I can burn. It hurts until it heals and I get that much darker."

Jos finished rubbing the sunscreen into his exposed skin while Shane stripped off the do-rag he'd covered his hair with and used his hand rag to wipe down his face and scalp before donning it again.

Coal mining must have been back-breaking and knuckle-busting work back in the days before big earthmoving equipment. It was taking far too long to accomplish this job with sweat work. The trucks filled slowly and Shane thought they might have to stay the night to accomplish the task. If they could scale while the ground crew broke up the coal, they would be able to go fifty percent faster, but Shane hadn't figured out a way to do that safely.

"Uhhh," Noah called. Shane looked down at him to read his sign. "If you break off rock all the way across, take break, down here, we gather faster. You up again."

"What's he saying?" Jos asked.

"He's suggesting a better way to do this. And, I'm going to say let's try it."

After Jos figured out a better way to anchor, finishing a whole row did indeed go faster, and they were ready for a break when they had done the row. Shane climbed up on the hood of the Big I to enjoy an MRE and a canteen of water, leaning back against the windshield. Jazz crawled up beside him, curls wrapped in a headkerchief and her face smudged with coal dust.

"Wow, it's hot!" She had a bit of a background tan, but she used the break to smear more sunscreen on. "You act like this is nothing."

"It is. It's a good twenty degrees cooler than what I'm used to."

"Is it ever cold in Miristan?"

"Up in the mountains they have real winter for six months out of the year. I spent one winter up in Padaresh in Shalimar Province."

"What were you doing there?"

Was that a flash of black back in the cottonwoods? A young man in dark grey cargo pants bent to pick something up.

"It was a mercenary base of operations. I drove trucks and flew planes, bringing cargo into forward bases." She shot him a look that he read as disbelief. "What?"

"You're really good. Playing poker would be hard against you. But there's something … you didn't want to talk about Padaresh before."

"The frozen armpit of Miristan. It was cold and windy and they speak a dialect I couldn't master." She laughed. "What do you think you know?"

She sobered. "I don't. I can just hear it in your voice."

Shane sighed, leaned his head back against the glass and closed his eyes. She was right. He was lying. Unfortunately, telling the truth would be a violation of the agreements he had signed.

"Just so you know, if you ever want to talk about it, I'll listen in confidence and never bring it up to you or anyone else, unless you do."

Shane opened his eyes in surprise. She leaned back against the windshield, too, her eyes closed, pert nose to the bright sun, a serene smile curving her pink lips. He wished he could be that comfortable in his skin, but he hadn't been for a long time, if ever.

"I appreciate it. I think you'd not like me so much if you knew what I was really up to."

"As a friend, I can dislike what you did halfway across the world six months ago and still care about your pain here today."

His eyes flew open. Fortunately, Jos knocked on the side of the truck to let him know it was time to go aloft again. He rolled off the hood, dropped to the ground, and put some distance between him and a very uncomfortable friendship.

Young Love

Jericho Springs Ghost Town

Pete picked up sign far faster than Poppy had thought possible. He'd been fairly motivated before her phone had fried, but now he didn't have a choice but to learn sign if he wanted to talk to her.

The midday heat drove them to the pond beside the Delaney cabin where reflections sparkled across the water. Now cooled off, they cuddled on the wooden dock, kissing. He eased a strap off her shoulder. She pulled back to look at his face, but he buried it in her neck causing her to laugh rather than try to stop his investigation. He eased her down onto her back and dropped his kisses down towards a breast.

Then he stopped, sat up, and stared towards the west.

"What?" she asked.

"Sound."

She sat up to look where he pointed, pulling up her straps and reaching for her t-shirt.

"What sound?" she asked after she'd pulled it over her head.

"B-a-n-g-i-n-g." His fingerspelling was still clumsy. "Sound – h-o-t-e-l."

"Shane's hotel?"

"Yes."

She pulled on her tennis shoes and headed in that direction. Pete followed, carrying his pants and shirt. Alex would kill them if he found out what they'd been doing. And, Shane was right that it could lead to places they weren't ready to go. She felt like she would love Pete forever, but they were really young and even safe sex was no guarantee you wouldn't get pregnant. She welcomed the distraction.

From the fringe of trees that separated the Delaney cabin from the old Jericho Springs Hotel, they watched as two men tested the window shutters that sealed the building. Shane said the security system had gone crazy with the pulse and so the seed corn was as safe as could be. So who were these men trying to break into the hotel?

"I ... talk ... to them."

"No! They could hurt you."

The men stood back from the shutters and talked, gazes on the façade. They looked a little alike and the older man could be either the elder brother or a very young father. They wore jeans and tennis shoes, nothing like the USDA suits or military fatigues.

"They say what?"

"They sound ... friend ... Shane."

"Emmaus ... no, not they."

"Friend ...." Pete made a vague sign that might mean 'long distance'.

"Maybe, but Shane, him not say him."

The two men walked away toward the bridge and then turned into the fenced yard of the Sullivan B&B.

"Who that?"

Pete's limited signs and poor comprehension constrained their conversation, but she knew that patience would eventually fix that.

"Bed and breakfast. New. You saw."

"Hotel?"

"Don't know. We tell Alex."

Pete donned his clothes and they headed back to the farmhouse. Poppy paused to scruff Mocha's head and signed "Where's Alex?"

"Dog know sign?"

He asked silly questions sometimes. Of course, the dog of Deaf people would know sign. How else would it know what you wanted. Mocha wagged her tail and led her to the spring shed where Alex was loading chiller containers into the back of his truck. The partially buried shed with the water sump in the corner usually served to age home cheeses, but now Alex used it to keep milk cool.

His blue eyes widened as Poppy explained about the men at the hotel, but when they explained that they didn't seem to be able to get in, he shrugged.

"I tell Shane, but not our business. Pete, Mark's looking for you. Barn – right side. Trucks. Poppy, stay."

Pete frowned but did as he was told. Alex waited for him to leave.

"Be smart, Star." That was his pet name for her, used only when nobody else was around. "He nice kid, but you're both young. Be smart."

She felt her cheeks flare red. Alex sighed and touched her on the nose with a rough fingertip.

"You - lots of time. No rush."

"Me ... world ... sliding off cliff."

"How will sex slow that down?"

She lifted her hands to retort, but nothing came to mind.

"Will you tell parents?"

Alex laughed. She had never heard him laugh, but she imagined it was a deep rumble, like thunder only without the risk of electrocution.

"Mark told me. Load up. Huffman's, sell."

"Me?"

"Yes. Two go faster."

Poppy sighed. Of course, now that he was on to them, he'd find ways to keep her busy and away from Pete, and Pete's parents would probably do the same. A part of her chaffed at being treated like a child, but how old was an adult in extraordinary times such as this?

Angry Farmer

Northwest Kansas

The two-lane blacktop had faded grey, but it still reflected the autumn sun effectively. After the tiny hamlet of Bird City had locked its doors to them, the USDA group had decided to turn north in the general direction of Omaha. They drank the water within a half hour, passing between harvested fields fronted with barbed wire, sometimes edged with cottonwood and live oak trees. The few previous farmhouses they passed had their gates closed and locked, sometimes with a dog menacing those who might climb over, but this one didn't. By wordless agreement, they turned up the lane and trudged toward the farmhouse. The overhanging trees cooled the air and

Galena wished she could just sit down and rest, but she was their leader so she walked out in front. She donned her jacket, hoping to look at least a little professional after days wearing the same clothes.

The pleasant white house with blue trim sat a stone's throw from a big red barn. A children's swing set sat near the generous front porch. A dog greeted them, barking as it ran off the porch. They didn't have any weapons, but Penelope picked up a rock and flung it at the beast. She missed, which was probably a good thing since the farmer came out on the porch with a shotgun at the ready. The dog circled them once, growling, until the farmer called it off. It ran back to sit next to him, now smiling at them with a fringed tail thumping the deck.

"Hi, I'm Galena Carboy. My friends and I broke down and we're looking for water and food …."

"I gave when you came through earlier," the farmer said. He was maybe forty and, although he was on the porch by himself, there were at least four people in the windows and another shotgun barrel visible.

Galena had nothing to offer in response. They were all wearing their USDA jackets. She'd approached him thinking it would be a friendly exchange. They needed help and he had water. But he didn't see them as needing help. He saw them as abusive thieves.

"I'm sorry, sir," Tanaka said. "We were following orders. And nobody knew the power would go out."

"I had grain enough to get through the winter until you all came around. So, I'm not interested in your reasons. Turn on around and go your way."

"We need water to do that." Galena held up their bottle. He stared at it a moment.

"For endangering my children's lives, no. I won't waste the calories pumping it for you. There's streams. Get water from God."

There were protests, but Galena knew that a leader led. She turned and walked back down the lane. They followed. Balsoms wept softly.

"These jackets are going to get us killed." Reinhold started to strip his off.

"It gets cold here at night this close to the Rockies. We need to get rid of the decals, but we can't afford to shed the jackets. Do any of us have a knife or scissors or …."

The rattle of a bicycle filled her ears. A teenage boy slowed and stopped well back of them, arching an object into the grass to the side of the lane.

"My ma's not as angry as my pa, but after you pick that up, you'd better keep going."

He turned and headed back up the lane. Reinhold cautiously approached the object in the grass. It was a two-liter soda bottle filled with water. He cracked the cap to take a drink.

"Maybe it's poisoned." Reinhold hesitated at Balsoms's suggestion.

"What's this for?" Raskin asked, indicating something taped to the side of the bottle. Galena approached to look more closely.

"That's a safety pin. Reinhold, you can take that drink. She gave us a tool to remove these decals."

The water didn't last long shared among eleven, but it buoyed their steps as they continued along the ribbon of highway.

Murder in the Breaks

Arikaree Breaks

Shane could sense Jos getting tired and his own left leg had started going intermittently numb from the climbing belt. While Jos struggled with setting the next anchor, Shane turned to look out over the canyon. The trees that had grown up in the middle of the artificial canyon didn't screen his group from the sun's intensity, so he could see why Evan's group had chosen to go further into the mine. There they had some shade and it looked like there was more coal available in the walls. It just meant more transport to the vehicles.

Below him, his group worked industriously. Jazz clung to the side of the Big I, one leg wrapped around an upright, the other braced on a horizontal, her biceps rippling in the afternoon sun as she pulled up a bucket of coal on a rope, drawing hand over hand. There was something *Clan of the Cave Bear* about it.

Andrew Bennett waved at him and called up.

"It's five o'clock. Shouldn't we be heading back to Emmaus?"

"That late? Time flies when your ass is going numb. Yeah. The trucks are just about full, so let's bag it. I'll go talk to the folks up top."

Jos looked relieved, which told Shane that the kid had been displaying his grandmother's famous pluck. Shane stripped off his gloves and faced the wall, working out the line he wanted to free-climb up to the rim.

The air felt pleasantly cool under the canopy of tough young cottonwood. The tension was off his rope, so he pulled the anchor, then pulled Jos' as soon as the rope was slack. He dropped the gear to the pit floor before turning toward the line shack.

He expected to find the sniper at some point, but the only evidence he found was a pile of fresh cigarette butts with several energy drink cans. He walked a bit more carefully, Spidey senses tingling, but he came upon the fence without seeing anyone.

Sighting down the chain link he could see the gates were chained shut. The fence kept people from driving into the pit and doing what his group had done. It wasn't meant to keep casual people from entering or leaving on foot. A short climb got him up and over the fence.

He crossed what must have been the parking lot of the pit back in the day, aiming for the line shack, mildly surprised that the blue dump truck was missing. He slowed, seeing that the front door of the shack hung ajar. Silence reigned. Shane's gaze swept the front of the building, looking for movement, scanning the roof, the nearby trees, the road headed east. The porch creaked under his boot as he eased across it.

The metallic smell of blood assaulted his nose as he swung the door all the way open. Flies buzzed in the silence. It had been warm in the shack in the early morning and it had gotten hotter during the day. Details distracted him from Bethany's severed trachea. Her hair had been sweaty around the fringes. The men had sweat stains under their underarms. All three had been stabbed. Darryl had wounds on his hands that suggested he'd tried to fight back. That friendly vibe Shane had trusted this morning had not served them well when a bad guy had come into their circle. It didn't look like any of them had gone for their guns. They had died maybe in the last two hours. He assumed whoever killed them had been after the truckload of coal.

He rifled through Bethany's pockets looking for the keys to the gate padlock when the porch groaned and he whipped around and centered the sight of his gun on Jazz's forehead. She broke left, putting the wall between him and her, jerking Andrew after her. Shane pointed his gun at the roof.

"Not a safe guy to sneak up on." Andrew leaned out cautiously as Shane holstered his gun in his back rig. "My finger was never inside the trigger guard."

"What happened?" Jazz's whisper suggested hushed voices were appropriate for a tomb.

"I don't know. I found them this way. They've been dead a couple of hours." Shane pulled out his multitool and began pulling on a brad-nail holding the paneling on the wall. "Rigor's just starting. See if you can find a key for the gate on the men. I've already checked Bethany."

Andrew patted down Darryl's pockets while Jazz tried to check Bob Lee's pockets, but she ended up puking. Andrew patted her quaking back before leaning over Bob Lee.

"Maybe they took the keys, whoever they were."

"They wanted the coal. Too lazy to collect their own." Shane spoke around the brad between his teeth as he worked on a second one. "They probably took the keys for the truck and the key to the gate was on the same ring."

He turned toward the door, catching Jazz by the shoulders to guide her ahead of him.

"There's no shame in feeling what you're feeling." He left her to go to the gate and try to pick the padlock with the two brads.

While he worked, he could hear Andrew and Jazz talking behind him. Andrew understood Jazz's shock. This wasn't his first dead body but he remembered that time. He distracted her with a quick story about some poor guy who had been barbecued in a forest fire. Jazz allowed that she'd seen a hundred people dead just last week. She didn't elaborate that Shane had killed two of them. Instead, she turned to where Shane was bent over the padlock.

"What are you doing?" Her voice was no longer shaking though he could smell vomit under the sweat.

"Trying to pick the lock so we can get out of the mine. But these are far from precision instruments and I'm failing at it."

"Is this your first attempt?" Andrew was now watching the road, but standing way too close, perhaps thinking he was shielding Shane from harm.

"No, but I left my lockpicks at home because I thought I wouldn't need them."

"What sort of a Boy Scout are you?" Joking was common in situations like this, though Jazz's mouth tightened. She would need to get over that. Delicate people wouldn't survive this brave new world.

"Never was one. Cai was. I got kicked out of Webelos for telling the scout master's wife that she was an idiot."

"Was she?" Jazz perhaps saw there were ways to control your horror, including using humor.

"On the subject of airplanes, yeah."

Jazz shuddered suddenly.

"Why would anyone kill three people for a half-a-truckload of coal?"

"I've seen people do worse for far less. And there was corn and salt too, which is gone."

"Look what the USDA did to Emmaus just because we wouldn't give up our food," Andrew added. The sun moved behind a tree and he pulled out a flashlight to improve Shane's lockpicking, but it didn't help. Shane sighed and admitted defeat. Jazz moved from disappointment to thinking outside the box.

"Can't you just bust the chain with the weight of the Big I?"

Shane blinked at her. It wasn't like the old truck didn't already have plenty of dings and scratches in its white paint. The winch on the front would protect the lights, turn signals and radiator. He pulled the keys out of his pocket and passed them to her.

"You drive stick, I presume?"

"Of course. Slow and gentle or fast?"

"Slow and gentle. It's going to struggle coming up the grade, but you can come to a stop at the top and then just go slow. With so few working vehicles, we can't afford to break one, or loose a headlight since we can't replace it."

She nodded, slipped through the gap between the gates, and jogged off down the gravel ramp. Andrew and Shane watched the sun as it touched the western hills.

"This feels like that movie."

"Which?"

"Tron. Remember, when they could unlock the connection with the transmission tower and all the programs could access the grid again?"

"No, but thanks for sharing."

"You are kind of young, aren't you?" Andrew might be in his forties, considering he had children who were in their teens.

"I have trouble sitting through movies, although if there was a book, I might have read it."

"It just feels like we're being released from our lock-outs."

"And you think that's a good thing?"

"The government is on the ropes – the movie would say it's been de-rezzed -- and that frees us to find better ways to do things. This quarry was abandoned, but we would never have done this two weeks ago because the law said we couldn't. Before all this, we'd have spent years asking permission. Now, we are willing to just come and take what we need because we know Big Brother can't watch us. And, it's perfectly lawful according to natural law. Why waste a needed resource? So, yeah, it'll be a good thing, in time."

"Except for the three people in there. There's no justice for them. The cops in the next town over won't have the means to find the murderers."

Shane watched Andrew struggle to find a response.

"Not yet." Shane could hear the Big I firing up down below in the silence that followed those two words. "But people will find a way to defend themselves and provide justice that doesn't require outsiders to impose it."

Those sounded like lofty ideals when they came from Jacob's mouth. Shane agreed the resource didn't belong to anyone, though he'd been willing to pay Bob Lee for the privilege of access just to avoid any hassle. Conservatives would say they were stealing and that it was wrong, no matter that the owners hadn't been around for decades. Years ago, when he and his friends had found the quarry, he'd not cared that much about the faded "no trespassing" signs. They hadn't been hurting anything. It surprised him that he cared even less about taking the actual coal. He liked the part of anarchist-libertarian thought that theorized abandoned property was up for grabs, but this was the real world they were living in now, and in the real world, idealists died holding out a hand of friendship to someone with a hidden knife. What would the world come to without law or authorities to assure the boundaries that kept people out of each other's way?

It had grown dusky by the time the truck lumbered up the ramp. Jazz paused on the flat, then slowly rolled forward until she stretched the chain to its farthest length and then revved the engine just a bit. The rear tires spun and Shane was about to tell her to stop, but he heard her drop it into 4-wheel low and go on the gas again. The gate popped open. He and Andrew grabbed the two halves of the gate to keep them swinging back at the truck as she drove through.

"I had to explain what happened to everyone, including Noah, and that took time." Jazz, Andrew, and Shane were standing back waiting for everyone to arrive.

"You guys never explained why you came up after me."

"I just felt like something was wrong," Andrew explained. "I'd been feeling it for a while and when you didn't come back right away, I went up to check. She tagged along."

"You think you've been deputized, Miss Tully?"

"Not to my knowledge, but when it comes to protecting the town, I think we're all going to have to step up."

Andrew frowned, but Shane grinned at her. He liked women with spunk.

While the other four trucks climbed the ramp one by one, Vin went down to inform

Evan of the events in the line shack and Jazz asked what they were going to do about the bodies. It was on the tip of Shane's tongue to say it wasn't their problem when Andrew said they should load them into his second seat and take them into St. Lucy.

"I'd want my people returned to me. And, who knows that their killers won't come back and attack the people who are still down in the pit? The sheriff might want to be aware."

Shane sighed. Of course, Rob and Jacob both would say they should promote cooperation with other towns. That he was covered in coal dust, had nearly shot Jazz and truly wanted to tear someone's face off was probably something for him to deal with in the privacy of his own head.

"Lead the way, man. I'm merely the hired muscle. You get to do all the talking."

A Silly Woman

Emmaus

Jill Delaney sat on a stool in front of the coal-burning cookstove that occupied one corner of her kitchen. All the doors were open as she tried to figure out how it worked. Her mother-in-law Vi had offered to show her several times, but they'd never found the time before Vi's death last year. It had been a pretty piece of enameled iron furniture—a great place for the potpourri pot, a few storm lanterns, and a plant. Years ago, she'd installed a wire shelving unit in the firebox where she stored her bakeware. The oven was a perfect size for the cereal boxes and the broiler pans nestled into the warmer. Who would want to mess up all that stylish storage by actually firing up the stove?

What a silly woman I've been!

Everything previously stored in the stove now rested on the countertops. She'd have to find somewhere for them, after she'd figured out how to use the stove. She picked up a slim book that she'd left open on cooktop. She'd been lucky to find this volume on wood cooktops in the floor-to-ceiling bookshelves in the den. Jacob had said it was there, but it had taken all morning to find it because Delaneys couldn't say no to books. She couldn't believe that in the years she'd lived in this house that she'd not read them all. Some dated back to the 1880s. The cookstove book's copyright date was 1925. It didn't seem to specifically apply to this cookstove, but it had probably been used by Jacob's mother to learn how to use her new-fangled kitchen gadget.

Jill had identified almost all of the parts and wondered where the rake had gotten to since the stove had been mothballed, when she heard a truck pulling into the driveway. It didn't sound like the Big-I. Before she could disentangle herself from the stove and go to the back door, Alex Lufgren was on the porch. He held a chiller can on his shoulder like it weighed no more than a bag of clothes.

"What are you doing here?" She'd been working by lantern light because the kitchen faced north, so she hadn't even noticed the sun had gone down.

"Delivering milk. It's my new enterprise." He put the chiller can on top of the stove. "You got a pitcher?"

"Sure. Actually, I have an old milk bottle or three."

"Great. Poppy's bringing in a can of goat's milk for Shane."

"You're a good friend ... a good son."

He blushed. He'd been in and out of their house since he and Shane had met in kindergarten and they had been his second family after his parents' death nine years ago, but they were all still working out this whole in-law thing.

"I probably owe you for all the babysitting." They smiled at each other. He'd really been a very attentive foster father-brother to his sister following their parents' deaths, but he'd also been a young man robbed of his late adolescence. The Delaneys had tried to help where they could.

"We were glad to do it." Poppy clattered noisily across the floor to put the smaller chiller on the breakfast table. Turning she signed, "What are we talking about?"

"How cute you were in lace dresses." Alex signed and spoke at the same time.

"Very cute!" Jill's signing was rusty and she'd never been all that good to begin with. It had been fortunate that Poppy hadn't been a stickler for grammar or even vocabulary.

"Keeping secrets." Poppy's expression suggested her irritation at the whole concept of being left out of their conversation.

"Hey. You know what we know." Alex paused in signing to crank the top off the chiller can as Jill pulled a milk jug out of the cabinet. Vi had been a collector, but she hadn't believed in not using items that had a function. Her dozen milk bottles of various sizes had become Jill's upon her death. Alex filled the half-gallon jug and recapped the chiller before he continued. "The world is going crazy, but we're doing what we can to fix it or ... er, deal with it."

Poppy sighed, made a face and grabbed the milk chiller to carry it out to the car while Alex filled another milk bottle with goat's milk.

"She's in a lovely mood today," Jill assessed.

"It's the loss of her phone. She actually has to talk to her friends. Or me. And, she thinks she's in love."

"That boy, Pete?" Alex nodded. "I thought there might be something there. Have you discussed it with his parents, or Poppy herself?"

"His parents want to all talk when Keri gets back. I'm in favor of just threatening to break his neck if he knocks up my sister."

"Are you sorry you let them move in?"

Alex sighed, mulling the thought.

"No. They feel right, like family. In the last few years, I've thought about what Poppy would need to do about getting married and I knew that would probably mean her moving away. Or, she'd have to marry a hearing guy, which doesn't really worry me except very few of her male classmates have learned sign. And this kid is learning sign and he's a hard worker. It's just ... she's so young."

"And you're her dad and those are perfectly ordinary feelings."

"Are they?" Alex sighed. "I would have rebelled if my father had spoken to me the way I spoke to her earlier."

"Boys are different. It's not that we don't hope they'll be virgins when they marry, but they can't get pregnant and they can't really be raped, so you just worry about them less."

Outside, the horn sounded, held a little too long.

"She is really being a pill today. We gotta get going. Mae is taking the rest of it off my hands for some grocery items she has unexpectedly come into."

"I don't believe she stole the Costco shipment."

"Neither do I, but I think she's received stolen property. But, hey, it's a survival situation, so—"

There was another horn blast.

"She is so going to regret that. What are you doing here?"

"Figuring out how to use the old cookstove. It's not quite as simple as the woodstove in the living room."

"No, they take some getting used to. When you're ready to fire it up, I'll come over and show you how it's done."

"You use the one at your house?"

"Sure, and I cook on it when it's heating the house because it's ridiculous to waste the heat. I use wood in mine, but coal will give you a longer steadier burn. But gotta go for now. I'll bring some eggs to church tomorrow."

"Thanks." The horn blew again.

"I haven't spanked her since she was five and nearly got herself killed crossing Old 24 without permission, but I am so tempted right now."

With that, Alex headed out the door, signing expansively that Poppy was going to find herself scrubbing toilets if she kept it up. At least, that's what Jill thought those signs meant. A couple of them were close to swear signs she wasn't supposed to know.

Jill closed up the stove and turned to look at the disaster wrought by cleaning it out. The broiler pans could go on the floor of the pantry and the bakeware could go on the top shelf of the Hoosier cabinet instead of that silly silk flower wreath. If she reorganized the pie press she'd have room for the cereal boxes, but they were almost empty anyway. She wouldn't need to hide those for long since there'd be no replenishment. Fear surged up into her chest and she got busy, pushing it back with mindless activity.

Strange Lights

St. Lucy, Kansas

St. Lucy resembled the darkest bowels of hell thanks to the Pulse. Most municipal generators fried and smaller generators could only run homes, not street lights. Shane's coal miners The Emmaus coal miners drove down the wide main street until they saw a building with some light in a window. It was just one window in the courthouse, but it was enough to suggest people might be there. Andrew and Zach banged on the door until a deputy came out. Shane watched tensely as they explained what had happened. Then two more deputies came out of the building and helped to carry the bodies which were well and truly stiff now.

Shane stared up at the stars to the north, which were obscured by a band of pale green. Jazz joined them and Shane let Jos take the driver's seat.

"What is that?" Jos asked as they were swapping in front of the truck. "Some kind of pollution? Something on fire, maybe."

"I think it's northern lights. I saw them in Alaska a couple of times." The conversation resumed when they climbed back into the truck.

"I thought you were there in the summer. Wasn't it daylight?"

"I flew a security detail into Deadhorse once on my way to Miristan. We were there for two nights. Well, the sun never came up over the horizon, so night is a relative term, but the aurora was really active."

"I've never seen them before." Jazz spoke in a whisper, way forward on the seat, her neck craned to see the dancing ribbon of color.

"You don't usually see them this far south."

"Maybe it wasn't an EMP." Apparently, Jos also thought a natural phenomenon required reverence. "Maybe it was a mass coronal ejection or…or—"

"I read about how the magnetic poles are supposed to be switching," Jazz said. "That's not supposed to be able to fry our electrical grid, but it theoretically could produce auroral displays way down here."

Shane felt a hollow grow in his chest as he stared at her.

"What?" she asked.

"Just thinking about how that would f-frack with intercontinental navigation. North becomes south, south becomes north."

"You mean the toilet will flush in the other direction?" Trust a teenager to go *there*.

"It does in Africa. It was fascinating for about three minutes, but I might have been a little drunk. There is a spot in the South Atlantic that screws with compasses. Supposedly that has something to do with the poles --."

All three of them startled when Andrew knocked on the window.

"They want to talk with you, get a statement about what happened at the mine. And their mayor is writing a note he wants us to take back to your dad."

Shane slid out of the truck. He had used muscles today that he'd not used in a few years, and he could feel it as he walked behind Andrew into the courthouse.

"Maynard Lowell," the sheriff greeted. "You found the bodies?"

"Yeah."

Sheriff Lowell was a short man with grey hair Shane thought had arrested him once back in high school. Lowell recognized his name, anyway. Guided by Lowell's questions, Shane gave a very brief description of what had happened.

"I honestly thought that the flash I saw in the woods was their spotter."

"Far as I know, there were just the three of them. They were helping the community by getting coal for our older folks. Bethany and Bob Lee left three kids behind, the oldest is twelve. Darryl's wife will have six mouths to feed."

"I'm sorry for their losses. From the tracks, I'd say they came up in a small car. And whoever drove the dump truck wasn't good at it. He kept overrevving on the shift."

"That's good to know. What about the folks that stayed behind?"

"They were going to set a watchman for themselves." Shane had avoided talking to Evan, who was just one of those annoying gym-coach types Shane had never been able to tolerate, so Andrew took up the report here.

Shane and Andrew paused on the sidewalk to looking up into the sky that flared with dancing colors.

"You know what that is up there?" Andrew asked.

"Hmm."

"My wife's from Alaska, you know? We met fighting fires in Idaho."

"Where there?"

"Goldstream. That's outside of Fairbanks. You been?"

"I flew through the airport, which could double as a Greyhound bus station. Sort of middle of the state, a bit to the east."

"Great memory."

"Never forget a navigational waypoint. You might need it again someday."

Laughing, Andrew walked away and Shane swung back up into the Big-I.

"Does anyone besides me think it's strange that we're making polite conversation after hauling three dead bodies here?" Jos asked.

"Yeah," Jazz grunted.

"Welcome to the new normal." Shane's stomach growled. "Is there any more of that MRE journey bread?" he asked.

Jazz checked the box and handed it to Shane, asking him if he wanted the peanut butter too.

"Nope, but while there's food to eat, I'm not starving myself because of something I didn't do."

Jos stared at the steering wheel, while Jazz gazed into Shane's soul for a long worrying moment before nodding.

"It might take the rest of us a while to catch up with reality."

Shane just ate his bread, because he didn't really know what else to say. The northern horizon looked like it was on fire before they got back on the road, driving east along Highway 36. Shane slipped the envelope from the sheriff into the visor and tried to spy light anywhere out there in the darkness. Jazz explained to Jos why Keri had kicked her out of her truck, something to do with a haywire heater.

A lonely farmhouse, way up a lane, shined a light in a single window. What a difference a week made. Had it really only been two weeks since the world had gone off the rails? The headlights picked up a car half in their lane. Jos shifted his foot off the gas and pushed in the clutch.

"Don't stop!" Shane pulled his 9 mm from the back holster. "Go around! Go fast!"

Something stirred in the shadows of the ditch. Jazz drew her own gun as Jos sped up, almost dropping the clutch, but chugging forward. Then they heard the gun report and, in the rearview mirror, Shane saw the flash of fire from Keri's passenger window. Her truck slowed and Shane started to unbuckle, preparing to drop out of the moving truck to defend his sister.

Andrew laid on his horn and Keri's truck regained speed, though it wavered between the lines considerably. The other three trucks cleared the ambush. The intervening headlights prevented Shane from seeing exactly what was going on, but there were a lot of dark shadows coming out of the ditches, evidence of an ambush.

"Should I stop, make sure Keri's all right?" Jos was clearly distressed.

"No. It's not safe out here. Keep going to Lufgren Crossing. Don't slow down for anything."

Keri had stopped crying by the time they reached the Crossing. She pulled into the bottom of the drive and stopped to run into the bushes and puke, so Shane and Jazz got out. Keri's fine-boned face was drawn and pale in the headlights.

"He had a gun. I didn't have a choice." Jazz wrapped her arms around her. Shane contemplated what he should do, but Keri had her own ideas. "I knew when I fired that shot at Rumdale that I might kill him, but it was him or Dad and …. I have a right to save my own life."

"You do." Shane hugged her now as Jazz stepped back to give him room. "It's all easy times discussing this around the fire at the lake when things are good, but we're in it now and chances are good you'd have been dead before I could have covered you."

She straightened in his arms.

"Alex?"

"He'll understand. Do you need me to tell him?"

"Tell me what?" Alex emerged from the darkness, flinching as three guns came around toward him. He held his hands up, shotgun in the left, which he leaned against a fencepost now that he knew it was them. "What's going on?"

"Poaching coal is apparently a dangerous business." Shane directed his gaze at Keri, but his attempted joke fell flat as unleavened bread. Alex frowned, perplexed, and then he saw Keri's face.

"What did you do?" Alex swept his wife into his arms as he accused Shane. He was so big she looked like a child against his chest.

"He didn't do anything." Keri's voice muffled in his shirt. She turned so they could hear her, or she could breathe. "He wasn't in a position to do anything. You don't blame him, and I won't blame you for that damn heater."

Alex frowned and Shane knew this could turn badly if he didn't intervene.

"We waited too long to leave. Everything was going so well that I wasn't paying attention to the time. We shouldn't have been trying to come back in the dark. That's on me.

"Shut up!" Jazz seemed to radiate light in her vehemence. She reminded him of a small cat Vi had once had who had grown mightily when irritated. "There were complications. Let's just blame the people who tried to ambush us! None of us would have killed anyone unless we were attacked, and arguing among ourselves doesn't change what happened."

"We didn't need the coal." Alex kissed the top of Keri's head.

"We don't, but others will," Keri insisted. "And I'm going back for more because this is the world we live in now and nobody gets to hide from it."

"You're not going back. It's too dangerous."

"You think Emmaus is safer? We were invaded by the freaking cow cops." Keri straight-armed him and climbed up into the truck. Without a glance backward, she drove up toward the farmhouse, her taillights glowing red in the darkness. What were you supposed to say after a speech like that?

"If we go again, we'll stay at the quarry overnight," Shane said. "It's a fortifiable position and we can see the dangers before we get to them in the daylight."

Alex growled. "She's not going."

"All due respect, Alex, how are you going to stop her?" Jazz asked.

"I'm going to tell her she can't go."

Shane shook his head.

"She's my mother's daughter. That's a fight you won't win."

"You're going to get her killed."

"Just living right now could get you killed, Alex. I didn't want to take her—not her or Jazz or Jos for that matter—but the truth is, they were an integral part of filling five trucks with coal in eight hours of work. If this town is going to survive the winter, we have got to work together and everybody has to play whatever role they can. You're a farmer. Crops and animals are what you do. And, Poppy needs the only parent she's got to not risk his life out there. But Keri is a teacher at a school that is no longer functioning, and she needs to define who she is going forward. She got her cherry popped and that hurts, but she gets that she'll be making tougher choices if she survives to spring. It's the world we live in now."

Alex rubbed a big hand across his face. In the quiet night, you could hear the scruff on his chin rasp across the calluses on his palm.

"What am I supposed to do, then?"

Shane remembered the night he'd stuck a gun in his mouth and pulled the trigger.

"I wish you'd been there when I got my cherry popped. The guy who was … great friend, but you read people a whole lot better."

Shane turned toward the truck. Alex turned toward the house, picking up his shotgun as he went. Mocha's tail followed him into the darkness. Jazz stood staring up at the eerie sky dance.

"What are you thinking?" Shane asked.

"That I'm tired and covered in coal dust and I'm never getting it off with cold water."

"Our generator's working. Mom promised me hot water when I got home. You can have it."

"You are incredibly confusing."

"I kind of embrace that."

Jos rolled down the window as they neared. "Can I drive the rest of the way?"

"Yeah. You need the practice."

"I'm sorry about the hesitation back there."

"It was a nice thought." Jazz climbed into the passenger side. "In the life before, that would have been the right thing to do."

"And, it isn't anymore." Shane climbed in behind her. "That's the sad fact that we all have to learn to live with."

Ill-Omened

Northwest Kansas

The road stretched on and on, a two-lane strip of asphalt stretching between trees interspersed by harvested fields. Galena's feet throbbed and the knee she'd blown out playing soccer in high school felt swollen. They'd been walking all day, hungry and thirsty. The water the farmer's wife had provided had been gone within the first hour. With low blood sugar and no idea where they were going, they hadn't tried to make good time. They'd picked out the stitches from their decals as they'd walked, more or less north, hoping to catch a ride or encounter a friendly town. Now the day was fading and the sky sparkled with stars as blue became black.

They stopped on a bridge. Tanaka pulled the water bottle out of his shirt.

"What do you think?"

Galena stared down into the black water.

"I don't think so. Any creeks around here would be contaminated with farm runoff. We could get really sick."

"Or, we could die of thirst."

Below and to their right, something splashed in the water and they heard Reinhold curse. Then there was more splashing.

"I guess they've made the decision for us."

"I'm not drinking unfiltered water," Lammers said. "You don't know what might be in it."

"I'm filling the bottle. We can't keep walking without water." Tanaka joined the others. Galena sighed, rolling her eyes skyward. Some sort of odd light flickered across the northern quarter of the star field.

"What the hell is that?" Reinhold asked.

"I have no idea." Galena stood awestruck as a ribbon of sea-foam light whipped across the sky.

"My wife's told me about this," Tanaka said. "She did one of those tourism things in Alaska with her folks when she was a kid. Must have cost them a bloody fortune from Japan. It's aurora."

"I grew up in Nebraska and I've never seen it."

"It doesn't usually come this far south. Or, maybe it just hasn't been dark enough in so long that we couldn't see it."

"You noticed, too?"

"Yeah. I don't see any town lights. They were using lanterns in Emmaus and the trucks they used to drop us off were all at least twenty years old."

"What do you think that means?"

"I don't know. Not sure I want to speculate. Hey, guys, let's get on the road. There's gotta be a town somewhere here. Someone with a working telephone or a vehicle to take us where we need to go."

Galena lowered her face into the creek and gulped a couple of big mouthfuls of the cold water. She didn't taste anything strange except for the lack of chemicals. The rest of the group had already reached the north end of the bridge. She could see Reinhold's white shirt. She jogged after them, a chill running down her spine. Folks had always described the aurora as beautiful, but to her, it felt like a harbinger of evil.

Dance

Emmaus

Shane admired that Jazz hadn't used up all the hot water, which he thoroughly enjoyed for the five minutes it took him to get the coal dust out of all of his cracks and crevices. The do-rag had kept most of the dust out of his hair, but his fingernails were rimed with black and it took three soapings for the water gathering around his feet to run frothy white instead of slate-grey.

The towel smelled of Jazz and he breathed the fragrance deeply. He knew better than to indulge the fantasy. *She* would make him pay for it. Except, if he were honest, he hadn't seen her since going over the side of the bridge. He saw Kitty Vance's purple face instead. At least that was sane. Maybe he could...*no, you can't.* It was cold in the bathroom, so he stopped dreaming, toweling off and dressing in sweats and a t-shirt.

Glister waited outside the bathroom door, politely banging his golden tail on the floor and looking down the stairs.

"They forget to take you out before they went to bed, boy?"

The collar and leash hung on a coat hook in the mud room because the yellow Lab was restricted from roaming until they had inspected the orchard behind the house for radioactive dead squirrels. Who had time for that?

Her white t-shirt alerted him to Jazz's presence on the picnic table. She lay flat on her back, watching the red, violet and green ribbons of dancing lights. The single ribbon had divided and the competing displays filled the entire northern half of the sky. When he approached she lifted her head.

"There's room." She scooted to her left, shifting her 9 mm under her thigh. Had Pygmalion felt this way about Psyche, seeing his efforts come to fruition? Shane took the seat on her right, putting his tailbone right at the edge of the seat and reclined back. "That's not exactly what I meant."

"I know. I'm ... I'm not ready yet." She didn't say anything for several heart beats. "After I spent that summer in Alaska, my grandmother told me a tale about what the Wyandots believed about the aurora. Not sure if it's true or not, but they believed they were the souls of their vanquished enemies and that if you whistled to the aurora, it would swoop down and cut off your head."

"And the gods will play soccer with it, but you can stop it if you clap."

"You know the legend?"

"The Greyeyes aren't the only Wyandots here."

"There are no more Greyeyes."

"Aren't there? Aren't you a Greyeyes?"

"My eyes are definitely green, like my mother's family, not grey like some of my grandmother's folks."

"Sign of white blood, right?"

"Yep. Some French voyageur, if family legend is accurate. Phillippe Machan. His son, Barsaillai Markan, lived his whole life as a Metis, comfortable with both worlds. His son, Joseph Markham immigrated to the Kansas City area when the Wyandots were 'strongly encouraged' to sell their land in Ohio. He married Etta Greyeyes, whose father was undoubtedly a white man, though nobody recorded the tomcat's name. He was probably a Scotsman."

"The French tended to stay with their Indian wives and children while the Scots returned back to their families in Europe," Jazz added. "So why not Markham or Markan or Machan rather than Greyeyes?"

"Wyandot are matrilineal. Joseph and Etta were Christians, but they still followed some of the old ways. Etta had siblings, too, and they married. But somehow all of them died and Joseph and Etta ended up raising a whole bunch. When white people started coming into the territory, Joseph sold his land in the east and moved here, where Etta's folks had an allotment. He built a sod house and, as an American citizen, homesteaded additional acres. This east side of town are all Metis lots backed up to the creek. This was all Indian land before the town relocated from Jericho Springs. Some of them sold out and moved to Oklahoma, but a bunch of Greyeyes stayed. Half the town are cousins from two or three generations back."

She turned her head to look at him. He looked back.

"But the Greyeyes name died out?"

"In Emmaus, yeah. There's a pretty good sized community of them up near Wyandot Lake. Jacob sent someone to talk with them about networking, sort of like St. Lucy."

"Do they have something besides corn? We have plenty of corn."

Shane laughed.

"If we only had enough for all 5,000 of us to survive the winter."

"Can Alex really feed the whole family this winter?"

"He and I have done the math. We're going to get real skinny and we still run out in March. But we can live on milk and eggs. He has enough feed for that."

"God, how did we back ourselves into this corner?"

"We'll figure it out." Shane wasn't nearly as certain as he sounded, but he knew the power of keeping positive attitudes. "Things like the apples bring us that much closer to survival."

They turned back to the aerial display. Glister groaned. The grass under Shane's bare feet was cold.

"Is it Marnie?" He tilted his head so he could see her expression.

"Why I'm not ready?" She nodded. He shook his head. "She and I were over a long time ago."

"And you moved on?"

"I dated a woman in South America for about six months until I found out I was being played." Shane laughed at that memory, painful at the time, but a great object lesson. "And there was a journalist in Miristan."

"Was?"

A hard lump formed in Shane's throat and his answer came out hoarse.

"It was a war zone, so let's not talk about it. You dated Paul Osimowitz. Did you move on?"

"I dated a guy in college for a few semesters."

"But Paul is still stalking you?"

"If I lived in Mara Wells he would be. He did every time I went home to visit. That's why I took the job here instead of there. For a good year, he didn't know I was anywhere near."

"How'd he find out?"

"Keri's wedding, I think."

"I could see my folks inviting Stan and him bringing Randi as his plus one, but Paul … that doesn't compute."

"I don't think it was them, but small-town Kansas gossip, that doesn't compute?"

Shane laughed.

"Yeah, of course. Everybody knows everybody's business and they all talk about it."

"Not yours. People seem real flinch-y about gossiping about you."

"I've been known to have a temper and I indulged that a bit when I was younger. Gossiping about me was one way to make me mad." Her face seemed somber in the low light. "I've learned to count to ten since then."

She didn't smile, just looked up at the sky. Maybe there was more than just his PTSD to stand in their way. Maybe he wanted there to be.

"What do the lights mean to you?" she asked softly.

"Electromagnetic energy in the ionosphere—"

"No. Metaphorically."

"Not sure an aeronautical engineer is qualified to speak metaphorically."

"You forget, you went to the high school I teach in. Some of the teachers consider you to be legendary. You were salutatorian of your class, right?"

"Only because Marnie cheated me out of valedictorian."

"Cheated?"

"We used to help each other with homework. She admitted in college that she would wait for me to go to the bathroom and then she'd jot down my math answers. And I rewrote several of her papers in a couple of English classes. We were seniors before I realized we were in competition for grades and by that time, it was too late."

"You sound incredibly competitive." He heard the humor in her voice.

"I was."

"Not now?"

"I'm learning better ways." He sighed as the light show flashed dramatically in wide loops. "That competition with Marnie pushed me to do my best. I might not have gone to Embry if I'd not wanted to show her that I was every bit as smart as she was."

"Hmm, I don't get that vibe from her and Cai."

"No. He was valedictorian of his class, so there's nothing for him to prove. I never would have thought those two would fit, and I still haven't seen it for myself, but Keri and Alex say they complete each other rather than compete with each other." His breath caught as he saw something in the sky. "It's a dance. See how the blues are running across the field with the violets chasing them? And then the reds and greens are following just behind, but opposite. It's like one of those line dances or … a ballet."

She twisted her head to stare at him, but he kept his eyes on the lights.

"What?"

"Did you know I was a ballet dancer?"

"That explains why you are so toned." A memory emerged. "You danced for Mrs. Sims, didn't you?"

"Yeah. Wait. There were some older boys who used to do lifts for us." He grinned at her. "You had hair down to your shoulders and Mrs. Sims kept saying she was going to put you in a tutu and a ballerina bun."

Shane laughed.

"You and Keri were little kids back then. Mr. Sing wanted us martial artists to take classes so we could improve our balance and body mechanics. Mrs. Sims needed boys to lift the girls. I only did it that one year, though. It drove Marnie crazy that I was touching other girls, and we actually almost broke up over it."

"Were you cheating?"

"No, not at all. The one real moral stricture I take from my dad and grandpa is monogamy."

"Is that another reason you won't lay down beside me?"

The sky display had thinned and retreated to mostly greens and blues. He sighed.

"Remember the other day in the feedstore when we almost kissed?" She didn't nod immediately, but she lifted her chin slightly. "I was going out to be hanged. I can do that—risk my life for the benefit of the town because I don't have to leave anyone behind. And, because of that mindset, maybe I shouldn't risk leaving anyone behind." She turned her head sideways, lips parted. "You're thinking again."

"You have a point. And, I'm living in your parents' home, so it would have to be platonic." She sighed as she saw the lights were fading. "If we stay here longer, will they come back?"

"Maybe. In Deadhorse, the display was on and off all night. I don't know about you, but I have to work in the morning."

She rolled up to sitting. "We have coal to unload. When are we going back?"

"If life lets us, day after tomorrow—which might not come, so …." Shane shrugged. They both stood. Glister stretched, chest to the ground, butt to the sky.

"Are you really okay with my living here this winter?"

"More okay with it than if you froze to death living elsewhere."

She held out her right hand.

"Friends?" she asked.

He sighed. She understood, but not really. He shook her hand anyway.

"Friends."

It was very dark inside the house, so they stuck close to the sound of Glister's claws against the floor to find the stairs and make their way to the second floor. Belle, the cat, hissed at Glister and fled Shane's room, growling softly.

"I suppose that was a midnight furring of my pillow. Good night."

Jazz turned toward the back of the house.

"Left hand door, right?"

"Unless you want to wake, Jacob, yeah."

"Left hand door for sure then. Good night."

Shane listened to her fumble along the landing to find the door, finally easing his own door closed when she closed the door to Keri's room. Glister grunted at him when he nudged him with his foot because his room was darker than the back side of the moon. He'd recharged his tablet with the generator and the notification light was blinking, intermittently bathing the ceiling in a pulse of light. He opened the screen and his mouth dropped open as he saw what was there.

Fear Not

New Jersey

The mysterious lights faded from the sky and, one by one, folks disappeared into the house. The bridge in Belvadere turned out to also be clogged with vehicles, but a neighbor with a tow strap had already been at work trying to clear it. He'd been willing to let the Sullivan group camp in his yard that night, as he hoped to finish the job in the morning. Perry and Julian whispered goodnight and climbed into their tent. Joseph held out a hand to Katharine and she took it.

Last night, they'd slept in the truck bed with one in the front seat and another standing guard. It had been horrible and none of them had slept very well. They'd picked up an additional sleeping bag today.

The tent's interior was pretty dark since it was a new moon, but Joseph had already laid out their sleeping bags, so it wasn't that complicated. When she had shrugged out of her jacket and pulled off her shirt, his hands touched her back, slowly caressing her.

"Maybe we should do this under the covers," he suggested. "You're cold."

"It's that time of the month."

"Oh." Joseph had always been an attentive lover and knew ways to make love without having sex. After satisfying each other, they cuddled, warmed by each other's ardor.

"When was the last time you heard from Allison?" Katharine asked.

"A few days ago. Dad left me messages along the way. She was fine then, so I assume she's fine now."

"Emmaus probably doesn't have power, either."

"But Dad has an amazing setup, Kat. Don't worry. She'll be fine."

"That cast should have come off a couple of weeks ago."

"Dad said he had it taken care of. You know, he raised three children. He's not inept."

"Just laser focused and in the midst of a chaotic event."

"He can handle it."

"What aren't you telling me?" She lifted her head off his chest so she could see him, though really all she could see was the light and shadow of his face.

He sighed.

"Nothing. It's a long way to Kansas, is all, and it won't do any of us a bit of good to worry about what's going on there."

"I'm her mother."

"And, I love her too."

"So, why did you come after me and leave her there alone?"

"She's not alone. My dad can handle it."

"Probably by taking her to Dr. Vashon."

"What is wrong with Dr. Vashon?"

"If he were any good he wouldn't be a doctor in Emmaus."

"He was a combat doctor. He likes the peace and quiet. We aren't going to fight, right?"

"No. I'm glad you came and found me. Julian did great getting me out of the city, but I wished you were with me the whole time."

"He seems like a nice kid."

"Yeah. He's a computer programmer. Compared to Perry, he might as well be a paperweight."

Joseph laughed.

"He must have some guts to brave a city in flames to get you out of there."

"I am grateful to him." It felt important to her that Joseph also be grateful

"So am I. I don't know that we can get him to Seattle, but we can get him to Kansas."

"That's halfway. It's better than where he is now. We have a long way to go, but at least you have a working vehicle. Where did you get it?"

Joseph told her a funny story about a farmer taking a helicopter as collateral for his truck.

"He might not have gotten the best deal on that trade. I'm thinking the helicopter is a lawn ornament at this point."

"How long do you think it will take us to get back?"

"A few more days. It'll take longer than it normally would; it's taken us nearly a week to get here. But with fewer people on the roads now, it'll be fine."

She listened to his voice and wondered why he was lying to her. He was one of the few people she knew who didn't, but tonight ... he mustn't want her to be scared, not for their daughter and, most especially, not for themselves.

Dust & Tears

Emmaus

Alex rolled over and reached for Keri only to find cold sheets. He looked around the dark room and didn't find her. He slept in shorts and a t-shirt, so he walked barefoot down the hall, listening to the house.

Mark and Alice slept in the bunk room with baby Lisa. Alex could hear the soft sounds of breathing. Pete rolled over in bed in the small bedroom. Alex eased Poppy's door open and by the light from the window could see his sister hugging her pillow. He closed the door and went in search of his wife. He finally found her in his parents' long-abandoned bedroom on the first floor off the living room. She sat in the rocker by the window, her feet drawn up and her mind somewhere out in the wood behind the house.

“Did I wake you?” she asked in a husky voice, sniffling.

“Your absence did.”

“I can’t get his face out of my mind.” She dissolved into tears on the last word. Alex sat down on the bed, holding her hand. She wept for a while before she spoke. “It happened so quickly. Jos slowed down for this broke-down car and then there were people moving. He stepped up on to the running board and – and he was reaching for me. I didn’t mean to shoot him, but it all happened so fast.”

“You didn’t have a choice.”

“You weren’t there. You can’t know.”

“But Shane was and he does know. We can’t do any better than his assessment.”

“My brother burned his conscience away years ago. What if I’m damned for this?”

“Damned?! Nothing can pluck us from His hand. Moses killed a man for far less than you did, and he was ultimately justified by faith. Think of Paul the apostle, and even that dude, Jephthah. That’s crazy talk, Keri. But you don’t have to be like Shane. He’s running from what he’s done and has to turn off his emotions. You can give it to Jesus and know it’s forgiven.”

"It doesn't feel forgiven."

"When my folks died I was angry for a long time. I wanted revenge and the guy going to jail for a few years wasn't enough for me. I wanted retribution. But eventually, I realized that I was only hurting myself. If I let it go and gave it to Jesus, I could feel better. Right after I did that, I saw the guy's obituary in the newspaper. He died of cancer. I felt actual compassion for him. It didn't make up for what had happened to my parents, but they wouldn't want me to be angry forever."

Keri sniffled.

"How do you do that?" she asked.

"Do what?"

"Talk me off the ledge."

"Did I?" She nodded in the darkness. "Good. I just know that we're in an impossible situation and we have very few options, none of them involving turning the other cheek. It's pretty to believe that if you'd just stopped and talked to that fellow that you could have worked something out but, clearly, you didn't think there was another option. So, cry. Be sad that this awful thing happened. Mourn him, if you need to. But know that you have as much right to live as he did, and the moment he stepped up onto that running board, he was threatening your right to live."

Keri sniffled again, wiping her cheek with her free hand.

"Thank you," she said.

They sat in quiet for several minutes.

"Are you going to forbid me to go when Shane goes back?"

"You're an adult. I can't forbid you. I suppose I could forbid the truck, but you'd probably still go. Right?"

She nodded.

"It just seems like something I should do."

"Shane and Jazz agree." Alex smiled at her, knowing he couldn't win this battle by making demands. "I don't have to like it, but husbands don't have to like everything their wives do."

"I don't like it much myself."

"Well, I don't think anyone would think you were a coward if you decided you'd sacrificed enough." Maybe what he couldn't forbid, he could persuade her from with reason.

"No one, but me."

"I sort of knew that's what you would say." There'd never been any hope that Alex could talk her out of what she had decided. All he could do was be supportive.

The light from the window provided definition to her face. She let go of his hand to wipe both cheeks.

"We have work to do before we go to church. I'm going to wash my face and put on clothes. Thanks." She kissed him and then headed for the door.

Alex sat on the bed wishing he could cry, too. The sun in the east window showed all the dust and cobwebs. Poppy sometimes came in here and poked around, mostly in their mother's things that Alex had never been able to sort through and throw out or give away. Keri had never said word one about sleeping in Alex's childhood room. The queen bed was enough for both of them and he'd moved his clothes into the room Pete was now using because she had needed the closet space. He'd need to do something different now. Maybe it was time to vacuum out this room and start using it for something more than storing memories and expressing tears.

On the Road Again

Missouri

Javier Chavez blinked tears from his eyes, trying to bring the room into focus. Looking toward the diffuse flashlight glow in the corner made more tears run, and he had to close his eyes for a moment. But, when he opened them again, he smiled.

"TV, you, door's there."

"Clear or blurry?" Ami asked. Definitely both. There were large parts of his vision where he couldn't pull things into focus. His eyes weren't burning, but when he looked toward the light, it felt like he was going onto a brightly lit beach from a really dark room.

"How many fingers am I holding up?"

Focusing took effort.

"Three?"

"Is that a statement or a question?"

"Both. It's hard to focus."

She made breakfast of MRE sides while his eyes slowly stopped tearing. His vision couldn't adjust to different light levels. He would lose focus, but he could see to feed himself for the first time in three days.

"Does this mean we can get going?"

Ami had spent most of yesterday afternoon looking for gasoline and had reported the tank was topped off.

"Yes, except we can make it about halfway to Emmaus with a full tank. It took me three stations to fill it, so ... I don't know."

"We will find more gas when we need to. It's really easier than you think. My eyes are still really sensitive to light though, so you're going to need to drive."

"I picked these up at a hardware store." She lifted something from the table, which was in the direction of the light, so it took a moment before he could recognize them as sunglasses. "You might want to put them on now because I'm going to crack the blinds to save the batteries and get you used to more light."

Putting the sunglasses on felt odd as he'd not worn any since coming back from South

America. It wasn't full daylight outside yet, but that half of the room became an underdeveloped photo. By the time he'd finished breakfast, he could make out details again.

"How long until sunrise?"

"Twenty minutes. It's cloudy, so it'll be a good day to start."

"Let's get loaded up."

"I've got it. You shouldn't be lifting anything just yet."

"Then open those blinds all the way so my eyes can get used to the light while you work."

He almost regretted that decision as a headache formed behind his left eye, but his gut said they needed to get on the road sooner rather than later. Between bouts of tearing, he practiced pulling Ami into focus.

"I like the hair style."

She'd pulled her curls up in a messy bun. Some of her hair escaped the fasteners and spilled down her neck.

"I can go days between shampoos, but I'm stretching that limit," she admitted.

"You smell nice."

"Cold showers are good for the skin, they claim. You ready to go?"

"Sure. You might want to stay right beside me, at least until my eyes adjust. I really lose detail in the light."

She had to guide him to the car. He blinked furiously as she went around to the driver's side. She didn't get in immediately, just seemed to be looking around intently.

"What's up?" he asked her.

"Nothing. Just…I'm not feeling safe right now."

"Speaking of that, where's my gun?"

"I slid it under the seat. Can you hit the broadside of a camel right now?"

"If it holds still, but other people don't know that." He found the gun in its back holster and lifted up his shirt to don the rig. Then he buckled up, missing the receiver twice before getting the tongue in. "Ready to go."

She took a deep breath and didn't let it go as she started the car and backed away from the motel.

Facing Home

Hutchinson

"Are you married?" Mike asked a few minutes into their journey. "I don't remember Ric ever saying."

"He didn't know until he got home." Mike shot him an incredulous look. "When you never answer your phone, it's hard to tell you big news."

"Yeah, he got a little reclusive there after our last tour."

"From our perspective, he's been reclusive for about five years."

Mike drove in silence for a while. Cai wondered what he was holding close to his chest.

"What's your wife like?"

"Capable. She's a doctor."

"So, you're not worried about her?"

"My parents will watch out for her. I suspect her father will, too."

"Who's her father?"

"Local trucker with a reputation."

Mike smiled like he might know folks with similar descriptions.

"Do you have kids?"

"No. We just got married in the summer. We'll probably wait a while, pay off our college debts first. You?"

"Alicia was in Santa Fe with her mom when this happened. I can't get through."

"Yeah. I tried to call Marnie this morning and there's still no connection. But we're going there, so ...."

Mike slowed for a truck that had broken down alongside the road. It seemed abandoned.

"We're expecting a kid."

"Wow. When?"

"February. She's hoping for a Valentine's baby."

Cai considered whether to ask the obvious question: Are you terrified for your kid in this world now?

"Do you know if it's a boy or a girl?"

"No. We hadn't done the ultrasound, yet. Those wouldn't work after this, right? So, I'm thinking we're just going to have to settle for being surprised."

Mike braked to a stop before the wreckage of two cars blocking the road.

"I can't negotiate the shoulder in this truck. Ric probably could, but I'll roll it. Let's see if we can move them."

Fortunately, one of the owners had left the keys in the car after realizing it wasn't going anywhere. They were able to roll it into the ditch to make room for their truck to pass. Cai wondered if his Subaru was still working.

"I miss Marnie." Cai buckled up.

"Yeah, it's been two weeks since I've seen Alicia. How long for you?"

"It's Sunday?" Mike considered a moment and then nodded. "It was Saturday. So a week. I didn't want Marnie with me when I was a slave, but I miss her now."

Mike frowned.

"Something?" Cai guessed the topic and figured they might as well get out in the open.

"Marnie ... is that a common name around here?"

"Shane tell you about his high school girlfriend?"

Mike snorted. For a cold-as-ice mercenary, he could smile warmly with his Hershey brown eyes

"He did, and that's not dysfunctional at all."

He didn't sound judgmental or like he was trying to take sides. He thought it was humorous.

"A lot of water flowed under that bridge before I started dating her."

"Okay. I could see that. A lot changes in, what, five years. And, I dated one of my brother's old girlfriends once. It wasn't a good idea because she was just using me to make Ray mad, but I don't think it was wrong or anything. Ric laughed when I told him that story."

"It took him a few minutes to get used to the idea, but he took it better than I thought he would."

"Not much fazes him long-term. Do you worry about them being together when you're out of town?" Mike had sobered now.

"No. No!"

"Because you don't need to worry. Ric got over her a long time ago. There was some *chica* in South America, and he dated this journalist in Miristan. I thought those two were going to get married."

"What happened?"

Mike stared out at the passing countryside and then his eyes widened. Cai looked forward. The truck's height gave him a fairly clear vantage point along the highway, and the mile-long traffic jam of abandoned cars.

"Wow! How are we getting past that?"

Disaster on the Horizon

Emmaus

Shane woke before dawn, hours before anyone else. He hadn't slept well and he felt like banging on doors, demanding they all get up and pay attention to his news, but he held his water until Jacob and Rob awoke.

"We have a problem."

"Good morning to you too." Rob picked up a coffee cup.

"His way of saying, 'Why don't have some coffee?' before easing into the crisis of the day." Jacob poured coffee into his own cup.

"Wish I could. It's already getting cold in the northern plains and my handler confirms that people are moving out of the remaining cities."

Rob stopped in the act of pouring from the coffee pot. Jacob frowned and stared into his cup. Jazz paused on the stairs.

"You assume they'll come here?" Rob asked.

"Some of them will. They have to know farming communities have resources."

Jill came in from outside with a platter of French toast.

"Coffee?" Rob asked her.

Marnie came down the stairs right behind Jazz.

"Hmm, French toast!"

Jill forked two each onto plates and they passed around the butter and a jug of maple syrup.

"We need to talk," Shane complained.

"Can't we wait until after breakfast?" Rob asked.

"Everybody runs in opposite directions then. This is important."

Marnie swallowed her first mouthful and mumbled, "What are you talking about? Nobody's mobile devices are working. Are you delusional?"

"The geosynch satellites are still up and I've got reception." Shane indicated the tablet. "I've been trying to set it up as something of an early warning system, hoping to not be surprised by the next government gabfest that comes our way. Last night, I saw a satellite snap of this, which is from yesterday at noon."

He passed the tablet to Jacob who passed it to Marnie without even looking at it. She spent a good deal of time staring at it before passing it to Jazz whose delicate forehead creased with concern before passing it to Jill. Rob sighed as he handed it back to Shane.

"That does look unsettling," he agreed. "We certainly can't help that many people, but …."

"We need to prepare to control that encounter."

"How long do we have?" Marnie asked. Finally, someone who got what they were talking about.

"They're walking for the most part. That big vanguard won't get here for days and may miss us entirely. But we've already got people leaving the smaller cities around here and heading our way. Some of them tried to stop us on the road last night." He opened another window on the tablet and ate some more breakfast while they passed it around.

"Shit," Marnie muttered. Jill's eyes widened. "Sorry, but it's not something we've needed to worry about all that much in my lifetime, but Jacob's been re-educating me.

With no electricity and really reduced running water, it's hard to stay clean. And then there's diseases. There's limited antibiotics and antiseptic and no antivirals. The last thing we need is people from other towns flooding into Emmaus."

They all stared at her.

"Think about this. It's the start of flu season and we have no vaccines. Those of us who have been getting the vaccines every year have immune systems that are out of practice with staving off the flu. Imagine what that means if there's a particularly virulent one going around?"

Jill nodded firmly. She understood that argument, but they didn't get the most important point.

"Feeding them would kill us." Shane hated their dismissive expressions as he reasoned with them. "Simple math says we need a certain amount of calories to make it to spring and what we have currently means some of our own people are going to starve to death because we don't have enough. We can't take in refugees and expect any of us to make it to spring." Shane considered the bite of food he'd just cut and put his fork down. His conscience had not been completely seared yet.

"So, what do we do? Build a wall?" Jacob's mouth twisted with dislike.

"Kind of. We block the main roads into town and put armed guards on the barricades." Jacob stared at Shane like he'd never seen him before.

"Did I have a hand in raising you?"

"Sorry to disappoint. Not really an idealist."

"We're not talking about idealism here, kid. We're talking about humanity."

"What would Jesus do?" Jill whispered.

"Your make-believe god could conveniently turn a little bit of food into a feast. I left my miracle wand in Miristan."

"You mock us while you contemplate sending people to their deaths?" Jill's flat voice was a sure sign she was judging him.

"Walls don't fix anything, kid." Jacob stood on principle, but the principles weren't very pragmatic.

"Pa, Shane has a point." Rob sounded grudging, but at least he was accepting reality. "Marnie's right about the spread of disease and Shane is right that we can't afford to take in refugees. We've got the commuter passengers and the people that came off the road before the rain. That's enough. We can't afford to feed more."

"But we're going to build walls?" Jacob objected.

"Be careful to entertain strangers, for many have entertained angels unawares." Shane might have thought of a clever retort to Jill's scripture citation if he'd not been shocked that he knew the verse was in Hebrews.

Jazz cleared her throat. She'd barely touched the food on her plate.

"Can I say something?"

"Of course, Jazz. There's no rank here," Jill assured her.

"I hate the idea of building walls, too, and we all need to pray about what God wants us to do, but that doesn't obligate the entire town … or Shane … to do what we want to do and … there's a lock on the door of my apartment because I don't want my stuff stolen. As a community, we have a right to band together to protect ourselves against threats. It's unfortunate, but, the world isn't sane anymore, and we have to confront that."

Rob growled. "You're right. Much as I hate it, you're right. We at least need to be prepared to defend ourselves. There're still no phones to Mara Wells, but we need to coordinate with Stan for roadblocks and manpower. How far out do we go?"

Shane pulled up another screen on the tablet, a map of the town and surrounding area marked up.

"I don't think we can hold more than the town by ourselves, but if that National Guard unit in Beulah is willing to throw in with us, I think we can hold it at these crossroads, which means we can still control those fields if people don't move on. Mara has the western approaches."

"What are you building the wall out of?"

"Pa, cut it out! Shane, you know road blocks won't keep them out. It can block the roads, but there's still all that off-road area."

"Barbed wire will help, and people who aren't comfortable in the country will avoid it. We just keep directing them around us."

"My God. We become the apocalypse."

"Grandpa, I know it doesn't set well, but we can't help these people. They'd be a drain on our resources. We all starve together or some of us survive separately."

"And what if there's another doctor, or someone who could fix the telephones, between here and Mara?" Jacob demanded. "We're just going to turn them away?"

Shane recognized immediately that he'd just lost the group. He couldn't argue against the idea of improving the community by absorbing immigrants. He sat back with a sigh. The silence became painful and then Jazz spoke.

"We direct them around us, but we offer them water. The Jericho Well is natural. It doesn't need power to get water out of the ground. It costs us nothing but the transportation. We can use that interaction to – uh, vet people."

"Brilliant idea." Rob smiled. "They'll resent us less if we have something we can offer, and we can offer a very limited number a chance to stay here."

"They'll come with their families." Shane visualized women in burqas leading their children up to an aid station. "You could end up feeding a dozen people in order to get three people with useful skills."

"Christiana has made herself invaluable at the clinic." Marnie reached for another slice of French toast. "She came off the commuter."

"Click has been providing valuable service. Dennis put out the corn field fire." Jacob ticked them off on his fingers.

"And, they are all extra mouths to feed." They all glared at him so that Shane held his hands before him like a shield. "I'm not saying we kick them out, but my role as the extreme realist is to point out what your soft hearts don't want to contemplate. They're going to put us that much closer to starvation. The other skills they have compensate for that, but they're individuals. They aren't coming with families. These people likely are."

"We don't have to take their families," Marnie mumbled. Her face showed her guilt. "We can make the offer and they can choose. Most won't let their families walk off down the road, but there may be individuals who would accept the offer."

Jacob nodded thoughtfully.

"Who do we make this offer to?"

"Doctors." That was the expected response from Marnie.

"Nurses." Jill sounded definite.

"Engineers." They all frowned at Shane's apparent change of opinion. He didn't object to feeding useful people. Yeah, maybe it was hard to keep up. "Or electricians and mechanics. We have a few already, but to rebuild the turbines so we can power this town and get out of the 1880s we need people with actual expertise."

Jacob nodded and Rob smiled, briefly.

"So what are we building these roadblocks out of?" Jacob sounded so reasonable that Shane actually smiled. Maybe Rob's reasonableness had soothed him. Shane had anticipated the question.

"Salvage yards. Pile up old cars as a semi-permanent restriction, mainly something for the guards to hide behind in case the migrants are armed. There's some connexes at the mine that we could use too."

"Are we just going to shoot people who try to break this cordon?" Jill sounded far too naïve for a woman who had served in Vietnam.

"Yeah." Shane could tell that was not the answer Jill wanted. "It's unfortunate, but if we wimp out now, we won't have the option for getting strong later."

"How do we know these people aren't going to just peacefully pass us?"

"They might. The AR-15s and barriers are just in case. But my experience is that people who have traveled hundreds of miles on foot are hungry and they'll be getting desperate by the time they get here."

"So, your plan for the day?" Rob asked.

"Get started hardening our northern border since that's the first to be challenged. I'm going to Bennetts this morning."

"After church, I'll go to Mara Wells and talk to Stan, ask him to introduce me to the National Guard in Beulah. As Emmaus' mayor, it's about time. According to Jason, the one truck we recovered had its tires shot out by a sniper. It had to be from Beulah. It was just past there when they stopped."

"Any word on what happened to those three USDA agents?"

"Nothing so far. They might just have walked away while we were trying to get the situation under control. Two others got away clean with the two trucks and then there was the driver of the shot-up truck. He was bleeding when he headed north. Judging by the description, I expect to find him curled up somewhere dead."

Jill shivered. It had to be hard to think of people they would have welcomed as tourists only two weeks ago as being the enemy now. When Shane moved to go past her, she put a hand on his arm.

"I know you're going to do what you feel is right." He wanted to pull away, but he didn't. "I just want to remind you that these people are people and if you don't have to kill them, you shouldn't."

A flash of black at his visual periphery and then just the briefest memory of Kitty Vance strangling to death.

"I know, Mom. I hope I can avoid it too."

Shane felt a heavy weight settle on his shoulders—the knowledge that he could so rarely avoid it.

"We're burning daylight." Jacob tapped his watch. "Days are getting shorter, nights are getting cooler and we've got a problem headed our way. There's a roan mare that could use some exercise and we need to start conserving gasoline. Go on now."

Entering the garage for his bike, Shane slowed. A shiver ran through him as he remembered that his uncle must have died in here. He paused to look at the rafters and wonder if things would have been different for him if his family had been able to talk about what happened to Eric. Would he not have agreed to go to Miristan?

Then I'd have nightmares about San Cristobal. And, because I would have lacked the skills I have now, I wouldn't have nightmares about Kitty Vance because I'd have been hung right alongside her.

Putting dark thoughts aside, he mounted the bike and rode eastward toward the ranch.

Seeing the Next Step

Wichita

Commander Crispin knocked on Ren's open office door. Phil looked up first from the documents on the desk in front of them.

"What's the situation?"

"The army in Wichita has surrendered. There's still limited skirmishes, but their commanders are on board with telling them to lay down arms. Casualties on our side have been much lower than on their side."

He also explained that the contingent of Knights I sent to Hutchinson returned with the surviving portion of an Army unit that set up some sort of petty fiefdom there. Although it was the Army's decision what to do with them, he expected executions.

Hutchinson was creating a market center under the auspices of former FEMA workers, using Knight Industry operatives for security.

"I've chosen to tell those Knights that they can contract with the center if they agree to give B&W 15%. I'm waiting to hear back on that."

"Your man Sanchez?"

"Report is that he headed westward to Emmaus with an Emmaus resident."

"Who?"

Crispin looked at his phone.

"Cai Delaney."

"Oh, good. I felt a responsibility to get him back home. Do we know where they're at now?"

"No. HQ is still repositioning satellites, but towers are essentially flag poles now. Voice is completely down. I'm mostly in text contact with my outlying units."

"Keep me informed on that and on what's going on with Hutchinson. That sounds like something that might work out well."

"Yes, sir. The big issue for us now is food. The city is just about stripped clean and people are starting to go hungry. What should we do about that?"

Ren leaned back in his chair and looked out at the blue sky and its white fluffy clouds.

Hard to believe the world could look so lovely when the reality on the ground was so starkly nasty.

"Honestly, I have no idea. What do you think? I don't like the idea of stripping Hutchinson for Wichita."

"Mr. Wilson was helping New York before the Pulse. Do you want me to check if food assistance is possible at this point?"

"Sounds good. What do you think the likelihood is?"

"For a short term, he might. For long term, I wouldn't count on it. Would you indefinitely feed strangers who didn't plan ahead?"

Ren sighed and poured him a cup of coffee. Crispin took the seat offered.

"Thank you, Mr. Sullivan."

"Ren. I need someone to listen while I work this out for myself."

"That'll be a first, sir. My background is having tea with mullahs who were going to pursue their own agenda and probably lie to me while they did it."

Ren smiled.

"I knew when I agreed to take charge of quelling the Army's abuses that I would have to also figure out how to feed people, but the problem is there's no food. Not enough to feed

300 million people. Not even enough to feed the population of Wichita. Before the Pulse, I saw the situation and I was trying to get Crystal to see it too. Her plan was to not feed 'less productive' neighborhoods."

Crispin's cheek twitched as if he had an opinion on that. What sort of person became a mercenary? Had he grown up in a poorer neighborhood?

"I ordered fuel and food up from the Gulf Coast before the Pulse, but I don't know how it's getting here if vehicles aren't running."

"Would your people go over and above like my boy Sanchez?"

"Pay day's Friday. Not sure how I pay them with no electronic banking system and loyalty only goes so far. So, I don't know. What's motivating Sanchez?"

"Trying to live up to an ideal. He served for several years with a partner who was a do-or-die agent. If Eric Faraday said he'd get the food to a village, the food got to a village. Beyond that, Wilson pays really well. And, I suspect, Sanchez is about to break his contract."

"Come again."

"His wife was in New Mexico when everything went down and it just makes sense that he'd go get her. Emmaus is closer to Santa

Fe than Wichita is, so I don't know if he'd come back and have her live in the barracks tent. Most of my guys will hold on because we were based in San Diego and don't have families to return to, but the ones that do...I just can't promise they'll stay here when their families are going hungry and winter's coming on."

"Of course not. Same with those crews coming up from the Gulf. I just don't know what to expect."

Crispin sipped his coffee.

"Seems to me, sir, that you can't make promises with half information. There's a saying in the military: 'You have to go to war with the army you have.' I think the same principle applies now. You need to recognize that you don't have unlimited resources and that all you can do is support people in what they mean to do, rather than dictate from on high."

Ren blinked at Crispin, surprised to hear his own thoughts echoing back at him. He nodded.

"Thank you. That clarifies a bit. There's what I, as a moral man, wish to do, and then there's what the practical man can do. And, maybe I need to remember I'm not the savior of the world. I'm merely a guy with a bank account I can't access just yet. Which means I have to decide my next move. What resources do I have?"

"Most of my forces will stick as long as we can feed them."

"And the communities?"

"I don't know, sir."

"Nobody's talked to them?"

"B&W doesn't hire us as PR agents."

Ren grinned. Weapons couldn't be expected to be good at public relations.

"Seems like maybe I should then."

Crispin's eyebrow arched.

"Let me know when you want to do that, sir."

Ren nodded.

"Sometime later today. No use wasting time getting it done."

"I'll coordinate with Phil, then." Crispin stood and left, taking his cup with him.

Spring came into the room a moment later and began cleaning up the coffee station.

"About the other day," he said. She blushed to the roots of her honey-brown hair. "Next time, don't let the person visiting intimidate you. You have my permission to tell them to wait while you come ahead and tell me what's going on." She nodded, staring at her hands. "Say what you're thinking."

"Um, well, I – I didn't think it would lead to a war."

Ren laughed, which startled her.

"It didn't lead to the war. That was already happening. We just hadn't declared it, yet. That's water under the bridge, anyway. So, I'm starting to delegate things and I need to know how this complex is fixed for food, water, beds, vehicles, fuel. Can you get me that information?"

"Yes. I think so. When do you want it?"

"Tuesday, about noon."

"Yes, sir."

She closed the door behind her. Ren thought she'd do just fine, and when the time came to let her know what he knew about her ... well, it would be the time of his choosing and that would probably work out for the best.

Toll Canyon

Pennsylvania

The trestle bridge cast bars of shadow and light down on the truck as they passed along it. The neighbor on the opposite shore moved his panel truck enough to let them pass through. There were already other vehicles waiting to go eastward. Bangor, Pennsylvania was a neat early American town touched with the beginning of autumn colors.

Julian chuckled to himself.

"Something funny?" Perry asked.

"The intertie. That used to carry electricity for hundreds of miles, providing power to millions of homes. Now it's just a giant erector set."

The reality of that was drilled home when Julian pointed out black scoring on several of the towers, evidence of flames. A pile of blackened timbers that had once been a house drew their attention to the left. Perry tried to concentrate on the golden autumn sunlight and not think about the people who might have died the night of the pulse.

He turned from the Belvedere Highway to Highway 611. The country to both sides of the highway was woods broken by intermittent homes and businesses, all built too close to the road in the way of times before automobiles.

"This is going well," he remarked.

Julian nodded. They'd only driven a few more miles, however, and rocky cliffs enclosed their route and a truck parked across the lanes prevented forward movement. Three men with semi-auto rifles at the ready fanned out around their truck.

"Sorry to do this, folks, but this is a toll route now. Looking for fuel or food."

"Cash?" Joseph asked from the cargo bed. It made sense that was his go-to position, but the time of money was rapidly fading.

"No, sir. Our families can't eat dollar bills. I see you got gas cans on the roof. For four of them, I'll call the toll paid."

"And, if we refuse?" Perry asked.

"You can back out and try to find another route but we aren't the only ones doing this."

Julian muttered a swear word under his breath. Perry rolled his window up and the conversation commenced.

"He's probably bluffing on the 'others have this idea' thing, but I don't like our odds of finding another route easily," Julian assessed. He'd been the one to gather the fuel cans and siphon the gasoline from dead cars, so his opinion mattered a bit more than anyone else's.

"He is bluffing about what others might do, but you're right, the map isn't in our favor," Perry added. "We need to get south to Highway 22 if we want to go west."

"So give him the fuel," Joseph said.

Perry looked at Julian because he'd grunted.

"Yeah. But don't give him the cans. We can get more gasoline, but we need containers."

Perry rolled down the window and told the highway robber what they were willing to do.

"That's fine," the head robber said. He conferred with his fellow pirates about which vehicle could use the fuel and Julian poured each can into the blocking truck's tank before putting the cans back on the roof. Three other cars passed from the west, having handed over fuel and food. They drove a mile before they pulled over and Julian put the full cans inside the camper shell.

"Next time, we'll not look so conspicuous," he explained.

"Why do you think there will be a next time?" Joseph asked.

Julian gave him an "are you brain-damaged" stare, so Katharine explained.

"Because people aren't good and they get worse when they start worrying about going hungry."

Getting back on the road felt anti-climatic, especially since the Delaware River continued to be at their left-hand side.

"Are you sure we're on the right road?" Katharine asked. "We seem to be going south, not west."

"It's rural Pennsylvania," Perry explained. "We'll be able to head west --." He slammed on the breaks as cars were parked in the road. Julian went forward to investigate.

"One of those intertie towers fell across the road probably the night of the pulse. Maybe we can go through the field."

Perry didn't like that idea much, but they didn't really have a better choice and it looked like other people had been using a ad hoc route for the last few days, so he had the others walk so they could push if he got stuck. He almost did at one point, but managed to rock free of the rut and pull out on the other side of the jam.

Eventually, Getters Island appeared on their left and Perry wove around broken down vehicles to turn west on US 22, but it was with the cold knowledge that they'd traveled half a day and were no further from New Jersey than when they started that morning.

Great Commission in Vexing Times

Emmaus

Brad Snow stared at the Bible page in front of him, trying to pray. His thoughts hit the ceiling and bounced back into his head, unheard. Really, what was there to say? *God help us. Help me to help my community.*

Beyond the door of his office, he could hear Emmaus Road Baptist Church beginning to fill up. The apocalypse was a great marketing plan. Last Sunday had been lower attendance than usual because folks had gone to fight the corn field fire, but Wednesday had been overflowing with people who hadn't darkened the door in decades. He'd not been here after 911, but he supposed it had been like that then, folks shook to the core, looking for words of solace. He'd tried to give them what they wanted, until the lights went out—and stayed out.

What word did God have for what they were going through? He surely didn't think this passage was the right one, and yet ... it was all he'd been given.

Ellen tapped on his door. When he didn't answer, she opened it.

"It's time, and it's a full house."

"I've got nothing."

"Since when has that ever stopped you?" Her waist-length braid was pulled over her left shoulder, dark against the light fabric of her dress. "I'll do what I can on the piano. Rob and Jacob Delaney brought their instruments. That'll help."

"Maybe we can just do another praise service." A forlorn hope. Ellen put a hand on his shoulder. "My God, why is this happening?" She didn't move. "I haven't felt this lost since the supply depot in Kabul."

"How fitting. Maybe after the service, you should talk to someone who would understand. Rob, maybe, or didn't Jacob serve in World War II?"

Brad heaved a big breath and let it out. Ellen went out the door. Brad bookmarked the passage and followed her. Rob had his guitar and Jacob had his fiddle. Donna, the organist, had died in the City Hall disaster. The pianist, Charlotte, had been traveling with her family when the bombs went off. Nobody knew where she was, or if she was.

Rob led them in songs like, "There's Power in the Blood" and "Sweet Sweet Spirit." He made a plug for folks who could to give to the church so that people wouldn't go hungry or freeze. They needed donations of bedding and clothes for the refugees from the commuter and roadway. If folks had homes that could take someone in, they ought to. Then, it was Brad's turn.

"God has given Me all authority on heaven and earth and, I say to you, you are going make disciples of
all nations, baptizing them in the name of the Father and the Son and the Holy
Spirit, teaching them to obey everything I have commanded you. And remember, I am with you always, to the end of the age."

It was literally standing room only, with people even in the usually-deserted balcony. It was a horrible time to choke on the sermon.

"I have no idea why God gave me that passage. We're not in an evangelical mood. Well, I know I'm not right now. I don't understand what has happened to our country or why we're going through this. I want some payback. And, when I ask God for guidance, I get the Great Commission—three times in two different Bibles."

They chuckled. Dell Conopher was actually here in church. His wife attended regularly. Kix sat slouched down on the end of his spine trying to hide in plain view, having not darkened the door of the church since he was ten. James and Jon Vance were there by themselves. Trisha was probably with David at the clinic, allowing Marnie Callahan—Marnie Delaney—to be here. Near the back row were a couple of Jason Breen's men with the tawdry women they called their "ole ladies". It was a passing miracle, and under ordinary circumstances, he would have pumped it for all it was worth.

"I don't have a sermon. My soul is poured out; I don't have an overflow today. Let's turn this into one of Noah's studies and get a little interactive. What does this passage mean to you?"

People stared at him. They weren't used to an interactive time during services. Brad struggled with the terror any preacher felt when he tried something new and saw blank faces staring back at him.

"I'm feeling challenged." Jacob Delaney had done his time in the pulpit during the two years it had been empty before Brad got here sixteen years ago. He'd filled in occasionally since. A thoughtful man, well educated in a classical sense. "We managed to hang onto the food, but it's not enough for all of us to make it through the winter. And, losing power means there are probably other people coming who will want what we have. They aren't evil people. They're hungry and desperate. How do we tell them we can't help and yet fulfill the Great Commission?"

A crater opened in Brad's chest as he realized he had nothing to say.

"Did the early Christians allow their children to starve in order to feed strangers?" Brad didn't know her name. She'd come off the commuter and she was some sort of a nurse. Very pretty and very dark. Looking at her set off memories of the Middle East and yet her English was perfect, her idioms American. She must have been a stranger to pretty much everyone in this room two weeks ago.

Now everyone was looking at him and he still had nothing to say.

"They were very generous among themselves." Alex Lufgren had his arm around Keri who looked like she'd not slept. "I think people sometimes went hungry to help a faraway church. But there wouldn't be a lot of Christians if they'd starved to death."

"They clearly opened their arms to newcomers." Mae Osimowitz looked smart in a nice dress and hat, the only hat in the congregation. "Paul took them to task for segregating within the congregation. But, Paul wouldn't have lived very long if he'd given away his tents."

"You have to wonder how much longer it took him to make those tents since he was talking to people in the marketplace about Jesus." James Vance was far too young for the adult responsibilities he'd acquired at his father's death.

Rob Delaney nodded.

"You have a point. He gave the gospel, but he didn't defraud himself the proceeds of his labor."

"I'll trade with anyone who has what I need and wants what I don't." Alex Lufgren stood and looked around the congregation. "I've said that for my neighbors, but I'll say that for strangers walking by the town."

"And what happens when people have nothing." Brad didn't know that middle-aged woman either. "Are you going to let them starve?"

"I can't feed the whole world. I'm not going to let my sister or in-laws starve because someone walking by needs food. But that doesn't mean I won't feel bad about that."

"Where does the Great Commission come into it?" Sharon Laughlin sat with her new foster son, who didn't look uncomfortable with church.

"We're going to provide water." Rob smiled at Jazz Tully who blushed. "It's not enough, but it's something and it won't hurt us to do that. And we can try to share our beliefs with people. Hopefully, it will help them on their journey."

"It doesn't say, 'feed everybody wherever you go'." Dell Conopher had a worn leather Bible open in his big hands. "It says, 'make disciples, teach them what I have commanded you.' Jesus fed folks, but He didn't feed the whole world. He also said the poor would always be with us. The best estimates are that 50% of us will be dead of starvation, cold, and disease by spring. That number gets worse if we give away the food we have now."

"What if we want to?" Jon Vance was a thinker for one so young.

Silence descended over the room. Keri Lufgren wiped a tear from her cheek before she spoke.

"Then, that's your choice. But, you'll endanger the town, because if they know you have food they'll assume the rest of us do. And, I know my brother would not be out building walls if there wasn't a credible threat from more people than we can easily fight off if they really want in."

"So, you're saying these people walking away from the cold are just like the USDA?" Jacob looked skeptical.

"How is it different?"

Jacob opened his mouth to answer, then closed his lips and shrugged, shaking his head, looking sad.

"What do you think, pastor?" Dell Conopher actually addressed him respectfully. That deserved a response which the Lord totally provided to his completely blank mind.

"I think it's an impossible choice that must be made with your individual understanding of scripture, while recognizing that your actions affect your community. There's nothing wrong with generosity. That's a God-appointed gift. But, find a way to do it that doesn't draw a target on the town. Recognize that if you give your food away early, your neighbors are under no obligation to feed you later—which doesn't mean they aren't allowed to."

By unspoken consent, Jacob and Rob lifted their instruments and played "Just a Closer Walk with Thee." Nobody came to take Brad's hand and say the "Sinner's Prayer", but two dozen people came to kneel at the steps of the choir platform, entreating God on personal matters. Twelve verses later, Brad prayed the last prayer and people began to file out the door.

Noah Lufgren met him as he was headed to his office. His wife Barbara accompanied him. She was hard of hearing, so her voice wasn't pretty, but she could speak understandably and understand when people talked, so she acted as interpreter between them.

"Did your folks want to talk about what would Jesus do in this circumstance?"

"They did. I let them talk it out and come up with their own answers."

"Me too. We have a plan. I wanted to tell you about it."

Coming Home

Sharon Laughlin rolled up to the garage she'd built herself fifteen years ago and hit the garage door opener. The boy, Danny, waited silently as the door closed and she shut off the engine.

"Are you hungry?" He nodded. "Come with me."

She'd left the windows open in the breezeway where her herb garden scented the air. She plucked basil on the way to the kitchen she'd remodeled a decade ago. She'd taken the cabinets down to bare wood, stained them and discovered a nice wood pattern in the honey tones, which set off the dark slate-look countertops. She loved to cook and often had friends over for a meal just to make the effort worth it.

"There's the pantry. There's jars of spaghetti sauce and noodles."

She lifted a clove of garlic and an onion down from the basket over her chopping block and reached for one of her chopping knives.

"You seemed to know your way around the Bible this morning."

"My grandma'd make us all go every Sunday."

"Sounds like someone I'd not get along with, but you'll be going with me for now."

"I'm not objecting. I had a lot of time to think in that cell."

"I expect you did."

"There's like five different kinds of spaghetti sauces here. You got a preference?"

"No. I thawed a package of ground beef. It's in the tray beneath the meat keeper."

He got it out for her after setting a jar marked "cheese" on the counter. He didn't know about farm work, but he'd done what he was told yesterday and fallen into bed right after dinner. He'd gotten up when told to and helped her gather eggs, though he was clearly afraid of the chickens. She had three nanny goats, but she'd let the cows go years ago.

"After we've eaten, we'll set up that room of yours. It needs a good sweeping out and there's no reason it needs to look like a cell. I've got plenty of quilts and sheets."

"Thanks. Do you don't have a husband?"

"No. This farm is getting a bit much for me, so having your help will be welcome."

"There's not a lot of food in this pantry."

"Of course not. If I'd not hidden it, the USDA would have gotten it. Tomorrow, we'll bring it all up here where it belongs. We can make it to spring and then, well, we'll see."

While she talked, she crushed garlic and stripped the peel off, dropping the mince in the warming olive oil in her favorite sauce pan. She pulled out another knife and suggested he chop onion.

"Do you miss your family?" she asked.

He didn't speak right away. His knife paused for a moment.

"The army shot my uncle outside Denver. I guess my grandma died in Chicago."

His eyes started to glisten, and he sniffled. Onions did it every time.

"What about your parents?"

"I never knew my father. Just my mother's baby-daddy. She was in prison for killing her pimp the last I knew. My grandma though …." Tears ran down his cheeks. "And my uncle."

"Good man?"

"Yeah. He could have ended up bad. Lots of men in our neighborhood do. But he got hit by a car when he was in high school and ended up in a wheelchair. The guy had to compensate him, I guess. So, he went to college, became a teacher. We were in Denver so he could talk to this student group. I went along because sometimes he needs help to get around curbs and showers and stuff like that. I liked going with him. I got to see new places. We were talking about where I might go to college."

They hadn't really needed a whole onion, but that meant they'd have the other half in something else. Sharon dumped half in with the garlic and stirred.

"It's a vexing time. So many died. You know your uncle isn't your fault, right?"

"I could have...I was too far ahead. But, if I'd been back with him...."

"No. I know it feels like that, but a kid with a revolver against the army was never going to work out for you."

She patted him on the back and reached for the spaghetti sauce.

"How are you at opening jars?"

She handed it over to him to open. It wasn't that she couldn't do it herself, but that he needed to feel competent.

"I killed a man, you know?"

"I know."

He handed her the opened jar.

"Do you think God's going to punish me for that?"

"I think there are consequences when we do something like that and that, maybe, the biggest consequence is a victim-shaped hole in your conscience that's probably never going to go away." He nodded. "There's a big white pot in that cabinet over there. Fill it three-quarters of the way with water and put it on the back burner."

He moved to do what she said. By the time he set the pot on the burner, she'd adjusted the gas to the flame she wanted.

"Do you like school?"

"Yeah. I was good. 'Straight-A's get scholarships', my grandma would say. I guess that won't matter now."

"Who knows what's around the corner? I like books. Turned my parents' bedroom into a library. Starting tomorrow, I'm going to assign you to read some of those books and tell me what's in them. And, we'll find lots of practical math problems."

"Like home schooling?"

"Exactly. A straight-A student shouldn't stop learning just because the apocalypse happened."

He snorted. She laughed. They were going to do just fine together.

An Uneasy Alliance

Shane and Andrew were still talking about defenses when Andrew's oldest boy, Josiah, came in the back door to announce Dan McAuliff was a few minutes behind him. Shane itched for the 9 mm he'd tucked into Rocket's saddlebag, but he forced his mind to be calm. Andrew was armed, and though he didn't act like he expected trouble, at a nod from him Rebecca Bennett shooed their daughters out of the house and then withdrew herself.

Dan looked older as he came into Andrew's living room and a little wary as he held his arms out to the sides to let him check him for weapons. Dan started speaking before Andrew was even done.

"Save me the whole 'I'm sorry, I didn't know' speech. You did it, and there's no taking it back."

"Yeah. I was wrong. Maybe ...."

"No, we're not playing that game. This crap is what I said was going to happen, and it did. There's nothing we can do to change that or give either of us back the last five years, so ... best scenario: one-quarter of this town starves to death by spring." Shane nodded, dumbfounded. "You and I don't have to be friends for me to care about that. Worst case scenario, your northern neighbors overrun this town, take all your corn and you all starve to death by Christmas. Except us, of course. We have a hardened silo behind high fences that can be electrified."

Shane didn't think his expression gave him away. Daniel must have read his mind.

"They're coming already, aren't they?"

"They will be, yeah. I'm wondering how you know that."

"Human nature is sadly predictable." Dan sighed, as if it did indeed sadden him. "So, you need think of how you plan to keep tens of thousands of people from coming in and making a bad situation into a deadly one."

"We're going to barricade the roads and direct them around us. The fields are already barb-wired to keep out deer."

"Deer aren't people. People are smart, downright cunning. Barbed wire will keep some out until others figure out how to cut it, and then it isn't going to keep anyone out."

"Plan B is to hose down the first arrivals and hope the others are too scared to climb over the dead bodies."

"You served in the military?"

"I was a contractor."

"A mercenary?"

Shane nodded.

"I'm going to guess your father and grandfather are really reluctant to build walls."

"Of course. I'm surprised you're not."

"I don't have a problem with communities working together to defend themselves. Patterson has an idea for that. It's audacious and it might work. If it does, you'd just have to guard the roads. That'll work until winter sets in. Even if you survive the zombie hoards now, you won't survive the winter."

"Some of us have a better shot at it than others." Andrew's attempt at humor fell flat.

"You're right. Those of us who don't sit on our thumbs have a better chance than others. How's that lady that owns the grocery store?"

Andrew and Shane exchanged glances before Shane replied.

"She's still 100% Huffy. Why?"

"Well, my folks need stuff, but we also have stuff. We're throwing in with Jason Breen to set up trade routes. Anders never sold our vehicles or pretty much anything else, so we're in good condition. If Mae's willing, we can help her stay in business and supply your town with needed goods."

"Is there a catch?" Shane asked.

"I doubt the government still exists or is in any position to come looking for us but, if they do, you have to protect us."

"I can't obligate my dad to that."

"No, but you can call him on the radio and give him the option. If you decline, we protect our own borders, maybe a few of our friends' and you all can go hang."

"How long is this deal good for?"

"What's your life worth, kid? The lives of your neighbors?"

Shane sat back on the solid wood chair, gaze on the checkered table cloth. He picked up his radio and keyed the mike.

"Click, you got ears on? Over."

After a moment, Click replied that he did.

"Can you relay a message to Rob? Over."

The relay system was annoying and took some time, but in the end, Rob agreed to the terms. Dan pulled a small brown bottle out of his jacket and asked for three glasses.

"I don't drink." Andrew brought two empty glasses and poured himself a glass of iced tea.

"And I'm not drinking that until I've seen you drink some and live several minutes."

Dan laughed, poured a finger into the tumbler and swallowed it down. He asked Shane where he'd been as a contractor and they had a bizarrely pleasant conversation until Dan poured a half-finger in each glass.

"To our future collaboration."

Shane licked dry lips, considering the glass. Dan was still alive five minutes after drinking and showed no signs of discomfort. Might as well not be a wimp. Shane picked up the glass.

"To our future collaboration." They downed the mellow aged bourbon together while Andrew toasted with iced tea. It warmed Shane's chest. Dan held out his right hand.

"Kid, I wish I could say there are no hard feelings, but that's not true. Just remember that my forbearance comes at a price."

They shook hands. Shane nodded at Andrew and left the house, swinging up into Rocket's saddle and turning her head towards home. He couldn't quite shake the feeling of a sniper's rifle at his back until he rounded the far side of Mission Ridge.

An Unwelcome Visitor

Santa Fe

Alicia Sanchez poured a can of soup into a pan and set it on the stove. Magdala was no better, and she didn't know what else she could do. Remembering Dr. Perrin's advice, she thought it might be a good sign that her mother was still burning with fever, but there was the risk that the fever could kill her.

Pepe tapped his claws against the tiles. He wanted a treat and Magdala had laid in a generous stock, though Alicia would have to access the hoard pretty soon. With Magdala's bed over the access door, it might get a little complicated if she continued being sick.

"There you go, boy."

He gave a little bark and then someone knocked on the door. Alicia swept Pepe into the bedroom and peeked through the muslin curtains to see Ron Bannon of FEMA on the porch. That couldn't be a good sign.

Mike had insisted that she take a concealed carry weapon before he left her. The belt had already grown too tight, so she'd slid the gun into a drawer. She pulled it out now before she opened the door, blocking it from opening too far with her foot

"Hey, hey, hey."

She stared at him. Her standard response to creepers like him was "no, no, no," but she didn't want this to turn ugly. "Do you need something?"

He held up a prescription bottle, shaking it back and forth.

"I brought antibiotics."

"Which won't work against a virus. What do you want?"

"Just to spend time with a pretty lady."

She sighed.

"No, thanks. There's lots of other women who would be glad to give you whatever you want in exchange for whatever useless thing you can offer them."

"Hey, I gave you an extra ration card."

"For grocery stores that are cleaned out and locked up. Thanks for that. I'm sure it'll be so helpful. Now go away."

She moved to close the door, which he tried to shove open. She brought the semi-auto around from her back and he pulled back, surprised.

"Go away," she insisted. Now she closed the door, throwing the deadbolt. Leaning against the door, she felt her baby move. Could they feel what was going on outside? It certainly seemed so.

Now she heard Magdala hacking. Before she could deal with that, though, she heard something falling over on the patio. By the time she reached the opening to the kitchen, Bannon was leaping the fence into the alley. She bolted the backdoor closed and blocked the dog door.

"Alicia Sanchez, you are a stupid woman and you'd better get smart before it costs you your life."

New Family

Emmaus

Keri's hand still shook as she poured iced tea into four glasses. She'd had a rough few days. Alice set Lisa in the grass and they all sat down at the table off the back porch. The little girl pointed across the driveway, clapping her hands and saying "perro." Mocha and she had become the best of friends in the storm shelter during the first few days after the bombs.

"I never thought I'd be having this conversation with anyone." Alex took a bite of chocolate chip cookie and sipped some tea.

"Neither did we." Mark rubbed the back of his neck. "I honestly didn't think we'd stay anywhere long enough for him to get attached to a girl."

"But, you had the talk with him, right?" Alice's gut clenched.

"The 'use a condom' speech? Yeah. But that probably doesn't make Alex feel any better."

Alex's fair skin flashed bright red now.

"Poppy says nothing's happened and I believe her, but ... I think they both want something to happen."

Mark nodded.

"So, what do we do?" Keri moved her glass around with her fingertips. She'd overdone the sugar.

They all stared around the circle.

"Chastity belt?" Alex managed to laugh as he said it.

"Saltpeter." Alice playfully slapped Mark on the shoulder.

"Birth control pills might be a more practical idea." Keri didn't have a child in the conversation. She could afford to be more practical.

"Does Marnie have a supply we could use?"

"I don't know, but we could ask her. What else can we do?"

"Tell him that if he gets her pregnant, he's going to have to raise a child in Apocalypse World."

They all stared at Mark, who looked perfectly serious.

"Do you think that would work?" Alice loved her son, but she wasn't certain she wholly trusted him. Boys his age were hormones with feet.

"It kept me from being a tomcat when Poppy was young." Alex blushed bright red again. "The idea that I would have two kids to raise with a stranger...yeah. I think it might work."

"I wasn't thinking it would stop them from ...." Mark blushed, too, though the Lufgrens couldn't tell because of his Coppertone tan. "I was just thinking that they're almost adults so they need to know the consequences. And, we need to recognize we can't control them."

"So, maybe the answer is birth control pills and a good discussion about responsibility." Keri finally took a sip of her tea as if a coda to her statement.

Alex sighed and nodded, taking her hand. Her smile didn't make it into her eyes.

"I wonder where they've gotten off to." Alice looked around and saw Poppy's bright blond head at the far end of the pasture. The shadow beside her was Pete. "Mocha, get Poppy."

The dog took off like a flash, sending goats running as he sprinted across the grass. It took several minutes for the teenagers to join them at the table. They came hand-in-hand, looking nervous.

"We've been talking." Alex signed while he spoke, this type of simultaneous communication so natural to him.

"We have too." Pete's sign was clumsy, but Poppy nodded. "Keri, could you interpret, please?" She nodded and moved her hands into neutral position. "I know you think you're keeping secrets from us, but he stinks at whispering." Alex frowned, then laughed. Of course, the child of Deaf parents wouldn't need to learn how to whisper growing up. "We haven't, yet, and we won't until she wants to ... So ...."

"We're not kids" Poppy said. *"I'm fifteen in November. Pete's fifteen in January."*

Alex sighed.

"No, you aren't. You could get pregnant and that's another mouth to feed at the worst time possible."

"We know that," Pete insisted. "It's why we're waiting. If this weren't such a bad situation, we'd probably have already. But, it's different now. We can't be kids. Alex, I've already asked her, and she's agreed. We'll wait

... try to wait. But if we can't ... then, I think we should get married."

Four jaws dropped. The teenagers were absolutely serious.

"You're awfully young to be making that decision." Alex's control of his emotions was admirable.

"You made that decision when you were eighteen-years old," Poppy said. *"We're not that much younger. And, Ms. Tully says people married younger back in the old days."*

"They did, but that doesn't mean you should be in a big rush now," Alice said.

"If we were in a big rush, we'd be asking to marry now," Pete said. "We're asking to be allowed when we stop being children."

Alex's face contorted. He held up his hands, and Poppy refrained from signing.

"Fine. You have my permission. Just ... don't be so rushed. Think about what you do."

This last part was for Pete.

"Yes, sir. Mom, Dad ...."

"Being an adult involves more than just having sex and getting married." Mark glanced to see that Keri was interpreting. "This is a world going off the rails and you risk bringing a kid into it."

"We know that, Dad. And, we will try to remember, but ... come on, guys. People married young back in those days because it was the only way they could keep from being stupid."

Alice wished she could talk to Poppy directly, but the language barrier stood between them.

"And you get that there's no running away if you get her pregnant?" Mark's eyes were on Pete's face. "You're responsible, and if you try to run away, Alex and I will find you and kick your ass."

Pete sighed and then spoke for himself, signing simultaneously.

"I know that."

"You don't get into each other's bedrooms until you're married, yeah?" Alex said, signing for himself. Poppy nodded immediately and Pete a moment later.

"And birth control pills," Keri suggested, speaking for herself.

Poppy nodded, then signed. "We won't until that."

Lisa howled with an elated laugh as Mocha licked her belly as she wriggled in the grass. Alice and Mark both went to get her.

"What do you think?" Alice asked in Spanish.

"I think we'll be grandparents by this time next year, but what are you going to do?"

Alice sighed and gathered Lisa to her. She had a few years before she'd need to make a decision with her little girl, but she supposed that there were worse things than Pete marrying a girl whose family were as nice as the Lufgrens.

She turned to her near-in-laws and announced her plan.

"I think it's time Mark and I learned sign."

Alex smiled and nodded.

"First sign. Family." He made A-okay signs with both hands, thumbs together, circling to pinks together. He indicated the whole group and then repeated the sign. "We are family."

It felt kind of like getting married.

Beware of Trolls

I70 east of Emmaus

Cai hummed. Mike didn't really object. Ric sang when he worked, too, and absolutely didn't care if it annoyed Mike. Cai hummed a tune Ric had also enjoyed. It had annoyed the heck out of Mike when Ric had done it, but it now intrigued him too much to frustrate.

"What is that tune?"

"Joyful, Joyful, We Adore Thee." He must have read Mike's expression. "Or Beethoven's 9th Symphony, Ode to Joy. Is that what he told you?"

"Yeah, except he didn't make it sound like a hymn."

"He wouldn't."

"He did say religion was real important to your folks."

"Yeah, but Shane's never cared about any of that. You?"

"I believe there's a god. I don't go to church, but I listened to *mi abuela*. She was always talking about Jesus."

"She a Catholic or …."

"No. She was some sort of … eh, Pentecostal, I think. They raise their hands and speak in something other than English or Spanish."

"Charismatic, sure. I used to fellowship with some in Lawrence."

"So, you folks do that?"

"Hand raising … some of us. Some Baptists might speak in tongues in private groups, but not in the church. It's considered disruptive. But we mostly believe the same things about Jesus."

"I remember that part, too. When I was a kid … I was a naughty little shit. Sorry."

"It's fine."

"So *abuela* says to me, 'You don't have to be good. Just talk to Jesus and he'll take the naughty away'." Cai stared at him. "So, I did. And, I was a pretty good kid until high school. Senior year, I just did stupid stuff and that led to stupider stuff and then I joined the Army. They kicked me out for a hot UA from the night before I left for basic. I couldn't go home and tell my dad I washed out, so I took a job with the Knights. When I finally went back home, my dad didn't care; he liked all the money I was making." Cai grinned, something in his smile reminding Mike of Ric.

"And your grandmother?"

"She said, 'You need to say that prayer again, *chico*.' But I didn't. Sometimes I think I should. She died last year and I think I won't see her again unless I get that right."

"If you sincerely prayed for salvation, then God still claims you, always …." Cai stared ahead. "What is that?"

The crossroads ahead was marked with a sign announcing "Harrisville". Someone had created a road block of junk cars piled up across the right-hand road and moveable barricades across the road in front of them.

"Keep cool," Mike ordered, easing his Glock onto his lap. "Eyes up. Don't make them nervous."

He rolled down his window as a stocky man in a ballcap approached.

"Howdy."

"Hi."

"Where you folks headed?"

"Northwest."

"What you hauling?"

"Supplies for the town we live in."

"What town is that?"

Mike didn't like this line of questioning and his hand tightened on his gun, but Cai pulled out his wallet and a badge.

"I'm a deputy sheriff for Emmaus. We're just trying to get home."

The fellow in the ballcap squinted at the ID.

"Delaney. You Rob's kid?"

"I am. Cai."

"I'm Cory Ledlow, mayor here. We heard things got bloody over that way when the USDA came through."

With the attention on Cai, Mike scanned the barricades and counted at least six rifle muzzles.

"I don't know about that. I was in Hutchinson."

"That explains the bruises. This fellow your helper or your jailer?"

"Mike is actually a friend of my brother. He's just helping me out. You guys heard about Hutchinson?"

"We've had people headed that way looking for people who were taken. They never got here. I guess because the towns to the west fought back. The USDA got their butts kicked over that way." That sounded like something Ric would be in the center of. "One of their trucks rolled up on the Interstate Wednesday night with a hole in his gas line. He said a town attacked them. From the looks of his cargo, they cleaned out a whole bunch of pantries. I can't argue with their gumption."

Gumption? These folks had some fun ways of talking.

"I hate doing this, but we can't let you into our town and, with our roadblocks, there's only two ways to go: back the way you came or up onto the interstate."

Mike scanned the signs.

"That's an off-ramp."

"Yup. There's a pileup we haven't had time to clear on the west-bound onramp. But there's no real traffic on the Interstate. Ain't a whole lot of vehicles still running."

"Well, thanks for the heads up." Cai's expression said it was time to go.

"Thanks, man," Mike said. He slipped his gun under his thigh before putting the truck in gear and doing what felt incredible wrong.

“How many guns did we have pointed at our heads while we were talking?” Cai asked.

“Half dozen. Makes sense. With what FEMA was doing, these towns learned not to trust real fast.”

Mike stared at the bottom of the off-ramp, what he knew warring with reality.

“There’s no cars on the Interstate. It’s been shut down by the military. If we get up there and drive, we can make Emmaus in a few hours. And, going west in the eastbound lane isn’t a problem, if there’s no traffic.” It felt all kinds of wrong to drive up the off-ramp, but the divided highway was deserted except for a few broken down FEMA, military and USDA trucks. Mike stared down the long road, a lump in his throat.

“This is like one of those movies. You know, the end-of-the-world ones.”

Cai nodded. Mike turned west. He couldn’t sustain the speed limit because of obstacles, but he figured he’d make a respectable 40 mph the rest of the time. Maybe ten miles on, he was slowing to get around a grouping of vehicles when he smelled it.

“What is that?” Cai pointed to the white vapor coming out of the hood.

"Crap," Mike hissed, slammed the truck into neutral, grabbed the fire extinguisher and dropped out of the cab. Flames shot up when he opened the hood. He sprayed them with the halon. Cai came up beside him.

"What happened?"

"Nothing good." Mike checked for any flames before indulging in a flurry of Spanish swear words.

"You done yet?" Cai lugged the toolbox to the front of the truck.

"Yeah. But we ain't fixing this. See those charred vacuum hoses? And I'm willing to bet every relay in the harness is at risk of shorting out."

"Why didn't Lawson catch this?"

"He probably did. Ric shot him. Why should he do us any favors?"

"Shane really didn't have any choice that night, but I could see where the guy would hold a grudge. Now what?"

The sun touched the western horizon. The Midwest had awesome sunsets, made even more stunning because the sky went over the horizon.

"That is the big question of the day. We need to lock up the load and go find another vehicle that can haul this trailer."

"How likely is that?"

"Not, but we gotta try."

"We've seen about three semis. Could we strip parts off ...?"

"I'm not a diesel mechanic. I know a few things, but I'm not Lawson. And those vehicles stopped when the EMP hit which means their electrical systems are probably fried. We need to find another working vehicle."

While he talked, Mike got a padlock out of the toolbox and locked up the rear doors. He remembered his *abuela* would always say to thank God for blessings. This didn't look like one, and he wasn't really sure anyone was listening, but he prayed anyway. Then he handed Cai one of the two AR-15s he'd brought along.

"You know how to use this?"

"I grew up in rural Kansas and the Arma Lite is the most popular hunting rifle in America. What do you think?" While he spoke, Cai checked the mag and sighted along the barrel at something down the highway.

"I think you need an extra mag."

"So, do we go together or does one of us stay here?" Cai slid the extra magazine into one of the pockets of the cargo pants.

Mike scanned the highway. In the scarlet hue cast by the sunset, he couldn't see anything moving.

"I'd feel better with someone at my back and we're not getting out of here without another ride, so we go together. You stay on my right and look forward and to the right. I'll handle the other quadrants. Yeah?"

They were near the top of an onramp and they paused at the railing to look out across the darkening landscape.

"See that?" Cai pointed at a light. "I'd guess that's a farm."

"So, light? Electricity?"

"Don't know, but almost every farmer I know that's stayed in business for any length of time has old trucks that should still be running. That rig still has a lot of diesel in it, right?"

"So maybe a swap?"

"Worth a try."

Mike grinned at his new partner and Cai's eyes narrowed.

"What? Am I reminding you of him again?"

"No. More like I'm wanting to follow your lead just like I wanted to follow his. You just seem to know what you're doing."

"I might have met a Kansas farmer or three in my lifetime, but I don't know squat about going through a war zone."

"Good thing I know that part."

Shadow quickly enveloped the onramp as the sun dropped in the west.

"After we get to Emmaus, what then?"

"I've got to get back to Alicia. Her mother is sitting on a good cache of food, so we can probably winter in Santa Fe. Getting there will be the hard part."

"Two women by themselves in this mess … "

"Alicia's got a good head on her shoulders, and her mother is as tough as nails, but, yeah. I don't want to be too long."

They neared the bottom of the ramp and Cai heard the scuff of a boot on asphalt. He swiveled the right and rear only to get clotheslined by a big guy in a hoodie.

Memories of Loves Past

Emmaus

This new stage in David Vance's coma had Trisha in tears. Yesterday David's eyes had been open and sometimes they seemed to track movement within their range. Today, he became agitated whenever anyone spoke to or touched him, flailing at them and moaning and groaning. Lila and Christiana tied his ankles to the bed frame while Marnie held his arms down until they could restrain those as well. Trisha wept while she nursed a bruise on her cheek.

Once restrained David calmed, breathing heavily, clearly tiring. Christina turned the lights down and he calmed further.

"Are you okay?" Marnie asked Trisha.

"He didn't break anything. Why is he doing that?"

"I'm only guessing without diagnostic equipment, but there's probably pressure on his brain. He's not responsible."

"Is he getting better or worse?" Trisha covered her mouth, holding back a sob.

Marnie had only ever seen Shane cry once … the day she'd told him he'd killed her sister and she never wanted to see him again. The resemblance was uncanny. Marnie knew the local gossip, but she thought there must be a closer relationship than Shane's great-uncle.

"The coma was the nadir. He's coming out of it. Yesterday, he was only moving his eyes and not responding to us at all. Now he's moving all four limbs and reacting … if inappropriately."

Her father, Jason, appeared at the observation window. Marnie motioned for him to go back to the lobby. David's eyes closed. Marnie peeled each eye open, checking his pupils with a pen light. She supposed they were lucky that was working. His right pupil was still a bit larger than the left one and a bit sluggish. The reflexes on his right side were reduced.

"I think we'll see more improvement in the next few days. I wish I could give you a better diagnosis and prognosis, but I just don't have the equipment."

Trisha nodded and moved back to the chair beside his bed.

"I'll stay," Christiana said.

"You're sure?"

"I am. You go get some rest."

The dark-haired girl shooed her out of the overnight room. The clinic had mostly ever had day patients, but two rooms had been installed 'just in case', and that was proving to be a Godsend now. Jason flipped through an ancient magazine when Marnie came out to the lobby.

"Maggie would love to see you," he said.

"I can't. I'm asleep on my feet. Take me home."

He shrugged and they walked out to his truck.

"Any word on Cai?"

"No." She sighed. "Shane's not telling me something, I think."

"You mean from the secret source of information?" She nodded. "At least he's telling us about the threats to the town."

"How's that going?"

"It's amazing what farmers can do when they put their minds to it."

"Isn't that using up a lot of fuel?"

"We'll get more. I've got crews out looking for whatever we need."

"Where and how?"

"Don't ask me no questions, I'll tell you no lies." She didn't like the sound of that. "I told them not to kill anyone or steal stuff, but if it's unguarded ...." He shrugged.

"Jesus," she whispered.

"Now don't go invoking your imaginary friend. If he doesn't want us to do these things, he should give us what we need."

They rode in silence all the way to the Delaney house.

"So, how long will you stay here if he doesn't come back?"

"They're my family, too, now." She slid out of the truck and went into the house without looking back. Jason didn't bother with nostalgia. He backed out of the driveway and was gone before she let herself in the back door.

The house echoed quietly. She grabbed a flashlight from the window shelf inside the door. Shane's door was open and Belle stared at her from the pillow, eyes glittering red in the light beam. Jacob's door was closed and so was the master bedroom. Jazz came out of Keri's room, wrapped in a robe, carrying a hurricane lantern. She stopped when she saw Marnie.

"You can have the shower." She turned back to Keri's room.

"We could share it." Jazz turned back toward her, perplexed. "That came out wrong. If we each keep our shower short, there should still be hot water for whenever Shane comes home. You can have it first since you're ready."

"Thanks."

Marnie rubbed her aching feet while she waited. The left side of her back cramped. Pregnancy really wasn't that pleasant. She identified the awful smell in her room as the orange sitting on the dresser. Jill was looking out for her, but it was making her gag. She met Jazz in the hallway.

"Want an orange?" She really didn't give Jazz a choice of answer. "I hope it tastes better than it smells."

Jazz frowned, but she took it. Marnie had been right. There was still hot water when she finished. Jazz, now dressed in sweat pants and a tank top, petted Glister's belly on the landing. Marnie could still smell that orange. Gagging, she saw it on Shane's nightstand. She closed the door.

"You're pregnant, aren't you?" Jazz straightened from the dog. Marnie sighed. No use denying it.

"I don't want to tell everybody before Cai gets back."

"Okay by me."

"How'd you know?"

"That orange smells delicious."

"Pregnancy is weird."

"That's what my mother used to say to her midwifery clients."

"Anabel Tully. Dr. Vashon used to talk about her."

"I'm sure not fondly."

"No." Marnie laughed. "I wish she were here. I'd put her to work. Want to come in and talk?"

Jazz settled into the wing chair. Marnie began to comb out her hair. She was out of conditioner, so there were more tangles than usual.

"Why'd you give the orange to Shane?"

"He's a good guy."

"Not really. He might have been, but nowadays, he's a good guy when he's on your side."

"What happened to you two?"

Marnie worked out a knot before answering.

"We should have ended in high school, but he's not written that way. I cheated on him several times in college and he always forgave me." She dropped a small bundle of hair into the trash can. "Cai got my sister pregnant ... well, someone got her pregnant. There's question as to who, but Cai was going to marry her. But, she told Shane that he might not to be the daddy. He told Cai."

"That sounds so unlike Shane."

"Why she told him and not anyone else, I don't know. Who knew Shane had a higher ethical standard for his family? Cai dumped her. Marie asked Shane to take her to Denver for an abortion. They say that's a simple procedure, harmless to the mother, but it isn't always. She got really depressed afterward and she jumped off Wolf Creek water tower the day she was supposed to marry Cai."

"Oh, God! That's awful! I'm so sorry!"

"I'm over it. Probably something wrong with me that I stopped crying eventually. But at first, I blamed Shane. I hated him for a while there. Maybe I would have relented a bit if he'd hung around, but he blew out of town a few weeks later and never came back."

"But you don't still love him?"

"I don't know that I ever loved him, not the way he loved me and not the way he deserved. We were comfortable. We knew each other too well."

"Keri said you were friends even in elementary school."

"He never went through the 'girls have cooties' stage and, even then, he was incredibly charming. I can understand why you give him citrus fruit."

"But you don't think it's a good idea."

Marnie began braiding her hair. Jazz fluffed her own curls, separating them as they dried.

"Something's changed inside him. Something really dark. And, truth be told … I think his heart belongs to someone else."

"What do you mean?"

"It's just a feeling. He's loved someone else and I don't think he's over it yet And I don't want you to get hurt. Something is broken inside Shane and I don't think you want to be the one to dive deeply into his dark recesses to fix it. A girl could really end up damaged that way."

Jazz rose to peek out the front window.

"He's home. Thanks for the advice."

"You're not going to take it, though, are you?"

Jazz hesitated as she was turning toward the door, and then closed the door behind her. Marnie heard her and Shane speaking in the hallway. Jazz was making an offer and Shane was accepting. Marnie sighed. Maybe Jazz wasn't wholly a lost cause, because she ended up in Keri's room and Shane in his, leaving Marnie to wonder what sort of thorn was lodged in Shane's heart that he could ignore a girl like Jazz.

What Shane Would Do

I70, 30 miles east of Emmaus

Cai rolled over on his side, drawing breath into his compressed lungs. The effort seared pain through his chest. He remembered the sound of an AR splatting three times and then a grunt. Up above on the ramp, he could hear voices speaking harshly and Mike sounding half-strangled in response. Cai gained his knees and reached for the fallen AR in the weeds. Nausea rolled through him as his left shoulder popped ominously, but the pain eased as he gained a full breath and his head cleared.

"...like a stuck pig. You ain't carrying no money. Where you coming from?"

Mike's answer, stronger now, was prosaic. Cai crawled over to the guardrail he vaguely remembered flipping over.

"You gots to give us something for saving your life."

"We ain't fooling, man." Mike cried out as one of them punched him. Cai had to take action and the question came again: What would Shane do? He thumbed off the safety and stayed low to the railing. They weren't looking in his direction, so he had time to decide what to do.

Mike sagged against the other railing, something dark and wet seeping down his shirt and pants as three men in watch caps and dark hoodies harassed him. Not seeing any guns was reassuring. One of the men used a hand to probe in Mike's wound and Mike stifled a scream.

"Hey! Cut it out!" Cai hollered, bringing the AR 15 up to his shoulder while keeping his body behind the barricade. This technique always worked for Shane in paintball. "Back away from him!"

"I thought you checked him."

"He wasn't breathing."

"Look, man, we're just trying to get by just like you."

"I'm not mugging people under bridges. You need to get walking in that direction." They looked where he pointed, but they didn't move. "Now!"

Cai heard the movement to his left and he turned without hesitation, aiming high to spray rounds above the fourth man's head. All four turned and ran in the direction Cai had indicated, leaving Mike and his AR 15 leaning against the railing.

"Damn. Stabbed."

Cai pulled up Mike's shirt to see a large gushing gash in his lower left abdomen. He set down the AR to strip off his own shirt. Mike immediately picked the rifle up, scanning the road where their assailants had disappeared. Cai bundled his shirt up neatly, pressed it over the wound and told Mike to hold it with his free hand while he stripped the mercenary's belt to use as a cinch. Mike growled in pain. Cai saw movement the way he'd sent the four men running, snatched up Mike's unattended rifle, thumbed off the safety and pumped two rounds into the air.

Mike blinked at him, perspiration glistening on his dark brow.

"We're in so much trouble." And then he laughed. That seemed like an abnormal response, but he'd seen that crazy twinkle in

Shane's eyes a few times during the early days after the bombs.

"This isn't going to hold you, but it should slow the bleeding. We need transportation now!" Cai looked around at the cars pushed off on the shoulders. Nothing looked old enough to be hotwired, assuming he could remember what Shane had taught him back in high school.

"How far's that farm?" Mike wiped sweat off his upper lip, leaving a smear of blood instead.

"Probably too far."

"We gotta try or I'm going to bleed to death right here. Help me up."

Mike took the other rifle in his left hand and Cai supported him. They wobbled down the road toward the crossroads that would take them in the general direction of where the light had been. Cai felt momentarily smart that he'd not sent the four muggers in that direction, but the fact was it had been complete happenstance.

"Stupid. Ric woulda been suspicious of the underpass."

"Sorry I'm not him."

"You're a lawyer. I'm the big bad mercen --." Mike doubled over in pain, panting heavily. Cai scanned the darkness nervously. "We gotta keep moving." Cai braced him again to get him upright. "Man, this hurts. I know you hum. You sing?" Mike's feet dragged.

"Yeah."

"Sing something. Ric used to sing on night patrols. Anytime where it wasn't silence."

Cai's mind went blank, so he seized on the last song he'd sang, a horrible choice for scuttling through the darkness. It required a lot of breath control to sound good. Instead of a blow against the darkness, it sounded like a flickering flame in a sea of black.

"When peace like a river attendeth my way. When sorrows like sea billows roll ...." Cai scanned the darkness again. He heard something in the darkness. An engine. "... It is well with my soul." *No, no it wasn't.*

Mike collapsed to his knees. Cai propped him against a tree outside a barbwire fence. His own pantleg was damp with Mike's blood.

"What is that song?"

"It's a hymn, my go-to comfort hymn. The other night when I was in that connex, it was cold and I wasn't sure they weren't going to execute me in the morning. And then there was this woman, she was in the connex next door. And we sang it together. It helped both of us face the morning."

Mike squeaked as Cai tightened the cinch.

"That was a dream, you know? There were no women in the connexes. They had a different use for that crowd."

Cai scoffed.

"I talked to her."

He could feel the smile fading from his face as Mike shook his head.

"*Mi abuela* would say angels are all around us." Mike sighed. "I'm not making it to that farmhouse. You need to leave me here and get help."

"I can't do that. If they come back ...."

"I'll shoot them, at least until I lose consciousness. You can run, get help, come back. It'll be good."

Cai opened his mouth to protest, but a flashlight beam swept them. Cai whipped around with the AR15, but Mike deflected the barrel to the sky.

"Don't shoot our rescuer, esquire."

"You folks okay?" The man behind the flashlight sounded older than Cai but younger than Jacob, with the cadences of Kansas.

"My friend was attacked by some people. He's bleeding."

As Cai said that, Mike slumped against him.

Farmer Henry Beach called his son, Calvin, out of the shadows, told Cai to cover them while they dragged Mike around to the farm house. Along the way, Cai told them the Cliff-notes version of what had happened.

Henry's wife met them at the door and they carried Mike into what was probably normally a den. After Calvin and a teenage girl brought electric light into the room, she examined Mike's wound and opened an extensive first aid kit to try to mend him. Henry drew Cai out to the kitchen, which was lit by a lantern.

"What were you doing out there in the dark before you were attacked?"

Cai explained what had happened in Hutchinson and how they were taking supplies to his hometown when their truck caught fire.

"I guess luck is not your super power. We'll deal with the truck in the morning. Emma will let us know if she needs us."

Henry checked the kettle on the stove, poured some water into tea mugs and the rest into a bowl with soap and a wash cloth.

"The wind turbine's working, but our battery backup was affected by the surge. I can't heat water enough for a shower, but if you want to take this into the powder room there, you can get cleaned up.

Cai thanked him for his generosity and turned to the bathroom.

"We have to stay human through this," Henry said. "If we give into the darkness, we've let Satan win."

Cai nodded, but that seemed inadequate. "Amen."

Community Outreach

Wichita

"Sir, where do you want to go?" Phil asked as Ren buckled in. Two Knights knelt in the pickup bed, but Ren had insisted on a small detail. Crispin wanted to object, but he'd agreed Ren was boss, though he explained the risks.

"The fight is mostly quelled except for that group dug in at St. Josephs, but that doesn't mean there aren't still Army out there who would love to notch their belts with the leader of what they view as a resistance."

"How many people actually know who is in charge?" Ren asked when Crispin paused. He saw that Crispin recognized a point there. "I need to see what's going on out there, maybe talk to some of the people. I'm not going to do like Crystal and decide which neighborhoods are worthy of eating. At least, not until I've seen for myself what's going on."

And so, as the night deepened in the city, Ren asked Phil to drive to Murdock, McAdams, and Millair, the majority-black neighborhoods deemed expendable under Crystal's leadership. Phil worked his way around the roadblocks downtown. The lack of street lights cast a sinister air over the city; lingering smoke added to the creepiness. The streets in the main city were mostly deserted except for patrols of Knights seeking stray Army personnel. Ren had not called a curfew, and it didn't seem necessary.

Phil turned off onto 9th Street North.

"I heard there's a gathering at the cemetery in that area. If you want to get a pulse of these neighborhoods that seems like an appropriate place."

Phil slowed down well back from the bonfire amid the trucks gathered on the fringe of the deserted cemetery. To the left were frame houses under mature trees and people in lawn chairs watching the spectacle. Most of the crowd were black folks though, here and there, whites gathered in protective clusters. Everyone was armed, and all attention focused on a man standing in the back of a pickup spotlighted by lanterns and using a karaoke machine to boost his voice.

The man in the truck answered questions for the crowd. Apparently, he'd been speaking with a Knight or two and was now reporting to his community on what he'd learned, most of it true. Ren heard his own name a few times and that he'd wanted to get rid of the Army because they were pushing people around worse than cops.

Food, fuel, and the lights were the big concerns, and the man in the truck bed said something interesting: fend for yourselves. Folks were welcome to join the teams he was sending out to look for trade. Apparently, a women's committee was organizing the men. Ren could see their colorful headscarves on the other side of the bonfire.

"I'm grateful the Army's gone. Gonna take some time to figure out the logistics, but they weren't gonna feed us anyway, so it's good we can feed ourselves."

Someone said something from the crowd.

"Sullivan don't care about us none, so we should just go on our way. We'll figure it out better than some old white man can."

Ren laughed. The speaker was probably right. He didn't have a clue what this community needed.

"That's all I know for now. Let's have some music and celebrate that the storm passed us by. There'll be more storms tomorrow."

The speaker hopped off the truck and walked rapidly into the crowd. The lanterns around the truck extinguished one by one. Ren wrestled over whether to go out into the crowd and talk to people or just drive away when he felt the Knights in the back of the truck move. The speaker now stood about five feet away, hands in the air. Ren rolled down the window.

"… don't want to hurt the man. I just want to talk with him."

"Sir?"

"It's why I came down here." Ren opened the door and stepped out into the cool night air. Someone had struck up what sounded like a zydeco tune.

"Ren Sullivan."

"I know who you are. I'm surprised to see you here. The leader of Wichita comes to pay us a visit. Should I be honored or worried?"

"Neither. I didn't set out to be the leader of Wichita. I was just put in an impossible situation: let the Army take me into custody as a puppet or put a true puppet up in my place."

"Looks like it worked."

"I hope."

"We're good with it. LeBron Collier, by the way."

"Nice to meet you." They shook hands. "So, impossible situations tend to put people in power who don't have a plan for what to do afterward."

The twisting light from the bonfire played on Collier's features, but he might have smiled.

"I'm good with that. Don't need no white people telling me how to live my life."

"What about all the things your community needs to survive?"

"This is a working community. Most of us are tired of being on the white man's plantation. We didn't take hand-outs before and we aren't interested in taking them now."

"Good, because I have no idea what help I can offer. I would like to facilitate a meeting with the community leaders to see if there's something we can work out."

"Okay. When?"

"Can you get the word out for tomorrow?"

"Yeah. It takes longer these days without email, but sure. What time and where?"

"You tell me."

"First Hope Baptist Church, sundown."

"I'll be there."

They shook hands and then Ren told Phil it was time to go. All the way back to SullCorp, Ren replayed the conversation over in his mind. *"We tired of the white man's plantation. We don't need your handouts."*

"You okay, sir?" Phil asked as they pulled into the parking spot in the secure parking area at headquarters.

"Just thinking about how we do things differently going forward."

Phil raised an eyebrow, but Ren just said goodnight and walked away.

Hot Wire

Emmaus

Walking through the pearlescent dawn, Dan McAuliff approached where Rod Patterson knelt in the brush with a car battery and jumper cables and one of his impromptu apprentices. Jason Breen stood behind them and watched.

"Josh said you wanted to see me."

"I figured how to hot-wire the fence."

Patterson plucked some grass and tossed it into the chain link. It sparked and sizzled into carbon.

"Once I get it all set up, we'll have 360-degree coverage, so if the town can't control its borders, we have a fallback position that can."

"I don't think we want to kill anyone, though."

"I've seen lots of people bit by hot fences," Jason said. "Never seen anyone killed. We're doing this at my compound, too, and I'm having some of the ladies make signs that warn people not to touch. I can get them to make a few for your fence too."

"I'd appreciate it."

"Well, you didn't leave Josh behind in prison, so I probably owe you. Can you imagine how bad it got in there after the power went out?"

"I've thought about how you get electrically-actuated gates to open without power. I think it became a deathtrap."

Momentary silence descended between the three of them. Was it in honor of the people who would starve to death on the wrong side of bars? Nobody said. They all three knew the reality of those bars closing and not opening again.

"Now we've got to hope the town can hold their borders," Patterson said.

Jason snorted.

"What?" Dan didn't like the look on his face.

"Farmers, shopkeepers ... Shane and Stan can't be on every barricade, and there's a lot of open fields out there. That's why I'm electrifying my compound. Now if I can just convince Maggie and Marnie to come inside."

Dan stared at the fence for a long moment, plucked a handful of grass and tossed it into the toaster.

"Would this work on barbed wire?"

"Yeah. That's what they usually use it on, to keep cows and horses from busting the fences. What are you thinking?"

"How many batteries it would take."

Patterson's eyebrows shot up into his hair line and Jason snorted again.

Watercolor Morning

Eastern Kansas

Ami stretched and slid up against the door, sleeping bag still tucked about her. The cool dawn outside washed the world in watercolor pastels. One expected a riot of bird calls at dawn, but she heard only a few, a testament of what the world had gone through just two weeks before. Javi still slept in the back, feet tucked into the space between the driver's seat and that door, his arm flung across his face, his unshaven chin visible.

She eased out of the sleeping bag and pulled on her pants and shoes before stepping out of the car to relieve herself. Javi stood on the other side of the car when she turned back. They'd spent all day yesterday working their way around traffic jams and barricaded towns and had finally stopped for the evening in this wood somewhere northeast of Wichita. Javi had been exhausted, his eyes so sensitive to light he'd resorted once more to the blindfold. He looked less ragged this morning, though he wore the sunglasses.

"You want to figure out where we are? I'll make breakfast." He actually had a frying pan and they'd bought some eggs from a farmer yesterday. While she worked to retrace their route on the map, he mended up the fire they'd started last night and fried the eggs.

"Well?" he asked.

"We're near Emporia City, Kansas. There's a little road going through lots of small towns headed north. It'll get us to I-70, which that farmer said he'd heard was the clearest route west."

"I thought it was closed by the military."

"If the military is in as bad a shape as we are, they don't control the interstate any longer. How are your eyes?"

"Not so bad. Still sensitive to light, but better. I can mostly see. It's a little fuzzy in places."

She treated them before they left. The narrow road north led through small towns hardly more than crossroads. She slowed at a panel van half in the ditch and blocking the right lane. Javi had his hand on his gun, but a man's figure slumped over the steering wheel.

"We should stop."

"Why? I can't save his life."

"No, but that's a pharmacy truck and there's probably some fuel in that tank."

The man behind the wheel was dead and the shelves of the van were filled with medical supplies.

"What do you think killed him?" She did a quick examination while Javi climbed into the back.

"Stroke, maybe. That's just a guess. Probably last night. There's rigor." She watched as Javi found a roll of garbage bags and opened one wide. "What are you doing?"

"Drugs, pharma, first aid supplies. They're useful as trade items and they'll come in handy if we need to shop your skills."

"These belong to someone."

"Yeah, but finders keepers. Better we get them than someone else."

Ami stared at this Special Forces kind of guy, practical beyond measure and able to ignore little things like morality and the law. He made perfect sense. His eyes would have been easier to heal if she'd had antibiotics the night of the flash. She helped him fill two bags with supplies and they left the shelves bare.

"I wish we had a shovel."

"We don't. And really, we don't have time. We need to get to Emmaus, hopefully before they harden their borders."

"You think they will? I mean, Kansas is kind of flat. How do you harden borders in this country?"

"These other towns are doing it. They kept us out. And, I don't like our odds of me being able to explain why they should let us in at Emmaus."

"You've been there?"

"No, but I worked with a guy who was from there. He was young, but if that was how they raise them there, his elders aren't going to trust a guy like me."

He held out a hand to help her out of the van. She didn't really need the assistance, but she took it because she was flattered. He stowed the meds in the back and came back with a siphon hose and a gas can. They stood in silence while he listened to the sound of fuel running from one tank to another, switching to the gas can when the level dropped to where the transfer slowed.

Ami hated the thought of the pharmacy man dying alone like that, his family not ever knowing what happened to him. She offered a prayer to her aunt and uncle's god because she didn't know what else to do for him.

Javi poured the can into the tank and went back to siphoning. Three cans later, he'd gotten all the fuel from the pharmacy truck that he could. They got back into the car.

"What's the fuel level?"

"We're back to 80%."

"That's Emmaus. Let's go."

The sun promised it would be warmer later in the day. Ami knew she wouldn't even think about the man again and, while that bothered her, she also knew it was a survival instinct. Thirty or forty million people had died already. What was one more life in comparison?

Horse Trading

East of Emmaus

His bruised shoulder throbbing, Cai hadn't slept much and with the cold grey of dawn, the creak of a screen door had awakened him. Farmers had to get up a lot earlier than lawyers. He dozed for a bit longer until he heard something out front that made him sit up on the couch. From the window, he saw farmer Beach pull the truck into the driveway using a matched quad of draft horses. Cai pulled on his shirt and shoes and went out front to ask why he hadn't asked him to help.

"You don't seem like much of a farmer, and I figured I'd let you sleep. Emma was up two or three times last night checking on your friend. His blood type's wrong for an infusion from any of us and she's worried his wound's infected. You're sure you're O-positive?"

"Yeah. My wife is a doctor. She practiced cross-matching on me. I'm positive I'm positive." That lame joke earned a grin from Henry.

"So, we need to take your friend to a doctor. What medicine we have, we gotta keep for our kids. You understand?"

"Of course. Will you hang onto the truck for me so we can come back for it?"

"That's why I pulled it off the road, but I might have a better idea."

Cai waited.

"I got a big hay wagon. For that diesel and a cut of your goods, I'd haul you and your friend over to Emmaus using the horses."

"How long would that take?"

"Most of the day. You'd have to feed me when we got there, give me and the horses a place for the night and then I'd turn around to head home."

"I need to ask Mike. It's not technically mine to barter with."

Mike lay sweating and chilled on a daybed in the study. He swallowed convulsively as Cai explained the situation to him.

"What do you think?"

"I think it's worth it to get you to medical attention. Seems like 10% would be fair."

Mike nodded.

"There's a package in the cab. Don't forget that."

"Sure. I'll even grab your personal gear."

"I wish I could help with the transfer ...."

"You can't, not in your condition. You just lay there and let me take care of this."

"Man, you sound like him."

"We were raised by the same people."

Cai joined Henry in the yard. Although he'd have felt odd carrying a gun when children were present two weeks before, he now didn't even feel the urge to apologize. Henry and 17-year-old Calvin also carried.

After Henry lined them out, the kids—including the six-year-old—got busy packing boxes into the wagon he'd backed up to the truck. It didn't take as long as Cai thought it would. Like a lot of farm kids, the Beaches were used to hard work and accomplishing tasks as a team.

"I'll be back tomorrow night," Henry told his wife and oldest son as they got Mike settled in the wagon.

"You need to make haste, Henry. I don't like the look of that wound and I don't think he's got the strength to stand an infection for long." Emma didn't seem to be really concerned that her husband of twenty years was making a two-day journey and leaving her and the kids alone. Calvin, the oldest boy, had an AR15 strung across his back and a pistol in a shoulder holster. He looked ready to take care of things, if need be. Cai prayed the need would never arise.

"I've taken the team that far before, so I don't anticipate a whole lot of difficulty. Cal, shoot first, ask questions never. You hear me?"

"Yes, sir."

"And, Emma, you and Flannery need to both carry today and tomorrow too, just to be safe."

"We will. Now, we got cows to milk and eggs to gather, so you best be on your way."

Cai glanced back over his shoulder as Henry climbed into the driver's seat. Emma dashed a tear away. She wasn't as brave as she acted. Henry picked up the reins and barked "Hey-up, horses" and off they trotted.

A Desert Land

Santa Fe

With the arroyo and every tap dry, Alicia had burned through two gallons of gasoline and still had empty buckets. Disappointed, she headed toward home when she saw a man standing on the corner with a sign that said "free water."

She pulled up and asked him about it. He answered her in Sonoran-flavored Spanish

"My wife and I are heading to Mexico tomorrow, but we have a pool full of water … well, half full now. We'll give it to anyone with buckets to haul it away."

Alicia grabbed her buckets and filled them. She wished she had more than four to fill, but it was maybe a week's worth of water and she thanked him profusely.

"It's sad to see what is happening to this country," Manuel said. "Twenty-five years and it's just not safe to stay. There's no food, the water's running out. How will you manage?"

"My mom and I have it worked out, except for water. And you've given me an idea with the pools. This water will be drinkable by tomorrow, sooner if I filter it."

While storing two of the buckets in the kitchen, she saw the truck in the alleyway.

"Popi," she greeted as he came in the back door. They embraced.

"You pregnant?" Rodrigo Esquibel had no right to look disapproving.

"I got married beforehand."

"He here?"

"Mike was in Wichita when everything went crazy."

"Wichita?" her brother, Pablo, asked. "I thought you lived in San Diego."

"Nobody lives in San Diego anymore, and he was working."

"We're headed to Mexico," Rod said. "We just swung by to see if Magdala wants to come ... and you, too."

"I'm going to wait for Mike. Besides, Mami is sick."

“Sick. What do you mean?”

“She’s got some kind of crud. I couldn’t find a doctor, but I found antibiotics. She’s only been on them since last night so, hopefully, she’ll be feeling better soon.”

“Well, we need to get into the supplies.”

“She shouldn’t be moved, and her bed is over the entrance so nobody can find it.”

“*Dios mio,* but you women make it complicated. I’m going to go talk to my wife now.”

“Don’t blame me if you get sick.”

Alicia looked at Pablo.

“You going with him?”

“A bunch of us are going. You should come, too. You could leave a note for your hubby.”

“No. I’m an American. Never really had a desire to live in Mexico.”

Rod came stumbling into the kitchen, eyes large and wild.

“We’re going.”

“Popi, what is it?”

“She died. She looked right at me and said ‘The Devil take you’ and coughed up blood. You can come with us if you want, but I’m not touching that body and, if you stay, I won’t help you bury her.”

Alicia heard the last of his outburst without comprehension. She turned and ran to the bedroom, aware that Pablo tried to follow her but was restrained by Rod. Magdala was in bed, Pepe standing guard. There was a little blood on her lips and her eyes were unfocused, her temperature rapidly cooling. Pepe barked and growled. Alicia never heard the truck pull away.

Tears spilled down her cheeks as she angrily muttered invocations against the heartless bastard her mother had married. Overwhelmed with grief and frustration, she took her tears out to the garage to look for a shovel. She was just setting the spade into the backyard soil when Mr. Pacheco came to the back gate.

"I heard Rod and your brother talking. Are you sure she's dead?"

"Yeah. I know how to check pulse."

"I am so sorry, *mija.* Is there something I can do for you?"

"I could use some help burying her."

"Of course. I'll go get a shovel and be right back."

Out of breath by the time they finished digging the hole, Alicia didn't know how much help she was in lifting Magdala into the garden cart and pulling her out to the backyard. Pepe howled from the bathroom. Mrs. Pacheco came over and they said a few words and Mrs. Pacheco removed Magdala's rings and necklace before putting a tarp over her.

"She'd want you to have those, if only for the trade value."

Alicia stared at them in shock and grief, but a practical part of her knew the woman was right. She put them in her pocket. It was only after Magdala had been laid to rest that Alicia thought that her mother would have objected to the mess they had made of the yard.

"If you need anything, you let us know," Mrs. Pacheco said. Alicia nodded and sat on the patio for a bit as the day grew warmer. Only the need to pee drove her into the house.

There was a dark red streak on the toilet paper when she finished.

"No! No! No! No! Oh, God, please, no!"

Passing Slowly to the West

East of Emmaus

The interstate stretched before them littered with a few broken-down cars, but it was otherwise deserted. The quad of draft horses was in fine form today, keeping up a moderate walk. Cai didn't think he'd ever seen the countryside pass so slowly. It might have been an interesting phenomenon if he hadn't been so anxious about Mike. Funny how you could know a guy for only a few short days and now feel like he was your best friend. Mike's fever was spiking. He complained alternatively of being hot and cold.

Cai sat in the seat next to Henry Beach, rubbing his throbbing shoulder and trying not to scratch his peeling sunburn. He longed to be able to dive into a lake and just float for a day or two. Instead, he answered Henry when he asked what he'd been doing in Hutchinson.

"I was a slave." Henry frowned at him. "That's where it was headed, anyway. Army picked me up on vagrancy, which was a lie, but ...." Shrugging made his shoulder click again. "The unit at Hutchinson was using people as slave labor, raping women, abusing the men. Mike and his guys freed us."

"Just did the right thing," Mike said. "You should sing, man."

"I heard you singing last night," Henry Beach said. "Interesting music choice for scuttling through the darkness."

"I was scared, and that song makes me feel brave."

Beach grinned and launched into a rendition of "There's Power in the Blood." Cai joined him. Mike's eyes closed, making it hard to tell if he was listening. But how could he not?

As soon as they finished, Cai launched into a Rich Mullins favorite. *"Well, the moon moved past Nebraska and spilled laughter on them cold Dakota Hills, and angels danced on Jacob's stairs, yeah they danced ...."*

Henry nodded and joined in. *"There is this silence in the Badlands and over Kansas the whole universe was stilled, by the whisper of a prayer ...."*

The team wasn't moving fast, but it had the advantage of sixteen legs over the people walking along the road. Beach slowed the team to give the knot of about twenty travelers a wide berth. Mike's hand tightened on Cai's pants.

"They could stop us if they wanted to. Don't slow down."

Cai glanced at Henry who flicked his whip to encourage the freight horses to go a little faster.

"Hey, mister, you got some food?"

As soon as the man called out, others turned and reached for the wagon. The crowd included men, women, and children, even some family dogs, all walking along the highway, as if they thought it still went somewhere. Henry flicked the whip again and the horses broke through to the other side ... only to encounter a larger crowd in less than a minute. Now they were reaching for the wagon and catching their hands in the harnesses.

"Hey, let go," Henry yellowed. "You're going to get trampled."

"Stop. We need food."

"There's nothing for you here."

The horses were neighing and the wagon slowed.

"Do something, man, or we're dead," Mike advised.

Cai reached for the AR-15 at his feet and pumped five rounds into the air over the crowd. They flinched back, the horses started going faster and Henry encouraged them with his whip.

"Good God, this is turning into a dangerous journey."

"Where'd they come from?"

"I don't know, but I'm not stopping to find out. There's an even bigger crowd ahead. I'm getting off this interstate before we get stopped."

"There's a least two towns between here and Emmaus to get through."

"Yup, and I'll worry about them when we get to them."

Henry guided the wagon down an open offramp onto a deserted section of Old 24.

"How long before we get to Emmaus?" Mike asked.

"I don't know. It's hard to gauge with horses."

Mike licked pinched lips.

"Sooner's better than later."

"I know." The wagon passed another group of hikers, but this time they maintained enough pace to keep going.

"He's fading. We need to get him to a doctor as soon as possible." Henry steered the team around a broken-down car. "Next time, you can't hesitate. You understand."

"Yeah." Cai ejected the magazine and replaced the rounds he'd just expended. He'd put an extra mag in one of the pouches of the cargo pants.

"There's at least five mags in my go-bag," Mike whispered. "And, an extra service pistol with extra mags."

Cai unzipped the bag and found what he needed, filling pockets. The next crowd they encountered, Cai brandished the AR-15 and nobody grabbed for the wagon. He made eye contact with a woman pulling two children in a Radio Flyer.

"It's working," Henry said. "Just keep looking tough."

"I'm going to go to hell for this," Cai whispered.

"But not today," Mike assured him. "Not today."

Quality of Life

Emmaus

Lila spooned up some rice pudding and held it in front of David's open eyes. He blinked a few times but made no effort to open his mouth. Lila stroked his jaw and gradually it opened. She had to push it closed after scrapping the pudding off on his teeth and then massage his throat to make him swallow. Half of it seemed to drool out. She tried again while Trisha Vance wiped tears from her cheeks.

"I wish we had the means to look inside his head and maybe find a way to fix it, but I can't." Marnie wanted to blame baby hormones, but she knew the big hole in her chest was because she felt totally inadequate to this job. She hadn't become a doctor to lose so many patients in two weeks that it now counted as a victory when one of them couldn't walk or talk but was still breathing.

"I know." Trisha sniffled. "And I get that you can't keep him here. This isn't a hospital, you don't have the staff."

"Well, you have a couple more days, until he's eating reliably. And hopefully, there'll be more improvement."

"What can we expect?"

"I don't know. He's not talking and his right side is weak. I'm pretty sure it's a skull fracture. There could be a subdural hematoma, but he's getting better, not worse, so I'm not going to risk blind brain surgery."

"Why isn't he talking?"

"Comas aren't like light switches, either on or off. They're more of a continuum. Yesterday, he was not following commands or responding to yes-no questions, but today he's tracking movement and swallowing food. I can't tell you what's going to happen, but talk to him, take time, use gestures, pictures ... hopefully, he'll improve over time. One reason I want to keep him here a few more days is the paresis—the partial paralysis on his right side. Right now, it's pretty much like taking care of an adult-sized baby, but he should grow stronger over the next few days. And he's entering a phase of recovery where seizures might happen. We want to keep an eye on that, for now."

"So, it's Monday. You think by Wednesday?"

"Maybe as late as Friday. We'll take our cues from him."

Lila rolled David onto his side so he could puke in a bucket she'd placed beside the bed in anticipation of vomit. Marnie assured Trish that this was perfectly normal, even expected. David closed his eyes when Lila moved to feed him more. Tired or fed up, it was hard to tell. Trish went in to sit with her son while Lila joined Marnie in the hallway. Down the hall, they could here Gilly Hopkins groaning with labor pains and her husband trying to sooth her. Gilly called him a filthy name.

"This is our future," Marnie whispered, fighting back tears. "Sending people home with no way to get better."

"You can only do what you can do. And, hopefully, the world rights itself in the next few months so we get back the tools we need to do what we were trained for. Come on. Gilly's baby won't wait, and you *can* do something about that."

Marnie sighed and linked arms with Lila to face her next challenge.

Relieved of Duty

Wichita

The dozen men who had controlled the military occupation of Wichita came in under guard and solemnly sat down in the chairs around the table. Ren had chosen the school board conference room to make a point that he had no intention of pressing.

Except for Sergeant Wright, whose left arm was in a sling, the defeated commanders looked none the worse for wear. He'd asked the Knights to minimize the casualties and his inspections so far had found no atrocities.

These men had not seen each other since they left the field. They exchanged nervous eye contact among themselves while shooting concerned looks at the Knights, who took up position in the back of the room. Captain Armstrong stared at the table, looking like he was ready to explode.

"For the uninitiated, I'm Warren Sullivan, owner of SullCorp. I never expected to be a revolutionary. Unfortunately, you forced me into that position by trying to enslave me to your command structure. We're not here to negotiate your surrender. You've already been captured, and I can do with you what I want. But, I am interested in hearing from you."

Armstrong responded by giving his name, rank and serial number. Ren really couldn't blame him for that.

"I'm not planning on killing any of you. When this conversation is over, you'll be allowed to bathe, eat, and rest, and then we'll pronounce your sentence, which isn't the death penalty." He looked at his roster. "Lieutenant Baxter. You want to tell me about rounding up the people of Millair?"

"I .... "Baxter was young, in his thirties, clean cut, and earnest. "I ... was ordered by my command to quell an uprising."

"How many people died?"

Baxter shifted uncomfortably.

"About a hundred civilian casualties."

"And a hundred dead didn't seem like a good reason for an uprising?"

Baxter didn't know how to answer. Not being in a position of authority any longer had stolen his power.

"Sergeant Marquette, tell me about the teenagers we found imprisoned at Goddard High School."

Marquette pulled himself up to his full military posture.

"They attacked my squad, injured one of my soldiers. We were holding them there rather than the jail because they were underage."

"They attacked your squad? Why?"

"How should I know? They saw uniforms and started throwing rocks."

"How many died?"

"A dozen, but they were attacking soldiers."

Ren nodded.

"What do you think you were accomplishing here in Wichita?" They didn't say anything. "Any of you?" Armstrong shifted. When Ren said his name, he looked up.

"I was told by my command that Wichita—Kansas—required civilian leadership to bring things under control. Crystal Lewis had an understanding with Colonel Marquette, but when she died, we needed another civilian representative. You were her second, so it made sense to come to you. I wasn't arresting you."

"Weren't you? It sure sounded like it to me. And, it doesn't matter now that I've done what I've done."

"You're correct, Mr. Sullivan." Major Halliday was the highest-ranked officer here. "What you've done here is treason and you'll hang for it, eventually."

"Could be, but if it's a sin to do a right thing, I'll gladly take eternal damnation. What I saw when I looked around was that the Knights were keeping the peace while your units were killing people. I can't speak for anywhere else in the country. That's what I've seen in Wichita. Now I've made my choice. As I said, none of you will be killed but, tomorrow, you'll receive your sentences. Enjoy your next twenty-four hours in the relative comfort of your imprisonment."

Ren signaled the Knights, who moved to escort the men out of the office. Phil and Crispin came out of their respective corners.

"Do you have a report for me?

"LeBron Collier is the son of the pastor at New Hope Baptist Church. He's a seminary student, just happened to be home when the bombs hit. He's got a reputation as a bit of a rabble-rouser, but a community-oriented one.

There's hints of a juvenile record, but the pulse wiped that out."

"I don't really care. He's a community representative and I want to connect with people who want what's best for the community." He glanced at his watch. The meeting at the church was an hour away. Although they could get there in ten minutes, he wanted to drive around the community a bit before stopping at the church. They took a small detail, four Knights in addition to Crispin and Phil.

Like most evangelical churches in the Midwest, New Hope didn't have a beautiful building, but it occupied a good-sized lot and had been on Ohio Ave. for more than a century. There was a new, larger sanctuary under construction beside the old one, but without windows or doors, it stood empty and likely to remain that way under the circumstances.

The sanctuary was as large as any Ren had seen, with bold rafters of a dark wood exposed against white wall board. Oddly, the pews weren't in keeping with the room. They were of a lighter wood with blue upholstery, like an afterthought. Ren hadn't been an ardent churchgoer since Lenore's death, but he thought he preferred the simpler architecture and harmonious pews of Emmaus Road Baptist Church.

Surprised by the size of the crowd, Ren took the front left-hand bench as a man he assumed was Pastor Collier began speaking. A middle-aged black man in a white button-down shirt, the pastor spoke briefly about community and drawing neighborhoods together, which gave Ren time to scan the crowd. There was a mixture of races represented in the pews. That spoke well for reaching more of the city than not. Pastor Collier ceded the floor to LeBron.

"I promised you I'd bring the man, and he's here. When I met him, I told him I didn't think we needed a rich white man to solve our problems, but I was spouting off. I'll take what help we can get. I would hear him out, anyway. Warren Sullivan."

About three people clapped as he rose and mounted the low platform. He'd never stood behind a pulpit and he didn't intend to do so now. There was no microphone as there was no electricity, so he would just have to trust to his own hot air.

"I never set out to be in charge. I merely didn't want to be an Army slave. I had the means to fight free and protect the town, but the problem with winning a war is that people think that puts you in charge. I don't have the means anymore to be in charge. The Pulse took out access to my bank accounts. I've got a fleet of trucks that no longer work. I think even my pipelines aren't flowing right now. So, I need your ... your guidance. To the extent possible, I want to know what you need and what I can help with. I will help as I can, but I don't have the ability to tax others to give to those in need. So, now, I'm going to sit down and you can tell me what you're thinking."

There were representatives, mostly pastors, from almost every neighborhood in Wichita, except for Delano and Crown Heights—neighborhoods with resources that thought they could ride out this storm. Ren hoped they were right. The others had been talking among themselves and they wanted his help to establish trading routes for fuel and food.

"I might have some trucks I could provide," Ren said. "But you must realize that there are nearly 400,000 people in this city. We can hope to provide enough aid to feed that many people but I can't promise it."

"We've heard you have connections with Bunnell & Wilson." Pastor Boy Collier had stood up. "That's the largest grocery wholesaler in the world and they own the Knights. You telling us that they can't bring food in?"

"They probably can, but they won't do it long-term."

"Who's asking for a handout?" LeBron spoke from a seated position. Several people echoed him. "You get the food flowing and we'll figure out how to pay for it."

"All we're asking is for something like existed before to come back," an older matronly woman said. "We don't need to exchange one ruler for another. We just want groceries and to pay with them from our jobs."

Ren blinked. He needed to put aside some personal misconceptions. These people didn't seek rescue. They just wanted a normal life.

"I'm afraid I don't have an answer on that just yet."

"But you'll work on it?" Pastor Collier asked.

Ren glanced at Crispin who was punching something into his tablet.

"I can work on it."

Crispin looked up and they made eye contact a second before he nodded.

"I've got no details yet, but I think it's entirely possible."

"We're just asking to make some contacts."

"I've got contacts. I'll promise to have more details by tomorrow this time. Mr. Wilson is a businessman, so he's all about the deal. You're going to have to decide what you can do to reciprocate."

Pastor Collier frowned, stroking a thumb along one side of his chin.

"All due respect," the matronly woman said, "but we're customers. Ain't his business how we're going to pay for food and fuel. It's just his business to get what we need to where we can buy it."

Ren grinned at her.

"You're absolutely right, ma'am. I'll let him know that." He paused a moment. "And, thank you for reminding me of that. In a crisis like this, folks tend to think someone like me has more power than I actually do. I needed to be reminded that I'm just as ordinary as you are."

"Ain't none of us ordinary, Mr. Sullivan. We're living through extraordinary times and that makes us special, for now."

"What's your name, ma'am. What do you do here in Wichita?"

"I'm Lenora Jacobson, and I own a corner market."

Ren laughed. Of course, she did.

Siege Discovered

Emmaus

Jos wished Granmae hadn't set him to restocking the shelves with the groceries he'd retrieved from the mine. The tedious work meant the market would stay in business for a while longer. He'd be leaving tomorrow for the Arikaree Breaks to gather more coal. He'd much rather be doing that than arranging canned soup on a shelf.

The bell at door tingled and he looked around the end of the shelf to see who had entered. Janice McCormick worked up at the Shack.

"Can I help you?"

"I heard you'd restocked. I was hoping to pick up some items."

"Of course. Let me know when you're finished and I'll meet you at the counter."

When she came into the aisle where he was working, he couldn't help make conversation.

"I'd think the Sullivans would be well-stocked."

"I suppose they are, but our cars aren't working and I can't get up there to check on Miss Allison."

"There are other workers, right?"

"Grace Kramer was off visiting family when the bombs went off. Melvin Kirsch, the groom, might still be up there taking care of the horses, but Larkin Caldwell, the driver, was killed by the USDA. If I had a way up, I'd want to check on Miss Allison, but that's a long walk all the way uphill and I'm not twenty anymore."

Mae had come down from upstairs while they talked and she took over the conversation right then.

"No, of course not. That is a long way to walk uphill. Jos'll go up and see how she's doing and report back to you. She's got food and probably a generator. She'll be fine, but you want to know."

"I appreciate that." Janice looked from Mae to Jos, not sure which one to thank. Jos smiled and nodded as if it had been his idea. Mae took

Janice's money and walked her to the door, chattering brightly as she went.

"Am I really going to go up there?"

"Of course, you are. I don't lie or make promises I can't keep. 'Sides, those high-fluting' Sullivans could owe us a favor or two. It wouldn't hurt us in the least."

"I hear there's a nice wine cellar up there."

"I'm never going to sell alcohol. But you should head out so you can get back here before dark."

"It's barely noon."

"You should stay and be polite to the young lady."

"You know I barely know her, right? She's always been home-schooled or gone to boarding schools."

"Well, that's no longer an option, so best she integrates with the rest of the community. You get going, now. You can even take the car to make the trip easier."

A half hour later, Jos parked in front of the closed gate of the Sullivan estate. He almost pushed the button to call up to the house, but there was no light to indicate it had power. He walked along the fence through the woods until the metal gave way to a low stone wall, which he jumped with minimal effort, finding himself among a stand of sumac trees. He couldn't see the roof of the house since the leaves were still on the trees, so he walked toward the gate once more and searched for an opening in the Siberian pea hedge. A wide driveway curved toward the house. His tennis shoes crunched on the gravel as he trudged toward it.

Granmae had teased him that if any local boy had a chance with "the Sullivan girl", it would be the one who came to her when she was all alone.

He rounded a bend and the house came into sight, but his steps slowed at the sight of a USDA truck parked near the house. A buzz of flies and the smell alerted him to the dead body near the stable. And then the bark of the nearest black walnut exploded as a bullet hit it.

Jos dove for cover, drawing his gun as he went.

Reunion at the Wire

Shane watched as one of Jason Breen's men hooked a car battery up to the barbed-wire fence along the backside of the Greyeyes allotment, pulling off some dried grass to test that the wire was hot. He glanced over his shoulder to see Sergeant Murphy glaring at him. They had not hit it off immediately, and Shane supposed that was his fault, but he couldn't very well let the guy take command when Rob had entrusted him with the job of leading the defense of the town. That his father trusted him with so vital a task required that he not cede his authority to a guy in fatigues who had just shown up this morning.

"I prefer having my squad together."

"You mean what's left of your squad. But I need people who are firearms proficient on every barricade, and that means your guys on the barricades I think we're are going to see the most people. But the good news is, your guys are in charge wherever they're stationed."

"You're not listening to me ...."

"No, you're not listening to me. You and your squad owe the town for medical care and food. You fulfill that duty by manning the barricades we need you to man. If you want to stop eating and having your colleagues consuming antibiotics, you're welcome to go wherever and do whatever. But as long as you like living where there's food and water, you work for me. And, when this is over, you and I can sit down over an unfortunately warm beer and talk about why I don't like what I just said and how I wish it could be different. Later because, right now, the first group of people should be reaching our borders any minute, and we have work to do."

Any minute was correct. Old 24 headed east showed a sporadic stream of humanity, all walking through the chill October morn. Folks carried bundles on their heads, over their shoulders, and clutched to their chests. Some people pulled garden wagons or Radio Flyers, while others pushed wheelbarrows and bicycles. Everybody looked bedraggled and foot sore and they all stopped and begged water and food. Many didn't immediately get the message that the barricades were meant to convey.

"My children are exhausted. Please let us in."

"My wife is near dead. Help us."

"I'm a doctor. I can be of great use to you. What's a sigmoid scope? Okay, I'm really a cab driver, but you should be more charitable."

"This is horrible," Joe remarked. "How can we do this?"

"We don't have a choice," Shane explained.

"Those are people out there."

"Yeah. But we only live if we stay strong."

Shane felt mildly guilty after the first dozen people he turned away, but that was quickly wearing off. If they turned south, they'd encounter the water wagon manned by Jazz and Alex and the Emmaus Road Baptist Deaf who were handing out small loaves of bread. That worked great because they didn't talk, so when asked questions, they could just pretend not to understand—which was essentially true except for Jazz and Alex, who were strictly using sign. Shane could just see them from the top of the tractor he was standing on. They'd put up a sign that provided the people on the road with all the information they needed.

-We give you what we can. Don't bite the hand that feeds you.

Rob and Brad Snow talked with people a little further south, assessing for aggression in the interaction with the Deaf congregation. So far, they'd not offered shelter to any of the migrants.

Shane eased the strap that ran across his shoulder, thinking he should switch arms for a while. Two of the mine guards were with him now. He preferred four, but Joe pled an inability to continue with the cruelty.

"I know it's necessary, but I just can't do this," he said.

Shane watched a family as they passed.

"You've got food in there, don't you?" The man wore a nice suit of clothes that was rapidly becoming rags. Shane pointed south. "Where is your compassion? My children will starve if winter doesn't catch us first."

Two sets of big blue eyes implored him to care, but Shane had known this would be hard duty. They couldn't afford empathy now.

Shane didn't get to stay on the Old 24 barricades for long. Sergeant Murphy soon called him to the interstate offramp where a familiar face waited by a gray Landcruiser the sort aging Vermont hippies favored.

"He says he knows you."

"Yeah, kind of. Keep the barricade in place until I've talked to him."

The dark-haired woman in the driver's seat watched him with eyes the shade of beaten gold. Shane paused to text Rigby before he engaged Chavez.

"You headed for the safe house?"

"If they'll have me."

"I guess that depends on whether they can feed you or not."

"Right. Your checkpoint on the corner—you've got four guards. Only one of them's got eyes. The other three couldn't spot trouble if it was wearing a sign."

"This your way of saying you can make yourself useful?"

Chavez rubbed above his left eye, pushed his sunglasses higher.

"I think you know how useful I'd be."

Shane chuckled, but he couldn't stand on sentiment. He needed to remember his job.

"And your friend?"

"She's even more useful than me. She's a doctor."

"Don't BS me, man."

"No, seriously. She's a doctor."

Chavez tapped on the glass and she rolled down the window. She looked to be fairly tall, slender but athletic, wearing a gun in a shoulder holster under a purple cardigan sweater. Her curly hair and dark complexion could be mistaken for African American at a distance, but Shane thought Middle Eastern immediately.

"Ami Ceylon, ... um, dang, uh, Shane Delaney. Your real name, right? He needs you to convince him that you're a doctor."

"I could show you my credentials."

"Credentials can be forged."

"Well, perhaps. Ask me a question or two then."

"Can you quote the Hippocratic Oath?"

"Classic or modern?"

"If you know there's two, never mind the quote. What is the highest ideal above all in the modern version?"

"'The power of life and death is an awesome responsibility. Do not play God.'"

"What are the twin traps?"

"Overtreatment and therapeutic nihilism."

She certainly sounded like she'd read the oath as recently as Marnie had.

"Can I get lice from my dog?"

"Doubtful. Lice are highly specialized and have difficulty even grabbing onto different kinds of human hair. Your hair being curly, you probably have never had lice."

Shane grinned at her because his hair was cut short enough that only a very observant woman would know it was curly.

"What's a sigmoid scope?"

"Essentially a camera we run up someone's bowel to check for tumors, polyps, what have you."

Shane's phone buzzed just then and he looked at the message from Rigby.

"If I let you in, the B&B will have to feed you, but you must agree to help in our clinic."

"Of course."

"I'll have them move the barricade to let you in. Javi, these are ordinary people. I have to remind myself every day of that. You feel me?"

Chavez stared at him from behind the sunglasses for a long moment before he nodded, accepting the certain knowledge that

Shane would put him down if he forgot that this was not a war zone. Shane had to remind himself about every half-hour that it wasn't, so he figured Javi would have to remind himself every ten minutes. Shane watched their taillights driving off to the west and shivered. Maybe he'd just let death inside the wire. Time to get back to his post.

He'd barely climbed the tractor again when far out to the east, Shane saw a wagon coming. Why would anyone who owned a farm decide to hitch up the draft horses and head south? Or west? Surely a farmer had food. One of the mine guards bumped his arm.

"You see that?"

"Yeah. Makes no sense. That wagon is loaded, too."

Shane watched as it drew closer. Horses that big could be driven through an electric fence without much difficulty. He got ready to make the farmer think twice about that, but before he needed to do anything, the wagon slowed to a stop and a fellow in Army pants and a Knight Industries black shirt dropped to the pavement and began walking toward them. He'd closed maybe a one-third of the fifty feet when Shane recognized his gait.

"Keep your eyes on everyone else." He dropped off the barricade and ran to embrace his brother, who carried an AR15 of his own and truly looked ready to use it. Cai wept as they hugged.

"Where the hell have you been?" Shane demanded.

"It's a really long story, but you need to come see what I brought." Cai scrubbed his face with the heel of his hand. He needed a shave. "I brought a friend."

"A friend? What friend?"

The farmer nodded companionably before turning back to watch the people passing. The high sides to the wagon meant what was inside was safe enough from casual thieves, but he was open carry just to be sure. Behind the driver's seat was a small space and tucked in there, blanket wrapped and quaking was a face Shane knew better than Cai's.

"Mike?"

"Hey, *amigo.*" Mike's voice quavered with weakness. "So glad to see you."

"What's wrong?"

"He got stabbed trying to protect me. We need to get him to the med center as soon as possible."

Shane nodded, one hand on Mike's forehead, the other on his pulse.

"You're headed to sepsis at this rate. Go north to the mine road and I'll let you in at the gate."

"Got it." Cai swung back up on the wagon. "How's Marnie, by the way?"

"I think she'll be better now that you're home."

Shane climbed the barricade and ran along the fence across a shorn field to de-electrify a gate guarded by mine personnel and Anders McAuliff. Shane wondered if Dan and he had even talked yet. He didn't really have time to ask. Anders told him to go with Cai, that he'd move to the more southernly position so Shane could accompany Cai into town.

"Your men understand that if these people try to break the barricade, they might have to use deadly force? Will they do that if you're not here?"

"The ones that have families here in Emmaus will. I'll radio down to the interstate barricades, see if I can get a couple of those National Guardsmen to come."

Shane complimented him and climbed onto the wagon to sit beside Cai, who gave him the Reader's Digest version of the last ten days. Shane sensed a massive amount unsaid.

"I feel like I've been gone for a year."

"A lot has happened. Kind of feels that way to me too. So, what's in the back?"

"A lot of supplies. Ren Sullivan ordered them taken to Emmaus and Mike tried to move the earth to make it happen."

"I probably should have attempted a smaller rock first." Mike's pallor glistened with sweat.

"You always were a stubborn, Chicano jarhead."

"Watch who you're callin' names, *pendejo*."

Cai frowned, but Shane grinned at him and his expression relaxed. If they'd been on the road for a few days, watching each other's backs, he should know that Mike didn't take a lot seriously and preferred if his friends did the same.

Main Street had mostly been cleared of broken-down cars and people were already losing their awe at seeing horse-drawn wagons. Soon they pulled up to the med clinic and Shane ran inside for a wheelchair. Mike could barely stand to get from the wagon to the chair.

"I've got him," Cai assured. "I know he's your friend, but I want to see my wife and you would be more valuable getting these groceries to wherever Dad decided such things go."

"Yeah." Cai grabbed a box from the wagon. Shane figured it was his personal business. "Mike, you all right?"

"I'm good, *amigo*. Come see me when you're finished." Mike knew about battlefield triage. Shane knew he'd be in good hands with Cai and Marnie.

"Shane Delaney." He held out his hand to the farmer.

"Henry Beach. Where to?"

"Around the block. There's a market that'll inventory this and get it available to distribution."

"Sounds good. Hey-up, horses."

Shane's radio squelched.

"Maverick, you got your ears on? Over"

"Yeah, Click. What's up? Over." The reporter had somehow gotten the radio station back up and running and since the town's handhelds couldn't broadcast over the ridge, he was transmitting messages between the checkpoints.

"Parker Bradshaw is at County Road S near Mara Wells. Stan hasn't answered yet. Can they let him in?"

"Doesn't he own a house there?"

"Yes, but nobody wants to make the decision without Stan's oversight."

"Oh, for heaven sakes, of course, let him in."

Farmer Beach and Mae were trying to figure out how to unload the wagon without Jos' help.

"Message delivered, Maverick. Over."

"Thanks, Click. Over and out."

Mae turned to Shane.

"I don't know why Jos hasn't come back from the Sullivans yet. I'm getting a little worried."

Shane sighed. Sometimes dealing with people who still cared wearied him. He keyed the radio.

"Sheriff Joe. This is Maverick. You got your ears on? Over."

The silence that followed was so long that Shane figured Joe was out of range, but then the radio crackled.

"Maverick, this is Deputy Joe. You should gather some folks to come up to the Shack. We found the USDA agents and … well, bring guns and body armor if you got it. It's not good. Over."

Farmer Beach's eyebrows shot up into his grizzled hair while Mae's mouth formed into a horrified "Oh."

"Jos?" she asked.

"Joe, is Jos Osimowitz with you? Over."

"He is, and he'll make a fine deputy someday ... if you-all will get here before things turn badly against us. Over."

"Over and out." Shane turned to Mae who looked agitated. "I don't have time for your shenanigans, Mae. I gotta go take care of this. We'll let you know what's going on as soon as we know."

He headed off down the street on foot, calling for Rob on the radio.

The End

The Story Continues

A Taste of "Gathering In"

The night of the pulse, Geo Tully and Wes Marcus were in the basement of Wes' aunt's home that had become their safehouse.

Wes held up a photo album that showed a man standing in front of the house with a shovel. The front door stood behind him, but not the view of the house that Geo was familiar with. The articulated arm of a backhoe could be seen on the edge of the frame.

"The porch is an addition," Geo acknowledged.

"And look at how deep the hole is behind him."

Geo turned to the front wall of the basement. The shelves had kept him from investigating here. They appeared to be attached to the wall, but when he ran his hand along the back edge of the shelving unit, he found a throw-bolt. He pulled it down and tugged on the shelves, swinging them out away from the wall. Hinged on the far side, they glided on hidden casters. Behind them was an open space that stretched the length of the porch. Geo tried the light in the ceiling, but it didn't turn on. He used the flashlight on his phone to illuminate the small room. A ham radio sat at one end, covered with plastic, while the other end was stacked with storage boxes.

"I knew that tower had to still have a use," Wes said. He squatted down to look under the table to radio sat on. "He left it disconnected. It'll take me a moment."

The light bulb in the main basement flared and popped off. Wes smacked his head on the underside of the table. Geo's phone light went out.

"What is that smell?" he asked.

"My phone just fried, I think."

They fumbled around in the dark to find the stairs and make their way to the kitchen. Duke, the Labrador retriever, stood in the livingroom, staring at the window and whining.

Geo peeked out the curtains. The neighbors were coming out on their porch, staring around.

"You smell that?" Wes asked. "I'm going to go check for fire."

"Do you hear that?"

Duke whined louder. Loud voices filtered in through the glass. Geo watched as the neighbors ran off their porch. Wes swept the front door open.

"What the hell?" Geo growled.

"They need help," Wes said and ran into the street.

"Stay, Duke," Geo ordered and followed his stupid partner into the street, where the neighbors could get a full view of their high-and-tights. A municipal bus sat at the corner, smoke pouring out of its windows as the people inside tried to get out, screaming, kicking, punching at the glass, but when one window shattered, it just fed the fire that was killing them.

Wes ran to the rear passenger door and tried to pull it open, convulsing and chewing his tongue, smoke rising from his body.

Other Lela Markham Titles

Meet Lela Markham

Hi. I was raised in a house made of books in Alaska and told tales from the time I could talk. A teacher eventually made me write one of them down. I hated the exercise, but it was the spark that ignited a fire that has never gone out.

My daring husband, two fearless offspring and I live the adventure of a lifetime here on the Last Frontier where the midnight sun encourages wandering the wilderness and the long dark winters favor reading, writing and staring at the northern lights … hence the moniker Aurorawatcher.

It's all about the aurora watching!

www.ingramcontent.com/pod-product-compliance
Lightning Source LLC
Chambersburg PA
CBHW031019030726
47497CB00004B/917
9780998173238